Forgotten  *Notes*

Forgotten Notes

a novel

SIAN ANN BESSEY

Covenant Communications, Inc.

Published by Covenant Communications, Inc.
American Fork, Utah

Printed in the United States of America
First Printing: January 2001

08 07 06 05 04 03 02 01   10 9 8 7 6 5 4 3 2 1

ISBN 1-57734-789-7

*To be born Welsh
Is to be born privileged.
Not with a silver spoon
In your mouth,
But music in your blood
And poetry in your soul.*

Anon.

*Dedicated to
my husband, Kent,
and my parents, Noel and Patricia Owen,
for their unfailing love and support.
And to my Welsh ancestors—
thank you for a priceless heritage.*

Glossary and Pronunciation Guide

Aga: a large cast-iron stove, fueled by coal
Aled (ălĕd)
aunty: used as Americans use "aunt"
bach *(bäch; the "ch" is aspirated as in German)*: Welsh, literally translated "small, little"; used as a diminutive form of affection
boot: trunk of the car
Boxing Day: December 26. Ancient custom where landowners' children boxed up their previous year's gifts to distribute to the tenants' children.
Cerys (*Keris*)
cheeky: impertinent
Cornish pasty: a hand-held savory pastry filled with meat, potatoes, and gravy
daft: silly, foolish
Deniol (*Daynyol*)
dual-carriageway: two lanes of traffic on each side of the highway
Eisteddfod (* āstĕthvŏd*): Welsh folk festival
flat: apartment
Llangollen (*thsh-an-gaw-thsh-ĕn*)
motorway: freeway
Mynydd Mawr (*mŭnith mauer*): Welsh, literally translated "large mountain"
Nain (*Nine*): Welsh for grandmother
pavement: sidewalk
Pen-y-Bryn (*Pen-a-brin*)
plaster: adhesive bandage ("band-aid")
Pystill Glas (*Pistithsh glass*)
queue: line of people
runner beans: a variety of green bean, similar to french beans
serviettes: napkins
sledge: sled
squash: a fruit-flavored drink, made by mixing a liquid concentrate with water
St. David's Day: March 1. A celebration of the patron saint of Wales. Traditionally, people wear daffodils or leeks.
sweets: candy
tad: little
Taid (*Tide*): Welsh for grandfather
tallboy: wooden clothes closet
telly: television
wellies: rubber boots, usually black or green
wool: yarn

❦ *Prologue* ❧

15 May 1881

Dear Father,

    I have only a few precious moments to write to you before our ship casts off for America. I could not leave without putting your mind at rest regarding my welfare. The thought of your distress over my sudden, secret departure has been the only thing marring my happiness. For I am happy, Father! And safe and well.

    I hope you can find it in your heart to forgive me for leaving with no word of good-bye. It was perhaps the hardest thing I have ever done.

    Glyn and I are married. We have loved each other since the first day we met. Our lives would have been forced to follow separate paths had we stayed in Pen-y-Bryn. I could not have born such a lonely, loveless life.

    I have followed my heart, but I grieve for those I've hurt—especially you, Father, and Joseph Lewis. He is a good, kind man. I will always admire him and be flattered that he showed interest in me—but I could not love him as a wife should love her husband. And he, of all people, deserves that. I have taken the small oval portrait of you and Mother. I will treasure it always. I have also taken the pearls that Mother gave me. It was all I had of my own to help augment Glyn's hard-earned savings. We will manage. We love one another dearly and look forward to our lives together in a new land.

    I must go. My thoughts are with you.

    Your loving daughter,

    Mary.

Chapter 1

Sarah Lewis sighed and tucked a stray wisp of long, chestnut-colored hair behind her ear. She sat up straight, stretched her aching shoulders and glanced longingly at the beam of bright sunlight pouring in through the small casement window above her head. After days of gray, wet weather the warm sunshine felt like a healing balm. She sighed again, and wished she could enjoy the beautiful summer day outside. But until inventory was complete, she was relegated to sitting in the chilly, uninviting back room of the shop, surrounded by dusty boxes and shelves of cans.

Sarah had been tempted to find a reason for doing inventory at another time. But then she would have had to face Aunty Lil. That was one of the disadvantages of working with family members—they knew you so well. Although she probably wouldn't have let on, Aunty Lil would have seen through any excuse she could have mustered. Then feeling guilty all day would have ruined Sarah's time off anyway. And so she found herself perched on the top of a rather ancient step stool alternately glaring at the rows of cans before her and the stack of papers on her knee.

It had been different when her dad was alive. She had always helped him do inventory. Perhaps that was why it fell to her lot now. Her father had made Sarah feel as though her assistance was invaluable, even as a young child. They had worked as a team. Sometimes she counted items and her father acted as scribe; sometimes they reversed roles. There were still pages in the old books on the office shelves with Sarah's large childish numbers meticulously listed in columns.

The shop had been in the family for almost three generations now. It was called "the shop" by everyone in the small Welsh village of Pen-y-Bryn quite simply because it was the only shop. Sarah's grandfather, Joseph Lewis, had been the first shopkeeper. Her father and aunt had taken over a few years before her grandfather's death. Now her aunt ran it alone with part-time help from Sarah and her mother.

The problem with being the sole retail establishment for the village was that it meant you had to stock everything from three-inch nails to cauliflower; pipe-cleaners to milk. As a child Sarah had always thought the back room of the shop was her very own Aladdin's grotto. If you dug deep enough you could find almost anything. But now, as she sat chewing on her pencil and surveying the crowded shelves, it looked more like a lot of tedious work.

She heard the doorbell chime in the distance and the heavy tread of footsteps entering the shop. But Sarah didn't pay any heed to it until she heard her aunt's voice from behind the front counter.

"Can I help you sir?"

Sarah stopped tabulating numbers midstream, and raised her head with interest. A stranger? Having lived here all her life, Aunty Lil knew everybody in the community by name. They didn't get many visitors to Pen-y-Bryn. It was sufficiently off the beaten path to preclude the tourist traffic that frequented many of the other villages in mid-Wales.

"Sure! I'll take two of these candy bars please." He had a deep voice with a very distinct accent. Sarah heard the objects being placed on the counter and money exchanging hands. As the cash register rang out, the man's voice continued "I was also wondering if you could recommend somewhere my mother and I could stay near here? A guest house or bed and breakfast maybe?"

Sarah held her breath. There was only one bed and breakfast in the village. It was her house.

After her father's death two years before, she and her mother had been the only ones left at home. Her two brothers were already married. Kevin and his wife Mair lived on a farm about five miles away. John and Eileen were in south Wales for the time being. John was a banker and was transferred to a different branch of the bank every few years.

Since her sons were out on their own, Sarah's mother had decided to renovate their bedrooms. With some help from Kevin they added a small but serviceable bathroom to that part of the house, and listed the home as a 'bed and breakfast' establishment. Aunty Lil had clucked her tongue disapprovingly throughout the venture, but it had given her mother a much-needed diversion after the loss of her husband and, although the opportunities were infrequent, allowed her to use her abundant homemaking skills in making guests feel comfortable.

Sarah knew that if Aunty Lil had any hesitations about the character of the American in the shop, she would direct him to stay at the Black Swan Hotel in Llansilyn, six or seven miles away. The fact that he was American was not in question. Even if she had not heard his obvious accent she would have known. No one in Wales called chocolate a "candy bar"!

She heard footsteps again, this time her aunt's measured tread along with the man's. They were talking but Sarah couldn't make out what was being said. Overcome with curiosity, she inched her way down the step stool and quietly placed her papers on the floor. Quickly she tried to brush the dust off her pink T-shirt and faded jeans. The hair that had worked loose from her ponytail fell forward again. She brushed it back impatiently. She wasn't very presentable, so she would just peek.

She walked softly to the connecting doorway and was just in time to hear Aunty Lil say, ". . . and I'm sure you would find it suitable. If you follow this road just around the corner there . . . ."

They were walking towards the outer door and Aunty Lil was pointing down the lane that passed the shop and led to Sarah's home.

To her frustration, Sarah could see her aunt well, but her view of the visitor was obscured by shelves. She got an impression of blonde hair, long legs in blue jeans, and what appeared to be a tan, light-weight jacket covering broad shoulders.

". . . It's not more than a few hundred yards. A gray stone house with a navy-blue door. You'll see the sign in the front garden."

To Lil's obvious surprise, the man then grasped her aunt's hand and shook it. "Thank you so much. You've been very helpful."

Aunty Lil colored with pleasure. "Well, you're very welcome, I'm sure." The doorbell rang again and he was gone.

Sarah stepped into the shop. "Aunty Lil, who was that?"

"Well I never!" Aunty Lil was still slightly pink cheeked and looking a little bemused. "Umm, what was that dear?"

"Who was that man? You sent him on to our house didn't you?"

Aunty Lil ran her work-worn hands down her serviceable but faded floral apron, seemed to collect her thoughts, and finally focused on Sarah.

"Why yes dear, I did. He seemed to be a very nice young man. Yes indeed. Very polite too, and handsome. Didn't quite catch the name . . . Peterson, Pedersen, or something like that." She absentmindedly began rearranging the apples sitting in a box next to the counter. "Do you know, he reminds me of someone . . . perhaps . . . yes, y'know, I'm sure I've seen him on that *Dallas* program on the telly."

Sarah burst into laughter. "Aunty Lil, the only Americans you've ever seen are the actors on *Dallas* and the President when he's on the news."

Aunty Lil looked a bit sheepish. "Well, I dare say you're right dear. And he did look a bit young to be President."

Sarah grinned. "Oh well, if anyone can find out who he is and what he's doing in Pen-y-Bryn, Mam will!"

"You can be sure of that, bach. The whole village will know within the hour." Aunty Lil gave a sniff that was intended to mean that she didn't approve one bit of her sister-in-law's tendency to chatter. Sarah hid a smile at the intentionally subtle reproof. She knew that beneath that prickly exterior beat the kind heart of someone who loved Sarah and her mother dearly. After all, they were almost all the family Aunty Lil had left.

Lillian Lewis was her father's only sister. She had never married and had lived in the flat above the shop ever since she was a young girl. She had co-owned the shop with her brother, Edward Lewis, and they had worked together daily. But each evening Edward, Sarah's father, had walked a short quarter of a mile down the lane from the shop to his own home, where his wife Annie and three children, Kevin, John, and Sarah were waiting with his dinner.

Mindful of his sister's single status, Edward and his wife had always tried to involve Lillian (or Lil as she was known by) in their family activities. She spent a great deal of time with Edward's family, and there could be no doubt that each of Edward's children held a special place in her heart. But she always found pleasure in returning to her own quiet haven above the shop. She was, by nature, fiercely independent and had capably taken control of the reins, running the shop quite successfully after her brother's death.

There was no question that she missed her brother. But in her mind, by continuing to operate the shop, she was showing her love for him, and doing what he would have wanted. She even felt it her duty to try and guide his widow against some of her more frivolous schemes (such as opening a bed and breakfast.) But to Lil's chagrin, Annie didn't give much heed to Lil's opinions unless they coincided with her own. Annie, it seemed, had her own share of the independent streak.

"How are you getting along?" Lil's question brought Sarah's thoughts back to the job at hand.

She groaned. "Oh, it's coming. But it's painfully slow."

Lil gave her a sympathetic nod and went back to rearranging apples. Her nonverbal message was clear. Time for pleasantries was over. It was back to work. Reluctantly, Sarah returned to the lists, ladder, and boxes.

🍂 🍂 🍂

By Sarah's small wristwatch it was precisely forty-two minutes later when the front door bell rang again and Mabel Jones trotted in. Sarah stifled a giggle. The grapevine was really humming today. This must truly be news of note! Well worth setting aside her paperwork, she reasoned, and she stepped into the shop front just as Mabel set her wicker basket on the counter and launched into her gossip. Big news indeed. There was none of the usual opening small talk. She got right down to business.

"Well Lil, you'll never believe who's staying at Annie's place. Not in a million years." Mabel paused for effect, then continued. "No, you'll never guess so I'll have to tell you."

Leaning forward on the counter as though about to impart something top secret Mabel whispered, "Glyn and Mary Jones' granddaughter!" Despite her somewhat dramatic overture, Mabel Jones could hardly have asked for a better reaction from her audience. She leaned back and nodded slowly as fright, surprise, questioning disbe-lief, then reluctant curiosity flitted across Lil's face in turn.

Before Lil could say a word, Mabel continued. "Her name's Iris Pearson. She's here with her son. I didn't catch his name. Came to see where her grandparents came from. Can you imagine that? All the way from America just to see where Glyn and Mary used to live. And then to end up at Annie's. Well I never!"

Sarah sensed immediately that there was something underlying this conversation that she didn't understand. It wasn't so much what was being said as much as what was not being said.

"Who are Glyn and Mary Jones?" she asked.

Both ladies looked up startled. Neither had been aware of her silent entrance. A quick look passed between them.

"Oh for goodness sake Lil, Sarah's all of twenty-two," Mabel exclaimed.

"Twenty-three" Sarah corrected her.

"Are you really, bach? My how time flies! Well, I think you're old enough to hear the story. Besides it was long ago. Only us old ones even remember." She looked at Lil, as though awaiting approval.

Aunty Lil pursed her lips and frowned slightly. "Well the whole village will be buzzing with it before the sun sets" she sighed. "She's going to hear it anyway, more's the pity. I suppose it's best that she hears it here. Then I can correct any embellishments that may find their way into the story." She gave Mabel Jones a pointed look.

Mabel responded with a wry smile. "All right, all right. But Lil, you know as well as I do, there's hardly any facts to this story. The wonder of it was all the guessing people did. People had all sorts of grand ideas. Some of them were right romantic too. Mind you, there were some that weren't an' all."

"Mrs. Jones, why don't you tell me what you can?" Sarah was beginning to get a bit impatient with all the piecemeal information being bandied about.

"Right you are. And quite a story it is too. You see, Glyn Jones lived with his mam and dad up on Mynydd Mawr in the small farm house Tom and Cerys Roberts redid a few years back." Sarah nodded. She knew the old farm house. She delivered groceries there often.

Cerys was a sweet girl, not much older than Sarah. She and her husband Tom had worked hard renovating the rather dilapidated main building to create their now cosy home.

"'Course in those days there weren't as many roads as there are now and that old house was pretty isolated and by all accounts quite primitive. Glyn's dad was a shepherd working for the Bixtons from Deniol Manor. Poor as church mice they were. Shepherding didn't pay well. Why they'd have even been without a roof over their heads if it wasn't for Squire Bixton letting them use the old farmhouse up there. Glyn's mam helped out a bit by taking in needlework. Quite a seamstress she was. People used to say her stitches were about invisible.

"When Glyn was old enough he went to work for the Squire too. Doing odd jobs around the manor. He was a nice boy they say. Always willin' to work and cheerful too.

"Anyway, it was at the manor that Glyn first saw Mary. Mary Williams, as she was then, was the daughter of the minister. Reverend William Williams took care of the preaching for the four chapels in the area. His church work kept him traveling quite a bit, but he checked in at Deniol Manor regularly. I think the Squire thought it would be good to be seen with the Methodist minister every once in a while even though he was Church of England himself. They were on quite friendly terms by all accounts.

"Young Mary often accompanied her father to the manor. Her Mam had passed away when she was a baby. She was a lot like her Mam I think. Yes indeed, a pretty little thing and quite the apple of her father's eye. I think he had high hopes for her—marrying well you know. And she might 'ave too if she hadn't gone an' fallen in love with Glyn."

Mabel Jones paused for a second, glanced over at Lil, then continued.

"Love at first sight, they said it was. For both of them. They didn't see each other much at first. Just at the manor. But they must have started seeing each other at other times too. Though no one knew it at the time of course. A big secret it was. They both knew her father would not 'ave approved at all. Not with all his high hopes for Mary. Glyn, for all his handsome looks and cheery disposition, just wasn't good enough.

"Well now, this is where the story gets a bit mysterious. No one really knows what happened for sure. One day everything was normal; the next day Glyn Jones and Mary Williams were gone. And no one ever saw either of them again. Reverend Williams was transferred to another diocese. Glyn's mam and dad moved away too. Some say the Squire made them go because of Glyn. But nobody seems to know for sure. Some of the other servants at the manor said that Glyn had talked about going to America. But they'd never really taken him seriously. Where would he come up with that kind of money?"

Mabel got a faraway look in her eye. "My, but there were all sorts of stories going round." She paused and glanced at Aunty Lil again, then added lamely, "but none of them were ever proven of course."

Sarah could well imagine the types of stories that were being spread about the couple. She had lived all her life aware of the village grapevine and the distortion caused by gossip. Truth and hearsay often had fuzzy edges. She felt instinctively sorry for Glyn and Mary who had probably been the fuel for all sorts of fabrications.

Aunty Lil cleared her throat, as if in an attempt to return the conversation to the here and now. "Well I dare say we'll all find out what happened soon enough. If this Mrs. Pearson is who she says she is, then she'll know more than the rest of us put together."

Mabel Jones wasn't quite ready for Lil's pragmatic return to reality. "But Lil," she said, "just think, after all these years, to suddenly turn up like this. And at Annie's of all places"!

"Well that's my fault and no one else's," retorted Lil. "The young man came into the shop and asked about a place to stay. He seemed a nice enough boy. I told him about Annie's bed and breakfast.

Sarah could tell by Aunty Lil's defensive answer, that there was still more to this story than she'd been told. But Mabel had not seemed to notice. Instead she pounced on another jewel. "Lillian Lewis, you've seen him!" she gasped. "Why didn't you say something? What's he like?"

Lil, obviously anxious to end her part in the story as quickly as she could, responded brusquely, "He was tall, blonde, and very polite." Then she turned and went back to rearranging apples in their box.

"Well I never!" breathed Mabel Jones and shook her head wonderingly. "What a day for Pen-y-Bryn."

Sarah took one look at her aunt's face and knew that discussion of this topic was over for the time being. But her curiosity was roused. The story she'd just heard should not have created a strained atmosphere in the shop, but it was most definitely there nonetheless. Even impervious Mabel Jones seemed to sense Lil's guarded apprehension. She opened her mouth to say something more, then abruptly changed her mind.

Instead, it was Lil who spoke first, and immediately steered the conversation onto more mundane things. "What can I get for you today, Mabel?"

Mabel glanced vaguely around the shop, as if searching for something. Her gaze fell upon a box of shining, red tomatoes.

"Oh, those look nice. I'll take a quarter pound of the tomatoes please."

"Yes, they do look good don't they? They're fresh in today." Then as an afterthought, Lil called to Sarah over her shoulder. "Sarah, be sure to take some home to your mother this evening. They won't be this nice for long."

Sarah nodded, silently acknowledging her dismissal. As she turned towards the back room, Aunty Lil was ringing up the tomatoes on the cash register. She and Mabel Jones were talking about the rising price of eggs. Things were back to normal. On the surface anyway.

☙ ☙ ☙

An hour and a half later Sarah shut the door of the shop behind her and thankfully stepped out into the waning sunlight. In one hand she held a small brown bag containing some ripe, red tomatoes. Aunty Lil had handed it to her when she stopped by the office to say good night. Sarah had thought that she looked a little pale, but hadn't commented on it. Aunty Lil had not seemed to be in a talkative mood. She had nodded, obviously pleased, when Sarah had told her that the bulk of the inventory was completed. Sarah too was glad to have it behind her—for a few months at least.

She stepped lightly into the lane that ran past the shop and looked around her with pleasure. Sarah loved this little village. She always had. Born and brought up here, she had left for four long years to attend nursing school, and although she had enjoyed her studies and the thrill of working at the hospital for a while, she was glad to be back. Unlike many of the young people she'd gone to school with, Sarah had no grandiose plans for moving to the big city. She enjoyed the peaceful serenity that came with village life. She loved the slower pace, the fact that your neighbors were your friends and relatives, and the close link to heritage and traditions.

Sarah had jumped at the chance to return to the village when she heard about an opening for a school nurse at the local Primary school. She enjoyed working with the children. And having the summer holidays to herself was an extra bonus. She spent some of her holidays and Saturdays helping at the shop, as she had today, but she also set aside some of her free time to enjoy her other great loves: music and exploring the countryside.

Nestled deep in the heart of the Berwyn mountains of Mid-Wales, Pen-y-Bryn village was a perfect location for leisurely country rambles or more arduous mountain hikes. The surrounding mountains were not as rugged or forbidding as their neighbors in the Snowdonia mountain range. The elevation here did not exceed 2,500 feet and the mountainous terrain was primarily covered with scrub grass and heather. Sheep dotted the landscape and were the primary source of income for the residents of the area. The hillsides were scarred by long, meandering stone walls built by long-forgotten shepherds in an era before the advent of cement or bricks. Some of the walls were crumbling now, but they had withstood the weathering of time remarkably well.

A river that had its beginnings as a mountain stream above them coursed through the village, winding its way down the valley. Apart from the farms that lay scattered around the surrounding hillsides, most homes were grouped together near the river. The village was positioned in a rough T formation with the horizontal bar of the letter T running alongside the river. This was the main road that led into the neighboring communities on either side of the valley. Here too were located most of the homes, the shop, a small post office, the Red

Dragon pub, a small petrol station and, a little further down the street, the church. The vertical bar of the T shape was a smaller lane that crossed the river and led to the newly built Primary school, the Welsh Methodist chapel, and a scattering of homes. This lane led out to most of the farms nearby. It was also the lane that Sarah took to walk home.

It was not a long walk. She enjoyed the exercise after having been cooped up in the shop all day. Summer evenings in Wales were long because of their northerly latitude, and it felt good to soak in a little of the remaining sunlight and warmth. She waved to a few people as she passed by, and exchanged greetings with one or two.

Although Welsh was the first language for most homes in Pen-y-Bryn, everyone also spoke English—it was a necessity nowadays. It always made Sarah smile to hear the children at school flitting from one language to the other, without really being aware that they were doing it. It never ceased to amaze her that even the four-year-old pupils rarely confused the two languages. Perhaps it was because the languages were so different; the sentence structures could not be intertwined. The Welsh language had a definite lilt to it so that when the children spoke in English, their Welsh accents almost made them sound as though they were singing the words. Sarah didn't notice it now as much as she had when she first returned from nursing school. She wondered suddenly if the American visitors would notice it—if it would seem as obvious to them as their accent did to her ears?

Sarah quickened her pace. Would the Americans be at her home when she got there? She crossed the bridge over the river. Above the sound of the babbling water she could hear the happy voices of children playing on the swings in the school yard over to her right. Even though school was closed for the summer, the school yard was still a favorite playing area for the younger inhabitants of the village.

There was an occasional bark from a distant dog, and the constant drone of busy bees amongst the flowers and tussocks of grass that lined the curb. There were no pavements in the village, partly because there was very little traffic, but also because most of the homes and establishments that lined the lane were built before such amenities were conceived.

The houses were made of stone and roofed with purple or gray slate from the quarries to the north of them. The wooden doors were painted various bright colors, and on this sunny day many windows were open and brightly colored drapes and lace curtains rustled softly in the evening breeze. Most of the homes were divided by thick, lush privet hedges or whitewashed picket fences. Thanks to all the recent rain, the lawns were a bright emerald green, covered with a smattering of tiny yellow and white daisies.

As the lane made a slight bend, Sarah reached her own home, which stood a little further back from the road than most of its neighbors. As she opened the creaky garden gate, Sarah noticed that there were no strange cars parked outside and concluded that their guests were gone for the time being. She walked up the graveled garden path lined with her mother's rose bushes. The smell was glorious. She did not stop at the dark-blue front door but continued along the path that curved around the side of the house. Here the tall privet hedge shielded them from the prevailing wind and gave them some privacy from neighboring homes. It was an almost impenetrable wall and Sarah felt momentarily chilled by its darkening shade.

Seconds later however, she reentered the sunlight of the back garden. The rolling green lawn stretched to the back hedge interrupted only by a large apple tree and an old, rather rusty swing set that had belonged to Sarah and her brothers when they were little, and remained there today only because of earnest pleading from Kevin's four-year-old son, Aled. Three lawn chairs stood together beneath the apple tree, and a black and white soccer ball lay forlornly up against the hedge—a memento of Aled's last visit.

To the other side of her lay the plot of ground that her mother fondly called the kitchen garden. There were clumps of various herbs, including parsley, chives, thyme, and mint. There was a riotous strawberry patch, which currently glistened in the sun because it was full of glass jars. Annie Lewis always carefully placed the small unripe fruit within the jars to mature and ripen free of the threat of thieving birds. The glass jars worked like miniature greenhouses, producing huge, luscious berries. There was a row of peas and a row of runner beans, staked up with bamboo canes. There were also half a dozen potato plants. And unless Sarah was mistaken, it looked as though someone had been at work recently, digging one of them up.

She turned and entered the house through the back door. It opened into a small boot room where, true to its name, sat a couple of pairs of wellies, Sarah's hiking boots, an assortment of jackets and coats, and a couple of walking sticks. The red-tiled floor continued through another door that led directly into the sunny kitchen.

Sarah stepped inside. Pushed up against one of the walls was an old pine kitchen table with four wooden chairs tucked underneath it. The red-and-white-checked table cloth on the table was topped with a white earthenware bowl of fruit.

In the corner was the big black Aga oven, a large cast-iron coal stove. Annie Lewis kept it shining. Just now, it was emanating a wonderful aroma of baking cakes. Next to the Aga was the far-less-used electric oven that Edward Lewis had insisted on buying for his wife. She found it useful for boiling eggs, but that was about all. She had used the Aga oven all her life and considered herself too old to change her ways.

The third wall housed most of the kitchen cupboards and the sink. Above the sink was a low, large kitchen window that faced the back garden. Three flower pots containing gently nodding, bright-red, white, and pink geraniums sat on the window sill. Annie Lewis stood at the sink scraping some new garden potatoes and placing them into the pan near her elbow.

As Sarah walked in her mother looked up. "Hello dear. How were things at the shop today?"

Sarah planted a kiss on her mother's soft, lined cheek. "Oh inventory was long, dusty, and a bit tedious, but it's almost finished now. I think the shop was fairly quiet."

Her mother nodded absently. "Yes, it would be, being market day an'all."

"Oh I almost forgot! Aunty Lil asked me to give these to you."

Sarah handed her mother the brown bag. Her mother opened it and looked inside.

"How nice! These will be lovely with our supper. I've almost finished these potatoes. Why don't you put the kettle on."

Sarah walked over to the kettle, checked to see that it was full of water, and plugged it into the outlet. Then as casually as she could, she asked "Do we have guests tonight, Mam?"

Her mother gave her a knowing look. "And I'm supposed to believe that you've been at the shop all day today and know nothing of any visitors in the village?"

Sarah laughed a little shamefacedly. "Oh Mam! Come on, tell me about them. Aunty Lil met the man in the shop but I didn't see him. I know she sent them here. Then Mabel Jones came in agog with the news, and Aunty Lil shut up like a clam. But when I get home, you're here in the kitchen as calm as a summer day. No visitors. No strange car. Where are they? Who are they? What're they doing here?"

Annie Lewis dried her hands and smiled at her daughter's impatient expression. "Alright, alright! Bring me a cup of tea and we'll chat while the potatoes boil."

A few minutes later, mother and daughter were seated at the kitchen table. The last valiant rays of the lowering sun streamed through the window, and bright beams of light reflected off the shining pans simmering on the Aga, highlighting the faces of the two women.

Other than their ready smiles, there was little to indicate that they were related. Sarah had inherited her tall, willowy figure from her father. Annie was significantly shorter than her daughter and comfortably plump. Her hair had once been a shimmering brown, similar to Sarah's, but was now salt-and-pepper gray, and permed in short curls. Her calloused hands carefully holding the tea cup told of years of laundry, dishes, and gardening. Her face, so noticeably lined beside her daughter's smooth one, testified to her cheery disposition. Laughter lines were clearly visible.

Annie Lewis took a sip of the scalding tea and sighed. "My, it's good to get off these old feet of mine for a few minutes."

She looked over at her daughter and chuckled. "It's alright. I'm not going to doze off, not that I wouldn't like to, mind you! Now your father—my word, I used to say he could go to sleep hanging on a clothes line. It only took two minutes off his feet and he was gone."

"Mam!" exasperation showed in Sarah's face and voice. Annie Lewis chuckled again and leaned over to pat her daughter's hand.

"I know, I know, your mother's rambling again. Very well. Let me see." She wrinkled her forehead as if trying to organize her thoughts.

"Our guests tonight are Mrs. Iris Pearson and her son Brian Pearson. They drove up this afternoon. I showed them the rooms and they seemed pleased. The young man brought in their luggage and I offered them a cup of tea. They didn't want any. I can't imagine driving all that way and not wanting to stop for a cup of tea, can you?"

"All what way? Where did they come from?"

"Well now, I think it was Oxford. But it was London before that. Yes, I think they've been touring 'round a bit. Anyway, they didn't want tea. After Mr. Pearson brought in the luggage they said they'd go out for a bit to get a feel for the place. I think they'll be back in time for some supper later.

"I've got some ham, the peas and new potatoes from the garden, and with Lil's tomatoes we should be alright, don't you think? And the cake of course. That's still in the oven. Help me remember to check it. I mustn't let it burn."

"I'm sure supper will be lovely Mam. It will be a treat for them to have a home-cooked meal if they've been traveling for a while."

"Well yes, it will, won't it."

"Did they tell you what brought them to Pen-y-Bryn?" Sarah asked.

"Why, to see where Glyn and Mary Jones came from of course. Didn't Mabel tell you that when she came in to the shop? I'm sure I told her when she walked by earlier."

"She did mention it, but she seemed to think it a bit strange. And it is isn't it? I mean to come all that way."

"Well, I think maybe we take things a bit for granted. You grew up here. All your family's from this area. All your life you've known where they were from and what life was like for them." Annie's eyes twinkled. "You've even got old Aunty Sally! She may be a bit fuzzy about what she had for dinner, but she can tell you anything you want to know about growing up in this valley. When it comes to the old days, her memory's like a steel trap."

Sarah smiled. It was true. Aunty Sally, as everyone in the village called her, was somewhere between ninety-five and one hundred years old. She never would tell anyone for sure. When young children pleaded with her to tell them her age she would cackle with laughter and just say "Well, young scamp. I'm as old as my tongue and a little bit older than my teeth!" And they had to be content with that.

Sarah watched her mother's face and saw understanding there.

"These people haven't got what we see and hear every day Sarah. They know where their ancestors came from but can't picture it. They don't have people around who remember either. Goodness me, we even talk differently. I was speaking my best English and I know poor Mrs. Pearson was having a time of it trying to understand me."

"So you really think that this Mrs. Pearson is Glyn and Mary Jones's granddaughter?"

"Well she'd have no reason to make something like that up would she? She seemed like a very nice lady. There was something quite genteel about her. And her boy was very nice too. Very polite and helpful."

"That's what Aunty Lil thought too."

"That's right; I'd forgotten Lil had met him. Yes, well he would have had to make a good impression or he would've been off to the Black Swan, wouldn't he?"

Annie and Sarah Lewis exchanged a knowing look and laughed.

"Poor Lil, I really think she feels that she has to watch over us like a mother hen," Annie sighed. "Maybe it's because she never had children of her own to fuss over."

Talking of Aunty Lil reminded Sarah of the older lady's strange reaction to Mabel Jones's news.

"Mam, when Mrs. Jones came in and told Aunty Lil who the visitors were, Aunty Lil acted like she'd really had a shock. Like it meant more to her than just a story about people long ago. And when Mrs. Jones said how strange it was that the Pearsons would be staying at our house, she got quite defensive. It wasn't like her at all."

Annie Lewis nodded her head slowly.

"Yes, it would affect her like that I suppose." She paused for a minute then continued. "What exactly did Mabel tell you about Glyn Jones and Mary Williams?"

"Well she just told me that Glyn Jones was the son of a shepherd on the Brixton land and worked up at the manor, that he fell in love with Mary Williams, the daughter of a minister, and that they suddenly disappeared, presumably together. And that no one heard anything about them afterwards."

Her mother nodded again. "Yes, well that's it in a nutshell really. There's one thing she may have missed out. And that's not because she doesn't know it—Mabel Jones makes it her job to know everything! It was just because Lil was there. You see, your grandfather was officially courting Mary when all this happened."

"What?" Sarah exclaimed. "How did . . . I mean . . . wait I don't understand this at all."

Annie Lewis took another sip of tea and gazed into her cup thoughtfully.

"It all happened a long time before Taid married your grandmother. You'll remember that he was quite a lot older than she was."

Sarah nodded. There had been over twenty years difference in age between her grandparents.

"Well, when Taid was in his early twenties he was already showing signs of becoming a good businessman. He had inherited some money from his mother and had opened the shop. It was smaller then, of course, and didn't carry as many goods. But still most folks could see that it had a lot of potential. And if anyone could make a go of it, your grandfather could.

"As you know, he was always a good chapel-going man, and even then attended his Sunday meetings regularly. He met Mary Williams at church. Her father, Reverend Williams, must have been impressed by your grandfather's prospects—and his religious activity probably didn't do any harm either. Anyway, when your Taid asked the Reverend for permission to court Mary, the Reverend gave his consent.

"Everything seemed to be going fine. He saw Mary a couple of times each month. Courting was so slow and proper in those days. Not like nowadays.

"I think he must have really been in love with her. She was supposed to have been quite a beauty.

"Then out of the blue she was gone. Without a word to the Reverend or your grandfather. I'm sure it was terribly hard on her father, but she just about broke Joseph Lewis's heart. He tried not to let it show by all accounts, but it hardened him for a long time. People thought for sure he'd never look at another girl again.

"He was over forty when he met your grandmother at Sunday School. She was a sweet girl and slowly warmed up that broken heart of his. Four years later they were married. And as far as I know, it was a very happy marriage. They had your Dad and Lillian as you know.

"Your Dad never paid much heed to the story of Mary Williams. As far as he was concerned it was water under the bridge. It was harder for Lillian—perhaps because she was a girl. I don't think she could quite forgive Mary Williams for slighting her father. Somehow she got it into her head that every story told about Glyn and Mary showed her father in a bad light.

"She's never said as much, mind you, but sometimes it's what's not said that tells you more than what is said."

Sarah nodded, silently recalling that she had thought the same thing only hours before.

Annie continued "As a girl, Lillian would always get really upset if anyone brought up the story of Mary Williams. It was like an open wound to her. A weak link in her father's armor perhaps. I don't know. It all seems very silly now. But there you are; there's no accounting for people's feelings sometimes."

They sat quietly for a few minutes, each caught up in her own thoughts. Sarah felt an ache of sorrow for her Aunty Lillian. How hard it must have been to carry that hurt around for so long. Especially as it seemed so inconsequential to an outsider.

Her reverie was broken by her mother, who suddenly leaped off her chair.

"My lands, the cakes!"

Annie Lewis flew across the room and heaved open the Aga door. She lifted the cake pans onto the counter and stood back to look at them. She gave a few disgusted tuts with her tongue.

"If I cut off the edges and cover them with some nice icing I may be able to salvage them. Oh dear, how could I have been so silly?"

Sarah joined her mother at the counter and gazed down at the browner-than-usual, golden-brown cakes. "They'll be fine Mam. You're cakes are always lovely."

Her mother looked unconvinced. "Well, I don't know about that indeed." Then she sighed and smiled at her daughter. "Go on with you. I'll see what I can do with these cakes."

Sarah gave her mother an affectionate squeeze. "Alright, miracle worker! Call me when you want help getting supper ready."

Annie was already hunting for icing sugar and a bowl.

"I will dear. Now go and relax for a little while."

ざ ざ ざ

Sarah walked out of the kitchen and into the hallway. The floor was a continuation of the red tile in the kitchen, but here it was covered with colorful throw rugs. A couple of old prints hung on the pale green walls. They were paintings of local scenes: a nearby waterfall and the view from Mynydd Mawr.

Immediately in front of her was the front door. To the right was the doorway that led to the formal dining room, and a little further on was the doorway to the front parlor. The two rooms were also connected from within. To the left was the staircase that led up to the next floor, and the door that led to the sitting room.

Sarah turned and ran lightly up the stairs. Four doors led off from the main landing. One was Sarah's room; one was her mother's room; one was the bathroom, with a bath and sink; and the last room housed the toilet. There was another short flight of stairs at the end of the landing. This led to the two guest rooms and small bathroom (complete with toilet).

Sarah entered her room, which had changed little since her childhood. The window was open a fraction and a small breeze teased the pale pink curtains. There was a twin bed with a pink and white eiderdown. An old wooden rocking chair that had belonged to her grandmother sat in the corner. Comfortably ensconced in the chair was an ancient, obviously well-loved, one-eyed teddy bear. To one side of the window was a small dressing table decorated with a few small framed family photos and a collection of knickknacks gathered on various long-gone holidays. A tallboy stood against the other wall. It was made of a heavy, dark wood and had scrolled corners. It opened to reveal a row of clothes on hangers and a long mirror attached to the inside of the door. A narrow chest of drawers stood beside it.

Sarah glanced down at her still-dusty T-shirt and jeans, opened the tallboy and pulled out a pair of light blue cotton trousers with a matching top. After running to the bathroom to wash her hands and face she quickly changed and stood in front of the mirror combing out her long dark hair.

She looked at her reflection critically. Her hair reached halfway down her back and fell in gentle waves. She had always considered it rather a nondescript brown color, but in the sunlight it glimmered with gold and red. Her eyes were also brown and she knew she should be grateful for inheriting her father's thick dark eyelashes that made mascara nonessential. Her skin was fair, and to her constant frustration, colored rapidly when she was embarrassed or teased. There was a dusting of freckles across her nose that tended to spread when she was out in the sun too long.

Even Sarah had to admit that she had finally outgrown the tall, gangly frame that had set her apart from her shorter friends for years. At 5 feet, 8 inches she was still taller than most of them but her body was now shaped as just about any young lady would wish. She looked down at her ringless fingers. They were long, tapered, and feminine. But they were deceptively strong. More than ten years of playing the harp had given them unusual strength and agility. She flexed them carefully. She needed to practice.

Sarah replaced the hairbrush on her dressing table and left her bedroom. On the landing she hesitated, then on impulse, she ran up the short flight of stairs to her left. Even though she knew the Pearsons had not yet returned, she tiptoed into the first room. It was very like her own except there was a double bed, and the colors were pale blue with lace trim. Instead of the old rocking chair there was a welcoming armchair with cushions that matched the curtains and bedspread.

On the floor at the end of the bed was a battered leather suitcase that was still closed. There was a green canvas bag on the dressing table, alongside a camera, a makeup bag, an apple, and a wilted banana. Sarah took all this in with a swift glance then stepped out, and while berating herself for being so nosy, entered the next bedroom.

This room was more masculine with navy-and-red-plaid curtains and bedspread. Brian Pearson had obviously agreed. His navy blue suitcase sat on the floor. A gray rain coat was draped over the armchair in this room. Instead of a dressing table there was a desk that her brothers had used to do their homework. Sarah stepped closer. She saw the brown bag with the chocolate bars he'd bought at the shop. In addition to a small pile of papers that looked like a collection of receipts, ticket stubs, and brochures, there was also a little loose change and a few books. Sarah recognized one book as a paperback on the current bestseller list. The other two were leather bound and sat in what looked like an open small brown leather bag. Curious, Sarah picked one up. Much to her surprise, the spine read "Holy Bible." She put it down quickly, aware that although she was in her own home, she was trespassing. Quietly she left the room and walked thoughtfully down the stairs.

What kind of man carried a copy of the Bible around with him on holiday? Certainly no one she knew (other than the minister of course). And what was the other book? It looked just like his Bible— a bit thinner maybe—but as though they were a set of books that came together. They had both appeared to be well read.

Her mother and aunt had been impressed by Brian Pearson, but Sarah was anxious to form her own opinion. Somehow she felt sure that he was going to be unlike anyone she had met before. For some inexplicable reason it made her nervous. She was normally a cheerful, outgoing person who had little difficulty making new friends. This feeling of apprehension was alien to her. She tried to shrug it off and focus her attention on other things.

Sarah walked into the front parlor. As a child, she had called this room "the cold room," because at that time each room was heated by an individual fireplace. The front parlor was used so infrequently that the fire remained unlit for weeks at a time, and they kept the room shut off to contain its igloo status. Several years ago her father had insisted that they install central heating. They had lived with messy construction for weeks, but had subsequently all agreed that it had been well worth it. The hot water radiators now in every room were warmer and far more convenient than the fireplaces had been. Her mother still lit a coal fire during the winter months, but it was more for its cosy appeal than from necessity.

Out of habit perhaps, the Lewis family still did not use the front parlor often, preferring instead the cosier sitting room across the hall. The front parlor was used by the bed-and-breakfast guests and more formal visitors. Sarah used the room as her practice room, primarily because it usually afforded her the most privacy.

The harp drew everyone's attention when they first walked into the room. It stood tall, gold, and regal in the corner opposite the door. Sitting next to it was a small round stool and a music stand. The rest of the room was furnished quite simply with a brocade sofa and two matching arm chairs. There were a couple of low, polished wooden coffee tables near the sofa and a shelving unit containing an assortment of books, a few magazines, and some glass and china ornaments that her mother had collected over the years. There were two large ferns in terra cotta urns standing on either side of the fireplace. The fire was laid with coal and wood kindling but not lit. It would probably remain that way until the colder autumn weather arrived. On the mantlepiece above the fireplace were a few photographs and two ceramic black and white dogs.

Sarah smiled at the dogs. They had been christened at least a dozen times by each of the children as they grew up. Kevin's son Aled had taken over where she and her brothers had left off. She was pretty sure that their latest names were Mot and Bet, because those were the names of Kevin's sheep dogs. It was a joy to watch the way Aled hero-worshiped his dad and tried to emulate him. Despite all his teasing of her when they were young, Sarah loved Kevin dearly, and knew that Aled could do a lot worse than to become just like his father.

Sarah walked over to the harp, pulled out the small stool, and sat down. The sheet music that she needed was already on the stand where she had left it the day before. Gently, she lowered the heavy harp until its broad spine rested against her shoulder. Placing her feet on one of the pedals she released it and brought her arms around either side of the large instrument. With her head bent low next to the strings Sarah plucked one, then another. Leaning over, she picked up the large key sitting on the music stand, then placed the key over the small bolt at the top of each of the strings. She twisted it minutely, plucked, and listened again.

Ten minutes later she gave a satisfied nod and ran through a multi-octave scale again. She had long since learned that having perfect pitch was a mixed blessing. It enabled her to tune her instrument without the aid of a piano, but it also made her far more critical. She could hear the smallest discrepancy from the sound of a pure note. Listening to an instrument that was not tuned correctly was akin to nails on a chalkboard.

Sarah had been playing her harp regularly over the last few weeks in preparation for the upcoming Eisteddfod, which was to take place in Llangollen where the International Eisteddfod was held annually. She had already performed many times at the local level, and Saturday's performance was to be her final event of the year. The competition would be intense, but she felt that she had prepared as well as she could.

After warming up her fingers and the strings with several scales and arpeggios, Sarah began the intricate piece that she had prepared for competition. It required all her concentration; the finger work was difficult and there was considerable use of the foot pedals too. Soon she became oblivious to her surroundings and was totally engrossed in the glorious music she was creating. It was not until she'd played the last note, relaxed, and let the harp gently fall forward onto its base, that Sarah became aware of her audience. He was standing in the doorway watching her. She took a small, sharp breath, momentarily startled. She did not know what she had expected him to look like, but it was not this.

He was tall, well over six feet she guessed, broad shouldered but lean. He wore a light blue collared T-shirt, jeans, and Nike athletic shoes, whose style was unfamiliar to her. She assumed they were basketball shoes. He had wavy blonde hair cut short and brushed back from his face. From this distance his eyes appeared to be blue. And in the few seconds she had taken to ascertain all this, they had not left her face. He was, undoubtedly, the most handsome man she had ever met. Furious with herself, yet unable to prevent it, Sarah felt color infuse her cheeks.

"Hello," she said, desperately trying to sound calm. "I'm sorry. Have you been there long? I didn't hear you come in."

Brian Pearson blinked and it seemed to break the spell. He smiled and stepped into the room.

"It's I who should apologize," he said as he moved forward. "I was uninvited and I was staring." Sarah smiled and lowered her head to hide it. He caught the movement and said, "Uh oh! You noticed." His laugh was a pleasant sound.

As he drew closer he held out his hand to her. "Hi, I'm Brian Pearson." Sarah withdrew her arm from around the harp and put her hand in his.

"Sarah Lewis" she said. His grasp was firm and warm.

"I've never been this close to a harp before. I've seen them in the distance at concerts, but it's hard to appreciate their beauty when they're just a small part of the whole orchestra." He touched the instrument. "It really is a work of art."

Sarah smiled. Anyone who appreciated her beloved instrument was a friend indeed. "This harp is quite old. It belonged to my grandmother. When I was little I practiced on a smaller one that was very simply made. It didn't have any of the scroll work or gold leafing that this one has."

"How long have you played the harp? You play beautifully."

Sarah gave him an appraising look. Rather to her surprise, his expression indicated that he was totally in earnest. She had received deferential compliments on her playing before, but Brian Pearson was not just being polite; he seemed to have genuinely been touched by her music.

"I've been playing since I was ten. The piece you heard has always been one of my favorites. I've been practicing it for a few weeks now, in preparation for Eisteddfod competition."

Brian's face registered confusion. "For what competition?"

"Eisteddfod."

"Aee . . . sth . . . " Sarah laughed as Brian tried to pronounce it. "It's alright; it's a Welsh word. It's the name of an age-old popular Welsh folk festival that's held throughout the summer at different levels: locally, nationally, and internationally. There are lots of different events but primarily it is a competition for the arts—music, poetry, and dance. The competition is stiff at the national and international Eisteddfod, so it's really an honor to be allowed to perform."

"That's great! When is the 'aeesthvod' you're competing in going to be held?"

Sarah smiled again at Brian's attempt at the word, conceding that he deserved points for trying. "The International Eisteddfod is going on this week in Llangollen, a town about an hour's drive from here. The solo harp event is on Friday. That's when I'll be there."

"Hey, I'll have to talk to my mother. I bet she'd enjoy going to something like that."

"Well, it would be one way of getting a very big dose of Welsh culture in a small amount of time."

Brian laughed again. "If I use that selling point, I can guarantee we'll be there." Then he sobered up and said, "Besides I'd love to hear you play again."

Before she could respond there was a loud clatter from the hallway. A door slammed and there was the sound of running feet. Both Brian and Sarah turned to face the doorway.

"Aunty Sarah! Aunty Sarah! Where are you?" a young voice shouted.

Sarah called out "I'm in the front parlor, Aled."

There was an impression of multiple legs, fur, and speed. Aled Lewis, closely followed by his father's sheepdog, hurled himself through the doorway and into Sarah's arms.

Sarah gave the young boy a big squeeze, then reached out to grab the exuberant dog.

"Oh Aled, it's lovely to see you, but we've got to get this wild animal out of here before your Nain comes in."

"What wild animal?" Aled asked in bewilderment, his eyes roaming the room.

"The dog, you daft thing" Sarah giggled. "Down Mot! Down!" She yanked at the dog's collar as the dog continued to leap up and lick her face. "Jump off my knee Aled and let me get off this stool." Aled obediently got up and Sarah, still grappling with the dog's collar, stood up too.

Suddenly remembering that they were not alone, Sarah turned to Aled and said "Aled, this is Mr. Pearson. He's one of Nain's guests." Then to Brian she said "Mr. Pearson, I'd like you to meet my nephew, Aled Lewis." Brian bent down and held out his hand to Aled. Aled gave Sarah a quick look. She nodded imperceptibly and he stepped forward and put his own small hand into Brian's.

"Hi Aled! I'm very pleased to meet you."

Aled grinned and turned to Sarah "Aunty Sarah, Mr. Pearson talks funny."

Sarah gave Brian an apologetic look. "Aled, that's not a very polite thing to say. Mr. Pearson comes from America and people there don't learn to speak Welsh or English quite like we do."

Aled looked shocked. "Didn't he go to school?"

Brian burst out laughing. He crouched down and looked Aled in the eye. "Aled, I can tell you're a very bright young man. Can you speak English and Welsh?"

"Of course!" Aled was obviously amazed to learn that some adults were not bilingual.

"Well, you're way ahead of me then. I can't get my tongue around any of the words I see on all the road signs here."

"Aw, that's easy!" Aled paused momentarily, then offered, "Want me to help you?"

"Sure! That would be great," Brian replied enthusiastically.

Sarah smiled down at the pleased expression on her young nephew's face. She couldn't help but be impressed by the way Brian was relating to him.

"What d'you want to know?" Aled was anxious to begin his tutoring.

Brian was thoughtful for a moment. "How about numbers?"

Aled's face lit up. "I can count all the way to one hundred!"

"Wow, that's awesome! But maybe I should start by going up to ten. What d'ya think?"

"Alright," agreed Aled unperturbed. "It's un, dau, tri, pedwar, pump, chwech, saith, wyth, naw, deg." The young boy rattled the words off in short order. Brian raised his hand in mock horror.

"Whoa there, buddy! Remember, I haven't heard these words before. Let's do it one number at a time okay?"

Aled giggled and turned to Sarah and in a loud whisper said, "He really does talk funny Aunty Sarah. He told me 'whoa' just like the cowboys say to their horses." Sarah bit her lower lip to try to prevent herself from giggling along with Aled. She gave a little cough to cover her laughter and tightened her hold on Mot's collar.

"I'll take Mot out into the garden while you two work on your numbers. I'll be back in a minute."

"Alright," Aled said and returned his attention to Brian. "The first number is 'Un.'"

Brian slowly repeated "Un." He looked up over Aled's head as Sarah left the room. When she glanced back, he grinned at her and gave her a quick wink. It was so quick that she wondered if she'd imagined it.

❦ ❦ ❦

By the time Sarah returned from taking a reluctant Mot outside, everyone had congregated in the front parlor. Annie Lewis was sitting on the sofa next to a very attractive, white-haired lady. Sarah's brother, Kevin, was having an animated conversation with Brian Pearson, and Aled was hopping around both of them on one foot.

As Sarah entered the room, Annie Lewis called out to her daughter. "Sarah, come and meet Mrs. Pearson."

Sarah walked over to the sofa. She was surprised to see that despite her age, Mrs. Pearson was dressed in tailored khaki trousers and a checked blouse. Sarah didn't think her mother had ever owned a pair of trousers. Mrs. Pearson shook Sarah's hand. "I'm pleased to meet you, Sarah." Unlike her son, Mrs. Pearson's hand shake had a soft, fragile quality. Her voice was soft, too. Although her American accent was readily apparent, it did not jar the ear as so many others did. There was a gentle kindness that radiated from her.

"It's nice to meet you too, Mrs. Pearson." Sarah said.

"Oh, please call me Iris" said Mrs. Pearson. "Everyone does." Sarah smiled and nodded, but inwardly she wondered if she could ever call anyone so much her senior by her first name. It seemed very disrespectful and against all her childhood training.

"Hello, Sis." Kevin walked over and gave her a hug. "How was inventory?"

Sarah groaned. "Boring!"

Kevin gave a her a sympathetic pat on the shoulder, but before he could say anything more, Aled called out. "Aunty Sarah, you should hear Mr. Pearson. He can count to ten now."

Out of the corner of her eye, Sarah saw Mrs. Pearson look momentarily startled. Sarah smiled at Aled and said "Do you think he's ready to show us?"

Aled looked like a proud parent. "Oh yes! Come on, Mr. Pearson. Show them."

Aware that all eyes were on him, Brian looked a bit self-conscious. He leaned over to Aled and whispered "Help me out if I get stuck, okay?"

"Okay," Aled whispered in conspiratorial style.

Brian cleared his throat and began. He stumbled through the numbers with only one prompt from Aled. When he finished, everyone clapped enthusiastically and he gave an exaggerated bow.

"He doesn't sound quite right yet, but he just needs to practice doesn't he?" Aled turned to his aunt for reassurance.

"Oh I'm sure he'll get better every day if he practices," Sarah assented seriously. Aled looked pleased and missed the smile Sarah exchanged with Brian.

"Kevin," Annie Lewis's voice reminded Sarah there were others in the room. "Are you and Aled going to be able to stay and have supper with us?"

"Oh no, Mam." Kevin replied. "We just dropped in on our way back from town." He paused. "Actually it was Sarah I needed to talk to."

Sarah looked over at him expectantly.

"I'm afraid I've got a problem, Sis. Edward Davis asked if I'd drive over to Newtown with him on Friday, to check on the sheep at market. I really ought to go because the prices they fetch will affect us next week. But I told you I'd help take the harp to Llangollen that day. I was wondering if you'd feel alright asking Gareth next door to help you load up and then p'raps one of the officials at the Eisteddfod could help you at that end?"

Kevin looked unhappy when he saw Sarah's crestfallen expression. "I'm really sorry, Sarah!"

Then Brian's voice broke in. "Hey, I'd be happy to help out if Sarah's willing to show me what to do. Mom and I were hoping to go to the 'aesthvod' anyway."

Iris Pearson looked startled. It was obviously the first time she'd heard these plans. But she covered her surprise quickly. "That sounds like a perfect solution," she said. Brian gave her a grateful smile. "What exactly is a . . . whatever it was Brian just said?" All the adults laughed.

"Aw come on, Mom. I was just starting to think I was getting the hang of this language!" The laughter erupted again.

"Well dear, I don't want to make you feel bad. I probably wouldn't be any the wiser if one of these fluent Welsh speakers had said it, would I?"

Brian grinned at his mother. "Mothers are the greatest! They're always trying to salvage their children's self-esteem."

This time it was Iris Pearson who laughed.

Kevin turned to Brian. "Brian, that's a very generous offer, but I don't want you to change any of your own plans. We can work this out fine without inconveniencing you and your mother."

"We'd be happy to do it. I was talking to Sarah before you came in. She told me about this folk festival and it sounds like just the sort of thing Mom would like to see. I heard Sarah playing the harp and she was telling me about the competition she's entering. I'd like to be there to hear her."

Sarah was surprised and flattered by Brian's comment. She felt suddenly nervous and gave herself a mental shake. What was wrong with her? She'd played before family, friends, and strangers many times before. Why should having the Pearsons there, or rather Brian Pearson in particular, make such a difference? It was a question she wasn't given time to pursue.

"Would that be okay with you, Sarah?" Brian asked.

"Certainly." Sarah was amazed that her own voice sounded so matter of fact.

"Well, that's it then!" There was gratitude and relief in Kevin's voice. "Thank you very much, Brian." He shook the other man's hand. "Mrs. Pearson." Kevin nodded at the older lady. "Aled, my boy, it's time we headed home. I can smell your Mam's supper cooking from here."

Aled looked up with an awed expression. "You can, Dad? Gosh, I thought it was Nain's supper we could smell!" Kevin grinned and tousled his son's hair affectionately. "Come on lad."

"Bye Nain, bye Aunty Sarah, bye Mrs. Pearson, bye Mr. Pearson. Don't forget to practice your numbers!"

"I won't, Aled. Thanks for all your help, little buddy."

Aled beamed and grasped his father's hand. "C'mon Dad, I think I can smell Mam's supper too!"

When the flurry of good-byes and waving had subsided, Iris Pearson turned to Annie Lewis and said "What a cute little boy."

Annie smiled proudly. "He is sweet, isn't he." Then her smile was replaced by an aghast expression. "Goodness me, we've all been sitting here this long time and I haven't offered anyone a cup of tea. Oh, you must be dying for one by now! What will you think of me? I'll go and put the kettle on straight away." She rose quickly and was halfway to the kitchen before anyone could voice an objection.

Sarah saw a concerned look pass between mother and son, then Brian said, "Sarah, why don't you tell my mother more about the folk festival and I'll go and see if I can do anything to help your mother out." Sarah looked at him blankly. Guests had never gone to help out in the kitchen before. She gathered her wits and would have stopped him, but Mrs. Pearson leaned forward eagerly and said "Yes dear, do tell me. I've never even heard of this festival before." And so Sarah found herself describing the International Eisteddfod while listening to Brian's footsteps receding down the hall.

🐦 🐦 🐦

A little later Sarah was sitting at the kitchen table eating supper with her mother and the two Pearsons. It was most unusual. She put it down to Americans being far more casual than their British counterparts. Never before had guests persuaded her mother not to bother setting the dining room table. The Pearsons seemed more than happy just to fit into the family routine and did not want to be looked upon as visiting strangers. She glanced surreptitiously at Brian Pearson. Maybe it wasn't Americans in general, but rather this one in particular.

"You're sure I can't get you a nice cup of tea?" Annie Lewis asked the Pearsons for the second time since they had sat down together.

Iris Pearson smiled patiently. "No, really Mrs. Lewis, we're fine. This meal is lovely. It's so good to have some home cooking again. These potatoes taste so fresh they're almost sweet."

Annie responded warmly. "They are good aren't they? I dug them out of the garden this afternoon. I always say you can't do better than fresh garden vegetables."

"I'm sure you're right. I grew up on a potato farm in Idaho. Potato harvest was such a big operation that they closed schools for a couple of weeks so the children could go work in the fields. We usually had a real good crop of big baking potatoes. But I must say, they never tasted like these."

"In Idaho, you say," Annie looked thoughtful. "Now where exactly is that?"

"It's in the Western United States," Iris Pearson said.

"Is it anywhere near California?" Annie asked, a little vaguely.

"It's north and east of California. I'm afraid we don't enjoy the same warm climate as California, but our cold nights and warm summer days are perfect for growing potatoes."

"Well now, tell me," asked Annie, "is that where Glyn and Mary ended up when they left here?"

"Eventually, yes. It's rather a long story, and there are quite a few holes in it. In fact, that's one reason why I begged Brian to bring me here. We know that Glyn and Mary ended up in Idaho. They had a farm there. They started with a few sheep . . ."

"Which was his father's livelihood," interrupted Annie.

"Yes, that's right," Iris Pearson continued. "I suppose he felt that it was an occupation that he knew. It was very isolated country at that time, but he was a hard-working man and managed his farm well.

"We also know, obviously, that they originally came from Pen-y-Bryn. People have told me that my grandmother talked about this place a lot. She must have loved it here. I can see why now. What we've never really known is what happened between leaving this village and arriving in Idaho. We've never found a written record. Mary died giving birth to my mother. My uncle was only two at the time, so neither of them had personal memories of her. My grandfather never really got over losing her. He threw himself into his work and died less than a year later in an accident with a plough horse. The farm and everything on it was sold, and the money given to a neighboring family who took in my mother and uncle and raised them as their own."

"Poor man!" Annie sighed at the end of Iris's account. "Fancy going all that way and losing her so soon after."

"It must have been very hard for him," Iris agreed. "I'm just glad they can be together again now." She gave her gentle smile and turned her attention to her supper once more.

Sarah looked at her curiously. What a strange thing to say. Iris Pearson acted as though she knew where her grandparents were, as though they were still living somewhere. She wanted to ask her what she had meant, but the conversation had moved on.

Brian picked up the story. "Because Glyn and Mary died when their children were so young, we know almost nothing about them.

We're not sure why they ended up in Idaho or even how they got there. We were hoping that by coming here we could unravel some of the mystery. We know there's no one around who remembers them personally, but perhaps there were stories passed down within families?"

Annie Lewis shook her head sadly. "I'm afraid you will be disappointed, Mr. Pearson."

"Please call me Brian," Brian interrupted.

Annie gave him a brief smile. "I've known about Glyn Jones and Mary Williams for as long as I can remember. As you said, it was a story that was passed around. In fact I'm afraid the story may have been added to a bit over the years. But the reason the story never seemed to die was that it was such a mystery. No one knew what had become of the couple. Mary's father moved away, and so did the Joneses. As far as I know, no one ever heard from them again."

A look of disappointment flashed over Iris Pearson's face. Brian, however, was not so easily dissuaded.

"Tell us what you know of the story, Mrs. Lewis," he asked.

Annie Lewis paused to take a sip of tea, then recounted the story Sarah had heard earlier in the day. Was it really this afternoon that she'd heard it for the first time? It seemed so familiar now. As she listened to her mother, Sarah experienced some of the same frustration that she saw played out in the Pearsons's expressions. What had happened to that young couple from the time they left their Welsh homes to the time they settled in their new one? It was as though that period of time no longer existed. And yet it had obviously been life-changing. Sarah felt herself leaving the realm of casual observer and becoming emotionally involved in the plight of these people. There had to be something, someone, somewhere to go to for a clue.

There was a brief silence when Annie finished her story. Sarah could tell that both Iris and Brian Pearson were disappointed. In an effort to cheer up his mother, Brian said, "Well, Mother, we could drive out to the manor that Mrs. Lewis told us about. You could see where they met and where Grandpa worked when he was young."

Iris Pearson nodded.

"I could take you to the home where he grew up too, if you like," Sarah volunteered.

"Is it still there?" Brian asked in surprise.

"Oh yes. Of course it doesn't look exactly the same any more. Some friends of mine recently finished renovating the old farm house. They bought the surrounding land when the current squire at Deniol Manor sold off some of his property to cover expenses at the manor, and they've done a lovely job. They left the basic structure of the old house intact. And of course the location hasn't changed a bit."

"That would be great. You're sure your friends wouldn't mind a couple of American tourists descending upon them?" Brian asked anxiously.

Sarah smiled. "Not if I forewarn them. I have to make deliveries up there tomorrow morning anyway. So you can either come up with me or, if you'd rather, you could go up alone in the afternoon."

"Deliveries?"

"Every Thursday I take supplies from the shop to some of the outlying farms. It saves the farmers or their wives an extra trip into the village. Tomorrow's the day and Cerys phoned in her shopping list already. If you're interested I could give her a ring right now."

Brian looked at his mother questioningly. She had been listening to Sarah with interest. "That would be wonderful, Sarah," she said.

"Alright, I'll be back in a minute." Sarah left the table and walked into the hall to use the phone. True to her word she was back shortly. "I spoke to Tom. He'll be out in the fields all day, but he mentioned it to Cerys, and she said she'll be home. You're welcome anytime."

"How very gracious of her. Thank you so much, Sarah," Iris Pearson said gratefully.

"Where exactly is the farm?" Brian asked.

"It's about eight miles further up the valley from us. You follow the road that goes past our house until you come to a fork in the road. There's a postbox in the wall right before you get there. You take the left fork and follow it past three or four smaller lanes, then . . . "

"Wait! Stop!" Brian held up his hands in surrender. "I vote we either go with you or follow you up!"

Sarah laughed. "Come on, it didn't sound that bad!"

"Maybe not for you! Driving these narrow, winding lanes, on the wrong side of the road with my mother squealing every time we meet a tractor bearing down on us is bad enough," he paused to grin as his mother made a noise of denial, "but doing so following a local's directions would be suicide. I'd end up in Oxford again!"

Sarah wished that she could come up with a suitably stinging retort, but Iris Pearson saved her the trouble by saying "Brian!" with the tone of reproof that only mothers can use.

He looked over at Sarah apologetically. "Hey, I didn't mean that personally! I just can't believe how fast everyone goes on these winding lanes. There are no numbers or compass directions on any of the street signs. I've pretty much decided that if you don't know where the road is, you'll never find it!"

"What do you mean 'compass directions'?" Sarah asked with confusion.

"Well most of the towns near us have a Center Street or Main Street in the middle of town. From there the roads are patterned in a grid with each street having a number, like 100 North, 200 North, 300 North; or 100 East, 200 East, and so on. So if you know someone lives at 343 North 200 East, you'd go two streets right of the center of town and three and a half streets up. Does that make sense?"

"Yes, I see. So the whole town is built along straight roads that run perpendicular or parallel to each other?"

"Right!"

"Umm. Well, that would be easier I suppose. But it sounds terribly unimaginative."

Brian laughed. "I can't argue with that one. There's a lot more creativity to your winding lanes."

"Don't listen to him, Sarah" Iris interjected. "He's just giving you a hard time. He loves it here. Just today he was telling me how amazing all the hedges are along the lanes."

"Oh yes, all the better to block your vision of oncoming tractors!" Brian teased his mother.

"Brian!" Iris reproved again. "You're impossible!"

This time it was Sarah who laughed. "It's alright Mrs. Pearson. I think we should teach him a lesson. Why don't you meet me at the shop at about nine o'clock and I'll drive you both up there. We'll let him be the passenger on those winding roads for a change."

Iris Pearson exchanged a smile of conspiracy with Sarah. "That would be perfect. And if we hear one single moan, shudder, or shout from him about speed, corners, or passing vehicles, we'll never let him hear the end of it!"

Annie Lewis, who had been enjoying this interchange, looked up from her cup of tea and said "It looks to me like you're outnumbered, young man."

Brian gave an exaggerated sigh and shook his head. Then with a glint of mischief in his eyes he said, "Henpecked! I'm totally henpecked!"

All three ladies laughed, and Sarah couldn't help thinking that she'd never seen a less likely candidate for henpecking in her life.

2 June 1881

Dear Father,

We have been on board ship now for almost two weeks, but it seems longer. It took me a few days to become accustomed to the motion of the sea beneath my feet, but I can truthfully say I scarcely notice it now. Indeed, I have fared far better than many fellow passengers. Some of whom, to this day, are confined to their beds with seasickness.

Our sleeping quarters are cramped but adequate. I quit them at the earliest convenience each morning and spend most of my day on deck. I fear that my complexion is suffering greatly from the constant sun and wind. However, I am pleased to be getting daily exercise and sea air.

When we first left harbor we were followed for a few days by flocks of seagulls. Their piercing cries were quite deafening. However, to my surprise, I find that now that they are gone I miss them greatly. Perhaps it is because their absence is a constant reminder of how far from Wales we have come. I cannot contemplate the thought of never seeing those familiar green hills again, or of not looking upon your face once more. There will always be a special place in my heart for my homeland.

My occasional longing for all that is familiar has been helped considerably by the friendship of a young family we met while boarding ship. Will and Catriona Evans are traveling to America from Merthyr Tydfil. They and their two young daughters are the only passengers on board with whom Glyn and I can speak Welsh. (I had not anticipated how hard it would be to have to converse in a language other than my native one. I am grateful for your diligent tutelage. My limited command of the English language has been invaluable on this voyage.)

I think perhaps the Evans struggle similarly with the language barrier onboard ship, for we speak together at every opportunity. Glyn and Will have formed a strong friendship. Poor Catriona is often confined to her bed with seasickness, but I have enjoyed accompanying her girls on deck. They are a delight and help to keep my mind and hands busy.

We have been told that the coast of America is only a few days distant. I will mail this letter to you as soon we reach landfall.

Your loving daughter,
Mary.

Chapter 2

Sarah could not sleep that night. She lay in bed for a long time reliving excerpts from her day: Brian in the shop with Aunty Lil; Mabel Jones's story about Brian's ancestors, later retold by her mother; Brian's response to her music; Brian and Aled together; Brian talking; Brian teasing. It was always Brian. She had never been so deeply affected by a man in so short a period of time. There was something about him. Did others feel it too, or was it just her?

She wished she could shake it off—this feeling of wonder, uncertainty, and, if she was willing to admit it, this feeling of attraction. It was unsettling to say the least.

Sarah had gone out with a few young men over the last four or five years, but she'd known that none of the relationships would ever develop into anything serious. It was one of the few things in her life that she regretted. She'd always wanted to have her own home, a loving husband whom she could love in return, and children. She wanted her own children.

She'd seen both of her brothers marry, and many of her school friends had, too. But most of them had met their future spouses when they had gone away to college. She had not. And despite its limited social life, she had made the conscious decision to return to Pen-y-Bryn. She was happy here. But there were times when she worried about her future. Her mother was getting older. Would she be as happy here when she was alone? The thought filled her with a great emptiness.

Sarah tossed and turned in bed. Her head was so full that sleep would not come. Why couldn't she get Brian Pearson out of her thoughts? That he was overwhelmingly attractive, she couldn't deny. Thinking about him as she had first seen him, standing in the front parlor doorway, still took her breath away. But it wasn't just his appearance.

He didn't fit the loud, aggressive stereotype Americans promoted on the big screen or TV. He had self-confidence, certainly. That was evident by his comfortable manner when meeting others, and his easy bantering at the supper table. But he wasn't overbearing. There was a kind gentleness in him that she had rarely seen a man display. She had seen real emotion in his eyes when she finished playing the harp. He had been tender with Aled. And he obviously cared deeply for his mother.

But she knew so little about him. She assumed he was from Idaho, but realized that even that could be wrong. What was his occupation, when he wasn't touring with his mother? Did he have any brothers or sisters? Or a girlfriend? That sudden thought made Sarah feel sick. What was she doing? Lying here sleepless because of someone who, for all she knew, was already engaged to a beautiful blonde in America. She punched her pillow furiously—this was ludicrous. She sat up in bed. Lying down was getting her nowhere. There was only one way she could clear her mind.

Silently, she slipped out of bed, put on a dressing gown and slippers and crept downstairs into the front parlor. She closed the door carefully behind her and turned on one of the small lamps on the coffee table nearest the harp. Using its warm glow, she adjusted the harp's strings and sat down to play. This time she played from memory. First a rousing piece that helped her release her frustrations. Then she moved on to a gentle, lyrical ballad. It was a haunting melody and when she brought it to its close she felt emotionally spent. She raised her head slowly from the strings. And there he was, just as he had stood before.

They gazed at each other across the room. "I couldn't sleep," Sarah said softly, and immediately felt stupid for having said something so obvious.

"I couldn't either," Brian said simply, and walked into the room. He was wearing a white T-shirt and gray loose-fitting trousers made of sweatshirt fabric. His feet were bare.

Suddenly self-conscious, Sarah looked down and tightened the belt of her dressing gown. It was faded and worn, but it was modest.

"You have an amazing gift, Sarah," Brian spoke quietly. She could tell that he was sincere.

"Thank you," she replied. "I've always loved music. Playing the harp is a pleasure, but it's also a therapy for me."

Brian nodded his understanding. "Like tonight."

"Like tonight." Sarah repeated. "I'm sorry if it disturbed you. I really thought that by closing the door I would prevent the sound from traveling very far."

"I would never have heard you if I hadn't already been awake. I hope you don't mind me coming down?"

Right then Sarah couldn't have told him if she really minded or not. She just knew that whatever relief she had found in her music had been reversed as soon as he'd walked in. Yet, deep down she was illogically glad that he was there. She realized that this was her opportunity to get answers to some of the questions that had teemed through her mind earlier that night.

She left the harp stool and walked over to the sofa and sat down. Then looking up at him she said, "Tell me about Idaho."

Brian looked momentarily disconcerted at the sudden change of subject. "Idaho?" he asked.

"Yes, that's where you're from isn't it?"

"Well, yes. Although I haven't lived there on a permanent basis for a few years now." He walked over and sat down near her. "What do you want to know?"

"Oh, I don't know. Tell me about your family and your home. What does it look like? Where do you live when you're not there?"

"Whoa, slow down!" Brian chuckled. "Okay, well we come from a small town called Rexburg in southeastern Idaho. It's basically a rural community, but there's a large Church-owned junior college there. My dad was a Chemistry teacher at the college, but he died about a year ago of a sudden heart attack." Brian's eyes had a faraway look, as though he was seeing things from the past. He shook it off and continued.

"My mother grew up on a potato farm just outside Rexburg—it's very near the farm where Glyn and Mary Jones lived. My parents met when they were both students at the junior college. I was born and brought up in Rexburg, along with my four sisters."

"You have four sisters?" Sarah asked in amazement.

Brian laughed. "Yep, you see I wasn't joking when I told you I was henpecked!"

Sarah laughed with him. "Are they older or younger than you?"

"All older. Linda's the oldest. She's married and lives in Texas. Her husband works for an oil company there. They have four children. Valerie's next. She's married and lives in Utah. Her husband's a dentist, and they have three children. Ellen married another Idaho farmer and lives just a few miles from home. She has four children. And my twin sister Mary got married at Christmas time. She and her husband are attending Brigham Young University. That's also in Utah."

Sarah looked at him with interest. "You have a twin sister?"

"Yes, and believe me, I am reminded constantly that she is still older than me by fifteen minutes!"

Sarah laughed again. "It sounds like we both had the raw end of things growing up," she said. "I had two older brothers who tortured me with creepy crawlies, frogs, and newts. I've been the object of all their teasing for as long as I can remember."

"I've met Kevin, of course. Where does your other brother live?"

"John's a banker so he's transferred to various bank branches around the country every few years. Right now he and his wife live in South Wales. We don't see them as often as we'd like to, but they keep in touch."

"That's great. Families are real important."

Sarah looked at him in surprise. What an unusual thing for a man to say. She wondered again what made him so different from other men that she'd known. She liked talking to Brian. He was interesting and humorous. He didn't talk down to her—he made her feel that what she thought, said, or did were important. But still, it seemed as though it was something more. She was just scratching the surface. There was depth to him that she sensed she had not yet even begun to discover.

"You said that you don't live at home anymore. Where do you live?"

"Right now I'm living in Salt Lake City. I've been there about three years attending the University of Utah Medical School."

"You're going to be a doctor?" Sarah's delight was spontaneous.

"Yes, I hope so." Brian's voice warmed to Sarah's enthusiasm.

"That's wonderful. I'm a nurse."

A look of surprise flashed across Brian's face. "You are? That's awesome. But I thought you worked at the shop."

"I do help out there a lot during the summers and on weekends, but most of the time you'll find me at the local Primary school. I'm the school nurse."

"You're kidding. That's great! Where did you do your schooling?" Brian asked with interest.

"In Birmingham. After qualifying I worked for a few months at the Orthopedic hospital in Oswestry. Then, when Mrs. Price retired as the local school nurse, I applied for the position. I suppose I was ready to return to village life." She paused and looked slightly embarrassed. "And I know it sounds trite, but I love working with the children."

"I bet they love you too." Brian said with feeling.

Sarah felt herself blush at his praise. She was thankful for the concealment afforded by the limited lighting, and anxiously redirected the conversation away from herself.

"Is this your first trip to Britain?" she asked.

"Yes. Mom and Dad had been planning this trip for years. I sometimes feel that I'm a very poor substitute for Dad, but I had some free time during the summer and didn't have little ones to take care of at home. So I was the logical choice. Mom has been working on her genealogy and is really hooked . . . "

"On her what?" Sarah interrupted.

"Genealogy. It's the study of your family tree. Mom's been trying to find the names and birth, marriage, and death dates of her ancestors. She's always been fascinated by her Welsh line, but hasn't been able to go much further back than Glyn and Mary Jones. Her main goal on this trip was to uncover the mystery of their arrival in Idaho and find out more about their families here."

"No wonder she was so disappointed when we couldn't tell you anything new at supper time."

Brian's face fell. "Yeah, she felt bad. But I don't think she's given up yet. Perhaps we can see if the local church has any family records."

Sarah thought for a few minutes. "It might. But you'd probably be better off trying the chapel first. The chapel is this side of the river. The church is on the other side." Sarah noticed Brian's look of confusion. "The church is the Church of England; the chapel is Welsh Methodist. Mary's father was a Welsh Methodist minister so my guess would be that if there are any records they'll be at the chapel."

"Oh I see. Yeah, I'm sure you're right. Gee, we'd really be up the creek without your help, wouldn't we?"

"I wish we could help you more. You've come so far. It's the least we can do."

Brian smiled at her. "Typical British understatement! You're doing a lot already, and we really appreciate it."

He stood up, and before Sarah knew what he was doing, he had reached out and pulled her to her feet. "Come on sleepyhead. I think we've talked long enough. If I'm going to risk my life on those roads with you at the wheel tomorrow, you've got to get some sleep."

Sarah smothered a yawn. He was right. She bent down and turned off the small light and together they walked out of the room. Brian left her at her bedroom door with a soft "goodnight," and before she could respond he had disappeared up the flight of stairs leading to his own room.

❦ ❦ ❦

Sarah woke the next morning to the sound of birds singing in the trees outside her window. Despite staying awake until the early hours of the morning, she felt rested. She stretched luxuriously, then jumped out of bed. She dressed quickly in a pair of comfortable jeans and a multi-colored T-shirt. After rooting through one of her drawers for a few minutes, she uncovered a narrow blue ribbon that matched one of the colors in her shirt. She swept her hair back into a ponytail and tied the ribbon in place. Then she stepped back and gazed at herself critically in the mirror. She knew that she couldn't dress up to deliver groceries, but it was important to her that she look nice today. She pulled a face at her reflection. Oh well, she would have to do.

As she reached the bottom of the stairs and started down the hall towards the kitchen, Sarah heard voices. She quickened her pace and entered the room to see her mother standing over Brian at the Aga. They both turned when she walked in.

"Good morning dear," Annie smiled at Sarah. "How pretty you look."

"She does indeed," added Brian with a twinkle in his eye.

She was startled again at how much his presence affected her. She felt the color mounting on her cheeks but tried to appear nonchalant. "Thank you. What are you two up to?"

"Your mother is coaching me in the art of making a British breakfast. It smells awesome, but the doctor in me is wondering how anyone in this country lives past thirty. I've never seen so much cholesterol on one plate!" Brian showed her his plate loaded up with fried bread, bacon, sausage and egg, baked beans and fried tomato. "Even the tomato, the one redeeming item of nutritional value, has been fried!"

Sarah laughed. "There's a simple answer to your question. Farmers around here eat a breakfast like that then spend all day in the fields burning off every calorie. The rest of us eat this." She opened a cupboard and lifted out a box of dry cereal. Blazoned across the box were the words "Fortified with twenty essential vitamins and minerals. No Fat."

Brian sat down at the table, looked at his plate and groaned. "Do you mean to tell me that you're going to sit here and eat that in front of me while I wade my way through all of this?"

Sarah laughed again. "I'm afraid so. But if it's any consolation, I bet yours will taste better!"

Annie walked over to Brian and handed him a glass of orange juice. "Don't you pay any attention to her, Brian. She's always been as skinny as a stick and I can't seem to do anything about it. Now you're a big strong young man. You need this sort of breakfast. Not that bird food she eats."

Brian grinned as Sarah rolled her eyes at her mother's words. She finished her cereal quickly and took the empty bowl over to Annie at the sink, then dropped a kiss on her mother's lined cheek. "Thanks for breakfast Mam. I'd better run over to the shop and organize the deliveries if I'm to be ready when the Pearsons arrive." Then she turned to Brian. "Do you happen to know what shoe size your mother wears?"

Brian looked startled by the strange question coming out of the blue. "Uh, seven or maybe eight. Gee, I'm not sure."

"Hmm, your sizes must not be the same as ours. I was just thinking that your mother probably didn't pack any wellies for this trip and I'd hate to have her ruin her shoes up at the farm."

Brian now looked totally blank. "Wellies? What are wellies?"

It was Sarah's turn to look surprised. "Don't you have wellies in Idaho?"

"I have no idea. It all depends on what wellies are."

"Come with me." She beckoned him to follow her to the boot room. In a corner of the room was a small pile of black rubber boots. Pointing to them, Sarah said, "Those are wellies."

"They're rubber boots," said Brian.

Sarah grinned at him impishly. "They may be rubber boots where you come from, but over here they're wellies!" She knelt down and pulled out a pair from the back. She sat back on her heels and tried to brush a layer of dust off the boots. Then she handed them to him. "These were my dad's. Try them on and see if they'll fit you."

Silently Brian took them from her, untied one of his athletic shoes and pulled on the wellie. "They'll be great. Thank you."

"You're welcome," Sarah said simply. She turned and dug through the pile again. "These are my mother's. D'you think they'd fit your mother?"

Brian looked at them. "I'd say they were about right. But are you sure your mother won't mind."

"Not at all. She'd feel far worse if you didn't use them and ruined good shoes in the farmyard."

Just then they heard voices coming from the kitchen. Sarah stood up and said, "It sounds like your mother's up. Why don't you take the wellies into the kitchen and see if they'll work for her."

"Okay. Thanks, Sarah."

She handed him the boots. For a fleeting moment their hands touched, then he turned and pushed open the door to the kitchen.

Sarah stood motionless for a few seconds, trying to come to terms with her response to his nearness. She heard him say, "Hi Mom!" and her own mother's voice said "Oh good, you've found some. I do hope they'll fit." Then Sarah picked up her own wellies, tucked them under her arm, and quietly let herself out of the house.

A brisk walk through the village did much to clear Sarah's head but she wondered if her emotions would ever be the same.

The shop was not scheduled to open for another thirty minutes, but her Aunty Lil was already there, dusting off some of the shelves. Sarah took a deep breath and mentally ordered herself to ignore her inner turmoil and behave normally.

"'Morning Aunty Lil," she called as she entered the shop through the back rooms. Her aunt looked up.

"Hello dear. How are you this morning?"

"Fine, thank you. I came in to see if you've received any more delivery orders before I start loading up the van."

"Of course. Let me see." Lil walked into the small office with Sarah close behind her. Lil pulled a large ledger book off a shelf. It didn't matter how high-tech other supermarkets became, Lillian Lewis would always do her book work in books. "It looks like we've just got the Robertses, Parrys, and Dave Joneses today. Mind you, the Roberts's order is rather big. D'you think you can manage it all, bach?"

"I'll be fine. Besides, I should have some help this morning."

Aunty Lil looked at her in surprise. "Who would that be?"

"Mr. and Mrs. Pearson. The people staying at our house," she clarified. "They were hoping to see the house that Glyn Jones lived in, so I told them I'd be going up there today. I called Cerys last night and she said they'd be welcome. Anyway, they're meeting me here at nine o'clock and driving up there with me."

Lil's stricken face filled Sarah with concern. Unsure of the cause of her aunt's obvious distress, but anxious to make her feel better, Sarah said encouragingly, "It's alright, Aunty Lil. They're very nice people. Mam and I have really enjoyed having them. You've already met Brian, of course, and I'm sure you'll like Mrs. Pearson too."

Lil pulled herself together quickly and said a little too cheerfully, "I dare say I will, Sarah, but I don't suppose I'll be able to meet them this morning. My word, there's so much to do before it gets busy." She gestured in the vague direction of the shop, gave a weak smile, and handed Sarah the book. "I'll go and bag the vegetables if you'll pick up the flour and sugar from the stockroom. There are plenty of boxes there, too."

Sarah realized that her aunt was once again avoiding the subject of the Pearsons and the Joneses, but felt it was not her place to force the issue. She accepted the order book and headed to the stock room, determined to be ready when Brian and his mother arrived.

♘ ♘ ♘

They were right on time. Sarah saw them walking down the street from her home as she was loading the last of the boxes into the back of the van. Brian was carrying the wellies in a bag. Sarah waved at them and they waved back. By the time they had reached the vehicle she had closed the door to the shop on a relieved Aunty Lil and was opening the front door of the van.

"You timed that perfectly," she said with a welcoming smile.

They both smiled in return and Sarah noticed for the first time that Brian had inherited his blue eyes from his mother.

"You should have told me to come earlier, Sarah." Brian said. "I could've helped you load up the van."

"Oh, I managed fine," Sarah assured him. "But you could help me when we unload at the farm. The Robertses have the biggest order today."

"You bet!"

Sarah couldn't help thinking that she knew of no one else who would have answered in quite that way or with such enthusiasm. She was glad that she could spend the morning with him.

Iris Pearson turned to her. "This is very good of you, Sarah."

"I'm happy to do it Mrs. Pearson. As you can see I was going to the Robertses anyway, and now I have a lackey to help me out."

"A lackey!" Brian feigned offense. "I've been called a lot of things before but I don't think 'lackey' is one of them!"

They all laughed, then Sarah said, "Why don't you both go around to the other side of the van and jump in? I'm afraid we'll all have to sit up at the front because none of the other seats are in. But I think we'll fit."

The Pearsons did as she asked. Sarah got in and started the engine. She was secretly relieved when Mrs. Pearson slid in first and sat next to her. She would have had a hard time concentrating on her driving had Brian been sitting that close. When she heard the door slam shut she said, "Alright, let's go. We'll be going down the road past our house and heading up the valley. It's mainly farm land. You'll see a lot of cows and sheep, but I think you'll enjoy the drive."

Sarah pointed out the chapel and the school as they drove by, and waved to a few passing motorists. After a while Iris Pearson said, "I just can't get over how green it is. The grass, the hedges, the trees, everywhere you look. It's just beautiful."

"It does look pretty doesn't it? I love this time of year. Mind you, the day you arrived was our first really warm, sunny one all month. We're seeing the result of a lot of rainy days right now. I think you'll be glad you have the wellies when we get to the farm. Most farms are just beginning to dry out and are still quite muddy."

Sarah paused as she came to a junction. "This is the fork in the road I described last night. If you took the one to the right it would take you to Deniol Manor. We'll be going left."

Sarah drove the van up the narrow, winding lane; they did not pass another vehicle and she drove confidently. She knew the road like the back of her hand. Tall hedgerows grew on either side of the road forming a tunnel effect. The windows were down in the van and all they could hear was the sound of their own engine, an occasional sheep bleating, cows lowing, or birds singing. There was a sense of timeless peace, and the occupants of the van sat in companionable silence, enjoying the feel of the morning sun streaming through the open window.

Then, above the sound of their own engine they heard the engine of another vehicle. As it drew closer, Sarah instinctively slowed down. About fifty yards before taking a sharp bend in the road she beeped the horn. There was an answering beep and Sarah stopped. Without comment, she turned her head to look through the rear window and skillfully began reversing the van down the road. Iris Pearson looked questioningly at her son but he only shrugged his shoulders. They sat quietly until Sarah had efficiently maneuvered the van into a small layby at the side of the road. Moments later, a dark green landrover drove by. The driver beeped his horn again and waved. Sarah waved in return, then put the van in gear and moved forward again.

"Wow," said Brian "I'll never make comments about women drivers again. That was impressive."

Sarah smiled at his praise. "There's an unwritten rule on these country roads. If you meet a car coming the other direction in an area that's too narrow for you both to pass, the car nearest a layby has to reverse. There are passing places every so often. Once you know what to look for, you'll notice them."

"There's one." Brian pointed to the area they were passing. It wasn't much more than a large nick in the hedge, but in a pinch, a car could squeeze in to allow more room on the road.

Sarah nodded. "That's right. Luckily, almost all the drivers on this road know every foot of it. When we meet as we did just then, each driver knows who's closest to the layby, and that person automatically reverses."

"That's amazing." Brian continued to be impressed. Then he teased, "And the honking. Was that some sort of country code? One honk for one car, two honks for two cars?"

Sarah laughed. "No, that's habit. I'm afraid our warm sunny days don't last too long here. When we're driving in the rain or cold and the windows are up, you can't hear the oncoming cars like we did today. We all honk when we get to particularly bad bends in the road just as a precaution."

"It sounds to me like the drivers in Wales are a lot more courteous than the ones we have at home," said Iris Pearson.

"More skilled, too, if you ask me" Brian added. "I'd like to see some of the kids in driver education try successfully reversing down a winding lane into a small layby like that, at the speed Sarah managed it."

"Now wait," Sarah broke in, enjoying the praise yet beginning to feel that her skills were being exaggerated. "You have to remember how many times I've driven along this road. I wasn't as sure of it myself when I first got my licence. And I know I'd be frozen to the steering wheel with fear if someone put me in a car on the motorways in Los Angeles."

Iris Pearson nodded her head. "There are a lot of things in this life that just take getting used to aren't there?"

Sarah thought about the truth of that statement for a few minutes. There had been many instances in her life when time, rather than any great show of courage, had been the determining factor in overcoming her fears. She wondered suddenly if that was all that was needed for Aunty Lil to face the Pearsons—just a little bit of time to get used to the idea. She hoped so.

Sarah turned the van off the lane and stopped in front of a large gate. "Okay Brian, your official duty as lackey has begun. Would you jump out and open the gate for us? I'll drive through and wait for you to close it behind us."

"You bet!" Brian was out of the car and opening the gate in seconds. A minute later he was back and they continued up the graveled road. They went through another narrow gate before finally pulling into the large cemented farm yard.

"Well, here we are," Sarah said as she turned off the engine. Both of the Pearsons looked at the old stone farm house immediately before them. Sarah let them sit quietly for a few minutes; then she saw Cerys emerge from the kitchen door. She waved and turned to the Pearsons. "You might want to put on your wellies before you get out of the van. I'll introduce you to Cerys and let her show you 'round while I get the groceries out of the back." She pulled on her own boots and jumped out of the van.

She had just opened the back doors when Brian appeared at her elbow. "I'll carry these things in for you," he said. "That's what lackeys are for, remember?"

Sarah blushed. "Brian, I was only joking."

"I know that. But I'd like to help you."

Sarah looked up at him standing beside the doors. Why did everything he said to her sound so personal? Did he mean it that way, or was she reading more into his manner than she should? She wished she knew if he felt her nearness the way she felt his.

Sarah felt that she was floundering out of her depth—she barely knew him and yet she felt a bond. He knew little of her culture, yet she sensed an empathy within him. As she looked into his deep blue eyes she knew there was goodness there; she couldn't understand how she knew it, but she did. She also knew that if she kept on looking into those eyes, her knees would cave in.

Cerys saved her from disaster by coming around the back of the van in the nick of time. "Hello Sarah. You're early today."

"I made yours the first stop. How are you?" Sarah turned and gave Cerys a hug. Her short, plump frame was even more pronounced now that she was expecting her first baby.

Cerys smiled and patted her swollen girth. "Oh, apart from a bit of backache and swollen feet, I'm fine."

Sarah gave a sympathetic smile. "Poor old you. I don't suppose you give yourself much time to rest either, do you?"

"Oh, I can't stand to be idle. There's so much to be done before the baby comes."

"Hmm, that's what I thought. You just mind you don't overdo it Cerys Roberts!" Sarah wagged her finger at her playfully.

Cerys giggled. "Yes, Nurse Lewis," she answered demurely. Sarah rolled her eyes and turned to Brian, who had been watching this exchange with enjoyment.

"Brian, this is my cheeky friend, Cerys Roberts. Cerys, this is Brian Pearson."

Brian extended his hand. "It's nice to meet you Cerys. It was very good of you to allow us to come at such short notice." Then as his mother came around the side of the van he added, "Cerys, this is my mother Iris Pearson." Cerys shook Iris's hand and the two women exchanged smiles.

"Welcome to Deniol Farm. I'm afraid my husband Tom is out at the main pasture at the moment, but he may be back before you leave. Why don't you come in and have a cup of tea, then I can show you 'round a bit."

"Oh please don't bother. We don't need any tea and we certainly don't want to impose on your time," Iris said.

"Goodness, you're no bother," Cerys said with a wave of her hand. "Besides you heard what the good nurse said. I need to put my feet up every once in a while." Cerys grinned at Sarah mischievously. "Come on, I'll show you the way." She glanced down. "Oh, I am glad you brought wellies. I'm afraid it's a bit muddy crossing the farm yard, but it shouldn't last too long if this nice weather holds out for a few more days." She turned and began waddling back towards the old, gray stone house.

"You go ahead Mom," Brian said. "I'll help Sarah with these boxes."

"Can I carry anything for you, Sarah?" Iris Pearson asked.

"No thank you, Mrs. Pearson. I think we can manage," Sarah answered, then she turned and without looking at Brian, jumped into the back of the van. "There are three boxes for the Robertses, Brian. If you can take the heavy one, I can manage this one." She shoved a box full of flour, sugar, and cans towards the open door where Brian grasped it easily.

"Where's the other box?" he asked.

"It's in the corner there. It has 'Roberts' written on it in red." Sarah pointed into the van.

"Is it very heavy?"

"No, the one you've got is the worst. I can come back for the other one easily."

"I'll come back for it." Brian's tone brooked no argument.

"Thank you," she said quietly, and she backed out of the van, picked up her box, and led him across the yard.

By the time they reached the kitchen, both Cerys and Iris had taken off their wellies and were sitting at the table. There were a few leftover dishes in the sink. A tabby cat was curled up on a rug in front of the black Aga. Copper pans shone from their hooks above the stove, and a hamper of damp clothes sat beside the door.

"There you are." Cerys greeted Brian and Sarah as they came in with their cargo. "Just put the boxes here in the corner. I don't think there's anything I ordered that will spoil, so we'll just leave them for the time being." Brian and Sarah obediently put down their loads, then Brian left again.

"He's gone to get one more box," Sarah explained to the watching women, and walked over to join them. Brian was back minutes later, and deposited the last of the boxes with the other two.

"Thank you very much Brian," said Cerys. "Now, how about a nice cup of tea?"

"We won't have any, thank you, Cerys." Brian said as he sat down.

"But you must have something! Would you prefer coffee? I think I have some here somewhere." Cerys rose to look. Sarah noticed that Iris Pearson was looking distinctly uncomfortable. What was it about tea? Sarah realized suddenly that the Pearsons always refused it.

"No thank you, Cerys. Please don't bother." Brian stopped Cerys mid stride, but after seeing her look of distress said, "D'you have any of that orange squash drink?"

Cerys thought for a second. "Let me see. I think I might have some left from the last time Tom's brother's children were here." She walked to the cupboard near the sink and opened it. "Yes, here it is. Oh dear, I'm afraid it's a bit old. Do you think it will do?"

Brian got up and walked over to her. "I'm sure it'll be great. Mom and I tried this for the first time in Oxford. We really liked it. Show me how much to pour into the glasses before I add the water."

Cerys passed him the glasses and stood near him as he poured. After he had added the water he carried the two glasses to the table and passed one to his mother. "Thank you Cerys," Iris said. "This is lovely."

"Well, if you're sure it's alright." Cerys still looked a bit troubled. "It doesn't seem right somehow, not giving you tea." She shook her head. "Sarah would you like a cup?"

"A small one would be lovely, Cerys. Thank you." Cerys bustled over to the counter to pour the brewing beverage.

A little while later the Pearsons began their tour. Cerys walked them through the rooms of the small farm house first. She pointed out the renovations they had made and told them how the house had looked when they first bought it. It didn't take much imagination to realize that life in that home had been spartan indeed. There had been no indoor plumbing and two fireplaces had provided the only source of heat. The stone walls were sturdy but cold. The Robertses had added insulation along with central heating and running water.

Prior to its modernization, the home's one redeeming feature, and still its greatest asset, was the view from the upstairs windows. Each window faced out onto rolling fields, scattered trees, the river in the distance, and, on one side, the majestic Berwyn mountains.

Through one window Cerys pointed out a distant roof with several chimneys, just visible above a copse of trees. "That's Deniol

Manor" she said. "Glyn Jones probably would have cut across these fields to reach it. It would have been a lot quicker than going by road in those days, especially since he would have been on foot."

Iris Pearson stood at that window the longest, gazing out at the distant roof. Sarah wondered what she was thinking, but thought it too personal to ask.

When they stepped out of the house and into the yard, a battered green landrover was parked next to the white van. Brian turned to Sarah and whispered "Is that the same car that passed us on our way here?"

Sarah shook her head and smiled. "No, I'm afraid battered green landrovers are part of every farmer's equipment here. It usually makes recognizing people a bit tricky, but you recognize Tom when you pass him."

Minutes later Tom Roberts appeared and Sarah saw a look of amused understanding flash across Brian's face. Tom was a large man. He was almost as tall as Brian, Sarah noted with interest, but about double the width. And even if his size did not arouse attention, his thatch of unruly dark red hair did. Tom Roberts was easy to spot in a crowd.

"'Morning Sarah!" Tom called when he saw them, and pulled at the brim of his flat cap in greeting to the others.

"Hello Tom. I hear you're busy these days," Sarah greeted him.

"Oh aye! Always busy, always busy!" he said cheerfully.

"Tom, I'd like you to meet Mrs. Iris Pearson and her son Brian Pearson. They're staying at our house at the moment, but they wanted to see where Glyn Jones came from. Mrs. Pearson is Glyn Jones's granddaughter." Sarah made the introductions and Tom shook the Pearsons's hands.

"Well I never! Well, you've come to the right place. Cerys has been showing you round, has she?"

"Yes, she's been very kind. Your home is lovely, Mr. Roberts" Iris answered.

"Well thank you, ma'am. It's a modest house, but the land's good."

"Is any of your land arable, Tom?" Brian asked with interest.

"Not much, no. We usually do one or two fields with hay, just so we have winter feed on hand in case of a bad winter. But mainly we're a dairy farm. The farms a bit higher up tend to do sheep, but it's good grazing down here for the cows. Has Cerys shown you our milking parlor yet?"

Brian smiled at the obvious pride in Tom Roberts's voice. "No, we were just on our way out of the house."

Tom made a mock noise of disgust. "Come with me lad. I'll show you the interesting stuff while these women discuss curtains, baby clothes, and cooking." He gave his indignant wife a wink.

Brian grinned, "Sounds great!" Then he followed the burly man towards a large white building several yards away.

"Well really!" said Cerys, in mock indignation, "If anyone around here's cheeky, Sarah, it's that one!" She pointed to her distant husband with affection.

"I don't know, Cerys," Sarah teased, "I think you deserve each other!"

The three women stood in the warm sunshine and chatted pleasantly. It wasn't long before they saw Tom and Brian emerge from the building at the other end of the farm yard. Cerys waved and the men waved back. Sarah watched them approach. They were deep in conversation and she could hear their laughter. They appeared to be enjoying one another's company. Sarah was surprised at how much this pleased her.

"I'll tell you something, Mrs. Pearson," Tom said as the men reached them. "Your young man here may not be a farmer, but he certainly knows machinery, and asks a lot of intelligent questions." This was praise indeed from Tom Roberts. Sarah caught Brian's eye and they exchanged smiles.

Iris Pearson smiled too. "It must be in his blood," she said.

Tom laughed. "Aye, you may be right there. Good Welsh farming stock." He gave Brian a slap on the back and shook his hand again. "It was good to meet you, Brian. You're welcome back anytime."

"Thank you Tom. If I ever decide to leave the medical profession I'll come here for some farm training," Brian joked.

Tom laughed again. "You do that. You could do a lot worse, even if I say so myself." He turned to Iris. "Mrs. Pearson, best wishes to you."

"Thank you, Tom." She shook his hand.

"Well, I'll be off now. Be seein' you round, Sarah. Take care of yourself."

"I will, Tom. Thanks again." Sarah waved as Tom heaved himself into the landrover and started the engine. She turned to Cerys and gave her a squeeze. "We'd best be going too, Cerys. It was lovely to see you again."

"You too. Come again before too long."

"I will. And you put your feet up every once in a while!" Sarah admonished.

Cerys groaned. "I'll do my best." She shook hands with Brian and Iris and accepted their thanks again before they followed Sarah to the van. They all waved as they pulled out of the farm yard.

"What a pleasant couple," Iris said with a sigh.

"They are nice, aren't they?" Sarah agreed and slowed the van so Brian could get out to open the first gate.

❦ ❦ ❦

Soon they were on their way again. Sarah glanced at her watch, thought for a minute, then asked, "Would you mind terribly if I made one other delivery before taking you back? It's right on our way."

"Of course not, dear," Iris said. "It's much more interesting for us to do this than to just aimlessly drive through the area ourselves."

Sarah turned onto another small lane to her left. They wound through a wooded area before emerging at the base of a steep hill. She put the van in low gear and they crawled up the steep road until the gradient leveled off and a cluster of buildings came into view. "That's the Parry's farm" she said.

"Wow," breathed Brian "check out that view!" From his side of the van the whole valley opened up. They could make out the village church spire and the flat roof of the school in the distance. The river sparkled as it meandered across the valley floor. Every so often sun would glint off a moving vehicle. The emerald-colored fields were dotted with white sheep and black and white cows. Green hedgerows and gray stone walls broke the landscape into an oddly shaped patchwork. They sat and admired the scene for a few minutes.

"I don't know how they could stand to leave it," Iris whispered. Brian heard the break in his mother's voice and put his arm around her shoulders.

"Life was hard for them then, mother," he said gently. "They were led by the Spirit to do what they did. We must be grateful to them. It was quite a sacrifice."

Although Brian's words puzzled her, Sarah was touched by the compassion he showed his mother. She suddenly felt like an outsider and wished that the Pearsons could have had this moment alone. Feeling uncomfortable, she looked down at her hands on the steering wheel. Brian saw the movement, and as though he sensed her discomfort, he smiled at her over his mother's head.

"Thanks for stopping, Sarah," he said. She nodded silently, and moved the car slowly forward until they reached the farmhouse.

"I'll just be one minute," she called as she jumped out of the van. She ran around to the back and opened the doors.

"Which one is it?"

His voice made her jump.

"I'm sorry; I didn't mean to startle you." Brian stepped closer and touched her arm. "Are you okay?"

Sarah's heart raced. She told herself it was only because he'd startled her and had nothing to do with Brian's proximity. But she didn't dare raise her eyes to his.

"I'm fine," she said, avoiding his face and peering into the van. "It's just one box this time. I think I put it in that far corner." She pointed to a box with "Dole Pineapples" emblazoned across the sides.

"I'll get it," he said, and reached inside to pull the box forward. "This one?"

"Yes, that's it. If you're sure you don't mind carrying it, I'll show you the way to the back door."

"Lead on!" Brian said, and hoisted the box into his arms.

No one answered Sarah's knock at the back door so she opened it a crack and called out "Mrs. Parry?" Silence. She opened the door wider and pointed to the kitchen table. "Just put the box on the table. I'm sure she'll be in before too long."

Brian did as he was told and put the box down with a thud. When he stepped outside again he flexed his arms and said "I don't know how you do this on your own. These boxes are heavy!"

Sarah laughed. "Oh, you've forgotten; I grew up having to wrestle two older brothers."

Brian grinned, "Well that may be, but I can't imagine they've asked to take you on any time recently." Sarah saw the admiration in his eyes and felt herself blush.

"No, not too recently, but I have arm wrestled Aled a lot!" she said to cover her embarrassment. Brian burst into laughter and she laughed with him.

27 June 1881

Dear Father,

It has been three weeks since our ship docked in New York and we finally have our tickets west. We are to leave by train tomorrow with our friends, Will and Catriona Evans.

I no longer remember what my preconceived notions about America were. They must have all blended into the amazing collage of sights and sounds that have made up my experience of the last few weeks.

Our arrival at Castle Garden was an ordeal that I hope never to relive. We were herded (much like the sheep at home), into a large room where we queued up for hours to suffer the indignity of a cursory medical examination before speaking with an immigration official. Glyn and I were grateful to be in line with the Evanses. It took all four of us to understand the questions and instructions issued by the young man who studied our papers. His accent and English were extremely difficult to comprehend. Whether he finally gave up trying to communicate with us, or whether we passed his criteria for entry, I am still not sure. However, he waved us on and we quitted that place with utmost relief. The Evans's little girls were beside themselves with exhaustion. Glyn and Will carried them while we walked to find a modest boarding house where we could all rest.

It did not take Glyn and I more than one day in New York to realize that we are very much out of place here. I have never seen so many people or buildings. There is constant noise, and considerable squalor. My heart breaks for the young children I see begging on the streets. I wish I could do something to help them, but Glyn will not allow me to approach them. He is most protective of me.

During our voyage, the Evanses told us of their plans to emigrate west. They have relatives in the Territory of Utah. It is apparently a vast valley, surrounded by high mountains. Will hopes to establish himself there as a cabinet maker. (That was his occupation in Merthyr Tydfil, and Catriona lovingly boasts of his skills.) He feels that there will be much demand for his work in the newly emerging settlements. Indeed, he is so confident of this, that he has asked Glyn to consider joining him as an apprentice. He seems unperturbed by Glyn's lack of experience in woodworking and is most encouraging regarding the venture.

After considerable thought and conversation, Glyn and I have decided to accompany the Evanses to Utah. We are already anxious to be out of the city and within sight of mountains, fields, and streams once more. I am also grateful that the much dreaded time of parting from Will and Catriona has been postponed. They have become dear friends.

There is something about their family that sets them apart from others. They seem to radiate happiness in a most peaceful way. We often sit together in the evenings and sing the songs from home that we love. Will's and Glyn's voices combine to create a rich harmony. It brings back memories of the Pen-y-Bryn male voice choir and I soak up every note.

I hope you are well. I think of you often.

> Your loving daughter,
> Mary.

❧ *Chapter 3* ❧

It was noon by the time they drove up outside Sarah's home. Annie Lewis was just putting the final touches on dinner when they walked in.

"There you are, and right on time too. How did it go?" she asked.

"Great," said Iris with enthusiasm. "The Robertses were very kind and showed us around their farm—the scenery was beautiful. Sarah was a wonderful tour guide." She smiled at Sarah with gratitude.

Annie nodded, pleased. "Any news from Tom and Cerys, Sarah?" she asked, always anxious to be abreast of local happenings.

"Not really, Mam. Cerys seems to be managing alright. She's only got six weeks left now. And Tom is as proud as punch of his new milking machine. Poor Brian was given the grand tour of the milking parlor."

"Hey, that was the best part of the trip!" Brian defended, and brought a smile to the women's lips.

"Well, I'm sure you're all hungry, so come and sit down and have a bite to eat," Annie said.

As they sat down at the table, Annie began serving up a meal of roast lamb, mint sauce, mashed potatoes, gravy, and vegetables. It smelled wonderful. After taking a couple of mouthfuls Brian groaned. "If you keep feeding me like this, Mrs. Lewis, someone's going to have to roll me home!"

Annie Lewis looked as if nothing would please her more. Sarah, on the other hand, felt her appetite dissipate. She had known Brian less than twenty-four hours, and yet the thought of him leaving gave her an empty feeling. What was wrong with her? She'd always been so cautious around men. Friends teased her that she was waiting, unrealistically, for a knight in shining armor to appear. Perhaps they were right, for although she had many male friends, she had never really let one into her heart. But Brian seemed to have just walked right in. It was as though they'd always known each other. He sensed her emotions without a word passing between them, and it both thrilled and frightened her. She glanced at him. As though he felt her look, he turned and gave her a gentle smile.

"My, it's good to have a man around to feed again. Women just peck at their food." Annie looked pointedly at Sarah, who blushed and continued to move a piece of meat around her plate with her fork.

"It really is delicious," Iris said.

"Well, thank you. I always say you can't beat a good meat-and-potatoes dinner." Then after a short silence, Annie Lewis continued. "So, what are your plans this afternoon?"

Iris Pearson said, "We were thinking of walking over to the church to see if they have any family records there."

Brian broke in, "Sarah suggested that we try the Welsh Methodist chapel first, Mom, since Mary Jones's father was a minister of that religion."

Annie Lewis nodded her agreement. "Yes, I daresay that's the place to start. I hope Reverend Davis is there this afternoon. The chapel won't be locked of course, but he'd be the best one to direct you to the old records."

"We'll go and see what we can find," Brian said.

About an hour later, when the meal was over and the dishes washed, Sarah picked up her wellies once more. The Pearsons had gone up to their rooms a little earlier. Her mother was sitting down, relaxing with a cup of tea. "I'll be back in a couple of hours, Mam," she said as she opened the back door.

"Alright bach, take care now," her mother replied.

The warm sun felt good as she walked through the back garden. She stopped to watch a little fat robin yank a worm out of the ground. He flew away with his prize dangling from his beak and headed for a gap in the tall hedge. She smiled as she heard him fluttering through the branches. There had been nests in that hedge for many years.

One of her earliest memories was of finding tiny broken blue egg shells lying on the ground beneath the hedge. Weeping, she had carried the fragile pieces in her small hand to her father, convinced that something awful had happened to the birds. Her father had lifted her onto his shoulders and taken her back to the spot, where he'd carefully parted the hedge to show her the nest full of hungry, chirping baby birds. She could still remember her joyful wonder. They had checked on the birds regularly afterwards and had even witnessed their first flight. Sarah sighed sadly. She really missed her father.

She climbed into the van and tried to dispel the crowding memories of making the shop deliveries with her dad. Sarah knew that in many ways she was very like him. They had enjoyed a rare comradery, and had loved driving around the countryside together. She wondered suddenly what he would have thought of Brian Pearson. Instinctively, she knew that they would have got along well together. The thought cheered her. She headed out of the village with a smile on her lips.

ૐ ૐ ૐ

When Sarah arrived back at the shop about an hour and a half later there was only one customer there, and her aunt informed her that it had been rather a quiet day.

"I think everyone's enjoying being outside in the sunshine," said her aunt. "They don't want to be bothered with shopping, and I don't blame them one bit. It's given me a chance to catch up with these accounts." She pointed to a small pile of papers on the counter.

"If you think you can manage for the rest of the afternoon, then maybe I'll go home now and spend a bit of time practicing," Sarah suggested.

"That's right; it's your big day tomorrow isn't it? Well you go right on home and do what you need to. I wish I could be there tomorrow. I'll be thinking of you, though."

"Thanks Aunty Lil. I hope I've got over my nervousness by the time I get on stage. Now I'm just looking forward to having it behind me," Sarah said with feeling.

Lil Lewis gave her an understanding look. "You'll sound grand. Just let your natural gift shine through. The judges would have to be deaf not to give you first place."

Sarah giggled. "Oh Aunty Lil, I think you're just a tad biased! But thanks anyway." She gave her aunt a quick hug. "I'll stop by and let you know how it goes as soon as we get home tomorrow. I'm not sure what time that'll be, but sometime in the early evening, I imagine."

"That's right, dear. Good luck to you!" Lil waved as Sarah left.

Sarah drove the van home instead of walking. She backed it into the driveway as close to the house as she could. The one big draw-back to playing the harp was transporting it. She was grateful for the use of the shop van. It made a difficult job a little easier.

When she went inside, Sarah found a note on the kitchen table from her mother. It read: 'Sarah, Have gone to see Aunty Sally. Will be back soon. Mam.' Sarah smiled indulgently to herself at the last words. Aunty Sally was too elderly to get out very often so she loved to have visitors. She could talk about the old days for as long as her guest could stand it. Sarah knew she'd have the house to herself for a while.

She didn't waste any time, and was soon engrossed in prac-ticing—first her scales and arpeggios, and then her performance piece. When she had reviewed the trickiest parts several times and gone over the entire piece until it flowed perfectly, Sarah sat back and flexed her shoulder muscles. She was tired. Her shoulders, arms, and fingers ached, but she knew she'd played well.

She tidied her sheet music into a small pile and stood up. A wave of nervousness swept over her as she thought about the competition the next day. Walking to the window, she gazed outside at the sun that was just beginning to lower behind the Berwyn mountains. Shadowed areas appeared as dull purple ink stains, and the green lower slopes shone in contrast. Sarah could hear the cattle lowing as they returned from milking. A bee buzzed past the window. Sarah blinked, made a decision, and briskly walked back to the kitchen.

Picking up her mother's note and grabbing the pencil that lay nearby, Sarah quickly wrote: 'Sorry to have missed you. Have gone for a walk. Don't wait for me before eating. Love, Sarah.' She grabbed an apple from the bowl and an old lightweight jacket from a peg in the boot room. She put the apple in one of the jacket pockets and tied the jacket sleeves around her waist. Then she let herself out the back door and walked around the house.

Just as Sarah reached the front gate, the Pearsons rounded the corner of the lane. Sarah waved and waited while they approached. "Hello, how did the research go?"

Iris Pearson pulled a face. "Not too well I'm afraid. It was fascinating to walk through the graveyard. I just can't believe how old some of the headstones are. We saw lots of Joneses and some Williamses."

Sarah laughed. "I'm afraid every Welsh village is teeming with Joneses and Williamses."

Iris looked a little rueful. "Yes, I'm beginning to see that now. This is rather a daunting job, especially with the language barrier."

Sarah looked puzzled so Brian explained, "We did go inside the church, but the minister wasn't there. There was a lady cleaning the brass. She told us Reverend Davis would be gone for the day, but she showed us where the old registers are kept. We spent some time trying to find the ones in the time period we think Glyn and Mary Jones would have been born, but we couldn't read the entries. Some of them were marked with an X of course, but the writing was all done in Welsh." Brian looked apologetic. "I'm afraid it didn't mean much to us."

It was Sarah's turn to look apologetic. "Oh dear! We didn't even think about that. How stupid of us. Will you have time to go back when the minister is there?"

"We'll make time," Iris said firmly.

Brian grinned. "I think that's a 'yes.'"

Sarah laughed. "I'll tell you what. Next time you go, Mam or I could go with you. Then if Reverend Davis is gone, perhaps we can help you understand the entries."

"Oh, that would be marvelous. Thank you Sarah." Iris Pearson beamed with pleasure. She glanced towards the house. "Is your mother home?"

"No, she's gone to visit an elderly lady in the village. She . . . oh!" Sarah stopped short. "Good grief! I can't believe we didn't think of her before!" Brian and his mother were both looking mystified. Sarah hurried to explain. "There's a lady in the village called Aunty Sally. Everyone calls her Aunty Sally because she's old enough to be everyone's aunt, great aunt, or great-great aunt. I don't know exactly how old she is—actually I don't think anyone does. But she's certainly the oldest person around these parts. She stays at home almost all the time now, but she loves to have visitors. Even though she's a bit fuzzy about everyday things, she's got an incredible memory for details from the past. It's quite amazing. She remembers names, dates, how people are related and all sorts of stories from her youth." Sarah paused. "What I'm trying to say is, that if anyone in Pen-y-Bryn knows anything about your ancestors, it will be Aunty Sally."

Iris Pearson looked excited. "D'you think she'd let us visit her?" she asked.

"She'd be thrilled to have a new audience. I'm afraid all of her regular visitors have heard the same stories over and over again. If you're interested, why don't you talk to my mother when she gets back? I'm sure she can arrange it."

"Sarah, you're a marvel." Iris said. Brian's expression said even more, and Sarah blushed. "I'm only sorry I didn't think of it before." Then, redirecting the subject from herself she added, "I'm afraid Mam's not back yet, but you're welcome to go on in and make yourselves at home."

"Thank you dear," said Iris.

"Did the rest of the deliveries go okay?" Brian asked, seemingly reluctant to leave.

"Yes, I got back quite a while ago. I'm just going for a walk now." Sarah grimaced. "I need to burn off some nervous energy!" Brian immediately looked sympathetic.

"Tomorrow's competition?"

Sarah nodded.

"Would you like some company or would you rather be alone?"

Sarah looked up, surprised by his question. " Well, I . . . er . . . " She looked into his deep blue eyes and heard herself say, "I'd love to have your company if you'd like to come." He smiled.

"That alright with you, Mom?"

"Of course dear. I'll see you both a little later." Iris entered the garden gate and walked up the path to the door.

Sarah stood still, watching her go. Then Brian smiled down at her. "Ready?"

"Oh, yes!" She looked away, feeling silly, and pointed down the lane that followed the river. "This way."

"Great!" he said, and fell into step beside her.

They walked in a comfortable silence. Gradually, the distant sound of vehicles and children playing was replaced by the song of birds, the rustling of leaves in the breeze, and most of all, the low roar of water rushing downstream.

"It's so peaceful here," Brian said quietly.

Sarah nodded. "It is. But, silly as it sounds, even village life can get too frenetic for me sometimes. I have a couple of favorite walks I take when I want to escape. This is one of them. It feels like you're far away from everyone here."

They walked on, following the meandering river. "Look," Sarah said as she drew closer to the hedge and lifted some of the lower branches. Hidden underneath was a clump of tiny wild strawberries. "Here, try one." She picked a couple of the minute berries and handed them to Brian.

"They're so sweet!" he exclaimed.

Sarah smiled. "My father used to tease me that they tasted sweeter because they were meant for the fairies."

"Did you come here often with your father?"

"Yes, we loved to walk together. He taught me to appreciate every season along this lane. In the spring we'd search for the wild snowdrops. They're delicate white flowers that bloom along the hedgerows. It was always such a thrill to find our first one because it was nature's way of telling us that winter was over. Later there were other discoveries—bird nests, rabbits, and the new lambs in the fields.

"In the summer we'd look for wild strawberries; we came to know the best places to find them. Then he'd make whistles out of young willow tree limbs. It would take him almost the whole length of our walk to carefully remove the bark, whittle out the inside, and restore the bark. By the time we got home, I would be playing tunes on the whistle.

"In the winter we'd come out all wrapped up and in our wellies. It always looks like a Christmas card when the snow has just fallen. Icicles hang on the branches over the river, and the air is crisp and clear."

"You miss him a lot, don't you?" Brian asked.

"Yes. Sometimes it's hard to believe he's really gone, even now after two years."

Brian nodded. "I know."

Sarah glanced at him and remembered that he too had lost his father recently. So he did know how it felt.

"Were you close to your father too?" she asked.

"Yes. I guess we had a unique relationship because I was his only son. He sounds a lot like your father. He loved being outdoors. We'd go camping and fishing together every summer."

Brian paused for a minute, then a little more quietly he said, "My dad was a wonderful role model. He taught me just by the way he acted. I don't ever remember him doing a dishonest thing in his life. He was patient with us kids, even when we did something really stupid." Brian pulled a rueful face. "Like the time I took the TV apart to see how it worked, and couldn't put it back together again." Sarah giggled. Brian grinned sheepishly, paused, then took a deep breath.

"I think what I admired the most about him, was that no matter what was going on in his life, everyone knew that he loved my mother, he loved his children, and he loved the gospel."

"The gospel?" Sarah asked, puzzled.

Brian stopped walking and turned to face her. "The gospel. You see Sarah, my father knew without question that there is a God, our Heavenly Father, and that He sent His son, Jesus Christ, to the earth to atone for our sins, and that the Holy Ghost can witness this to us."

Sarah looked up at him. "Well, I believe that too."

Brian smiled at her gently and reached out for her hand. He wrapped his strong fingers around hers. It was as though a current passed through them both. "I know you do," he said. "But Dad also believed that the church Christ established on the earth had been changed so much by men during the centuries that followed Christ's death, that many important truths were no longer on the earth. People like Martin Luther, John Calvin, and John Wesley obviously felt the same way when they broke from the Catholic Church.

"However, my father believed that unlike some of the early reformers, there was a man in the 1800s who was given authority from God to restore the true church to the earth. His name was

Joseph Smith. The church that Joseph Smith reinstated was the Church of Jesus Christ of Latter-day Saints. It's sometimes called the Mormon Church."

Sarah took a small step back. "Your father was a Mormon?" she whispered.

"Yes." Brian paused imperceptibly. "I am too, and so are the other members of my family."

Sarah tried to pull her hand from his but he held it tightly. She turned her head away from him, recoiling from his nearness.

"Sarah!" his voice pleaded. "Don't reject me because of a label." She said nothing. "Please Sarah. Your friendship means a great deal to me."

Sarah shuddered. A Mormon. What did that mean? She didn't know, but she knew she'd never heard anything good about them. But Brian was a good person, wasn't he? Had he deceived her, her mother, Aunty Lil? She didn't know what to think.

"Sarah?" Brian cupped the fingers of his free hand around her chin and turned her face towards him. His expression mirrored her grief-stricken one. Sarah dropped her eyes and surprised him by pulling her hand free.

"I must go home now," she whispered, embarrassed by the catch in her voice.

"I'll walk back with you."

She shook her head. "There's no need. Good-bye, Brian." She turned quickly and began to run back the way they had come.

When she finally stopped running she was halfway home. She felt as though her heart would pound right out of her body. What was she running from? She didn't know. Fear? Fear of Brian? No, that was ridiculous. Fear of his religion? That was ridiculous too. How could his religion affect her if she was forewarned against it? Fear of her reaction? That was closer to home. She was afraid that the growing attraction she felt for him would blind her to his deception.

She kept walking, misery gnawing at her. But had he really deceived her? She had never asked him what his religion was. There had never been any reason to bring it up. He was the one who introduced the subject. Sarah's jumbled thoughts tumbled over each other as she continued walking towards home.

Should she tell her mother that Iris and Brian Pearson were Mormons? How would she react? Sarah groaned and put her hand to her head. So many questions; her head hurt. She was confused, and upset, but she didn't want to take the time to analyze why. She just wanted to be home and escape the multitude of teeming emotions she was experiencing.

As her house came into view, Sarah broke into a run again. Glancing over her shoulder, she saw no sign of anyone behind her. Her steps slowed as she reached the garden gate. The last thing she wanted to do right then was to meet anyone else, particularly Iris Pearson or her own mother. If they were in the kitchen she needed to avoid the back door; if they were in the front parlor, she would walk right past them if she used the front door. She paused in indecision, glanced at her watch and guessed that her mother would be finishing up supper preparations. Taking a deep breath, she quietly opened the front door.

She could hear voices but they were coming from the back of the house—the kitchen. Breathing a sigh of relief, but still careful lest she make any unusual noise, she tiptoed indoors and gently closed the door behind her. She pulled off her shoes and crept down the hallway and up the stairs.

Sarah reached her bedroom door without discovery, entered, locked the door behind her, and threw herself onto the bed. Only then did she allow herself to release her pent-up emotions. She wept until there were no more tears. Then, exhausted, she fell into a fitful sleep.

ಠ ಠ ಠ

When she awoke, her room was dark. Momentarily confused, she raised her head, saw that she was still fully clothed, and sank back onto the bed as memory flooded back. She lay still, staring at the ceiling with unseeing eyes. She wondered when Brian had returned. What excuse had he given their mothers for arriving home alone? And what excuse could she contrive for having locked herself in her room without a word to anyone?

Painfully she forced herself to relive her walk with Brian. She remembered the closeness they'd shared as she spoke about her father, his empathy because of the loss of the father he had loved so much. Then had come his revelation about his religion. Why had she felt so deceived? Did it stem more from her own shock at being told something that she'd never suspected, rather than any wrongdoing on Brian's part? Sarah tried to detach herself emotionally from the experience.

What did she know about Mormons anyway? That they were some sort of American cult that believed in polygamy. Sarah had to admit she knew very little. What did she know about Iris and Brian Pearson? Again, very little in theory, but something deep down, something that bypassed reason, told her that they were good, genuine people. She could not believe that they were tricksters who had pulled the wool over the eyes of all the villagers in Pen-y-Bryn. Something within her had responded deeply to Brian Pearson. She had to have more confidence in her own feelings, her own ability to judge character.

The more she thought about it, the more she realized that Brian had done nothing to blemish his character. The fact that he professed beliefs that she denounced should not detract from the fact that he had emulated his father's honest character. He had told her forthrightly that he was a Mormon. He had asked for her friendship, even her understanding. But she had run away.

Slowly Sarah got up, turned on her bedside light, took off her clothes and dressed in her nightgown. She put on her robe, cinched the belt tightly and sat down at her dressing table. She pulled the bedraggled ribbon out of her hair and stared at it. It seemed an eon ago that she had tied it onto her ponytail. Dropping the ribbon into a drawer, she mechanically began brushing out her long hair.

"You are not a pretty sight, Sarah Lewis," she whispered to her reflection. Her eyes were puffy from crying and there were pink blotches on her cheeks. But the greater problem lay below the surface. Sarah lowered the brush and bowed her head. She knew what she needed to do, but she wasn't sure if she had the courage to do it. She clenched her fists. It wasn't going to get any easier the longer she waited. She glanced at her watch. Twelve-twenty A.M. She had no right to wake him at this time of night, but she knew that she'd never sleep until she'd done it. With a last glance at her watch, she rose and walked to the door.

Sarah paused as she stepped out of her room. All the lights in the house were out, and everything was silent. She tiptoed past her mother's room and up the small flight of stairs that led to the guest rooms. When she reached the small landing, she stopped again. There was a chink of light filtering out underneath the door to Brian's room. Her determination faltered. She stood, desperately wanting to retreat, yet willing herself to move forward. The grandfather clock in the hall downstairs struck the half hour. Sarah jumped and quickly moved to the door. Before she had time to reconsider, she knocked.

There was a moment of silence, a creak as someone rose, then footsteps. When he opened the door, Sarah took an instinctive step backwards. To her astonishment, except for his shoes, Brian was still wearing the clothes he'd worn earlier that evening. The lamplight behind him left his face pale and shadowed but she could tell that his eyes were tired. He ran his hand through his hair as his eyes adjusted to the gloom.

"Sarah?" His whispered voice did nothing to calm her tremulous nerves.

"Brian, I know it's late and I shouldn't have disturbed you but I . . . " Sarah pulled the ties on her robe more tightly. "I . . . had to come to apologize." Sarah felt a load lift off her as she spoke the words. There was a moment of silence, and Sarah raised her eyes to look into his.

Very quietly he said, "The first time I set eyes on you I was sure you were a very special woman, Sarah Lewis. Now I'm convinced of it."

He held a hand out to her and hesitatingly she extended her own to meet it. With a thankful smile, he gave her hand a soft squeeze before releasing it.

She took a small step back and said softly, "I must go, and let you get some sleep. You haven't even been to bed yet."

"We seem to have the same sleep disorder, don't we?" he teased. Sarah gave a shaky smile and nodded. She took another step away from him.

"Goodnight, Brian," she whispered.

He stood silhouetted in the doorway. For a second, it seemed as though he was going to say something more, or call her back, but he didn't.

"Goodnight, Sarah," he replied softly.

She turned and ran quietly down the stairs. She felt his gaze follow her as she left, and didn't hear his door click shut until she had reached her own bedroom.

Dear Father,

We have been deceived. Will and Catriona have confessed to being Mormons! I can scarcely take it in. How can these people who seem so good, profess such wickedness?

Glyn expressed surprise at their revelation, but does not seem unduly upset. He tells me that he knows nothing of Mormonism and is willing to accept the Evanses as friends regardless of their religious beliefs. But I do know about Mormonism. Surely it is not right to ignore such evil?

Every day the train takes us further west. There is no going back now, and for the first time I fear for our future. Please pray for us, Father.

Your loving daughter,

Mary.

Chapter 4

Morning seemed to arrive too soon. Sarah forced her tired body out of bed and groped her way to the bathroom. Even after splashing cold water on her face, her eyes still looked a little worse for wear, but she hoped that a shower and some makeup would help.

She moved quickly and quietly, dressing in jeans and a sweatshirt. Then she gathered together some hair accessories, a pair of soft black leather ballet slippers, a brush and some makeup, and dropped them all into a canvas bag. Next she opened her tallboy and withdrew a long maroon-colored, velvet dress covered in protective plastic. With the dress carefully draped over one arm and the canvas bag in the other hand, Sarah left her room and made her way downstairs.

Entering the front parlor, she placed the bag on the floor and the dress over the back of the nearest chair. She pulled out a well-used brown leather music case and gathered together the sheets still sitting on her music stand. She glanced through each page, making sure that they were in order and that none were missing. Satisfied, she placed them in the music case and set the case on the floor next to the canvas bag.

Sarah then slipped out into the hall and opened a small recessed cupboard underneath the stairs. She pulled out a large box and dragged it as quietly as she could back into the front parlor. Once inside the room, she opened the box to reveal what appeared to be a dark brown tarpaulin. She lifted it out and as she began unfolding it on the floor, it opened into a roughly triangular shape. Grasping it by two of the corners, she walked it over to the harp, then stepped onto the small stool and lifted the tarpaulin above the harp and slowly lowered it over the instrument. It fit perfectly. She jumped down and moved around to the front of the harp. There were six sets of ties along one side of the cover, which she drew together carefully around the front of the wooden frame. When she had finished, the instrument was totally covered.

She went back to the box and pulled out a rectangular wooden board with four sturdy castors on one side. She placed the board next to the harp, closed the now-empty box, and returned it to the hall cupboard. Then she headed into the kitchen.

Annie Lewis was already there, hard at work making a mountain of sandwiches. Sarah braced herself for a barrage of questions about her behavior the night before.

"Good morning, Mam," she said, as cheerfully as she could muster. Her mother looked up.

"Sarah! How are you feeling, bach? I hoped you'd sleep as long as you could. Brian told us that you'd had to come home early with a bad headache. I told the Pearsons it was just pre-competition nerves, you know. But I was a little worried about you. You usually take these things in stride. Are you feeling better?"

Sarah smiled and gave silent thanks to Brian for his timely, albeit unoriginal, excuse. "I feel much better thank you, Mam. A bit jittery maybe, but not too bad."

"Oh, I am glad. It wouldn't do to come down with something today of all days. Dear me no." She glanced out of the window. "Looks like it's going to be a nice morning. 'Course, you can't really tell how it will be in Llangollen from here, but we can always hope, can't we?"

Annie rinsed off her hands and dried them on her apron. "Now then, you need some breakfast."

"Don't worry about me Mam, I can get it."

"I know you can. But I'm thinking that today you need something a bit more sustaining than a bowl of those lightweight flakes you usually have."

"Oh no you don't! A sure way to make me sick is to feed me one of those breakfasts you gave Brian yesterday. Grapefruit and a piece of toast will be great."

Annie Lewis knew from past experience that arguing with her daughter would get her nowhere. So she just shook her head and clucked her tongue disapprovingly. "You don't eat enough to keep a fly alive, child!"

Sarah laughed. "Mam, you've been telling me that for as far back as I can remember. I must be defying all odds!"

"Oh go on with you!" Annie said with a small smile, knowing full well that she was fighting a losing battle. Sarah gave her a quick hug, knowing equally well that it would be a battle waged many times again.

"What's all this food for?" Sarah asked when she saw the sandwiches stacked up on the counter over her mother's shoulder. Her mother turned around.

"Oh, I'm just making up some lunch for us all."

"Mam! That's enough to feed a whole male voice choir!" Sarah exclaimed.

"Don't be silly. You'll be surprised how quickly it's eaten up. We'll all be very glad of it once we're at the Eisteddfod. Those food booths are far too expensive, and the food doesn't taste fresh either. I'm sure Brian will be ready for several of those little sandwiches by lunchtime."

An amused male voice at the door said, "I'm sure Brian can manage a couple of those great-looking sandwiches at lunchtime, on the condition that he's allowed to eat the same breakfast Sarah's having."

The two women swung around to see Brian standing at the kitchen door. Sarah felt her heartbeat quicken, and a wave of nervousness swept over her. She felt suddenly unsure of herself in his presence. She longed for a return to their easy comradery, but with her new knowledge, wondered if it would be possible. Would he make any reference to their walk, or even their time together last night?

Annie Lewis unknowingly bought Sarah a little time to compose herself by greeting Brian enthusiastically and urging him to sit down at the table.

"Now don't you go without a good breakfast just because Sarah won't eat one, Brian," Annie said. Sarah hid a smile at her mother's words and walked over to the table where she set down her food.

"No, really, Mrs. Lewis." Brian glanced at Sarah's plate. " Half a grapefruit and a piece of toast would be great."

Annie looked quite distraught. "But you can't possibly survive until lunchtime on that!"

Brian grinned at her. "Alright, make it two pieces of toast!"

Sarah smothered a giggle as her mother gave a sigh of defeat and went to cut some bread. Brian pulled out the chair beside her and sat down. She turned to look at him and gave him a tremulous smile. As she looked into his blue eyes she was moved to see the same hesitation that she was experiencing mirrored there.

"How are you feeling today?" he asked quietly. Sarah saw the concern in his face and swallowed hard. He deserved more than easy platitudes. The singing kettle drowned her words from Annie Lewis's ears.

"I'm not sure." She picked at a loose thread on the edge of the tablecloth. "I'm still confused and a bit troubled." She paused. "But even though I don't understand any of this, I feel that I can trust you." She looked up at him again.

Brian's expression told her more than any words could convey. Wordlessly he reached out and covered her hand with his.

"Will you let me explain some of this to you sometime?"

Although Sarah shied from reliving her distress of the evening before, she knew that unless she confronted her feelings, she could never totally put them to rest. They would always be there as an invisible barrier between Brian and her. Understanding more about Mormonism would help her understand him. And Sarah knew that understanding this man seated beside her was extremely important to her.

She took a deep breath. "Yes," she whispered in a solemn voice.

She felt the pressure from his hand on hers increase. She looked up to see his eyes full of gratitude.

"You're quite a lady, Sarah Lewis."

His words brought back memories of their late-night conversation, but she was saved from further discussion by her mother who arrived at the table with Brian's breakfast.

"You be sure to tell me if you're still hungry when you finish this paltry breakfast, Brian," Annie said, looking at his plate with disdain. Brian laughed.

"It looks great, Mrs. Lewis. Thanks."

"Hmmm." Annie was not convinced. Just then the door opened once more, and Iris Pearson walked in.

"Good morning. Oh dear, am I the last one up again?" Iris said in dismay.

"Think nothing of it, dear," Annie reassured her. "You're on holiday."

Iris smiled at her. "You're very kind. But I do hope I'm not holding you all up."

"You're fine, Mother," Brian said. "Why don't you come and eat while Sarah gives me instructions on loading the harp into the van." He turned to Sarah. "Are you ready?"

Sarah stood up. "Yes, that sounds like a good idea. I've got the harp wrapped and ready to go. We've just got to get out the ramp and the blankets."

"That's right, you two go ahead. Iris can have her breakfast and help me pack the lunches," Annie said.

Brian opened the door for Sarah and they walked through the hall, out of the front door, and over to the waiting van. Sarah opened the back doors of the vehicle, then turned and opened the garage door. Leaning up against the back wall was a metal ramp. She pointed it out to Brian, who retrieved it and brought it over to the van.

"Kevin made this for me," Sarah said. "See, this tongue on the ramp fits into the groove on the back of the van." She showed Brian how the two fit together. He lowered it into place, then pushed down hard on the ramp to make sure it was secure. Sarah handed him a pile of thick blankets from a box in the garage.

"We'll lay one of these down on the floor of the van before bringing in the harp, then we'll use the others as padding once it's in position."

"Okay," Brian said, and jumped inside to place the first blanket down.

When they returned to the front parlor, Sarah showed Brian the small dolly she had put next to the covered harp. "If we lift the harp onto the dolly, we can guide it out of this room and down the hall to the front door. We'll have to lift it over the steps, but then we can replace the dolly and roll it to the van."

Brian nodded his understanding. "Okay, you hold the dolly steady and I'll lift the harp onto it." Sarah knelt down to hold the rectan-

gular piece of wood. With very little apparent effort, Brian hoisted
the heavy instrument onto the dolly. When it was steady, Sarah rose.
Then standing on either side of it, the two of them guided the
cumbersome object through the house. They went through the same
procedure at the front door, and finally arrived at the van. At this
point, Sarah climbed into the van ahead of the harp and guided it in
as Brian lifted it from the dolly. They placed the extra blankets
around the harp to try and minimize its movement during transit.
Within twenty minutes the whole project was complete.

Brian slammed the van doors closed and turned to Sarah. "Whew,
maybe you should take up the flute!"

She laughed. "I wish I'd been given a penny for every time my
Dad and brothers have told me that. I'd be a rich woman." Then she
teased, "And you've had an easy time of it. Up until a couple of years
ago, we had to get it into our old Volvo estate. That was quite an art,
let me tell you!"

Brian looked puzzled. "What's a 'Volvo estate'?"

"You know, the kind of car that has a long body and hatchback
door instead of a boot."

"A station wagon?"

Sarah shrugged her shoulders. "I don't know. Is that what you call
them?"

"Going by your description, I think so. But what d'you mean by a
'boot'? Cars don't have boots," Brian said.

Sarah looked perplexed. "Of course they do. Unless it's an estate
of course. What do you put luggage in?"

"A trunk."

"No, I mean when you go somewhere in a car. What do you call
the place at the back where you store the luggage?"

"A trunk." Brian repeated.

They looked at each other and it was as though the absurdity of
their conversation suddenly struck them simultaneously. They burst
into laughter.

"I can't believe it!" Brian chuckled when their laughter subsided.
"And I thought we were both speaking English!"

"I am," Sarah teased. "You're speaking American."

Brian looked a bit rueful. "I guess, you've got me on that one."

Sarah chuckled. "Come on. Let's go and get the other bags in the front parlor and see if our mothers are ready."

They walked back into the house together. Sarah gathered up her dress from the chair and Brian picked up the two bags. They entered the kitchen to find the ladies just finishing loading up a large box with food.

"Are you ready?" Sarah called.

"Just about," her mother replied. She took off her apron and hung it on a peg behind the door. "Give me two minutes to powder my nose and I'll be there," she said and bustled off down the hall.

Brian placed the bags on top of the box of food and picked them all up. "Let's take these out to the car and wait for your mother there," he suggested. Then he led the way outside again. They didn't have to wait long. Within a few minutes, Annie Lewis came out, locked the door behind her, and joined them.

"Shall I drive our car and follow you?" Brian offered, indicating to the leased red Ford Escort parked alongside the house.

"That sounds like the best idea, if you don't mind," Annie said. "It's too bad we can't all fit in the van." She peered inside as if to check that the seating was as she remembered it.

"No problem," Brian said cheerfully. Then he turned to Sarah. "Don't forget I haven't a clue where we're going. Don't lose me— especially on one of those roundabout things!"

Sarah smiled. "Don't worry, we only pass through one roundabout the whole way there. If by any chance we get separated, just stay on the A5. There will be signs posted for Llangollen and I imagine there'll be a lot of traffic all going the same way."

"Okay," he called and helped his mother into the car. "See you there."

ॐ ॐ ॐ

The journey took just over an hour, and as Sarah had predicted, the closer they got to Llangollen, the heavier the traffic became. They passed through several villages along their winding route. The rolling hills, fields, rivers, and stone walls remained with them the whole way. Even to Sarah's seasoned eye, the countryside looked beautiful. It was green, lush, and remained largely untouched by modern man. It gave her a feeling of security to think that her own ancestors had probably viewed this area much as she was now seeing it. Only the power lines and noisy cars buzzing by detracted from the picture.

She was careful to keep an eye on her rearview mirror. Brian was staying close. Sometimes she would lose him for a few miles, especially when the road was very winding, but before long she would catch a glimpse of red and see him behind her again.

Sarah was glad that no other car separated them as they entered Llangollen. She was sure that the original planners of the International Eisteddfod had no idea that the festival would become so popular; the small town was really not built to cope with the huge surge in traffic. Every road was a bottleneck. Men wearing flourescent orange vests stood at every major junction trying to control the flow. Most cars were heading over the bridge that spanned the river, and into the large field that had been commissioned as a parking area.

As she moved forward, Sarah made sure that she waited for a gap in the traffic large enough for the van and the red car. They inched forward slowly until they crossed the bridge. Large signs indicated the area for Eisteddfod parking. Sarah slowed as she reached another of the men waving the cars on, then wound down her window and held out a blue ticket.

"Which way do we go if we're contestants?" she called to him. He walked forward.

"What's that, love?" he asked, trying to hear over the sound of many engines.

Sarah showed him her contestant pass. "I need to get as close to the grand marquee as possible," she explained. "We have to unload a harp."

The man eyed her pass, and nodded. "Right you are, love. Turn right here and keep going past all the parked cars. There'll be another man down there who can show you where to go."

"Thank you so much," Sarah said. "Can the red car behind me follow? I need his help with the harp."

The man peered around the van to view Brian's car. He grimaced. "Shouldn't be letting you do this, but . . . " He gave her a good-natured smile "Go on with you! I'll let him through just this once."

"Thanks," Sarah said and gave him a grateful smile. The man waved at her and then indicated that Brian follow. "Best of luck!" he called as they moved on.

They drove slowly, mindful of the effect bumps and ruts could have on the harp. When they reached the far side of the parking area, they could see the grand marquee and dozens of other smaller booths and pavilions ahead of them. Sarah stopped again when she reached the next attendant. She showed him her pass and explained that they were transporting a harp. The older man nodded and pointed out the docking area near the marquee, and the smaller parking area along side it. Sarah waved her thanks and moved on. Brian stayed close behind. She stopped briefly beside the parking area and indicated with hand gestures that Brian should park there. Then she drove a little further and carefully backed the van into the docking bay. By the time she had finished her maneuver, Brian and Iris Pearson had joined them.

"Good job!" Brian said to Sarah as she jumped down from the driver's seat. He had opened the door for her. She smiled with relief.

"Thanks. That traffic was pretty bad. You did a brilliant job just staying with me."

"I had no idea it would be such a big event," said Iris Pearson, looking around her with an awed expression. "There are thousands of people here."

"It gets bigger every year," Sarah said. Then she gave a small moan. "I think I'm starting to get nervous again!"

Her mother reached out and patted her arm. "Don't you worry about a thing, bach. You'll be wonderful."

A young man with a large round badge that read "Official" walked over to them. "Are you contestants?" he asked.

"I am," Sarah said, and handed him the blue ticket that she had shown to the attendants.

The man glanced at it and nodded. "Solo harp," he read aloud. He turned to Sarah. "Is the harp in the van?" he asked.

"Yes," Sarah said.

"Right, then," the man said, assuming a businesslike tone. He consulted a clipboard under his arm. "Solo harp contestants are supposed to be ready in the grand marquee by one o'clock. Competition starts at one-thirty." Sarah nodded.

"It'll probably take us twenty minutes to move the harp from the van to the stage." He glanced at his watch, then back at the group. "Are you planning to stay here until then or were you going to walk 'round a bit?"

"Oh, I think we should take a look around," said Annie Lewis. She pointed to the Pearsons. "These people are all the way from America. They've never been to an Eisteddfod before."

"Well, I hope you'll enjoy it. Yes indeed. I think there's a big group of dancers from somewhere in America competing today. Maybe you'll see them. You can't miss them. They're all dressed like cowboys and cowgirls."

Iris Pearson smiled politely and said, "Thank you, we'll keep a look out for them."

"Yes, you do that. They'd probably be pleased to see another American." The man turned back to Sarah. "Now, miss, I suggest that if you're not going to be in the marquee with the harp, you might want to keep it in the van until . . ." he looked at his watch again, ". . . oh, maybe noon or soon after. That way we can get it inside in plenty of time, and you can stay with it until the competition's over. How does that sound?"

Sarah gave a resigned sigh. She didn't want to move the van and go through the whole exercise again in two hours. But she hid her frustration and gave the man a polite nod.

"Alright. Where should we park till then?"

The man pointed to a spot not far from the Pearsons's car. "That would be grand."

Sarah climbed back into the van and started the engine.

"I'll see you back here in a couple of hours," called the man. She waved in acknowledgment and drove the van into the nearby vacant parking spot.

Once the van was parked and locked, the Pearsons and Lewises walked together to the ticket booth on the other side of the parking area. They bought tickets for general admittance and for the solo harp competition.

"You'll want to be there at least half an hour early," the ticket attendant warned them as she handed Brian the competition tickets. "It will fill up fast."

"Thank you. We'll do that." Brian said, and smiled at her. Sarah noticed the attendant perk up immediately, and felt rather sorry for her. It probably wasn't very often that someone as handsome and friendly as Brian came to her booth.

Brian touched Sarah's elbow and guided her through the gate. For the umpteenth time, she wondered if he was as aware of her touch as she was of his.

He dropped his hand from her arm but stayed close beside her as the four of them made their way into the large field. On either side of them were rows of booths. There were several large tent-like structures ahead of them, and the grand marquee stood behind them all. There were signs pointing out eating areas, lavatories, first aid, and telephones. Each sign was written in Welsh first, with English translations and an appropriate symbol beneath. People were milling around in various types of dress. Most people were dressed casually, but some were obviously competitors; their clothing ranged from formal to the national costume of their native land. It was a colorful sight.

The sounds were colorful too. The predominant language was Welsh, but there were many other tongues in evidence. English could be heard frequently, but it vied for popularity with several other languages. It was difficult to identify many of them. Above the babble of voices, they could hear the music coming from the competitions going on in the grand marquee. The music was broadcast live on loud speakers placed strategically around the outer area.

They slowly moved forward, stopping every once in a while to view the displays in various booths. Some of them were informational, such as the one sponsored by the Welsh Water Authority and the United Dairymen. There was a large, very popular one run by the Welsh Tourism Council. The Pearsons joined the visitors there for a time, and left with some pictorial brochures.

Local artisans had also set up booths. There were paintings, sketches, and photographs of scenes around Wales, as well as pottery pieces ranging from large bowls to small candlesticks. A small booth showed off the workmanship of an elderly silversmith. His jewelry was delicate and unique, with a lot of the pieces patterned on old Gaelic designs.

Iris Pearson was most taken with an exhibit of items made from the purple slate mined in the mountains nearby. The soft stone had been polished to create flower vases, book ends, name plaques for homes and businesses, and clock faces. After much deliberation she decided to buy a hexagonal clock. She had it wrapped in tissue and newspaper for protection, then handed the heavy object over to Brian.

"Whose suitcase is this going home in?" he teased his mother.

She gave him a quick smile. "Yours of course!"

He rolled his eyes and groaned.

Brian, for his part, was intrigued by a showcase of Welsh love-spoons. The young man sitting behind the table was busily whittling on a piece of wood with a sharp narrow knife. He looked up as he heard Brian ask Sarah, "Tell me about these."

Sarah said, "Traditionally a love-spoon was made by a young man for the woman he wanted to marry. It's made out of one piece of wood. One end is shaped into the cupping end of a spoon, and the handle is carved into all sorts of designs. Each spoon is different, because no two pieces of wood are exactly alike, and no two couples are exactly alike." She looked over at the man behind the table. "Isn't that right?" she asked.

"That's right, miss," he said, then turned to Brian. "You'll notice that some spoons are a lot more detailed than others, sir. As the lady said, it all depends on the message the young man wants to send his girl. The interlocking hearts, of course, is a favorite. So's the inter-locking rings. This one 'ere, . . . " he pointed to one of the larger spoons, ". . . has little beads carved out of the wood that are held in place inside a hollow area of the wood. Each of these beads is supposed to symbolize a child that they will have together."

Brian raised his eyebrows and looked at the man with amuse-ment. "I assume the man must be pretty sure of his chances with his girl before he gives her one like that," he said. To her embarrassment, Sarah felt herself color.

The man gave her what he thought was a knowing look, then said, "Oh, yes sir. In the old days, it was like giving an engagement ring."

"I see," said Brian. "Well, they're real works of art. Thanks for showing them to us." The man's face fell as he realized he was not, after all, going to make a sale.

"Yes, sir. Thank you, sir."

Brian and Sarah moved on to where their mothers were admiring some paintings.

"D'you recognize this one, Brian?" his mother asked.

"It does look familiar, but I can't think why," he replied.

"It's the same waterfall that's in the painting in the Lewis's hallway," she told him.

"That's right! I remember now. Is the waterfall near here?"

"It's called Pystill Glas, or Blue Waterfall in English. It's on the other side of Mynydd Mawr, so it's actually closer to Pen-y-Bryn than Llangollen," Sarah said. "It's a bit of a hike, but from home, you can get there and back on foot in less than a day."

Brian looked at the painting again. "It looks beautiful," he said.

Sarah followed his gaze. "It is," she said simply. "It's one of my favorite places."

He looked at her and said, "I'd like to go there one day."

Sarah felt her heartbeat quicken. Was he asking? "I . . . I could take you, if you really want to go," she heard herself say.

Annie Lewis's enthusiastic voice saved Brian from responding. "Why yes, that's a grand idea. If the good weather holds, and you've got enough time, I'm sure you'd enjoy that, Brian."

Iris Pearson added, "If it worked into Sarah's schedule, perhaps you could go while I go to see Aunty Sally tomorrow."

Brian looked surprised. "I didn't know you'd managed to set that up."

His mother looked pleased. "Yes, I talked to Annie about it when she arrived home yesterday. She called and talked to Aunty Sally's daughter and arranged for me to go over there tomorrow morning."

"That's great," Brian said. "Thanks Mrs. Lewis."

Annie Lewis smiled. "No trouble at all Brian. Aunty Sally will be pleased to have someone new to talk to."

Brian turned to Sarah, "How about it, Sarah?"

Sarah felt as though all eyes were on her, and she wondered fleetingly what had ever possessed her to offer. But if she was honest with herself, she knew she really wanted to show Brian a place so dear to her heart. "Let's hope the weather stays good," she said and smiled at him. The smile he gave her in return did nothing to help her irregular heart beat.

"Good, good," said Annie Lewis. "Now let's find somewhere to have a bite to eat before you have to go, Sarah."

Sarah felt her stomach knot up. She looked at her watch. Where had all the time gone? She groaned. "We'll have to hurry, Mam."

"I know, dear," her mother said in a placating tone. "Why don't you and Brian go back to the van and get our lunch. Iris and I will go over there," she pointed to an eating area a few yards away, "and find a table."

"Sounds like a great idea," said Brian. "Then I can get rid of this lead weight too!" He raised the wrapped clock in his arms.

His mother gave an embarrassed laugh. "I'm sorry, dear."

"Oh, I guess you're worth it, Mom!" he teased. "Come on, Sarah. Let's go."

❦ ❦ ❦

Twenty minutes later they were all seated at a round table making very little dent in Annie Lewis's enormous packed lunch. Annie and Iris had eaten a moderate amount. Brian had made a valiant attempt to eat a 'man-size' portion. Sarah had eaten very little, and Annie was looking worried.

"Sarah, if you don't eat something more, you'll pass out on stage."

"Oh Mam! Please!" Sarah held her stomach. "I'm too nervous to eat anything right now. I'll eat in the van on the way home, when the competition's all over."

"Are you sure, bach?"

Sarah groaned and rolled her eyes. Brian took pity on her.

"Okay ladies, if you've finished I'll take this box back to the van." He rose.

Annie said, "Thank you, Brian. I'll just finish up this cup of tea, then your mother and I can walk over to the marquee. Why don't we meet you there after you've unloaded the harp?"

"Sure. I've got my ticket. If I don't find you, we'll meet back at the van after the competition." Brian lifted the box and looked over at Sarah. "Ready?"

"Yes," she said and stood up with relief.

"Good luck, Sarah," said Iris Pearson. "I'm sure you'll do a great job."

"Thank you. I hope so." Sarah walked over to her mother and gave her a hug.

"Best of luck, child. Your father would be proud." Annie Lewis whispered in her ear. Sarah fought back the tears that memories and nerves produced. She nodded, then joined Brian as he wove his way through the tables and chairs towards the exit.

They had almost cleared the eating area when Brian paused, and Sarah nearly bumped into him from behind. "What . . ." she began.

"Sorry," said Brian "Hang on a minute." He put the box next to Sarah's feet and walked over to the nearest table. Then to Sarah's astonishment he began speaking to the occupants in a language she didn't recognize. To her untrained ear, it sounded as though he was fluent, too. A few minutes later he was back.

"Are you willing to do a good deed?" he asked expectantly.

Sarah hoped that she didn't look as confused as she felt. "A good deed?" she repeated.

Brian explained. "As we were passing this table I overheard the family talking. It sounded as though they were having a hard time being understood here. I speak Spanish . . ."

"So I noticed," interrupted Sarah.

Brian grinned. "Yes, well . . . I speak Spanish, so I asked them if I could help. They're from Patagonia. It's an area of Argentina originally colonized by Welsh people. They speak Spanish and some Welsh, although I imagine the accent's not what you're used to! But they don't speak English.

"Anyway, the people working at this concession stand are from England and can't understand Welsh or Spanish. So the bottom line is, these people haven't been able to order any food."

"How awful, especially for their children." Sarah's sympathy was automatically extended to the two young, dark-haired, dark-eyed children sitting forlornly at the table.

"You'll help?" Brian asked.

"Of course. What d'you want me to do?"

"Well, I'll see if there's anything in particular that they want, and go with the father to the counter and help him order. And I was wondering if you'd be willing to share some of your mother's lunch with the children to hold them over until we get back?"

"I can't believe I didn't think of it myself. Of course I will. You go ahead, and I'll try and cope with their Welsh dialect."

Brian grinned. "Awesome!"

Sarah smiled. She was beginning to get used to his accent, but some of his expressions really were strange.

"Brian," she called as he turned to leave.

"Yes."

"Don't forget, we don't have much time!" She pulled an apologetic face.

Brian reached over and squeezed her hand. "I won't!" Then he hurried to the table, exchanged a few more Spanish phrases, and left with the father of the family in tow.

Sarah walked over to the family and smiled. She hoisted the box onto the table and began handing sandwiches to the children. She offered one to the mother too, but she declined it with a small shake of her head.

Sarah found that if they spoke slowly she could understand most of their Welsh, but it certainly had a different lilt than she was used to. The dark-eyed children smiled their thanks and began eating immediately. They were well into their second sandwiches when Brian returned with a triumphant and extremely grateful partner. After receiving repeated thanks from the family, Brian and Sarah made their escape and started running towards the parking area.

"Brian," Sarah asked as they jogged along, "when did you learn to speak Spanish?"

"Several years ago," he said. He paused then continued. "I lived in Peru for two years."

Sarah was amazed. "What were you doing there?"

There was a longer pause. Then he said, "I was working as a missionary for our Church."

They jogged on in silence. Sarah's mind was reeling. A missionary! Her idea of a missionary was a very good, kind, elderly person who wore dark, drab clothing and a habitually tired countenance. Sarah glanced over at Brian, trying to match his long loping stride. He couldn't be much further from her image of a missionary if he tried.

"How old were you then?" she panted.

"I went when I was nineteen and returned home when I was twenty-one." They ran on a little further. "I won't say that it was an easy experience," he continued. "But, it was a wonderful one. I learned so much."

Sarah wished that she could ask him more, but didn't even know where to begin. She saw him give her an anxious look and realized that he was concerned about her reaction to this information.

"When this competition is all over, and we're not both out of breath," she added with a wheeze, "will you tell me more about your mission?"

She saw his face light up. "I'd like that," he said, and Sarah noticed with dismay that he wasn't nearly as out of breath as she was.

There was no opportunity for further discussion because when they arrived at the van, they saw the man who had met them earlier. He was standing at the dock looking at his watch.

"I was beginning to wonder if you were coming after all," he commented.

"Sorry," panted Brian as Sarah got into the driver's seat.

"Oh we'll manage," the man said affably. "Bring her in really close now," he called to Sarah as she began reversing the van towards the two men. "That's it. Stop!" he shouted. Sarah turned off the ignition and went around to the back. The men were already at work, and it wasn't long before the harp was carefully placed on its dolly just offstage in the grand marquee.

"Just give me a holler when you're ready to reload it," the man said as he turned to go. "I'll be around all afternoon. Best of luck to you, miss."

"Thanks for all your help," Sarah said. The man waved and left them. Sarah looked at her watch.

"I have to hurry and change, bring in my music, and tune the harp before the competition starts." She was beginning to feel a little panicked.

"Hang in there! We'll make it." Sarah noticed his use of the word "we," and felt better just knowing he was on her side. Brian placed his hands on her shoulders and smiled down at her. "You start tuning the harp. I'll go get your clothes and the music from the van. Then you can go change and I'll stay with the harp until you get back."

"Thank you," she said gratefully. He kept his hands on her shoulders a minute longer and the tender look in his eyes made her tremble. Then he smiled and was gone.

Sarah sat down and forced herself to concentrate. She bent her head low, plucked, and started adjusting the strings. She had almost finished when Brian returned. He stood to one side, quietly watching her until she raised her head from the last note.

"I'll check it again when I get back, but it should be pretty close."

"You're truly amazing," he said in awe.

Sarah blushed. "I'd better go. I'll be as fast as I can." Brian nodded and stepped over to stand beside the harp.

She followed the painted signs to the competitors' changing room. It was already crowded but she squeezed into a corner and quickly changed into her long dress. It was a very simple design, but she knew that the burgundy fabric set off her coloring well. The dress had a square neckline, a fitted bodice, short puffed sleeves and a very full skirt; the skirt had to be full to allow her to sit comfortably behind the harp. She put on the black ballet slippers and dropped her other clothes and shoes into her bag.

Once she was dressed, she swept her hair up into a neat chignon. A few shorter wisps fell in soft curls to frame her face. She touched up her makeup, gathered her belongings, and slipped out of the room. According to her watch, she had been gone less than twelve minutes.

Brian was dutifully standing beside the harp when she reemerged off stage. He looked up as she approached and seemed to be momentarily speechless.

"Sarah, you're beautiful!" he said in a hushed tone. But it was the open admiration in his eyes that set her pulse racing.

"Thank you," she whispered, furiously wishing that she did not blush so easily. She stepped closer and placed her bag beside the harp. She noticed that several other participants were also now standing in the wings. She looked around and recognized three other girls from previous Eisteddfods. They exchanged smiles.

Sarah could feel the nervous tension building in the room. She stood still, closed her eyes, took a deep breath and tried to relax. Brian, seeming to sense her need for quiet contemplation, said nothing. But she could feel his support and strength as he stood beside her.

When the announcement came for the beginning of the solo harp competition there was a noticeable drop in the buzzing of the unseen audience. Sarah opened her eyes and as she did so Brian slipped her hand into his and held it firmly. Instinctively Sarah responded by curving her fingers around his. She looked up at him and for a long moment was conscious only of the emotion flickering in his deep blue eyes. It was as though there was no one there but the two of them.

The harp music broke the spell. The first competitor had begun her piece, and they turned to listen, but Brian kept her close, his strong, long fingers intertwined with hers. When the music ended and the applause began, Sarah said, "She did well."

Brian nodded his agreement. They watched as the stage crew efficiently exchanged harps and the next participant walked onstage.

"I'm seventh out of eight contestants," Sarah whispered. "I don't know if I can stand the wait."

Brian squeezed her hand. "They're saving the best for the end," he said.

Sarah moaned. "I think you're biased!" she whispered.

"Who, me?" Brian replied, feigning innocence.

Sarah giggled, and realized with gratitude that his easy bantering had helped ease her stress.

Their patient waiting finally came to an end about forty minutes later. The stage crew approached and took charge of the harp. Sarah picked up her music and clutched it in trembling hands. Just as she was about to follow the men onto the stage, Brian pulled her to him and whispered, "Just remember, whatever the judges decide, you'll always be number one in my book!" Then he lightly brushed her forehead with his lips, and just as quickly, released her. In a daze, Sarah walked out in front of the audience.

She acknowledged their applause with a small smile, then walked over to the judges and handed them her music. She turned, walked back to the waiting harp, and sat down on the stool. She laid her fingers across the strings and noticed that they were quivering slightly. She flexed them carefully and laid them still again. A hush fell over the audience. Sarah straightened her position and looked over to the judges table. At a nod from the head judge, she bent forward slightly and began to play.

Sarah was not aware of the passage of time. Her nervousness left her. She was doing what she loved. She became totally engrossed in the music as it came to life beneath her fingers. When her piece finally came to a close she raised her head slowly and looked out into the sea of faces before her. It was as though the enraptured audience gave an audible sigh. Then the applause began. She stood and curtsied once, then again as the applause continued. The stage crew unobtrusively appeared at her elbow to remove her harp. She followed them off stage.

Brian was waiting for her. She went straight into his open arms.

"Oh, it's over! It's finally over!" She wasn't sure if she wanted to cry with relief or with joy.

"You were magnificent, Sarah!" His voice was husky with emotion. She raised her eyes to his and his lips found hers. Everything and everyone around them blurred into insignificance.

ॐ ॐ ॐ

It took the judges just five minutes after the final competitor had left the stage to hand the master of ceremonies their decision. When Sarah heard her name called as the first-place winner, she couldn't believe her ears. Some of the other girls backstage rushed forward to congratulate her. Brian, who had had his arm around her waist as the results were announced, hugged her close, then pushed her gently towards the stage entrance.

Sarah felt as though she were living a dream. She wondered when she would wake up. The audience gave her a standing ovation as she accepted her award. She thanked the master of ceremonies, curtsied to the judges and audience, and made her escape. She was besieged by well wishers backstage. It was totally overwhelming. By the time the frenzy died down, she felt completely drained. Her face ached from smiling, and her stomach had finally decided that enough was enough. She was hungry.

She was surprised at how disappointed she was to find Brian gone. Her harp was also missing, so she assumed that he had found help to take it back to the van. Her clothing bag sat in the corner, where she had left it. Clutching her award in one hand and the bag in the other, she hurried to the changing rooms.

To her relief, most people had already left. Because contestants for other events would be arriving within minutes, she changed quickly. She was careful to hang up her dress and replace the protective plastic. Then she pulled the pins out of her hair and shook it free, enjoying how good it felt to have it loose once more. She gathered up her belongings and walked towards the door.

Just before leaving, she stopped beside a large mirror and gazed at the reflection she saw there. Was she really the girl who had just won the solo harp competition at the International Eisteddfod? It still seemed unbelievable. Yet, there was the trophy in her hand. Was she really the girl whom Brian Pearson had taken in his arms and kissed? That too seemed unbelievable. She touched her lips gently. Her response to that kiss was like nothing she had ever felt before. She knew that she was beginning to care deeply for the American. She hardly knew him, and yet when she was with him, it was as though they'd always known each other. It was wonderful, yet it scared her. He was on holiday and would be part of her world for a very short time. She could not allow herself to become too attached, only to have him walk out of her life as suddenly as he'd entered it.

Then there was his religion. She gave an involuntary shudder. There was so much she didn't understand, and she knew that she would have to face it as surely as she knew that she dreaded it. But that was still to come. She held the trophy close. Today was for celebrating.

Her mother, Brian, and Iris were all waiting for her at the van, and her mother ran forward to greet her.

"Sarah! Oh Sarah, I'm so proud of you!" In her excitement her mother reverted to her native tongue. Sarah responded in Welsh.

"I still can't believe it, Mam."

"Oh, you were wonderful. I was nervous for you. But I shouldn't have been. You were wonderful!"

The Pearsons were standing quietly, watching their interaction. Even though they couldn't translate what was being said, their smiles testified that they understood.

"Thank you for taking care of the harp, Brian," Sarah said in English.

"No problem," he smiled. "The man who helped us unload it came back to help me put it in. He was tickled pink that you'd won. He acted like you were his prodigy! And as for these two," Brian's eyes twinkled as he teased the older women, "you've never seen anything like it! Telling everyone, 'I'm her mother,' and 'I'm her friend.' They were bursting with pride and couldn't get to you fast enough."

"Brian! We did not!" Annie Lewis and Iris Pearson cried out in unison. They looked so indignant that Sarah and Brian burst out laughing.

"Come on!" said Brian. "Let's get Sarah home so that the whole village can share in her triumph."

"You're absolutely right, Brian," said Annie. Then a look of concern crossed her face. "Oh, but Iris, did you want to see any more of the Eisteddfod?"

Iris Pearson smiled. "I've enjoyed every minute of it, but Brian's right. I think we should head back now." She looked over at Sarah. "Besides, I think someone is probably pretty exhausted."

Sarah smiled at Iris's perceptive comment. "It's just beginning to hit me. I suppose I've been going on adrenalin for quite a while."

It was Brian's turn to look concerned. "And now that I think about it, the doctor in me says it's about time you had something to eat."

To Sarah's embarrassment, her stomach chose that exact moment to rumble loudly. She groaned. "It sounds like my stomach seconds that motion," she said, and within two minutes her mother had food and drink in her hands.

As soon as Sarah had finished her sandwich, they set out once more. Sarah drove the van with Brian close behind in his car. By leaving early they missed most of the heavy traffic they had encountered on the way in, and arrived back at the village in the early evening.

❦ ❦ ❦

Instead of driving directly home, Sarah pulled up outside the shop. Brian stopped behind her. Sarah jumped out of the van and ran back to the car. Brian wound down the window as she drew near.

"I promised Aunty Lil I'd let her know what happened as soon as we got back," she explained. "You're welcome to come in with us, or else you can drive on home if you'd like to."

Brian looked at his mother questioningly. She leaned over Brian to speak through the window. "Why don't you and your mother go in? Brian and I will wait for you at home. I'm sure you could use a bit of family time alone."

"You're more than welcome to join us," Sarah insisted.

"Thank you, Sarah. You're very sweet. But you go ahead with your mother now and we'll see you when you get back."

"Well, if you're sure." Sarah put her hand in her pocket and pulled out a key. "This is the key to the back door. Let yourselves in. We won't be long." She handed the key to Brian.

"Thanks, Sarah."

She stood still and watched as he put the car in gear and backed up a little, before moving around the van. She raised her hand as Brian and his mother drove on. She was stunned by how hard it was to see him drive down the lane. He was only going as far as her own home. She would see him soon. If she felt like this now, how was she ever going to deal with him leaving for good? The thought felt like a lead weight landing on her shoulders. She tried to block it out of her mind as she walked back to the van. Her mother was just stepping out of the passenger side.

"They decided to go on home, did they?" her mother asked.

"Yes," Sarah replied. "I gave them my back-door key, so they can get into the house."

"Oh, that was a good idea. You know how your Aunty Lil is. There's really no telling how long we might be with her."

Sarah hid a smile. She knew full well who'd be doing all the talking once they got inside. It wouldn't be her and it wouldn't be Aunty Lil. She looked over at her mother fondly. "Why don't you carry the trophy in," she offered.

"Ooh, may I really? That'd be lovely," her mother crooned, and lifted the award with careful hands.

Sarah smiled and closed the van door behind her mother. "Come on then." She led the way around to the back of the shop and opened the door that led to Aunty Lil's flat.

When they reached the door at the top of the stairs, Sarah knocked, opened it a crack, and called out, "We're back, Aunty Lil!"

Lil's voice called back, "Oh that's grand! Come on in and tell me all about it."

Sarah opened the door further and she and her mother entered. They walked into a small sitting room with two rather ancient armchairs pulled up to a fireplace. A plethora of photos sat on display along the mantlepiece. Most of them were pictures of Sarah and her brothers. A black and white cat was curled up on one of the chairs. There was a copy of the local newspaper spread over the arm of the other chair. A bulbous lamp with a faded pink lamp shade sat on a nearby coffee table. The carpet's paisley design had originally been quite vivid in color, but, like the rest of the room, it now had a faded look.

"I'm in the kitchen," Aunty Lil's voice called out once more. "I'm just putting the kettle on for a spot of tea. Come in and join me."

Sarah and her mother moved on through a doorway that led directly into the small kitchen and dining area of the flat. Lil was plugging in the electric kettle. She turned as they walked in, and her eyes immediately lit on the trophy in Annie Lewis's hands. Her own hands flew to her cheeks.

"My stars, child! You did it! Oh Sarah, bach!" She ran over to Sarah and hugged her. "Oh your dad would be so proud. He always said you'd do it one day." She took a step back. "May I see it?"

Annie handed the trophy to her sister-in-law. Lil turned it around slowly. When she had viewed it from all sides she breathed, "Well, what an honor!" Then she handed it back to Sarah and said, "Come on now, sit down and tell me all about it."

So the three ladies sat down around Lil's tiny kitchen table, and over their cups of tea they told Lil about their day at the Eisteddfod. As Sarah recounted her experience, she discovered that it was hard for her to separate her emotions of the day. Which ones were due to the competition and which ones were due to Brian's presence? She ended up giving a rather bare-bones chronology of events which, to both her amusement and relief, her mother padded out with the thoughts and feelings of a proud mother.

Eventually Annie Lewis glanced at the clock hanging on the wall above the table. "Goodness gracious, we must go!" She looked at Lil apologetically. "I'm sorry Lil, but we must get back home. The Pearsons have been waiting for us for over an hour now." Sarah saw the shutter come down over her aunt's face.

"Well, thank you for stopping by," Lil said and somehow it seemed as though the warmth had gone from her voice.

Sarah stood up and gave her a hug. "I promised I would, Aunty Lil. You're the first person we've told."

Lil gave her a grateful smile. "I'm right proud of you Sarah. I told you, you've got a gift. I'm glad those judges were able to see past the ends of their noses and recognize it!"

Sarah burst out laughing. "You may have to give those Eisteddfod judges the benefit of the doubt from now on, Aunty Lil!"

Lil gave her a rueful smile. "You may be right, bach. You may be right!"

🍂 🍂 🍂

It took them only a few minutes to arrive home. When they pulled into the driveway, a small, bouncy reception committee was waiting in the front garden. Aled and Mot raced to the van. Hopping up and down on his short stubby legs Aled called out, "Aunty Sarah, Mr. Pearson wouldn't tell me if you won. Did you win? Did you win?"

Sarah laughed at her young nephew's exuberance. "Let me get out of the van and I'll tell you," she said through her open window.

Aled obligingly yanked on Mot's collar and pulled him down from the door that he had been standing up against on hind legs. Sarah quickly opened the door and as she closed it behind her she held out her trophy to Aled. Aled's eyes were as big as saucers. "You won! You really won!" he whooped. Then he turned and ran for the house just as fast as his little legs would carry him. "Mam! Dad! Come quick! Aunty Sarah won! She won!"

The next few minutes were a mass of hugs, kisses, congratulations, laughter, and teasing. "D'you mean to tell me that Dad, John, and I went through all those years of lugging that horrendous instrument around Wales and all you get is this tiny trophy? Where's our trophy?" Sarah's brother teased when they had all gathered in the back garden.

"They didn't even offer me one," Brian added with a grin. "And I was Johnny-on-the-Spot, still panting from the exertion!" Everyone laughed.

They were seated on deck chairs under the shade of the old apple tree. Kevin had already introduced his wife, Mair, to the Pearsons. They were on their way back from the market at Newtown and had stopped at the house, anxious to know how Sarah had done in competition.

Most of the adults were drinking cups of tea. Iris, Brian, and Aled were enjoying tall cool glasses of lemonade. "What are your plans for tomorrow, Brian?" Kevin asked. "You're not thinking of leaving any time soon are you?"

"We'd like to stay a couple more days, if that's okay with your mother," Brian replied and looked over at Annie Lewis.

"Of course! We'd love to have you for as long as you can stay," she responded quickly.

"Mom has a bit more looking around she'd like to do," Brian continued. "We still haven't spoken to Reverend Davis and I think Mom's hoping to visit Aunty Sally too."

Kevin nodded.

Annie Lewis broke in again. "If the weather stays good, Brian and Sarah were thinking of walking up to Pystill Glas tomorrow while I take Iris to see Aunty Sally."

Kevin grinned. "Yes, a ten-mile hike uphill and a conversation with Aunty Sally should take about the same amount of time!"

"Kevin!" his mother reproved. Everyone else laughed.

When the laughter died down, Kevin turned to Sarah. "If you decide to go to Pistyll Glas tomorrow, why don't you drive over and park in the farmyard. You can cut up onto the old trail through our back pasture. It'll save you an hour both ways. It probably won't matter on the way there, but you may be glad of it on the way back."

Sarah nodded. "That's a good idea. Thanks Kev. We'll probably do that." She looked over at Brian.

"Sounds great!" he said.

"Can I go with you?" said a young voice at Brian's elbow. Aled had been uncharacteristically quiet over the last few minutes. He had been listening to the adults talk and absently throwing a stick for Mot to retrieve over and over again.

Brian looked at Sarah for help. "I'm afraid this walk is a bit too long for you, Aled. It's going to take us all day and it's rough ground," she said.

Aled was not to be dissuaded. "I can climb Mynydd Mawr easy!" he boasted. "Please can I go with you, Aunty Sarah? I'll be really good and I won't ask to go to the potty even once!" Sarah did her best not to smile, and out of the corner of her eye noticed other adults doing the same thing. Aled's mother, Mair, tried to help Sarah out.

"Aled, bach, I need you at home tomorrow to help me make strawberry jam. You can help me pick out the best strawberries and you can eat the scrapings off the pan," Mair coaxed.

"Oh Mam!" Aled moaned. "That's girl stuff. I want to go on a big walk to see the waterfall with Aunty Sarah and Mr. Pearson."

"Aled," Kevin's voice was more stern than his wife's had been. "You can hike up to Pistyll Glas when you're a bit older. But you can't go this time."

Aled heard the finality in his father's voice and hung his head. He jabbed the grass with the stick that Mot had been chasing. "It's not fair," he muttered. "I always have to stay home with Mam!" Mair looked uncomfortable but Kevin ignored him.

"Don't worry about him," Kevin said. "He'll have forgotten all about it in a few minutes."

Sarah watched Aled attacking an unsuspecting daisy with his stick. She wasn't as convinced as her brother that Aled would forget so quickly. She tried to think of something to take his mind off his disappointment. With a mental word of apology to the unsuspecting Brian, Sarah whispered to Aled, "Hey Aled! I haven't heard Mr. Pearson practicing his numbers today. Maybe you should test him."

Aled's digging stopped. He looked up, but was not quite in time to see his aunt mouth 'sorry' to Brian or to see Brian's understanding wink in return. "Mr. Pearson," Aled asked, "have you been doin' your numbers?"

"Weeell . . . " Brian pulled a rueful face.

Aled smiled and suddenly the sulky young boy was gone. "You'd better do them now, then," he said.

"Whatever you say, teacher!" Brian said and sat up straight, as if ready to accept punishment. Aled giggled and the other relieved adults smiled. Sarah didn't know what the others were thinking, but she thought Brian deserved ten out of ten for being such a good sport and for salvaging Aled's natural good humor.

She then sat in open-mouthed amazement as Brian calmly recited his numbers in Welsh from one to ten almost perfectly. Everyone, including Aled, clapped when he had finished. As he had done once before, Brian gave a mock bow and slipped in another quick wink at Sarah.

"I think he's been practicing in bed, Aunty Sarah," said Aled in a proud voice. "That's where I practice new words," he added in a matter-of-fact tone. Then, "He sounds quite good doesn't he?"

"He certainly does, Aled. I'm very impressed." And she was.

Brian grinned. "Hey, my mom and I were talking in the car on the way home from the 'aestethvod.'" Sarah noticed that Mair, who had not been with them when Brian was first introduced to that Welsh word, winced a little at Brian's pronunciation. Sarah however, mentally applauded his effort.

"You guys have all been so good to us." This time Sarah did wince. Kevin and Aled were the only "guys" present. If the others noticed, they were polite enough not to show it. Brian continued, "We wanted to do something to show our appreciation. We were wondering if we could take you all out to dinner tonight?"

Annie was the first to respond. "Oh Brian, that's very nice of you. But you really don't need to do that."

"I know we don't need to, but we'd really like to. You haven't needed to go out of your way for us over the last few days either, but you have. We're very grateful to you all. Besides," he added with a pointed look at Sarah, "we've got Sarah's victory to celebrate tonight."

"Brian's right," interjected Iris Pearson. "Please let us do this for you. Is there anywhere nearby that would be suitable? I'm afraid we'll have to have you guide us again."

"The Fish'n Chip Shop!" yelled Aled with glee.

"Shh, Aled!" whispered his mother.

"Come here Aled," said Brian with a chuckle. He put his arm around the young boy's shoulders. "Tell me about this 'Fish and Chip Shop.'"

"It's brilliant!" Aled said with enthusiasm. "They give you tons of chips, an' I like the fish cakes best, an' it's best when you have tons of vinegar on top."

Brian chuckled all the more. "Sounds awesome!" Aled looked pleased.

"Is there anyone who would violently object to a 'Fish and Chip Shop' dinner?" Brian asked and looked around. "Great! Well I think one big disappointment is enough for anyone in one day," Brian said, subtly referring to Aled's recent letdown. "I vote we go to the 'Fish and Chip Shop' for dinner."

"Yeah!" shouted Aled, jumping up and down with joy.

Kevin smiled at Aled's antics. "Thanks Brian. You've made his day."

"Hey, all I needed was an excuse!" Brian laughed. "Everyone told me I had to try British fish and chips before leaving. I'm as excited as he is!"

"Kevin," said Annie Lewis, "why don't you and Brian drive down to the Fish and Chip Shop and bring the food back here. We can eat outside or in the kitchen. And I'll make a little salad to help balance all those greasy chips."

Kevin rolled his eyes. "Honestly, a man can't have one decent deep-fried meal anymore without his mother or his wife fussing about fruits and vegetables!"

Brian laughed. "Sounds like you're as henpecked as I am Kevin!" he joked.

"Oh, go on with you both!" said Annie, trying to hide a smile.

"Can I go too?" pleaded Aled.

"Good grief, boy," Kevin said good naturedly, "you have to be there to tell them how much vinegar to put on."

Aled grinned from ear to ear and slipped his hand into his father's. "Great! Let's go!"

They stood up and Kevin started toward the car with Aled. As Brian walked past her to join them, Sarah reached out her arm and touched his. Brian stopped immediately and turned to her.

"Have you really been practicing those numbers at night?" she whispered. "I felt so bad about putting you on the spot like that, but you were marvelous."

Brian smiled. "Don't even worry about it. Actually, my nights have been busy with other things recently," he teased. Sarah felt herself color.

He saw her discomfort and quickly said. "It's a trick I learned on my mission." Sarah was startled. "I tried to memorize quite a few scriptures while I was in Peru. When I got home I found that I could use a similar technique with all the horrendous medical terms my teachers wanted me to learn. So now when I come across new or strange words I automatically file them away. It helps for pop quizzes," he added with a grin. Then, on seeing Sarah's confused expression, he explained, "Pop quizzes are unexpected tests."

The sound of a car horn honking made them both jump. "That's Aled," Sarah said with a smile.

"I'd better go." Brian gave Sarah's hand a squeeze, then ran across the lawn to the waiting car.

Sarah watched him go. When he had first mentioned his Church mission she had had a hard time fitting him into the role of a pious missionary. Now she wondered about this new information. The only men she knew who could quote scriptures were ministers. She had seen many Bible-thumping ministers spout scripture without referring to text. Somehow Brian seemed as little like a Bible-thumping minister as he had an unassuming missionary. It seemed that the more Brian told her, the more confused Sarah became. She shook her head; it made no sense to her.

On a logical level she wanted to wash her hands of him and all his strange ideas. But on another level, deep inside her heart, she wanted to be with him all the time. Sarah sighed. Mair walked over to her and followed her gaze as Kevin's car disappeared around the bend.

"What a remarkable man!" Mair said in a soft voice. "No wonder Aled's been plaguing us to come back and see him."

Sarah smiled. "He is good with Aled, isn't he?"

Mair smiled in return. "He's got him wrapped around his finger."

Sarah laughed. "I think it works both ways. Goodness only knows what Aled will make him buy at the Fish and Chip Shop. It's a good thing Kevin's there to make sure they bring home something edible."

By the time the men returned with their purchases, all individually wrapped in newspaper, the women had made a salad, cut up some fruit, and laid out plates, knives, and forks. Aled took one look at the table and wrinkled up his nose.

"Nain, you can't eat fish'n chips on plates like that. You have to eat it out of the newspaper with your fingers, or it doesn't taste right."

Annie Lewis chuckled. "I'll tell you what, you young scamp. I'll let you eat yours off the newspaper, and some of us older ones will use the plates. Would that be alright?"

"I s'pose so," Aled conceded with a sigh. "D'you have any tomato sauce, Nain?" he asked a minute later.

"I think I do, Aled. See if your Aunty Sarah can find some in the fridge for you."

It didn't take long for Sarah to find the bottle. She carried it over to Aled who was anxiously waiting with his fat, soggy chips unwrapped and lying on the newspaper they had come in. She helped him pour a big puddle of tomato sauce onto the paper.

"Want some tomato sauce, Mr. Pearson?" Aled asked Brian, who was sitting next to him.

"Sure," said Brian. Aled slid the bottle over to him. "Hey, this is ketchup!" Brian said.

"It's tomato sauce," mumbled Aled with his mouth full of food.

"Aled, don't talk with your mouth full," admonished his mother. Aled made a big effort to swallow the huge wad of chips.

"Your chips'll taste a lot better with tomato sauce," Aled promised Brian.

Brian grinned. "They taste great already. I've never had chips quite like this before."

Aled looked at him with surprise. "Why not?"

"Well, in America we call them 'french fries' and they're much skinnier than these and crispy instead of soggy."

"I don't like them when they're crispy. That means they're burned," Aled informed him. Brian suppressed a smile but Sarah could see the mirth shining in his eyes.

"This fish is delicious," commented Iris Pearson. Unlike her son, she was eating her meal with silverware and a plate. "What kind of fish is it?" she asked.

"Cod," answered Kevin. "The fishcakes are salmon, but the fillets are cod."

"It all tastes great," said Brian with enthusiasm. Sarah smiled. She wouldn't want to eat this greasy food very often, but it was true—every once in a while it really hit the spot.

They enjoyed their meal together. Sarah thought that if it hadn't been for her constant awareness of Brian, it would have seemed like a big family gathering. There was a lot of laughter and a pleasant atmosphere. She looked around at the happy faces and wished that she too could truly enjoy this time together, without fighting the doubts and concerns that plagued her about Brian and his family's religious beliefs.

All too soon Kevin, Mair, and a very tired Aled had to leave for home.

"If you decide on the hike tomorrow, maybe we'll see you at the farm," Kevin said as he shook Brian's hand.

"I hope so," Brian said. He shook Mair's hand too and tousled Aled's hair. "Thanks for recommending the fish and chips, little buddy," he said.

"Welcome," came the sleepy reply. "See you tomorrow!"

Iris Pearson wished them all good-bye in her own quiet way. It seemed all wrong that they would probably never see each other again. It left a sadness to an otherwise merry occasion.

15 November 1881

Dear Father,

As time goes by I gain greater and greater respect for my husband. Glyn's calm, forgiving approach to life is a perfect foil for my impulsive temperament (although I fear it sheds me in poor light as often as not).

I have long since regretted the hasty words penned to you as we traveled west. The Evanses have remained true and loyal friends despite my erroneous judgement of them. Indeed I have come to realize that much of what I believed about Mormons is false. We have come to know many of them. They are an industrious, God-fearing people, who care deeply for one another. I have witnessed firsthand the way in which they have united to create beautiful communities out of forsaken desert land. They have welcomed Glyn and me into their homes with open arms, despite our obvious religious differences.

Glyn and I have made a home for ourselves in a small town called Logan. It is beautifully situated on the Logan River at the mouth of a canyon, on ground sloping gently westward. Although it does not boast the lush, green, rolling fields of Wales, it has a majestic splendor of its own. The rugged mountains are awe inspiring and there is much wildlife nearby—including animals I have never seen before, such as moose, raccoon, and skunk.

Despite its humble beginnings, the town is growing steadily. Glyn has learned cabinetry skills quickly at Will's side, and they find themselves in great demand. A magnificent Mormon temple is close to completion. I have not entered the building myself, but Glyn speaks highly of the craftsmanship that has gone into its construction. He and Will have spent many hours there sharing their tools and talents with other volunteers.

I see Catriona almost daily and have made other friends among the women living nearby. The settlers here have come from all over Europe. Language barriers are challenging at times, but there is a marvelous feeling of fellowship amongst these people that seems to transcend their differences.

Glyn and I often talk of Pen-y-Bryn. We will always miss the village and its people, but we do not regret our decision to emigrate. We feel very fortunate. We are very happy here. We have our health, we have our home, and we have each other.

Our thoughts and prayers are with you.

Mary.

Chapter 5

Everyone went to bed early that night. Sarah worried that she would be unable to sleep because of the maelstrom of emotions she was experiencing. As she lay in bed, pictures and phrases from her day's activities flitted onto the canvas of her mind like an unedited movie film. But physical and mental exhaustion finally took over. She slept deeply and was wakened by the rising sun peering in through the curtains, and the sound of birds singing their morning song.

She crawled out of bed and went to the window. The sky was blue with a few puffy white clouds floating overhead. The air smelt cool and damp with morning dew. Above the song of the birds she could hear an occasional dog barking, cows lowing, sheep bleating, and a vehicle traveling in the distance. The village was waking up to a new day.

Sarah felt refreshed after her uninterrupted night's sleep, and she viewed the dawning day from her window with pleasure.

"Perfect!" she said to herself and hurried to get washed and dressed.

She was pleased to be the first one downstairs. She stoked up the Aga and made a cup of tea. Then after a quick breakfast, she began making sandwiches for lunch. Sarah had almost finished her preparations when her mother arrived in the kitchen.

"My word, you're an early bird today," Annie Lewis said when she walked in. "Don't tell me you've made your lunch too. Dear me! I could've done that for you."

"It was no bother, Mam. Besides," she faced her mother with a twinkle in her eye, "if I've got to carry this lunch up Mynydd Mawr I'd rather have one my size that one your size!"

"Well, I certainly hope you've made enough for Brian, young lady," her mother quipped with mock gruffness. She peered into the bags. "I think I'd better add another sandwich to his bag."

"Mam!" Sarah groaned.

"One little sandwich won't make his pack any heavier, but it could make all the difference between being hungry or not," her mother said ignoring Sarah's remonstration. And she proceeded to make another thick sandwich and add it to the already full bag.

Sarah knew there was no use arguing with her so she went into the boot room and rooted around in the cupboard until she found her navy blue backpack and her father's old red backpack. She shook them out, then took them into the kitchen. She put a lunch and a full water bottle in each one, and was in the process of rolling up a lightweight jacket to stuff into her pack when the Pearsons came in.

"Are we on?" Brian asked eagerly when he saw the backpacks leaning against the cupboards.

"If you still want to go, I'm ready," said Sarah with a smile.

"All right!"

He was wearing jeans and a blue and white T-shirt with 'Ricks College Vikings' and a Viking ship emblazoned across the chest. Sarah was also wearing jeans. Her T-shirt was dark green, and she had braided her hair into one long rope down her back and tied it off with a narrow green ribbon. She was wearing thick wool socks, and as Brian and his mother sat down to eat their breakfast, she sat down too and began lacing up her hiking boots.

"How rough is this hike, Sarah?" Brian asked when he noticed what she was doing.

"Most of it's not bad at all," Sarah said. "But there are a couple of patches that are a bit of a scramble."

"I'm afraid I didn't come very well prepared for a hike," Brian said, ruefully viewing his athletic shoes.

"Don't worry, you'll be fine as long as your shoes are comfortable and sturdy. I've got out my father's backpack for you, so just be sure you bring a jacket or a warm sweater."

Brian glanced out of the window at the cobalt blue sky and raised a questioning eyebrow. Sarah saw the look.

"Don't be fooled by the sunshine. The weather in these valleys can change in an instant. We don't have all this lush greenery without the rain that goes along with it. We'll be gone several hours, so it's best to be prepared for the worst."

Brian nodded. "Okay, I'll run upstairs and get one. I'll meet you down here in just a couple of minutes."

Fifteen minutes later they were ready. Their mothers walked with them to the road. Brian loaded their backpacks into his hired car and with well wishes from the two older ladies for a safe and enjoyable outing, they were off.

Brian drove slowly through the village. Out of the corner of her eye, Sarah studied his profile. His handsome features left her feeling breathless. She could sense his concentration as he approached a junction and shifted down the gears.

"Which way?" he asked and flashed her a smile.

"Oh . . . Uh . . . " momentarily caught off guard, Sarah couldn't even remember where they were going. "Sorry. Turn right here," she said, feeling like a total idiot.

As Brian moved the car forward he said, "It sounds crazy, but I'm more worried about driving on these quiet lanes than on the motorway. When I'm one car among many, it's easy to remember to stay on the left. Here, I keep having to prevent myself from moving over onto the right side."

"I'll warn you if you do," said Sarah with feeling.

Brian laughed. "You do that!" After a brief pause he continued, "I don't think I've been on this road before."

"Probably not," Sarah said. "If we'd gone left at the last junction you would have recognized the road we took up to the farms on Thursday. This road goes past Deniol Manor and on up the valley. It'll take us about fifteen minutes to reach Kevin's farm."

Just then they turned another corner and the roughly hewn stone wall edging the road became a red brick one. Behind the wall was a long row of manicured evergreen trees. The dense foliage precluded any view from the road, but in the distance, above the tree line, motorists could just glimpse half a dozen tall chimneys and portions of a purple slate roof.

"That's Deniol Manor in the distance," said Sarah as she pointed to the chimneys. "From this point on we are passing Manor land."

Brian drove on until Sarah touched his arm and said, "Slow down as soon as you pass this bend, Brian. It will be about your only chance to see the Manor itself."

He followed her instructions. As they turned the bend, he saw an elaborate gateway built into the wall. He pulled over to the side of the road. "D'you mind if I go out and look?" Brian asked.

"Not at all," said Sarah.

Brian quickly jumped out of the car and walked briskly over to the gate. He stood for a few minutes with his hands in his pockets and his back to her. She wished that she knew what he was thinking as he gazed out at the building that had played such an important role in his ancestors's lives.

When he got back into the car, they were both silent for a few minutes. Finally Brian said, "I feel like I'm living in two worlds." He shook his head with frustration. "It's hard to explain. I've heard about Glyn and Mary Jones and Pen-y-Bryn for as long as I can remember, but they always seemed so removed from me that they didn't affect my daily life very much. Then all of a sudden, I find myself here, seeing places where they lived and worked. Meeting people whose families they would have known." Brian looked over at Sarah. "Coming to care deeply about some of those people." Sarah's heart leaped as she met his eyes and he continued, "Now being here with you feels real and my life in the U.S. is like a dream. It's hard to imagine going back."

Sarah looked down. She didn't know what to say. She longed to have this man beside her hold her in his arms and say that he was never going to leave, but she knew that it could never be.

Brian leaned towards her, "Sarah, I . . ."

Sarah was not to find out what Brian had been about to say because suddenly there was a shrill whistle and a cacophony of bleating and barking. Around the corner came a huge flock of noisy, trotting sheep. They jostled forward, egged on by two sheepdogs on either side and a farmer wielding a stout stick from behind.

The farmer, dressed in old brown trousers, black wellies, a worn tweed jacket, and flat cap raised his arm in greeting but continued his instructions to the dogs through a series of high-pitched whistles.

Brian stared out of the car window open-mouthed as the sheep surrounded the vehicle. He sat back in his seat with a whoosh. "I think I've entered a time warp!" he said in amazement. Sarah took one look at his face and started to giggle. Not only was the situation ludicrous, the timing was unbelievable. Sarah decided she had to laugh or she'd cry.

Brian looked over at her. She could tell by the way that his lips were twitching that he was struggling to keep a straight face himself. "So, Miss Lewis," he said, "would you like to tell me how we get out of this mess?"

"Well, Mr. Pearson," she said, imitating his tone, "I think we should sit here and admire Hefin Thomas's flock until they are securely behind the pasture gate, then we slowly drive on."

"I see," Brian said, manfully maintaining his poise. "And about how long would you anticipate these fine specimens will be monopolizing the road?"

Sarah pretended to be studying the sheep while she fought off another attack of the giggles. "I'd guess about fifteen minutes," she said primly, then burst into gales of laughter. Brian's laughter joined hers.

"Oh, stop! Stop!" Sarah gasped a few minutes later. "My side hurts."

"I think maybe we can move now," Brian said, still chuckling. He carefully edged the car forward being sure to leave several yards between him and the last stragglers of the flock. Both Brian and Sarah raised their hands to the farmer as they passed him at the gate. He gave them a second salute with his stick.

"I hope Hefin didn't see us laughing our heads off in the car," Sarah said. "He'll think we're a couple of raving looneys."

"He might be right!" Brian answered. "I can't even figure out what we were laughing about now."

Sarah sighed. "Neither can I, but it was funny at the time!"

Brian stretched out his hand and found hers. He held it tightly. "You're a lot of fun to be around, Sarah Lewis."

Sarah gave his hand an answering squeeze. "You are too, Brian Pearson."

❦ ❦ ❦

It only took another ten minutes to reach Kevin and Mair's farm. Brian followed Sarah's instructions and drove into the farmyard without further incident. As their car pulled in, they could see Mair hanging clothes on the line at the side of the farmhouse. She looked up and shaded her eyes with her hand. At first she could not place the strange car, but as they drew nearer, recognition dawned and she waved. She dropped the damp clothes she was holding into the hamper at her feet and walked over to greet them.

"Good morning!" she called. "You've decided to make the hike then?"

Sarah got out of the car and gave her sister-in-law a hug. "Hello Mair. Yes, we're going to give it a go."

"Hi there, Mair!" Brian came around the car and reached over to shake her hand. Then he went back to retrieve the two backpacks from inside the car.

"I'm afraid you've missed Kevin. He's gone down to the south field. Part of the hedge there has a hole in it. He's going to try and mend it before moving the sheep in."

"Not to worry," said Sarah. "Maybe we'll catch him on the way back."

"That's right," said Mair. She looked around at the nearby buildings. "I'm surprised Aled hasn't come running out yet. He's been on the lookout for you ever since he got up this morning. He was here just a minute ago."

Brian and Sarah looked around the farmyard too. "I don't see him anywhere either," Sarah said. "Tell him we'll stop by at the farmhouse before we leave." She looked at her watch. "I don't suppose we'll be back much before four o'clock."

"I'll tell him. He'll be anxious to see you again."

Sarah and Brian donned their backpacks. Mair walked with them until they reached the gate that led into the north pasture. "Have a lovely time," she said as they parted.

"Thanks Mair," Brian said.

"We'll see you later this afternoon," Sarah called and waved. Mair waved in return, then began to retrace her steps to the waiting basket of damp washing.

Brian and Sarah walked through the lush green field, heading up a gentle incline. A handful of sheep stared at them with baleful eyes.

A few of the younger lambs skittered away as the intruding humans drew closer, but for the most part the sheep ignored their steady progress through the pasture.

The field was enclosed on all sides by a thick hedge. The small, dark-green waxy leaves let very little light through. Brian studied the closest one carefully. He must have been thinking about Kevin because he said, "It's hard to imagine one of these thick hedges developing a hole. They seem impenetrable."

Sarah nodded. "It doesn't happen very often, and the reasons are varied. But they're an awful pain to put right." She led him over to the thriving foliage. "Most of the hedges on Kevin's farm are hawthorn. They look lovely, especially in the spring when they're covered with little white blossoms. But they have an awful barb." She gently pulled back a young branch and exposed a dark, almost black twig thickly covered in angry, sharp thorns.

"Ouch! Those look nasty," he said.

Sarah nodded. "They are. In fact most people get a horrid rash if they're unlucky enough to brush up against them. Kevin and his workers have to wear thick long sleeves and long leather gloves when they're patching the hedges."

Brian grimaced. "I don't envy him that job."

Sarah grinned. "Well, let's get going before he sees you on his land and shanghais you into helping him."

Brian laughed. "Lead the way."

They followed the hedge uphill for quite a while until they approached the corner of the field. Brian looked at Sarah with curiosity. "Are we pole vaulting the hedge at this point?" he asked with one eyebrow raised.

"Where's your faith in your guide?" Sarah teased. Then added in a dramatic tone, "Wait one more minute and all will be revealed!"

They walked just a few more yards until Brian could see, deftly hidden in the corner of the hedge, three large slabs of stone laid down to form a rudimentary staircase.

"This is an old stile," Sarah said as she lightly stepped up and over. "They're strewn all over the hills, linking fields and property lines. I don't think anyone knows who built them. They've been here for centuries, but they're still used all the time."

Brian climbed over the stile as well. "I just can't get over how old things are here. Not just the castles and valuable antiques. So many of the homes and the things people still use everyday were created so long ago." He paused. "Maybe it's different on the east coast of the United States. They have more history there than we have in the west. But in our area, if something's over fifty years old, it's a treasured heirloom."

"So how long does that give you? Twenty more years?" Sarah quipped.

"Hey, you turkey!" Brian tried to grab her arm, but Sarah anticipated his move and ran off laughing. He chased her and even though Sarah was swift and surefooted, Brian had the advantage of longer legs and strength. He caught her and pulled her to a standstill, panting and chuckling. "Guess I'm not a museum piece just yet!"

Sarah, still out of breath herself, looked up at him. "Not yet," she agreed with a small smile. His arm tightened around her and he drew her close. Their lips met, and instinctively her arms wrapped themselves around his neck.

Sarah was shaken by her reaction. She knew that she had never before felt this way about a man. She was falling in love. No, she was already in love. It was wonderful and it was terrifying. She wanted all the answers but didn't even know all the questions.

She wanted to be with him. She wanted his love. But everything was happening so fast that it frightened her. There was so much she didn't understand or know about Brian, and she had never allowed her heart to rule her head before; she was in unfamiliar territory and felt vulnerable.

As though he sensed her turbulent emotions, Brian wordlessly released her. He held out his hand for hers and together they began their ascent towards the tree-lined ridge ahead.

They walked in silence, as though by mutual consent they had decided to soak in their time together without the clutter of idle chatter or the problems of deeper discussion. They enjoyed the feel of the gentle breeze in their faces and the sun on their backs. They heard the distant sounds of farm life, the twittering birds, droning insects, and the regular tread of their footsteps as they made their way up the barely discernable footpath. The smell of grass and occasional blossoms assailed them, and the views of the valley below became more and more panoramic as they climbed.

For Sarah it was as though her senses were more keen than they had ever been. The hike that she had known and loved for years had suddenly become even more poignant. Sharing it with Brian, and trying to see things through his inexperienced eyes helped her rediscover just how beautiful this small parcel of mid-Wales really was.

As they climbed, the terrain became more rugged and the grass more sparse. The lush greenery gave way to hardier vegetation like thistles, gorse, and heather that somehow thrived among the boulders and crumbling rocks. They encountered a lone, hardy sheep every once in a while, but the animals ambled off with disinterest as Brian and Sarah approached. There were a few stretches that required careful climbing because the ground was covered in loose shale. Sarah had to use both hands to steady herself a couple of times, but when they passed on to steadier ground, Brian took her hand again.

When they finally reached the crest of the mountain, Sarah chose a large boulder and sat down to rest. She could feel the heat from the stone penetrating through her jeans. Brian followed her example and sat at her feet. They both opened up their bottled water and drank.

Their eyes were drawn to the scene below them. Untamed mountain led down to a patchwork quilt of cultivated fields. Minute threads indicated distant roads, and individual tiny brown squares were the isolated farms, while small clusters gathered to form villages. Livestock appeared as black and white specks on a green canvas. The deep-blue sky above them was marred by only an occasional wispy white cloud. The slight breeze had died down, and the air was still . It was as though they were sitting on the top of the world.

Brian broke the silence. "Wow!"

"It's breathtaking, isn't it?" Sarah said.

Brian nodded. "It's incredible."

They sat soaking in the view for a few more minutes. Sarah was the first to stir. "It's downhill from here," she said. "The waterfall is in the valley on the other side of this mountain."

"How long d'you think it will take us to reach it?" Brian asked.

Sarah glanced at her watch. "Fifteen to twenty minutes probably." She looked up. "Shall we wait until we get there before eating?"

Brian ran his arm across his glistening forehead. "Is there shade down there?"

"Yes, and it'll seem a lot cooler because of the spray coming from the waterfall."

"Sounds great," said Brian with feeling.

Sarah smiled. "Come on then!" She rose to her feet stiffly and struggled to heave her backpack back into place. Brian moved to help her adjust the second strap, then she stood at his side as he reshouldered his own backpack with ease.

They both lost their footing at times on the loose shale, but by clinging to a few tenacious shrubs and larger rock outcrops, they were able to slither to a stop before sliding far. It was with a great sense of relief that Sarah found herself at last on firm and grassy ground.

They could already hear the waterfall. The roar of water began as a distant rumble but increased in magnitude with every few yards they walked. They came upon it with no forewarning, other than the increase in volume. They rounded a bend and there it was. It fell from the mountainside above them like a sparkling silver ribbon, shrouded in mist and encircled by multicolored rainbows. The water fell into a deep green pool and then on into a gurgling stream that danced its way merrily down the hillside.

On either side of the stream were tussocks of emerald-green grass, rocks of various shapes and sizes, and untamed bushes. Young saplings fought for space beneath mature oak and beech trees. At first glance the area appeared to be totally untouched by human hand, but closer inspection revealed a rustic wooden footbridge that spanned the stream just a few yards below the big pool.

Sarah led the way to the footbridge. About three feet wide and fifteen feet long, it was made of roughly hewn logs lashed together, and on either side was a thick rope handrail. They walked onto the structure and paused halfway across to look up at the waterfall. The spray assailed them, leaving their faces, hair, and clothes damp. It was exhilarating. Sarah closed her eyes and soaked in the powerful sound and vibration of the moving water.

By the time they had crossed the bridge and found a sheltered spot beneath an old oak tree, their clothes were completely dry once more. They sat on the ground and began unloading their lunches from their backpacks. They leaned their backs against the tree trunk and gazed out at the scene before them as they ate.

"This is awesome!" Brian said. "I can't believe this beautiful place is so untouched. If there was a spot like this in America," he said, "there'd be a parking lot over there." He pointed to a small group of trees. "There'd be a visitors' center over there." This time he pointed to a clump of tangled bushes. "And there'd be a paved path that linked them all together." He paused and flicked a persistent fly off his sandwich. "Oh, and there'd also be picnic tables and drinking-water fountains."

"That might be nice," commented Sarah as she squirmed a little to avoid sitting on a protruding root.

"In some ways," Brian responded. "But along with all those things come droves of people, making lots of noise with their cars, radios, and voices. It's hard to capture the spirit of a place when it's competing with all that other stuff."

They sat in contented silence for a few minutes, and Sarah experienced a wave of gratitude that Brian could sense the peace and majesty of this place that meant so much to her.

"How often do you come here?" Brian asked eventually.

Sarah plucked at a few blades of grass absently. "I used to come about twice each summer, usually with my father. It's too exposed to snow and rain storms to come any other time of the year. I hiked in alone after my Dad died, but I haven't been since then. That's been almost two years now."

Brian nodded with understanding. "Painful memories, along with the good ones."

Sarah marveled again at his perception. "I suppose that's it," she said quietly.

"My Dad and I had a favorite hike too. It's in the Grand Teton National Park. We'd try and go every summer. There's a beautiful, clear lake there called Jenny Lake. We'd hike around the lake, then up the mountain behind it. There was often snow at the top, even in the middle of summer."

Sarah watched the emotions flit across Brian's face as he told her of this place she'd never seen. It wasn't hard for her to imagine it. She knew by now that Brian's impression of a place would be very similar to her own.

"I've only been back to Jenny Lake twice since Dad died. I still love it there, but it's not as much fun to go alone." Brian paused and looked off into the distance. "Even though there were times on my hikes that I felt like he might have been with me in spirit."

Sarah looked at him quizzically. "You really believe he's still alive in some way, don't you?"

Brian turned to face her. "Yes, I'm sure of it."

"And your mother does too, doesn't she?"

"Yes. That's one of the reasons she's so thrilled to be in Wales. We both believe that one day we'll have the opportunity of meeting our ancestors and being reunited with family members and friends who have already passed on."

Sarah stared at him. "You mean as people? Like we are now?"

"Much as we are now, yes. Our Church teaches that because of Christ's atonement and resurrection, all people have the opportunity to live again. That their bodies and spirits will be reunited in a perfect state."

"So you are Christian then?" Hope filled Sarah's voice.

It was Brian's turn to stare. "Of course!" Sarah saw lines of deep concern furrow across his forehead. "Sarah, you have to believe that!"

Sarah lowered her head. "I don't know what to believe, Brian," she whispered. She looked out at the waterfall. "I've never known a Mormon before. I just remember hearing something about . . . about the sect practicing plural marriage." She'd said it! She felt her cheeks color and quickly lowered her head again in an attempt to hide it.

She heard Brian give a low groan and a twig break in two. She still did not dare look him in the face. After a minute of silence, Brian said, "It's true that in the early days of our Church a small group of people practiced polygamy. There were reasons for it at the time. But that time has passed. It hasn't been practiced for about 100 years. In fact, anyone professing to be a member of our Church who is also practicing polygamy now is excommunicated."

Sarah wished that her mind had been put completely at rest by this information. She was relieved to a degree, but she was still confused. What kind of church was this Mormon Church?

As if reading her mind, Brian reached out for her hand and turned her to face him. "Sarah, can I tell you a little about my Church? Can I help put some of those fears you've been harboring to rest, and maybe help explain why my mom and I believe what we believe?"

Sarah raised her eyes to his. Beneath the strong, handsome features she saw the sensitive, kind person she had come to know and care about deeply. When she gazed into his eyes, it reaffirmed what she had already guessed. There was a depth to this man that she had yet to unlock. She also knew instinctively that he was now offering her the key to that treasure. Her hand trembled in his. He felt it. She saw her own nervousness reflected in his eyes. Somehow that gave her the courage she'd been lacking.

"Yes. Tell me what you believe." It was not much more than a whisper, but Brian heard her. He squeezed her hand.

"I know most of this will be new to you and some of it may be confusing. If you don't understand, or have any questions, you just stop me, okay?"

Sarah nodded and he gave her a slow smile. Then, beneath the branches of the old oak tree and with the sound of falling water, busy insects, and singing birds as their only distraction, Brian taught her about what he called the gospel of Jesus Christ.

He told her of the gradual downfall of the church that Christ established during his earthly ministry, and the subsequent restoration of the gospel through a young man called Joseph Smith. He explained the coming forth of the Book of Mormon, and how this book complemented the scripture contained within the Bible. He rehearsed the restoration of the Priesthood and authority of God upon the earth. He taught her about the need for a latter-day prophet and the establishment of a church structure as it had been in biblical times. He also mentioned the need for temples, the divine nature of families, and that each human being is a special son or daughter of a loving Father in Heaven.

Sarah sat and listened in wonder. There was so much that she'd never heard before, so much she'd never thought about before, so much that despite its newness just felt right. She asked questions every once in a while, but not often. Brian was careful to explain things in simple terms, and he clarified new concepts with examples.

When she reached the point where she thought her mind would burst, Brian's tone changed. His voice slowed. He took both her hands in his and said, "I know I've stuffed you full of information, Sarah. It doesn't seem fair to ask you to take in so much so fast, but I know we don't have a lot of time. I just want you to know that what I've told you is true. I know it as surely as I know that I'm sitting here with you."

Sarah felt tears spring to her eyes as she saw the emotion in Brian's. "You can have that knowledge too. But not from anything I tell you. Heavenly Father loves all His children so much that He has provided a way for each of us to gain our own testimonies of the truthfulness of the gospel. If you really want to know if the Church of Jesus Christ of Latter-day Saints is true, or if the Book of Mormon is the word of God, or if Joseph Smith was a prophet, all you have to do is pray. Just ask. The Holy Ghost will let you know. You'll feel it deep inside."

The tears that had filled Sarah's eyes silently trickled down her cheeks. She had never experienced these feelings before. She felt a warmth from within. She felt good being with Brian, hearing his voice, listening to his words.

Brian released one of her hands, and with his fingers, gently wiped away her tears. "I know Heavenly Father loves you, Sarah. More than anything, He wants you to be happy. The gospel of Jesus Christ can bring you happiness now and forever."

Sarah felt a torrent of emotions. She wanted to stay under the oak tree with Brian forever: she wanted to be alone and sort through her tumbling thoughts. She felt totally overwhelmed, and didn't know what to think or say or do. She closed her eyes and leaned back against the tree, desperately trying to distance herself from everything, to look at things objectively. But it was no use. Despite Brian's sympathetic silence, she could sense his nearness. His words buzzed through her head like persistent bees. She opened her eyes. Brian's head was bowed. She reached over and touched his arm. He looked up immediately.

"I don't know what to think, Brian," she whispered. "It's all so new and strange. Just give me a little time to think things through."

Brian nodded but she saw the sadness in his eyes. She swallowed the lump in her throat with difficulty. She knew as well as he did that time was one thing they were lacking. He would be gone within two days.

Sarah looked over at the waterfall and noticed with a start the lengthening shadows from the tall trees near the stream. She glanced at her watch. Three twenty-five! Where had the time gone?

"Brian, it's almost half-past three" she gasped. "We'd better get going; it's a long way back." She began gathering up the few leftovers and stuffed them into her backpack.

Brian looked at his own watch in disbelief. "I can't believe it," he said. "Wait, Sarah, before we go . . . ," he thrust his hand deep into his backpack and retrieved a camera. ". . . I brought my camera up and haven't taken a single photo. Stay there!"

Sarah obediently stayed by the tree and watched as Brian ran over to the stream. She assumed that he was going to take a photo of the waterfall, but instead he turned and pointed the camera in her direction. "Smile!" he yelled above the sound of the water, and before she had time to react he was loping back with a pleased grin across his face.

"You didn't give me any warning," she accused.

"Sorry!" he said, not looking the least bit sorry.

"You beast!" Sarah said trying hard not to laugh at his smug expression. "Give me that camera. I'll take a photo of you over by the waterfall. You have to have something to prove you made it all the way here."

"Yes ma'am!" Brian quipped and raised his hand in salute.

Sarah snatched the camera from him. She studied it for a few seconds, then asked, "Okay, which button do I push?"

Brian rolled his eyes. "Women!"

"Watch it!" Sarah warned. "This woman could leave you stranded in the mountains if you're not nice!"

Brian threw back his head and laughed. He held out his hand for the camera. "Here, let me show you."

Sarah never was sure if she had all the settings correct, but within five minutes she had taken Brian's photo with the waterfall in the background, and they were making their way across the footbridge. They retraced their steps, scrambling up the steep slope that they had earlier slithered down. They passed by the large boulders where they had rested before, knowing that they could not afford that luxury this time. Because of their late start, their homeward trek must be completed more quickly than their outward one had been.

ॐ ॐ ॐ

Panting a little from exertion, they reached the upper meadows in good time. The lowering sun was obscured by dark gray clouds that had been gradually moving in from the west as they hiked. There was a slight chill to the air. Sarah stopped and looked up. "I think we may be in for some rain," she observed. "It can move in quickly over the mountains, but we should make it to the farm before it hits."

They continued on. The grassy ground was easier on their tired feet than the loose shale and rocks had been. The sheep were huddled together near the hedges. "They can feel the storm coming," commented Sarah as they trudged by.

"The birds are quiet, too," noted Brian.

Sarah looked around. There was a dark purple hue to the sky and the wind was picking up. She pulled a face. "I think this is going to be a bad one." They crested the last hill together and stopped in unison.

"Wow! What a reception committee!" said Brian.

Sarah looked confused. "What on earth's going on down there?"

From their vantage point Brian and Sarah could see that Kevin's farm yard was full of vehicles. There were a few people milling around the stationary vehicles. Others were clustered in small groups. There was one group at the farmhouse door and another at the gate to the north pasture.

Sarah's face suddenly paled. She clutched Brian's arm. "Brian, there's something wrong! That's Constable Lloyd's car and . . . " she gave a low moan as an ambulance turned off the road and moved swiftly up the lane to the farm.

Brian grabbed Sarah's hand and they flew down the slope. Their tired feet and aching legs were forgotten. They were only a few hundred yards from the gate when one of the group assembled there noticed them. He pointed in their direction and the others turned to watch their approach.

Gasping for breath, Sarah hurled herself at her brother. "Kevin . . . Kev, what's happened?"

Her brother held her at arm's length. His face was ashen and lines of worry were prominent. "Calm down, sis! Take a minute to get your breath back." Sarah shook her head vehemently.

"No! Tell me what's wrong."

Kevin steeled himself. "It's Aled," he said. "He's missing."

"Missing!" repeated Sarah stunned. "But how . . . I mean where . . . "

"We're organizing search parties now," said Kevin. "Mair has turned the house upside down looking. We've gone through all the farm buildings time and time again. No one's seen him since early this morning. We've got to start searching the hills, the mountain and . . ." he swallowed hard, ". . . the river."

"Oh Kevin!" Sarah sobbed.

A burly man with short gray hair pushed himself forward. Under normal circumstances he would have had a jovial face and cheerful disposition, but now he was grave. He gave Sarah a sympathetic pat then extended his hand to Brian.

"Constable Dafydd Lloyd," he said. "You must be Brian Pearson."

Brian shook his hand. "Yes, sir," he said.

"You didn't see anything up there that might help us, did you, lad?" he asked.

"No, Constable, we didn't. But we've been traveling at a pretty fast pace for the last hour or so. We noticed the storm coming in . . . " Brian looked over at Sarah's stricken face. "It's possible we could have overlooked something."

Kevin ran his hand through his hair in frustration. "Let's get going, Constable. We're getting nothing done standing here."

The police officer nodded. "We will Kev, we will. Tom's going to lead his group to the river and follow it up and down stream for a few miles. This group is heading into the hills. We'll fan out in pairs and cover as much area as we can before dark." He looked at his watch. "I reckon that gives us four to five hours." He looked over at the lowering clouds. "If the weather holds out," he muttered.

"I'll go back the way Sarah and I came," Brian volunteered. "It's the only area I know well enough to be of any help."

"Thanks Brian," Kevin gave him a look of gratitude. He turned to the Constable. "That's up the north pasture, over the shoulder of Mynydd Mawr to Pistyll Glas."

"I'm going with him," Sarah said.

Brian and Kevin both swung around. "Sarah, you've been out there all day. You're too tired to go again," Kevin remonstrated.

"I'm no more tired than Brian," contended Sarah. "Aled's my nephew. I'm going." Her tone brooked no argument.

Brian put his arm on Kevin's shoulder. "Let her go, Kevin. I'll look after her."

Kevin looked from one to the other. Then he ran his hand across his haggard face, the strain showing terribly. He was not up to a battle. "Be careful!" His voice was little more than a hoarse whisper. Then as they turned to leave, Kevin called out, "Sarah, we think he has Mot with him." Sarah experienced a surge of relief. Mot was devoted to Aled and wouldn't leave him, no matter where the child was. If they could only find the dog, they'd find Aled too.

Constable Lloyd acknowledged Brian and Sarah's departure, and began organizing the other volunteers into pairs. By the time Brian and Sarah reached the stile and looked back, the fields were dotted with searchers, each heading for their assigned areas.

Sarah walked with her hands clenched, straining her eyes in all directions. Every once in a while she would cup her hands to her mouth and shout "Aled! Mot!" The ensuing silence was both eerie and discouraging. Brian walked doggedly on beside her. Neither of them mentioned the cooler temperatures or the buffeting wind that had sprung up once they reached the more difficult terrain. Sarah barely noticed either condition. Her focus was solely on finding Aled. She ignored her sore feet, aching legs, and burning chest. Urgency drove her upward and onward.

When she slipped for the third time in as many minutes, Brian took her by the elbow and led her to a boulder. "You have to rest for a minute," he ordered.

Sarah tried to stand up again. "We can't!" It was almost a sob. "We've got to find him Brian. It's almost dark, and the storm . . ." As she spoke, the first drops of rain fell. They were large and heavy. Brian held out an upturned palm and looked skyward. Then he looked back down at her grief-stricken face.

"Sarah," he said in a quiet tone, "let's say a prayer."

Sarah stared at him. Despite the torture she was experiencing as she thought about Aled and the condition he might be in, she marveled at this man before her. She had never encountered anyone with this kind of faith, except perhaps the minister. And she had a hard time imagining him praying outside the confines of the chapel.

"Here? Now?"

"Here and now," he replied gravely.

She hesitated for only a moment, then gave Brian her hand. It lent her courage just to feel his strong fingers intertwine with hers. He knelt down on the rocky path and she knelt down beside him. When she saw him bow his head, she followed suit.

His prayer was unlike any prayer she had ever heard. She was given a glimpse into a part of Brian that she had sensed existed but had not before witnessed. She heard him express gratitude for his association with her family. He spoke of the love that he and the other searchers had for Aled, and of their deep concern for him now. She listened as he humbly asked for divine guidance in finding the lost boy, and pled for protection over him until he was found.

Sarah shoulders shook as she cried silent tears. She clung to Brian's hand, desperately wanting to share in his faith. She tried to block her fears from her mind and focus on Brian's voice. As she did so, a feeling of calm assurance began to permeate her troubled mind. Notwithstanding the strengthening wind, or the increasing rainfall, a warmth filled her.

They knelt together in silence for a few seconds after Brian closed his prayer. Sarah didn't want to let go of the momentary peace that surrounded her. Brian squeezed her hand.

"We'll find him, Sarah," he assured.

Sarah gave him a weak smile. "We've got to," she said. Her voice broke on the words. She stared off into the gray drizzling rain. "Which way?" she whispered.

Brian helped her up. "What's down there?" he asked, pointing to a dropoff on the other side of the ridge.

"It leads down to Pystill Glas too, but it's really steep, and you have to work your way around a few old rock slides."

Brian nodded, looking thoughtful. "Let's take a look," he decided, and led the way to the top.

"Boy, you weren't kidding!" Brian whistled through his teeth at the scene beneath him. The blowing rain made the sight appear even more austere than it normally would have. Large granite boulders stood sentinel above layers of gray shale. A few hardy shrubs defied nature and gravity by clinging to the vertical barren ground. There were also some tufts of scrub grass relieving the otherwise bleak mountain face.

Brian cupped his hands to his mouth. "Aled! Mot!" he yelled. He and Sarah stood and waited, scanning the ground below for any movement. Sarah added her shout to Brian's. They waited again, and were about to turn back when Sarah clutched Brian's arm. She felt her nails penetrate his flesh and heard his sharp intake of breath.

"Listen! Did you hear anything?" she hissed.

"Ouch!" Brian removed her hand and placed his own over the scratches.

"Sorry!" Sarah apologized with embarrassment. "I thought I heard a dog. Did you hear it?"

"I didn't hear anything. But it'd be hard to hear a train in this wind!"

"Mot! Where are you?" Sarah shouted against the gale.

They both strained their ears. They heard a faint but unmistakable bark float back on the wind.

"He's down there! Oh Brian, he's down there!" Hope mixed with horror as Sarah surveyed the drop once more.

"Hold on!" Brian held out a restraining arm. "We've got to do this right, or we won't be any help to Aled at all."

Sarah stomped her feet with impatience as Brian walked along the ridge, stopping occasionally to look down. After what seemed like an eternity, he beckoned to her. She moved close beside him.

"I think our best bet is to try going down from here," he pointed to a handful of secure boulders that marked a rudimentary trail. "It's going to be slick," he warned, running his hand across the wet surface of a nearby rock. "We'll have to take it slowly." He gave Sarah a pointed look.

"I know, I know! But he may be badly hurt. Let's go!" Sarah's anxiety to reach Aled was deepening. Every second counted.

"I'll go first, then if you slip you'll have a soft landing!" Brian's attempt at levity sounded a little forced. Sarah barely heard his concerned mutter, "I wish we had a rope."

But they managed it somehow. It was agonizingly slow. It was steep, slippery, and frightening, but inch by torturous inch they made their way down. They depended on the large rocks and shrubs for anchors. They stopped frequently to shout for Mot. Each time, he barked in response, and each time the bark became louder.

At last they reached a narrow ledge that had been hidden from view earlier by a deformed, scrawny scrub oak that hung over the crevice. And there, huddled against the side of the mountain was a very wet dog. Behind his canine guard, protected from the elements, was the body of a young boy.

"Aled!" Sarah screamed when she saw his motionless body.

Mot stood up and barked a greeting. Then the dog gingerly made his way forward, carefully avoiding the edge of the ledge. Brian reached the dog first. Ignoring the dog's soggy coat, he patted and praised the dog affectionately, all the while holding him firmly in place so that Sarah could squeeze past and reach Aled. Once Brian saw that Sarah was safely on the ledge, he released his hold on the dog and began his own crawl forward. Mot stood passively aside, but continued to watch the newcomers with alert eyes.

By the time Brian reached her, Sarah was already taking Aled's pulse. He didn't interrupt her. Instead, he reached into his pocket and pulled out a small pocket knife. Careful not to move the boy at all, Brian slipped the knife under the hem of one trouser leg. The fabric was wet, badly blood stained and torn above the knee. Within seconds he had the trouser leg ripped open two-thirds of the way up.

Sarah gave an involuntary gasp. Aled's leg looked awful. "Compound fracture," muttered Brian through clenched teeth. He looked up at Sarah. She dug deep to try and maintain some semblance of professionalism.

"His pulse is rapid and weak," she said. Her voice broke on the last word.

Brian looked over at her with sympathy, then turned his attention back to Aled. The cut across his leg was deep and had bled profusely. The bone was visible through the gash, and his leg was distorted.

"The bleeding has lessened, but it's been bleeding for some time. That and his pant leg probably kept the wound pretty clean. I wish I could splint it for him, but there's nothing . . . " Brian looked around the barren ledge in desperation. "There's nothing here that could support the leg."

Sarah ran her fingers over Aled's pale face. It was covered in ugly scratches. His skin felt rough and dry. His lips had a slightly blue tinge. "I think he's badly dehydrated, Brian," she said.

Brian nodded. "If he's been out here all day, we've got to get some water down him." He was rooting through his backpack. He handed Sarah his water bottle. "See if you can get him to take a little," he instructed. Then he pulled out his jacket and set it on the ground. Using his pocketknife, he hacked off one of the sleeves and tore it open along the seam. The lining, Sarah noticed, was soft cotton flannel.

Brian carefully slid the fabric under Aled's leg and wrapped it securely around the wound. As he did so, Aled stirred for the first time. Sarah knelt over him immediately.

"Aled!" she called softly. "Aled, it's Aunty Sarah. It's alright now."

Aled turned his head weakly and mumbled some words in Welsh before losing consciousness again.

"What did he say?" Brian asked.

Sarah turned to him with tears in her eyes. "He said 'I just wanted to go with you.'"

Brian groaned and wiped the rain off his face with an equally wet hand. "Well, that explains what he's doing here. He must have followed us when we left the farm. Perhaps he lost sight of us at the top and assumed we'd come down this way." He pressed a gentle hand on the young boy's cheek. "Sorry little buddy. We'd have waited for you if we'd only known." Except for his shallow breathing, Aled remained silent.

Brian turned to Sarah. "I'll go for help. I hate to leave you here, but if he comes round again, he's sure to speak in Welsh, and I won't be able to understand him. If he's in shock, it will help to have someone really familiar nearby."

Sarah felt herself tremble. "We'll be alright." She tried to convince herself as she spoke.

Brian looked down at Aled. "Sarah, I . . . " he broke off his sentence, paused, then turned to her. "Sarah, remember how I told you about how our Church believes that the priesthood of God has been restored?"

Sarah nodded, wondering why Brian would bring religion up at a time like this. Then he continued. "Well, one of the things that men who have been given the priesthood can do is give blessings to people who are sick or hurt." He took a deep breath. "I've been given that priesthood. I'd like to give Aled a blessing before I go. Would that be okay with you?"

Sarah stared at him. He was a priest? It was too much for her to take in. Brian must have seen the confusion in her eyes. He reached out to her.

"It's okay, Sarah. I'm still the same Brian!" He smiled. "I can't do too much for Aled medically on this ledge. But this is one way that I truly believe I can help him. We've got to do everything we can for him until he's safely in a hospital."

His final argument cinched it for Sarah. She had put her trust in this man before. Now was not the time to question it. "Give him a blessing, Brian." Then as an afterthought she added, "But hurry!"

Brian nodded, then turned his attention to Aled once more. Sarah watched as he knelt over the boy and placed his hands on Aled's head. Then bowing his own head he began to speak. At first the words seemed strange to Sarah, but she was struck by the simplicity and power they conveyed. She heard Brian promise Aled that his body would recover and that he would have the strength to endure until more help arrived. She heard her own name. Brian was asking for a blessing of safety on her while he went for help. Then it was over. Brian raised his hands and Aled stirred. For a second it seemed to Sarah that Aled smiled. Then the moment was gone.

Brian quickly pulled his jacket towards him and cut off the other sleeve. He handed it to Sarah. "Keep an eye on his leg," he told her. "If the bleeding continues, use this as a makeshift tourniquet above the wound."

She took the fabric and thrust it into her backpack to prevent it from becoming sodden. Brian laid his sleeveless jacket over the small boy's body. "I'm going to leave my backpack here," he told her. "It will just weigh me down and you can eat the leftover sandwiches. Keep trying to give Aled the water."

Sarah nodded and struggled to maintain composure. She didn't want to be left alone in this forsaken spot. But she knew that Brian was right. He had to go for help if they were to get Aled out of there alive. And Aled needed her with him.

Brian was looking back up the escarpment. Sarah followed his gaze and shuddered. She didn't know how they'd ever made it down, but the thought of going up again was inconceivable.

"Brian," she called and reached for him. He turned to her. "Be careful!" The words came out in a sob. He pulled her into his arms and she clung to him. They were soaking wet. Their hands and faces were mud streaked. Droplets showered down from Brian's hair as he moved, but they didn't care.

Brian cupped his hands around Sarah's face. Wisps of her hair that had pulled loose from the braid curled in damp ringlets around his fingers. He bent his head and kissed her hard on the lips. "I'll get help as fast as I can, sweetheart." Then he was gone.

Mot watched quietly as Brian passed him. Sarah watched with fear: fear for Brian's safety, fear over Aled's weakening condition, and fear for their well-being on the tiny ledge as the storm continued and darkness closed in.

She followed Brian's progress until he was hidden from view. Afterwards, she heard several small rock slides, and she held her breath each time, willing Brian to safety. She heard no human sound, and after a while the sporadic rock movements ceased altogether.

Sarah turned her attention to Aled once more. His pulse remained unchanged, as did his breathing. His hands were cold. Sarah tucked them beneath Brian's jacket, then checked the wound. Blood had soaked into the flannel lining of the jacket sleeve. She chewed her lip in indecision. The tourniquet might help, and it would be easier to apply before all the daylight was gone.

She pulled the second sleeve out of her backpack. With practiced fingers she gently applied the tourniquet. As she cinched it tight, Aled gave a soft moan. Quickly she moved towards his face. "Aled! Aled, bach, it's Aunty Sarah. Can you drink a little?"

Aled's moaning continued and he began moving his head slightly. Sarah carefully slid her arm under his neck and raised his head a few inches. Talking softly to him all the time, she managed to squeeze a few drops of water between his lips. She waited, then tried again. On the third try, Aled's eyelids fluttered open briefly. Sarah felt a cold knot of fear as she saw the usually bright, intelligent eyes stare at her dully, without seeming to recognize her. She cradled his head in her arms and wept.

🐚 🐚 🐚

Sarah had no way of knowing how long they had been waiting. Darkness had slipped in unannounced under the cover of the rain clouds, and she could no longer see her wristwatch. Mot lay close to Aled. She could see the whites of the dog's eyes as he lay with his head on his paws beside his young master. Sarah sat leaning against Mot's warm body. She was grateful for the dog's company. Aled had stirred frequently, but had not regained consciousness fully. She had repeatedly offered him water, but feared that he had consumed very little. Her ears were tuned to his shallow breathing, and she acknowledged each breath with thanks and relief.

The damp and the cold were starting to affect her. She pulled her knees up close and wrapped her arms around them. She had relinquished her own jacket to Aled long ago, and now relied on Mot for the little warmth she felt. She was shivering constantly now, and every joint ached. She had tried eating one of Brian's sandwiches, but it had been like eating cardboard. Sarah had forced it down, knowing that she needed the food, but she could stomach no more. Finally, she rested her head against her knees and prayed.

She tried to remember the way Brian had prayed, but her thoughts were muddled. She was just so cold. Without any form or structure she pled for help to arrive soon. She prayed for Aled. She prayed for Brian. And she prayed for herself. When she raised her head, the silence was total. Even the wind had died down. Alarmed, she instinctively moved towards Aled. But as she did so, she heard him take another rasping breath. Then Mot stirred.

Sarah felt the dog's body tense beside her. Immediately she tensed too. Mot raised his head, but Sarah didn't move, not wanting to distract the dog. Without warning, the dog rose to his feet. Sarah was brushed aside as he moved toward the far end of the ledge. Then he barked. The sound echoed eerily off the mountain side. Sarah inched closer to Aled. Mot barked again, more than once. She could hear the dog moving with agitation. Fear rose within her. What was out there? What could the dog sense, that she had yet to perceive?

Her taut nerves clanged as she heard the first rock slide. "Oh please, God!" she begged, "Let it be rescuers. Let it be Brian." The moving shingle slithered down the mountainside again. This time it was closer. Suddenly, above her, a beam of yellow light penetrated the blackness. Then another, and another.

Mot barked.

"We're here! Over here!" Sarah screamed up at the lights.

She could hear distant voices calling, but couldn't make out any words. The drizzling rain distorted the sounds. "Over here!" she sobbed. Another rock slide and the crunch of boots pulled her attention from the floating lights to the corner of the ledge. A voice, gasping for breath, greeted Mot.

On her hands and knees Sarah began crawling towards the sound. He heard her coming. "Sarah!" Strong arms wrapped around her and drew her close.

Without releasing his hold on her, he asked, "How's Aled?" Sarah winced. Guilt seared her as she realized she'd put her own need for human contact above the young boy's safety. She pulled away and began crawling back along the ledge as quickly as she dared. She could hear Brian close behind her.

Devoted Mot was waiting for them beside Aled's still form. "Good dog, Mot." Sarah reached out and patted the faithful dog. Relief surged through her as she drew close enough to hear Aled's breathing again. She sensed Brian right behind her.

"I applied the tourniquet," she said over her shoulder. "His pulse is about the same and his breathing is still regular but shallow. He's cold. I covered him as best I could . . . "

"You used your jacket too," Brian's voice was grim. She knew he'd felt her shivering in his arms.

Sarah ignored his comment and went on, "He's stirred but never totally regained consciousness. I've tried to give him water, but I don't think he's taken in much."

Sarah realized that Brian was moving behind her. She heard a zipper open and more movement, then suddenly there was a bright light. "Oh!" She covered her blinded eyes with her arm.

"Sorry, honey!" said Brian with contrition. "I should've warned you. I'll cover the light with my hand till you get used to it."

Gradually forms took shape in the darkness. As Sarah's eyes adjusted, she saw her discarded backpack up against the mountainside, with Brian's laying next to it. Mot's eyes glowed, and the white patches on his black body were pale smudges in the night. Another backpack lay at her feet. Brian must have brought it down with him. That explained his recent movement—he had been taking it off his back. It had held the big flashlight he was now carrying, and she saw a skein of rope tied to its base.

Brian had moved forward and had propped the flashlight against a rock. He was examining Aled in the pale glow. "They gave me two minutes in the ambulance before heading back." As he spoke he carefully removed the makeshift bandage. "I hope I grabbed what I need to splint this leg. See what you can find in the backpack."

Sarah obediently reached out and drew the backpack towards her. She pulled out a couple of rolled bandages and a boxed set of splints. Further searching unearthed some thick dressing pads and safety pins. She held them ready, watching Brian's deft hands at work, and waiting for the cues that experienced nurses recognize. Without any words passing between them, she passed him the items that he needed. It was as though they were in a hospital surgery room and had worked together for years.

At last, Brian sat back on his heels. "It's temporary, but it should help as we transport him down the mountain."

"You did a wonderful job." Sarah's praise was genuine.

Brian gave a tired smile. "Thanks," he looked over at Aled's pale face, "but the sooner we get this little guy to a hospital the better."

Sarah looked over at her nephew. The limited arc of light from Brian's flashlight left dark shadows over Aled's face and limp body. Her heart contracted to see him like this. "How are we ever going to get him . . . "

Her question was interrupted by a shout from above. "Sarah! Brian!" She recognized her brother's voice immediately. He sounded as though he was right above her head.

Brian swung the light upward and shouted back. "Right here, Kevin!" He held the flashlight steady as other dancing beams of light converged on the area above them. They illuminated the fine rain-drops that hung in the air like a mist. The cold was penetrating, but the wind had died down and the heavy rainfall had moved on.

"How's Aled?" The anxiety in Kevin's voice was apparent even at this distance.

"He's hanging in there!" Brian yelled back. "He's still uncon-scious. We've got his leg splinted. Let's get him out of here!"

There was a sound of movement above. Then Kevin's voice echoed through the mist again. "The stretcher's ready to go. We've got it anchored up top. Can you two manage down there?"

"We'll do our best," Brian shouted. "Let it down slowly till I yell 'stop.'"

Small rock slides began again. Brian turned to Sarah. "There are six or seven men up there, including Kevin. They're sending down a stretcher on a pulley. We've got to get Aled into it down here. They'll heave him up. There's a paramedic up there who'll get Aled to the hospital while we make our way up afterwards."

Sarah felt the nervous tension building again. It was a risky endeavor during perfect conditions, but at night in this weather . . . She shuddered. It didn't bear thinking about, but they had very few alternatives. They had to get Aled off this ledge fast.

A few minutes later, by the light of Brian's flashlight, she saw a large white object floating above the ledge. It bounced off the side of the mountain and sent a shower of rocks ricocheting down on them. Sarah ducked and cowered over Aled to try and protect him a little. Brian leaned against the mountainside with one arm over his head. When the worst was over, he stepped out gingerly and yelled, "Slow it down now!"

The white object stopped, suspended in space. "About four more feet," Brian shouted. He reached out as the stretcher inched its way closer. Once he had it in his hands, he quickly pulled it onto the ledge. "Stop!" he shouted. Then he straightened out the heavy fabric and checked to make sure that the ropes were not caught or tangled.

"Okay, Sarah," he said, "our job is to get this little tyke strapped in securely, without hurting him any more than he's already hurt."

Sarah nodded, trying to look more confident than she felt. Brian crawled over to her, eyeing Aled, then the stretcher. "How 'bout if I try to lift Aled and you guide the stretcher beneath him?"

Sarah nodded again, chaffing her cold hands. "I'll do my best."

Brian gave her a smile that buoyed her flagging spirits no end. She caught hold of the coarse cloth.

"Okay," he said as he positioned himself beside Aled. "On the count of three, I'll lift him, and you tuck as much of that under him as you can."

Brian counted and gently raised Aled off the rocky surface. He strained to keep the boy in the same position he had been lying in. Aled murmured something incoherent as Sarah struggled to maneuver the stretcher into position around Brian's bent legs.

"You got it?" Brian hissed through clenched teeth.

"Okay, try now," Sarah gasped.

Gently, Brian lowered Aled onto the stretcher. He slid his arms out from under the small body and flexed them gingerly. Once again he checked the position of the ropes.

"Good girl!" he beamed at Sarah. "We've just got to secure him in now."

In a matter of minutes, Aled was carefully covered, padded, and trussed.

"Where on earth did you learn to do all this?" Sarah asked, mystified.

Brian grinned. "Scouts. My mother made me! I had to have my Eagle before she'd let me drive the car!"

The explanation didn't mean much to Sarah, but the thought of soft-spoken Iris Pearson threatening her tall son with the keys to the car brought a smile to Sarah's lips.

"That's better," said Brian. "I haven't seen one of those smiles for a long time."

Sarah gave him another small smile. She was so grateful he was with her. His positive assurance filled her with hope and encouragement.

Together they carefully moved the stretcher to the center of the ledge. Then Brian cupped his hands to his mouth. "Okay Kevin. He's ready. Bring him up very slowly."

Standing on either end of the large cocoon-shaped stretcher, Brian and Sarah guided it up as the ropes tightened. Within seconds it was out of their reach. Sarah stood biting her lip in nervous agony as the precious cargo swayed above her head. Brian stood beside her, watching in silence until it disappeared from sight.

There were intermittent small showers of rock, but nothing alarming. They heard no human voice for what felt like an interminable time. Then, out of the darkness came Kevin's jubilant voice. "We've got him. He's safe. We're sending the rope down for Sarah."

"Alright!" Brian exclaimed.

Sarah felt a huge load of anxiety lift off her shoulders. "We did it!" She whispered the words with joy.

Brian looked down and put his arms around her. "We did, didn't we!" he said and hugged her close. The slap of a rope hitting the rock beside them startled them both.

Sarah looked at the rope and shuddered. "I can't climb up that thing."

Brian kept his arms around her. She tried to soak in some of his warmth. She was still cold and aching, but the shivering had lessened.

Brian's voice was reassuring. "Don't worry, you'll be just fine. I'll tie it around you, and the guys at the top will haul you up. All you'll have to do is use your feet to push off the mountainside if you get too close."

While inwardly protesting, Sarah allowed Brian to lead her to the rope. He tied it securely around her and helped thread her arms through her backpack. "Just hold on tight, push off with your feet, and you'll be at the top in no time." Sarah tried to ignore the knot of fear in her stomach. Her mouth was dry and her palms sweaty. Her shivering had begun in earnest again. She couldn't tell if it was the cold or nerves. Brian put a hand on her shoulder. "Make sure someone up there gives you a blanket or coat pronto. I'll be coming up right behind you."

Sarah nodded mutely. Then she gasped as something brushed by her legs. "Mot! Oh Mot, how could we have forgotten you!" She turned to Brian. "What about Mot?" she asked with a touch of panic. "We can't leave him here."

Brian knelt down and fondled the dog's ears. "Tell Kevin to put an extra man on the rope when I come up. I'll be carrying the dog."

"But Brian . . . " fear laced Sarah's voice.

"No buts," Brian interrupted. "This dog saved Aled's life. We're not leaving him here, and he can't go up on the rope alone. He's well trained. He'll hold still for me."

As if to underscore Brian's words, Mot barked.

"Go now. We'll both be with you in a matter of minutes."

"Be careful!" Sarah whispered. Brian kissed her cheek, then through cupped hands shouted upward again.

"Okay up top! We're ready!"

Sarah felt the rope go taut. She clung to it with frozen trembling fingers. There was a shuddering jerk, and within seconds she was floating above the ground. It was too dark to see anything around her. She hit the mountainside hard twice because she could not anticipate its approach. Stunned and bruised, she continued upward. Then suddenly there were lights, and men, and arms reaching out to catch her. She felt herself falling and there was blackness once more.

🐿 🐿 🐿

She was awakened by something wet on her face. She felt dizzy, sick, and cold. She tried to brush away the wetness only to discover it was attached to a dog. Mot was beside her, licking her face. Instantly, she knew where she was. She sat up and fought the wave of dizziness that accompanied the movement.

Shadowy figures were talking and moving all around her. Some were huddled in small groups. Others were intent on specific jobs. They seemed to be gathering equipment, ropes, and packs. Someone broke away from a nearby group and moved quickly towards her.

He must have just arrived, because he was still fumbling with the straps of two backpacks slung over his shoulders. He dropped down beside her.

"Are you okay?" he asked.

Sarah put a hand to her throbbing temple. "A bit light-headed," she said, "but, I'll be alright." Then as the realization dawned, gladness filled her voice. "At least we're all safely off the ledge."

"Prayers are truly answered," Brian breathed. His voice was so quiet that Sarah wasn't sure she'd even heard him correctly. But she sensed his grateful relief. She suddenly recognized that beneath his encouraging attitude and capable actions, his fear for their safety had been similar to her own. Somehow it made him seem more human, and she was glad.

He moved closer to her, then let out a cry of consternation. "Hey, you're still shaking like a leaf. Why don't you have a jacket on, or a blanket?"

Before Sarah could say anything, he was on his feet. "Hey Tom, we're going to have a serious case of hypothermia here unless Sarah gets a jacket or blanket or something!"

Sarah was surprised to hear a hint of anger in Brian's words. Another shadow separated from the group and moved towards them, carrying a bulky object. It was Tom Roberts.

"Didn't anyone think to check on her after you got her up here?" Brian asked brusquely. "The girl's been exposed to this awful weather for hours. Goodness only knows how long she's been shivering like this." As he spoke, he took the proffered jacket from Tom and threaded Sarah's arms through the armholes.

"Sorry Sarah," Tom's voice was contrite. "I suppose we all thought someone else would be watching out for you."

"That's alright, Tom." As she spoke, Sarah couldn't prevent her teeth from chattering. "Thanks for the jacket. It's wonderful." Then with a note of concern she added, "Whose is it Tom? Is someone else going without now?"

"Don't you worry about that," he said. "I reckon you've earned a jacket more than anyone else up here. Finding the lad and staying with him an' all. We're mighty grateful to you Sarah. And you too, Mr. Pearson." Then without another word he turned and melted back into the shadows.

Brian watched him go. "They're good people," he said. His tone now was far more mellow than it had previously been.

"Yes, they are," Sarah agreed. "In many ways the village is like a big family. What affects one person affects us all. If there's ever a tragedy, everyone rallies round. If there's something to celebrate, everyone's in on it."

Brian grinned. "Well, I guess the pub'll be busy tonight!"

Sarah smiled a little sheepishly. "I dare say you're right," she said.

A few minutes later Tom reemerged. "We're almost ready to head down," he told them. "Are you up to it, Sarah?" he asked with concern.

"Nothing could stop me!" Sarah replied with feeling, valiantly trying to hide the total weariness that she felt.

"Well then," Tom said heartily, "let's get off this cold wet mountain and back to civilization."

"Civilization, nothing!" called out another voice from the darkness. "It's the Red Dragon we want!"

There was the sound of men's laughter. Brian and Sarah exchanged knowing smiles. Brian stood up and reached for Sarah's hand. She gave it to him and he helped pull her to her feet. She kept her hand in his.

He leaned over and whispered in her ear. "We'll hobble down together."

Sarah knew that he alone had any concept of how exhausted, physically and mentally, she had become during this ordeal. Without making a big fuss, he intended to help her all he could. She was overwhelmingly grateful for his quiet support. But she was also aware that he had been down and back up the mountain one more time than she had, and twice more than the other men. Perhaps her slower pace would be a boon to him. She hoped so. The thought helped boost her morale, and she began the long descent, thankful that the worst was over.

It took them twice as long to go down this time than it had earlier that afternoon. It was hard for Sarah to believe that outing had been just a few hours before. So much had happened in the interim. This time her whole body hurt with every footstep. Scratches and bruises from her collisions with the mountain while on the rope were making themselves evident. She felt wet, dirty, and more tired than she had ever felt before.

When they finally spied the distant lights of the farmhouse, Sarah wanted to weep for joy. As they drew nearer, the door flew open and they were greeted with open arms, tears, hugs, and kisses. Her mother was there, so was Brian's mother, and Aunty Lil. Sarah was swept inside and plied with cups of tea, concerned questions, and comments.

There was no sight of Mair. When Sarah could finally get a word in edgewise, the other ladies told her that Mair had gone in the ambulance with Kevin and Aled. Sarah's fuddled mind registered that she hadn't seen Kevin on the mountain. Obviously he had escorted Aled down with the ambulance crew. The group of men she'd been with had dispersed and headed into the village in their respective cars. She had seen some of them talking with Brian on the other side of the room. They'd slapped him on the back and offered him rides. She guessed that his smiling shake of the head was a refusal to join them at the pub.

When the last of the volunteers had gone, Annie Lewis turned to her daughter. "Alright, bach, you need a nice warm bath and some attention given to all those cuts and bruises. I can't begin to imagine how you got them all." She walked over to Sarah and cradled her daughter in her arms. "I'm just so glad you're home safely. And Aled too. Praise the Lord!" Sarah heard the break in her mother's voice and realized what agony it must have been for her to sit here at the farm and wait for news.

"A bath sounds wonderful, Mam," she said simply and allowed her mother to guide her upstairs and into the bathroom.

30 May 1882

Dear Father,

You are a grandfather! William Glyn Jones (named after his grandfather and father) was born 16 March 1882. It was not an easy delivery, and it has taken me several weeks to regain my full strength, but I have been aided daily by neighboring friends and the wonderful support of my dear husband.

Little William has brought great joy into our home. He is a placid, happy baby. My greatest hope is that he will grow to be as fine a man as his father and grandfather before him.

Glyn is extraordinarily proud of him. He crafted a beautiful cradle for his son, and is now at work on a small harp for me. We are anxious that our son come to love and appreciate his Welsh heritage and rich musical tradition. Glyn sings to him each night, and I look forward to sharing the music of the harp with him soon.

I long to hear news of you. If you have found it in your heart to forgive me for leaving as I did, I pray that you will write soon so that I may know that you are well. My thoughts are with you daily.

All my love,
Mary.

❦ Chapter 6 ❧

Soaking in the warm bubbles was bliss. Sarah would probably have fallen asleep in the bath had the telephone not rung. Its piercing ring penetrated her sleepy head. Jolted, she wondered if it was news from the hospital. As quickly as she could, she got out of the bath and helped herself to Mair's bathrobe, which was conveniently hanging on the bathroom door. She towel-dried her hair and ran a brush through it.

When she paused to look in the mirror, however, she was aghast. Her face was slightly pink from the warm bath and the midday sun. New freckles were evident on her nose. No one would notice them now though. What drew immediate attention was the deep purple welt running down the right side of her face. Her cheek was a little swollen, and angry red scratches were clustered around her chin and one side of her nose. It was not a pretty sight.

Sarah ran tentative fingers over the tender bruise. She would feel it for days. She thought about her recent Eisteddfod performance, and was glad that was behind her. She didn't need to show this face in public until it had time to heal. Then she saw the reflection of her fingers in the mirror. Looking down at them, she saw that they too were scratched. Three knuckles had been bleeding, and four nails were broken. She flexed her fingers carefully. They would probably be sore almost as long as her face. Playing the harp would be nearly impossible.

Sarah sighed. She knew her minor wounds were nothing compared with what little Aled had to deal with. She wondered how he was faring. Then she remembered the ringing phone, and without any further thought to her appearance, she hurried downstairs.

The only sound came from the kitchen where she could hear her mother's voice. Sarah entered the cheery room. Her mother was standing beside the small table where the phone rested, and was just hanging up the receiver as Sarah walked in.

"Sarah!" she called. "How are you feeling now?"

"Much better thanks, Mam," Sarah said, as she walked over to the kitchen table. Every movement hurt. "I think I'll be a bit sore for a few days," she added as she slowly lowered herself into one of the wooden chairs.

Her mother walked over to her, put her hand gently under Sarah's chin and carefully raised her head so that she could scrutinize her daughter's face. She tutted softly. "Bless your heart! What you must have been through!" She kissed her daughter's forehead gently. "I've got some chicken noodle soup on the stove. Let me get you some."

Annie Lewis walked over to the stove and began filling a bowl with steaming soup.

"Was that the hospital on the phone?" Sarah asked.

"It was Kevin," her mother replied. She carried the bowl of soup over to the table and set it in front of Sarah. She passed her a package of crackers, then sat down on the opposite side of the table.

Sarah thanked her, then asked, "What did he say? How's Aled?"

"Aled's going to be alright." The relief in Annie's voice was readily apparent. "Kevin says he has a compound fracture on his right leg, a lot of cuts and bruises, and a concussion. He's been in and out of consciousness, and they're watching him quite closely. But the doctors say he'll pull through just fine. All he needs is a bit of time and good care." She sighed. "It really is a miracle he wasn't more badly hurt. I mean really, falling down all that way. It could've been so much worse. We've got a lot to be thankful for."

Sarah pondered her mother's words. A miracle. Had she witnessed a miracle? She thought about Brian—about his prayer when they were still searching for Aled. She thought about the way he had placed his large, strong hands on Aled's small head and prayed again. She had felt a power, a sense of peace. She even considered her own disjointed prayer when her hope and physical well-being had been disintegrating. Had she, Brian, and Aled been given divine aid? Was their safe return a miracle? Sarah didn't know what to think.

Annie was talking again. "Kevin said he and Mair are going to stay at the hospital tonight. They want to be there when Aled comes 'round. He won't know what's happened to him, poor little mite. Kevin said to stay here as long as we wanted."

"Where's everyone else gone?" Sarah asked.

"Brian needed to get cleaned up and didn't want to rush you in the bathroom here. So he went back home. His mother went with him. They were going to drop Lil off at her place on the way."

Sarah raised her head with interest. "Aunty Lil? How did . . . I mean, well . . . Did Aunty Lil and Mrs. Pearson get along alright?"

Annie seemed surprised by Sarah's question. "Why yes, of course." She stopped to think about it for a minute. "Well, now that you mention it, Lil was a bit strange at first. Didn't say much. Just held back. It was almost as though she was afraid of something. I don't know. I suppose we were all under a bit of a strain—not knowing what was going on with the search and everything.

"I've got to hand it to Iris. She pitched right in. She didn't know most of the people here, and couldn't understand us at all when we spoke Welsh. But that didn't stop her. She spent ages at the sink washing cups and saucers, and handing out cups of tea to all the men. Yes, by the end there, she and Lil had quite a production line going. Lil made the tea and Iris passed it 'round. I think they both needed to keep their hands busy to stop their minds from worrying."

Sarah sat back in her chair and smiled. She was so glad. She hoped that Aunty Lil had overcome whatever had been troubling her about the Americans. It would be very difficult not to like Iris Pearson. And if nothing else, she knew Aunty Lil was fair. Iris Pearson's willingness to help would have raised her in Aunty Lil's estimation no end.

Annie looked at her watch. "There's not much point in going home for what little's left of the night," she commented. "Why don't you go and lie down on Aled's bed, Sarah. We'll run home in the morning, then see about going over to the hospital. Kevin and Mair might want some rest themselves by then."

"What about you?" Sarah asked.

"Oh, don't worry about me. I'll lie down on Kevin and Mair's bed for a while."

"Alright." Sarah rose stiffly. Sleep in a warm bed sounded wonderful. Her mother gave her a tender smile.

"Off with you now. I'll turn out the lights and be up in just a few minutes."

♥ ♥ ♥

Sarah couldn't even remember closing her eyes. Total fatigue caused a deep sleep that lasted until her mother came in to rouse her. Last night's storm was but a memory. Sunlight was pouring in through the window. The sky was blue, newly washed by the night's rain. There was a clean, crisp flavor to the air. Sarah stretched, then immediately wished she hadn't. Her muscles cried out in protest. Slowly she got out of bed, and feeling like a geriatric, she hobbled to the bathroom.

Her face looked even worse in the morning light. It was more swollen and now the purple hue had been joined by tones of navy and green. The scratches were scabbed over. Sarah rooted through her sister-in-law's bathroom cupboard and found some antiseptic cream, which she applied to her abrasions. Then she found an emery board, which she used to try and redeem her broken nails.

Her soiled clothes lay where she had left them, in a discarded heap on the bathroom floor. Sarah gathered them up in her arms and went downstairs.

"Mam," she called. "Where can I find a bag for these clothes?"

Her mother placed a bowl of porridge on the kitchen table as Sarah entered the room. "Let me see," she pondered. "I think Mair keeps plastic bags in that cupboard under the sink. Give them to me and I'll go and look. You sit down and eat some breakfast."

Annie held her hands out for the clothing. Sarah looked over at the steaming bowl on the table and grimaced.

"Now don't you go pulling faces like that," Annie chided. "You need a lot more than half a grapefruit after what you've been through. Besides," she added with a triumphant smile, "Mair hasn't got any grapefruit!"

Sarah laughed. "Alright! You win. But this is my one bowl of porridge for the month!"

Annie made a noise that sounded like a humph and went in search of a bag.

About half an hour later they drove out of the farm yard. Annie had insisted on tidying up the kitchen and front room before leaving. There was no evidence left of the drama that had unfolded less than twelve hours earlier.

The roads were quiet. A drowsy aura surrounded the village as they entered, and they pulled into their driveway without encountering anyone. Both Sarah and her mother noticed Brian's car parked on the side of the road.

"I can't imagine what kind of hostess the Pearsons think I am," Annie muttered. "I send them home to sleep here alone. No supper. I only hope we're here in time to make them some breakfast. Dear me!"

Sarah smiled fondly at her mother as Annie hurried indoors and headed straight for the kitchen, still clucking her tongue in self-deprecation. Despite her tendency to focus heavily on keeping up appearances, Sarah knew that Annie's fretting stemmed from genuine concern for her guests' comfort. For Sarah however, clothing was the priority. Still clad in Mair's robe, she went upstairs just as fast as her aching limbs would allow. She gave a sigh of relief when she reached her own bedroom and closed the door behind her.

As she sat on the end of the bed to gather her thoughts, it came as a bit of a shock when she realized that it was Sunday. That explained the lack of activity in the village. Under normal circumstances, she would be putting on a dress in preparation for Worship Service at eleven o'clock. Sarah perused her wardrobe. She was pretty sure that she would be spending most of the day at the hospital, so she decided against wearing a dress, and opted instead for a pair of navy trousers with a favorite cream-colored shirt.

She ran a brush through her hair, leaving it long and loose in the hope that it would hide some of the discoloration on her face. She had decided against applying any makeup except the merest touch of lipstick. Her face was too tender to accept it. Besides, Sarah thought ruefully, she had lots of color—not quite the right color—but color nevertheless.

Annie was on the phone in the hall as Sarah went down the stairs. It sounded as though she was speaking with Kevin again. Sarah knew her mother would pass on any information, so she slipped past her and went into the kitchen. She was startled to find Brian already there, sitting at the table. He looked up as she walked in.

She noticed a long scratch along his jawline and tired smudges beneath his eyes, but above all she saw the look of shock on his face.

"Sarah!" His voice was filled with horror. He rose and moved towards her. He cupped his hand gently beneath her chin and raised her face to his. "Why didn't you tell me?"

Sarah averted her eyes and bit her quivering lip. She didn't want him to think that she was crying out of self-pity. She just hated to have him see her like this.

"How did it happen?" Brian's gentle tone and probing eyes sought hers again.

"Going up on the rope," Sarah's voice was little more than a whisper. "I hit the mountainside a couple of times. I couldn't see it. I hit before I had time to stop myself."

Sarah hung her head. She felt foolish. But Brian groaned, shook his head slightly and took her in his arms. "I'm sorry, sweetheart. I'm so sorry!" He whispered the words into her hair. She leaned against him, moved that he should care so deeply.

Wordlessly, they separated as they heard Annie Lewis say good-bye in the hall, put down the telephone receiver, and walk into the kitchen. Sarah could tell by her mother's cheery smile that the news was good.

"Aled's awake and eating breakfast," Annie announced. Sarah smiled. She knew that as long as Aled ate his meals well, her mother would be happy.

"How's the leg?" Brian asked. Annie turned to him.

"They've set it. I think they've had to give him something for the pain, but Kevin seemed really pleased with how well he's getting along."

Brian nodded with a pleased smile. "Did Kevin say if Aled's up to having visitors? Mom and I are scheduled to leave early tomorrow. We'd love to see him again before we go."

Sarah felt as though the bottom had just dropped out of her world. She tried to fight the numbing misery seeping through her body. She told herself it was a symptom of being overtired, and a reaction to yesterday's stress. She had always known that the Pearsons were only staying in Pen-y-Bryn for a few days. They were on vacation half a world away from their home. Of course they had to go back.

Sarah sat down heavily and tried to focus on her mother's words.

". . . and I'm sure Aled would love to see you. I think visiting hours are at about one o'clock. Why don't we drive over to the hospital together? Maybe we can sit with Aled for a little while and let Kevin and Mair get some rest." Annie turned to her daughter. "Are you up to it, bach? Perhaps you should stay at home and rest too."

Sarah tried to rally herself. She painted a smile on her face. "I'd like to go, Mam. I'll be fine." But deep down she wondered if she would be.

Iris Pearson entered the kitchen at that moment. Sarah was glad to relinquish the focus of attention.

"D'you have any news?" Iris asked Annie immediately.

Annie Lewis was delighted to tell Iris about her recent phone call with Kevin.

"We were thinking of going to see him this afternoon, Mom," Brian informed her. "Would you like to go?"

"Yes, I'd love to. I did talk to Reverend Davis yesterday, before all this happened. He suggested I go over to the chapel this evening, when his services are over. He said he thought he could help me find some of the records I've been looking for. We should be back by then, don't you think?"

"Oh, yes!" said Annie. "I'm afraid visiting hours are quite restricted. We won't be at the hospital very long."

"How did your talk with Aunty Sally go?" Sarah asked.

Iris Pearson turned to her, full of enthusiasm. "Oh she's a remarkable lady!" Then she saw Sarah's face for the first time, and her excitement ebbed. "Sarah, dear, your face!"

Sarah was beginning to feel that she should wear a mask. "It looks worse than it is," she tried to persuade an unconvinced Iris Pearson. Then, wanting to change the subject, she asked, "Did Aunty Sally have any new information for you?"

Iris's concerned expression remained, but she answered Sarah's question. "Her memory's amazing. She told me about her childhood.

She never knew Mary or Glyn, but she remembered the furor after they left. Apparently it lasted for some time. She added a few more details to the story we already knew, but it was really her outlook on what life was like then that was so fascinating. We spent a very enjoyable morning together."

Sarah smiled. "I'm sure Aunty Sally was thrilled to have you. She loves to have a new audience, because most of the villagers have heard her stories so many times before."

"It's too bad someone hasn't tape recorded her or written down her stories. It's terrible to think of all those experiences being lost when she does eventually die," Iris said.

"I wonder if anyone's thought of that before? We'll have to mention it to her daughter," Annie suggested.

"And send us a copy," added Brian with a grin.

"Yes indeed," agreed Annie.

❧ ❧ ❧

They all ended up going to the hospital in the Pearson's rented car. Because it was Sunday and the shop was closed, they invited Aunty Lil to go too. They picked her up on their way out of the village. She sat in the front with Brian. Iris, Sarah, and her mother squeezed into the back. The journey took about thirty minutes. Aunty Lil gave succinct directions to Brian, who followed them to the letter. They drew up in front of the Oswestry Orthopedic hospital without a single hitch.

After asking a few questions at the front desk, they discovered that Aled had been moved to the children's ward. They made their way up there and met Kevin in the hall outside. He looked haggard. There were dark circles beneath his eyes and a day's stubble growth on his chin. But his face lit up when he saw them. He gave his mother a brief hug and shook Brian's hand warmly.

"Can't thank you enough for what you did last night, Brian. You too, Sarah. If you hadn't found him, stayed with him, strapped him up so expertly . . . well we could've had a very different ending." Kevin's expression of gratitude changed to one of shock when his gaze fell upon Sarah. "Sarah, what on earth happened to your face?"

Self-consciously, Sarah put her hand up to cover her swollen cheek. "I had a disagreement with Mynydd Mawr!" She tried to make light of it although it throbbed continuously.

"Are you alright?" Kevin took a step closer to her, his voice filled with concern. "Did it hurt your eye?"

"I'll be fine. It'll just take a bit of time for the swelling and bruising to disappear."

Kevin turned back to Brian. "Is she telling me the truth, Brian?"

Brian nodded. "She's being very brave about it. She hasn't complained once about how much it must hurt. But I think she's right. It should be a lot better in a week or so."

Kevin turned back to Sarah. "I'm sorry it happened, Sis."

Sarah shrugged her shoulders. "It's nothing compared with what Aled's been through."

Kevin shook his head in wonder. "That child's amazing. We almost lost him last night in the ambulance. His breathing kept stopping. It was the worst experience of my life." He ran his fingers through his hair in agitation. "They wanted to get to work on his leg as soon as we got here, but he needed fluids and . . . " He shuddered. "Anyway, I hope I never have to go through anything like that again.

"Mair and I sat by his bed all night. About four in the morning, he woke up. Just like nothing had happened. He turned to Mair and said 'Mam, I'm hungry!' I tell you, I've never heard anything so wonderful in my life as those three words."

Kevin sighed. "He still hasn't said anything about being on the mountain. Maybe he can't remember it at all. We've been told not to say anything about it until he mentions it or asks us."

He shook his head again. "I think even the doctors are surprised at how fast he's bounced back. It's a miracle. It really is."

There was that word again! Sarah looked over at Brian and caught his eye. He gave her an understanding smile. She knew they were both remembering the prayers they'd offered up on the mountain. Sarah had never really thought about her own prayers being answered so directly before. She'd participated in prayers at church for as long as she could remember. But they were always form prayers, read by the minister out of prayer books. The prayers she'd participated in the night before with Brian had been prayers from the heart—prayers to a God from children in desperate need. There was a difference. She had felt it. Could their prayers have really helped? Once again, she wished she knew.

Kevin glanced at his watch. "I'm afraid they only give you one hour to visit patients here unless you're immediate family. And they only allow two visitors at a time." He pulled a wry face. "Some of these rules date back to the dinosaurs!" With an apologetic look at the others, he said, "Why don't you and Aunty Lil come first, Mam. I'll take you in."

Sarah stood with the Pearsons and watched Kevin lead her mother and aunt into the children's ward. When they disappeared behind the heavy swinging doors, she turned to see if there were any vacant chairs in the waiting area of the hall. A low, jovial voice behind her made her jump.

"Sarah Lewis! It's about time you came back to see us!"

Sarah, Brian, and Iris swung around in unison. Sarah smiled at the snowy-haired doctor approaching her. She held out her hand. "Hello Dr. Robinson. It's nice to see you again."

"I should say so, young lady. Been neglecting us, haven't you?" he teased with a twinkle in his eye. Then as he peered at her over his half spectacles he added, "My word, that's quite an elegant shiner you've got there! How did that happen?"

Sarah pulled a face. "It's a long story, I'm afraid. But I did it in the dark on Mynydd Mawr."

"Mynydd Mawr . . . Mynydd Mawr . . . of course, young Aled Lewis!"

"He's my nephew," Sarah clarified. Then, mindful of the Pearsons standing close beside her she said, "Dr. Robinson, I'd like you to meet some friends of mine. This is Iris and Brian Pearson. They're visiting us from America.

"Mrs. Pearson, Brian, this is Dr. Charles Robinson—one of the best orthopedic surgeons in the country."

They shook hands. "Pleased to meet you." Dr. Robinson said. "And after an introduction like that, I ought to add that we lost one of the best nurses in the country when Sarah left the hospital!"

He gave Sarah no opportunity to demure before returning his attention to Brian. "Are you by any chance the young chap that splinted the boy's leg out on the mountain? It seems to me that his father said it was a visiting American. Mentioned something about some medical training."

"Guilty on both counts," Brian said with a smile.

"Well, then I'm doubly pleased to meet you," Dr. Robinson said cheerfully. "That was an excellent job you did. Couldn't believe it when they said you'd done it on a mountain ledge. Where did you do your schooling?"

"The University of Utah Medical Center," Brian replied.

"Ah yes!" Dr. Robinson nodded.

"You've heard of it?" Brian asked with interest.

"Yes, indeed. Went to a big conference in Boston a couple of years ago. A couple of physicians from Utah were there presenting a paper." Dr. Robinson scratched his head and thought for a few seconds. "Let me see . . . um . . . Verl . . . no, Vern Hansen and Lowell Young if I remember correctly."

Brian nodded his head with enthusiasm. "Yes, I've worked with both of them."

Dr. Robinson looked pleased. "Have you, by jove! Well, well. Small world! They gave a very interesting paper on some excellent results they've seen using innovative operating procedures. Very interesting. I talked with them for quite some time afterwards. Sounds like you've got a very good program over there."

"We have some great doctors and they do a lot of good work," Brian agreed.

At that moment, Kevin and Mair joined the small group. Kevin extended his hand to the doctor. "Hello again, Dr. Robinson."

"Good afternoon Mr. Lewis. How's Aled getting along?"

"He's amazing us all!" Kevin said with a grin.

"Good, good! I'll be in to see him as soon as visiting hour is over."

Kevin turned to Sarah. "That reminds me, Sarah, Aled wants to see you and Brian. If you both go in now, Mam and Aunty Lil can come out and join us here."

"Alright." Sarah shook Dr. Robinson's hand again. "I'm glad you're working with Aled, Doctor."

"Oh, we'll have him climbing mountains again in no time!" Dr. Robinson chuckled as Kevin and Mair both groaned.

Brian shook the doctor's hand again too. "It was great to meet you, Dr. Robinson. I'll tell Dr. Hansen and Dr. Young that I met you."

"You do that. Best of luck to you, Mr. Pearson. Glad to know you'll soon be part of this honorable profession!"

Brian grinned and raised his hand as he followed Sarah down the hall.

❦ ❦ ❦

The solid white doors whooshed closed behind them as they entered the ward. There were six beds on each side of the long room. They were separated by curtain partitions, but most of the partitions were now open. The beds were metal framed and sat on sturdy black wheels. The walls, sheets, and bedcovers were white. There was an aura of sterile uniformity to the characterless room.

Splashes of color dotted the room in the form of flowers, stuffed animals, and brightly patterned pajamas. Each bed's occupant was sitting up, and most already had visitors sitting beside them. Those few who didn't, anxiously glanced from the large clock on the wall to the doorway where Sarah and Brian stood, and back to the clock again.

"There's Aled," said Brian and pointed to the right.

Sarah looked and saw her mother wave. Annie and Lil rose and waited for Sarah and Brian to reach them.

"We'll go and join Kevin, Mair, and Iris and let you three have some time together," Annie Lewis said. Then she bent down and kissed the top of Aled's head. "We'll see you again soon, bach."

"Bye Nain. Bye Aunty Lil. Thanks for the sweets."

Lil's lined cheeks were touched with pink. "You're welcome, Aled. I was pretty sure that lemon drops were your favorite."

"You mind you don't eat too many, now," Annie warned.

"I won't," Aled said and clutched the small, white paper bag even tighter.

"Good boy!" Annie patted his hand. She and Lil walked to the end of the ward together. They paused at the door to wave. Aled waved back, and they disappeared.

Once they were alone, Brian leaned over the bed and whispered in a conspiratorial style, "Well Aled, how're they treating you in here?"

Aled giggled. "Alright. They make me take yucky medicine, but the nurse is really pretty!"

Brian sat back and raised an eyebrow. "Is that right! Is she as pretty as your Aunty Sarah?"

Aled looked over at Sarah, who could feel herself blushing. After a couple of seconds of intense scrutiny Aled declared, "No, not as pretty as Aunty Sarah."

Brian gave an exaggerated sigh of relief. "Oh well, I'd better stick with her then!"

Aled's face brightened. Then, as a totally unrelated thought came to him, he said "Hey, guess what I had for breakfast?" He glanced from one to the other and squirmed with excitement. "You'll never guess!"

Sarah was pretty sure that she knew exactly what he'd had for breakfast—especially if Aled's delight was any indication, but she feigned ignorance.

"What did you have?" she asked.

"Red jelly and an orange lolly!" Aled squealed.

Sarah couldn't help laughing. "And what did your Mam and your Nain say about that?"

Aled's eyes grew large. "Oh, I didn't tell *them*. And you mustn't either. Or they'll make that nice nurse give me porridge tomorrow!"

Sarah laughed again.

Brian gave her a gentle prod. "What's red jelly and orange lolly?" he asked.

Sarah looked at him with surprise. "You really don't know?"

Brian shrugged. "Give me some clues."

Sarah was floored. "Well, red jelly is strawberry or raspberry flavored gelatin . . . "

"Oh, Jello! We call that Jello."

"Jello! I see. Well, an orange lolly is . . . um . . . it's like frozen orange juice on a stick—but it's not real orange juice."

"A Popsicle! Okay, I get it. Red Jello and an orange Popsicle. Mmm . . . my idea of a great breakfast!"

"Yeah!" Aled said with enthusiasm. "An' I got another lolly after my soup at lunch time. But it was yellow and I don't like yellow ones as much as orange ones." He paused again, then was off on another tangent. "D'you want to see my leg?"

"Sure!" Brian said. He helped Aled lower the sheets to expose the large cream-colored cast.

"It's my first broken thing in my body!" Aled announced proudly.

"It's very impressive!" Brian said. "How does it feel?"

Aled pulled a face. It's heavy. Sometimes it hurts and sometimes it itches." Then his eyes lit up. "But Dr. Robinson said I can ask people to write their names on it. D'you want to write your name on my leg, Mr. Pearson?"

"You bet!" said Brian and reached into his pocket for a pen.

He spent a couple of minutes writing on the bumpy surface, then he handed the pen to Sarah. "Shall we have your aunt write on it now?"

"Alright," said Aled, and obligingly leaned back so that Sarah could reach his cast.

Sarah read Brian's message: 'I'll be thinking of you, little buddy. Brian Pearson.' She felt a lump rise in her throat and began swallowing furiously. She bent her head and simply signed her name 'Aunty Sarah.'

"Aled," she said, trying to keep her voice as upbeat as she could, "the Pearsons are leaving early tomorrow. They're going back to America. They both wanted to see you before they go, so I'm going to go and get Mrs. Pearson now, alright?"

Aled turned baleful eyes on Brian. "Why can't you stay at Nain's house all the time? Don't you like it here?"

Sarah didn't want to stay to hear Brian's answer. She quietly stood up and slipped out before either of them realized that she'd gone.

When she brought Iris Pearson into the ward, Brian was regaling Aled with a humorous story. They were both laughing. Watching them together filled Sarah with pleasure and pain. Sarah pointed them out to Iris and let her make her own way to the bed.

10 October 1882

Dear Father,

A great change has occurred in my life since my last letter. I know it will come as a great shock to you, and so I confess I have procrastinated writing. Please believe that the path I have chosen was not an easy decision, nor one that I took lightly.

We had not long been in Logan before Glyn and I came to feel great admiration for the people of the Mormon Church. They are hard workers, generous and kind. They truly strive to live Christ-like lives. As a people they have suffered and sacrificed more than any I know, but they have retained a cheerfulness and optimism in the future without the bitterness that often follows such persecution.

I was curious to read the Book of Mormon that they spoke of so lovingly and mentioned this interest to my good friend, Catriona Evans. She loaned me her book. Glyn and I read it together each evening. As we read we became more and more convinced that it contained great truths. There is a power to the book that I have never experienced before. By the time we reached the last page, Glyn was ready for baptism.

You were in my thoughts constantly at that time. I could not do anything more that might hurt you, whom I love so dearly, without total conviction that I was choosing the right course. I prayed as I have never prayed before. The answer came, Father. I cannot deny it. I was filled with a burning warmth that encompassed my whole being. I have never known such joy. It is true! It is true!

I was baptized into the Church of Jesus Christ of Latter-day Saints on 23 August 1882 in the Logan River. Glyn was baptized two weeks before me so that he could perform my baptism.

I pray that you will be able to put aside the fearful prejudices that exist against the Mormon faith in Wales, and be happy for me. I am striving each day to draw closer to my God, as I know you would have wanted me to. I will forever be grateful for your example.

Your loving daughter,
Mary.

✺ *Chapter 7* ✺

Annie may have noticed that Sarah was unusually quiet on the return journey. When they arrived home, she turned to her daughter and in a tone that brooked no argument, said, "Now, Sarah Lewis, you go straight upstairs and rest. You're looking very pale. I'm sure you're worn out."

Sarah found that she really didn't have the energy or desire to disagree, so following her mother's orders, she excused herself and went to her room.

She wasn't sure how long she lay on her bed staring at the ceiling trying to empty her mind of its tumultuous thoughts, but eventually it must have worked. She fell asleep.

She awoke almost three hours later. Sarah stared at her watch with incredulity, then she compared it to the small clock sitting on her dressing table. She must have been truly exhausted.

She ran a brush through her hair and examined her cheek in the mirror. There wasn't much change since the morning—perhaps a few more shades of color, but still as big and still as ugly. Knowing that nothing more could be done to help it, she turned her back on the mirror and hurried downstairs.

The house was very quiet. She went directly to the kitchen, expecting to find someone there. But it was empty. Surprised, she backtracked and peeked into the other rooms on the ground floor. Silence met her in every room. She retraced her steps to the kitchen and made herself a cup of tea. Afterwards she let herself out the back door and walked over to the chairs beneath the apple tree. She sat down and let the peaceful sounds of the warm summer evening wash over her.

The drone of bees and song of thrushes in the hedge were inter-rupted by an occasional bleating sheep or lowing cow in the nearby field. She could hear cars in the distance, and the sound of children at play.

"Hi! How're you feeling?"

Sarah almost leaped out of her skin when Brian spoke. She had not heard his footsteps cross the lush grass.

"Oh, I'm sorry," he apologized immediately. "I was reading upstairs and happened to glance out the window and see you here. D'you mind if I join you?"

"Of course not," Sarah replied, her earlier tranquility jarred by his unexpected appearance.

Brian sat down beside her.

"Where are our mothers?" Sarah asked. "I wasn't sure where everyone had gone."

"They've gone over to meet Reverend Davis."

"Oh that's right!" Sarah remembered that Iris had mentioned her appointment at the chapel when they had made their plans earlier in the day.

"Your mother kindly offered to go with her," Brian added. "I think Mom was grateful to have a Welsh speaker along."

Sarah nodded. "Reverend Davis is a very kind man. He'll do all he can to help her too."

They sat without speaking for a few minutes. Sarah wished that she could control her racing heart. She couldn't understand what was wrong with her. She sensed that Brian was ill at ease too.

She focused her attention on a cheeky robin that had decided that she and Brian were harmless. It was moving closer and closer in search of worms. It was within a couple of yards of them when Brian reached over and grasped her hand. The bird took flight in a flurry of feathers. Brian tightened his grip and Sarah looked over at him with surprise.

"Sarah," he began, "this may be our only opportunity to talk to each other alone before tomorrow." He paused, as though searching for the right words. "I know we've only known each other for a few days, but it seems like I've always known you. And I don't need any more time to know how I feel about you. I love you, Sarah!"

Sarah sat in stunned silence. She could hardly believe her ears. She had hoped that he cared for her. She had already admitted to herself that she cared for him more than any other man she'd known. But to have him tell her that he loved her. It was more than she'd ever imagined.

But Brian hadn't finished. "I know more time will just strengthen the love I feel, and I can't bear to think of leaving you—even though I know I must go back. So I have to ask, right now, before it's too late. Will you marry me, Sarah? We could even call and get you a ticket to fly home with us on Tuesday."

Sarah's eyes widened. "Don't be silly!" she whispered.

It was Brian's turn to look surprised. "I'm totally serious," he told her.

Sarah recognized his conviction and felt tears coming to her eyes. She bent her head to hide them, but she couldn't hide the break in her voice. "Brian, I care for you more than any other man I've known. I've never experienced anything like what I've felt since you arrived. I've spent all day trying to block out the thought of you leaving because it hurts so much." She looked up and the tears flowed unabashedly down her cheeks. "But I can't say that I'll marry you. How can you even ask? It's madness. You hardly know me. We grew up half a world apart. I know nothing of your culture, and you know little of mine. And there's your church." Sarah paused, then in little more than a whisper she looked him in the eye and said, "I have a glimmer of how much your church means to you. But it means nothing to me."

"But Sarah," Brian pleaded, "it could come to mean something to you, given time."

"Time!" Sarah cried. "That's just it Brian. We haven't had enough time!"

"Sarah, I've prayed about this," Brian continued earnestly.

That was too much. "*You*'ve prayed about it!" Sarah almost spat the words out. "What about me? Don't I have some choice in this?"

Brian looked as though she'd slapped him across the face. "Yes! Yes, of course you do. I just meant that . . . "

Sarah interrupted him. "Brian, when . . . no, *if* I get married, I want it to be for life. That's not a decision you rush into after knowing someone for five days. Those kind of marriages last a year if they're lucky!"

"Not if you pray about it and know that it's right," Brian said with feeling.

"Brian, it wouldn't work!" Sarah's voice began to rise. "Don't you see? Our understanding, our backgrounds, are so different. You say you have answers to your prayers. As much as I like you, I can't put my future happiness on the line because of that. You're asking me to go with you to who knows where, and give up everything I know and love: my family, my home, my country, my customs, my religion, my job, even my harp! I can't do that just because *you* say it's right."

Sarah wrenched her hand free and stood up. "And don't ask me to pray about it—because I don't know how!"

Brian stood up beside her. She saw pain reflected in his eyes and pale face. Remorse caused her to lower her voice. She clenched her fists. "We've had a wonderful time together. I'll never forget it. I'll never forget you. But that's all there can ever be." She couldn't continue. She gave a sob, turned and ran into the house. She didn't stop running until she had reached her own room, then she closed the door and threw herself across the bed.

ಕ ಕ ಕ

After several minutes of uncontrolled weeping, Sarah forced herself to calm down. She had never spent as much time in tears or studying the ceiling above her bed in her life as she had since Brian Pearson's arrival. She told herself sternly that she needed to show more maturity. She'd made her decision. It was the right one. It was the only logical one. She just couldn't understand why she continued to feel so terribly miserable.

There was only one explanation. She wasn't in love. Being in love, if all the books were right, meant being filled with joy and happiness. All she felt was confusion and pain. She tried to use this theory to bolster her decision. Of course she couldn't marry Brian if, on top of all her other arguments, she wasn't even in love with him.

But she didn't want him to leave! The thought that she would never see him again, never laugh with him again, never be held by him again, was the most painful of all.

And so Sarah's thoughts eddied around in circles, getting her nowhere. She dreaded facing him again, but knew it had to be done. For the first time since it occurred, Sarah was grateful for her swollen, mottled cheek. It was excellent camouflage for her red puffy eyes.

"If Brian Pearson can propose to you with a face like this, he's either desperate or as blind as a bat," she told her reflection. But her words of bravado did little to lessen the sadness she saw in the mirror.

The doorbell rang. Sarah groaned and resolved to ignore it. She didn't want anyone seeing her like this. But it rang a second time. She slowly left the sanctuary of her room and walked to the top of the stairs. If she craned her neck, she could see through the glass in the door without being seen by the visitor. The distorted glass panes revealed a small angular figure with gray hair, wearing subdued gray clothing. Sarah had seen that picture many times before. She ran down the stairs and opened the door to admit Aunty Lil.

Lil Lewis took in Sarah's appearance with one piercing glance, opened her mouth to say something, then abruptly changed her mind and closed it again.

"Come in, Aunty Lil," Sarah invited. "I'm afraid Mam and Mrs. Pearson are over at the chapel. But I expect they'll be back in no time. Would you like a cup of tea?"

"Thank you, Sarah. That would be lovely. But don't go to any trouble."

"No trouble at all. Come on through."

Sarah led the way to the kitchen and while her aunt sat down at the table, Sarah took the kettle over to the sink. As she rinsed it out and refilled it with water, she glanced out of the window. Brian was still in the garden. His back was to her. He was standing with his hands in his pockets, looking out across the fields towards the mountains. As she watched, he hung his head and turned to face the house. Anxious not to be seen, Sarah hurriedly picked up the kettle and moved away from the window to plug it in.

Seconds later, she heard him coming in through the back door. Her hand on the kettle shook. She steeled herself, grateful that with her aunt in the room, she would not have to face him alone. She was desperately afraid that her former resistance would dissolve into nothing.

He stopped in the doorway when he saw her. Sarah's grip on the kettle tightened and she took a sharp breath when she saw the pain in his eyes. Not even during the worst moments on the mountain the night before had she seen his face look so bleak. She cleared her throat and willed her voice to sound normal.

"Hello, Brian. Aunty Lil has just dropped by."

Sarah could only begin to imagine how much effort it took Brian to tear his eyes from hers and assume a mask of polite friendliness. But he did it. He walked over and greeted her aunt in his usual gracious way. Sarah joined them with her aunt's cup of tea. She offered to get something for Brian but he declined. Then, with Aunty Lil making infrequent comments only when called upon to do so, they managed to maintain polite small talk together for an interminable twenty minutes.

It was as though they were slight acquaintances who had happened to meet after a long absence. Sarah hated every minute of it. She hated it all the more because she knew that she was the one who had burned the bridge between them. Misery consumed her for she knew there was no going back to what they once had.

During the course of the conversation, Aunty Lil looked at her curiously, but she asked no questions. Sarah was also aware of penetrating glances directed at Brian. But the polite facade continued without a wrinkle until, with relief, she heard the voices of Annie and Iris entering the house.

The two women entered the subdued kitchen with a burst of enthusiastic energy.

"Oh Brian!" exclaimed Iris. "You wouldn't believe how many names and dates I found. Reverend Davis was so helpful, and Annie," she patted her new friend's arm, "Annie was invaluable. It was so exciting to find people listed you've been searching for for years."

"I must say," Annie added with a smile, "I never would have thought that going through those musty old records could be so thrilling." Then noticing Lil for the first time she said, "Well hello, Lil, how nice to see you!"

Annie bustled over to heat up the kettle once more and Iris sat down to tell them in detail what she and Annie had found. The enthusiasm exuded by the two older women more than made up for the lack of animation present in their offspring. In fact, they seemed totally oblivious to anything out of the ordinary going on between the kitchen's occupants. Only Lil, with her silent watchful eyes gave any indication that she recognized that something was amiss.

At the first lull in the conversation, Brian stood up and apologetically asked to be excused. Iris looked up with surprise at this unusual turn of events.

"Are you feeling okay, Brian?" she asked with motherly concern. "You do look a bit pale."

Brian gave his first natural smile since he'd entered the kitchen. "I'm fine, Mom," he said. "I just need to get my stuff organized. We'll be heading out pretty early tomorrow."

Iris Pearson accepted her son's reasoning at face value. She nodded. "Good idea. I should do the same thing. I'll follow you up in just a few minutes."

Brian said good-bye to Lil and shook her hand. Then he left the kitchen and Sarah heard his heavy footsteps make their way up the stairs.

It didn't seem to strike anyone as peculiar that Brian took so long to organize one suitcase. Sarah kept expecting him to reappear. But he didn't. Aunty Lil went home after a second cup of tea. Iris Pearson retired early, presumably to do her packing, and Annie pottered around in the kitchen for a while before also heading upstairs for an early night. When the house was quiet and the world outside was falling asleep, Sarah wandered into the front parlor. Her long nap and heightened emotional status made sleep elusive. Instinctively, she looked for solace with her harp.

She sat down behind the instrument and flexed her sore, grazed fingers. They were still stiff and painful but, taking it slowly, she made it through a few of her easier pieces of music with only a couple of stumbles. Playing was therapeutic. When she came to a close she looked up, half expecting to see Brian in the doorway again. But he was not there. You have to get used to him not being there, she lectured herself. She put away her music, shut off the light, and made her way to bed with a heavy heart.

☙ ☙ ☙

Morning dawned with gray overcast skies and a light drizzling rain. Sarah thought it reflected her mood perfectly—dreary. A quick look at her clock told her that the morning was still young, but she could hear the sound of footsteps and soft voices on the stairs. When Brian had said he planned on an early start, just how early had he meant? Alarmed that she might miss seeing the Pearsons off, Sarah hurried out of bed and into some clothes.

By the time she reached the bottom of the stairs, Brian was loading the last of the cases into the car. Iris and Annie were exchanging fond good-byes in the hall.

Annie caught sight of Sarah. "Oh Sarah! I'm so glad you're up in time to say good-bye to the Pearsons. They're just off now."

Sarah came down the last few steps and gave Iris Pearson a hug.

"Thank you for everything dear," Iris said. She ran a gentle hand down Sarah's silky hair. "I do hope you'll recover from all your cuts and bruises very soon."

Sarah touched her cheek self-consciously. "I'm sure I will," she said as cheerfully as she could muster. "I hope your journey home goes well."

"Thank you dear," Iris said. "This trip has been wonderful. We'll have so much to tell and such happy memories."

Sarah wondered how happy Brian's memories would be. Part of her felt responsible for the division between them now. Another part of her vehemently denied any wrongdoing and blamed Brian for having tried to go too far, too fast. She kept telling herself that she'd done the right thing. But she wasn't very convincing.

"Ready Brian?" Iris's question drew everyone's eyes to the door. Brian stood silhouetted in the door frame. Even with the drab wet background and the moisture glistening on his hair and jacket, Sarah was overwhelmed once more by how handsome he was. She clutched the banister rail for support as she looked into those clear blue eyes again. She felt suddenly awkward, and didn't know what to say or do.

Brian met her gaze. For a fraction of a second it was as though they were the only ones present. Sarah longed to run into his arms and beg him not to go, but instead she tightened her grip on the banister. Some of her torment must have shown in her face, for Brian took a couple of steps towards her. Sarah took a sharp breath. Brian heard it and stopped.

"I'm glad I was able to see you before we go, Sarah," he said. He held out a brown bag to her. "I wanted to give you this and thank you for everything."

Sarah took the brown bag with tentative fingers.

"I'm sorry it's not wrapped better," Brian apologized. "You can open it after we leave."

Sarah nodded, unable to trust her voice. A single tear rolled down her cheek. She tried to brush it away before anyone noticed. But she was not fast enough for Brian. He closed the gap between them and put his arms around her.

"Take care of yourself, Sarah," he whispered in a hoarse voice.

Sarah closed her eyes and leaned against his broad shoulder. He rested his head on hers and for a precious moment Sarah felt her inner agony slip away. But all too soon, the moment was gone. Brian released her and walked over to Annie Lewis. They exchanged a brief hug and parting words. Then Brian and Iris walked out to their car. Sarah and her mother stood on the porch and watched them go. As they started down the road, Iris Pearson opened her window and waved. Annie and Sarah waved back. The red car turned the corner at the bridge, and disappeared from view. Brian was on his way home. Sarah followed her mother back into the house and bleakly wondered if she would ever be truly happy again.

It wasn't until she was in the hallway that Sarah remembered the package in her hand. She stopped. Her mother had already gone ahead into the kitchen. Sarah looked at the unobtrusive brown bag and then at the kitchen door, before turning around and retreating up the stairs to her room.

She closed the door and sat down on the bed. With shaking fingers, Sarah opened the bag. Inside was a book and a slip of white paper. She withdrew them. She recognized the book immediately. She ran her hand over the soft leather cover. It was one of the books she had seen on the desk in Brian's room the day the Pearsons had arrived. She read the gold lettering on the cover: The Book of Mormon: Another Testament of Jesus Christ. In smaller letters in the lower right-hand corner was printed Brian D. Pearson.

Sarah picked up the piece of paper and unfolded it. It was a short note. It read: *Dear Sarah, Please forgive me for not being more sensitive to your feelings. I hope you will accept this book. I know that nothing can bring you more happiness than living by the teachings it reveals—and more than anything, I want you to be happy. I will never forget you or the time we spent together. With love, Brian.*

Sarah refolded the paper and carefully placed it within the pages of the book. She moved over to her chest of drawers and opened the bottom drawer. With one hand she pushed aside a few sweaters, then she thrust the book into the back corner. The sweaters fell back into place and she shut the drawer with a slam. She had to get Brian Pearson out of her system and now was as good a time to start as any. Then she turned, and without a backward glance she walked out of her room and down the stairs.

Dear Father,

We have endured a long, cold winter here in Logan. There has been no thaw since our first snowfall in November of last year. The snow accumulation in the mountains is a sight to behold. As much as we look forward to the warmer temperatures of spring, there is considerable concern hereabouts that we will experience flooding in the valley. Our small home is situated upon a rise and Glyn is fairly sure that we will be untouched by heavy snow runoff. However, he is one of many who has volunteered to help those in the lower regions of the town, should the need arise.

I believe it impossible not to be impressed by the way in which the Mormons organize themselves in the service of others. I myself belong to a women's organization within our Church called the Relief Society. We gather weekly and learn much from one another. The meetings have helped me to grow spiritually, and have given me a greater appreciation of the cultures and talents of the other women. We work together with our hands and hearts. I have developed many new skills, and as a group we have been able to give aid to many needy families.

My own small family continues to be a great source of happiness to me. Young William is growing and developing daily. He is crawling now and displays an insatiable curiosity for the world around him. Despite the cold temperatures, he loves to be taken outdoors for short periods of time. Glyn often takes him for rides on a wooden sledge that he fashioned for him at Christmas time. They both return home with red cheeks, red noses, and smiles from ear to ear.

We thought of you yesterday as Glyn, William, and I celebrated St. David's Day. There are no daffodils here yet, nor leeks for that matter. But I was able to make a nourishing onion soup that tasted not unlike the traditional leek soup of home. Glyn and I spoke together of Pen-y-Bryn—such fond memories! Our greatest wish is that our son will grow up with a strong testimony of the Gospel of Jesus Christ and an appreciation of his Welsh heritage.

We pray that all goes well with you.

Your loving daughter,

Mary.

Chapter 8

The next few weeks seemed interminable. Sarah tried to fill every waking moment to prevent any time for thoughts of Brian to intrude. And it helped. But it was not failsafe. Sometimes she'd see something that would bring back a particular memory of him. Then thoughts of him would flood her mind, leaving her feeling bereft once more. She spent long hours walking the hills, but purposely avoided Mynydd Mawr, Pystill Glas, and the path along the river. She also found great comfort in her harp playing. But she couldn't bring herself to play her Eisteddfod piece. Those sheets of music lay untouched, carefully hidden under a handful of other music books.

There was always plenty to do at the shop, so Sarah spent many hours there. She completed the inventory and updated the book work. She worked several days behind the counter to give Aunty Lil a much-needed holiday. Aunty Lil couldn't bring herself to be away from the shop for more than a day or two at a time, but was pleased to take a short jaunt to the seaside resort of Llandudno one day, and a shopping expedition to Shrewsbury on another day.

The one bright spot in a run of dreary days was the afternoon that Aled returned home from the hospital. The family gathered at the farm to welcome him. Aled was still in a leg cast and using crutches, but his joy at returning home was contagious. There were hugs and laughter, a celebratory cake and ice-cream and, for the first time since the Pearsons's departure, Sarah experienced a time of real happiness again.

She went to visit Aled often once he was home. He was always so pleased to see her and was full of ways to fill her day. Since he was still housebound, his suggestions usually meant that she had to stoop to being defeated in checkers, or working on a jigsaw puzzle until her head ached. But it was good to feel needed and to be surrounded by his boyish exuberance.

Her visits only became uncomfortable when, in typical childlike fashion, Aled would relentlessly question her about Brian. Had she heard from him? Where was he now? When was he going to visit again? Had he forgotten them already? There wasn't much Sarah could say. She hadn't heard from either Brian or his mother. Aled's questions merely echoed the ones that filled her heart and mind in the quiet of the night.

As the end of the summer drew closer, Sarah spent a few hours each day in her office at the school. She was pleased to discover the supplies that she had ordered at the end of the previous year had been delivered. She methodically cleaned out all the cupboards and reorganized her equipment in preparation for a new school year.

And so it was that by mid-September, Sarah found her life once more in a well-established routine. She worked at the shop on Saturdays, played the organ at chapel on Sundays, and spent Monday through Friday with the children at school. Most of the time her days consisted of grazed knees, nose bleeds, and paper-cuts. But on some days, social workers would come to help her administer vaccinations or eyesight tests. One exhausting week they had to check all the children one by one because of a head lice outbreak.

Her office was rarely empty. There seemed to be many cases of imaginary bumps and bruises and invisible cuts. Sarah's innate modesty did not allow her to believe that this stemmed from any enormous popularity on her part. She thought it more likely that the children were merely anxious to escape their class work or to sample the sweets in the jar on her counter. Her most regular visitor was Aled. He was down to using only one crutch by the time school started, but liked to spend recess time in her office, particularly on rainy days, since it was still hard for him to keep up with his peers on the playground.

By November, Sarah felt that she had her feelings under control. Her terrible heartache, although far from gone completely, had dulled. She was able to respond to Aled's enquiries about Brian and

his lack of correspondence without the need to ward off tears. Even
her Aunty Lil seemed to sense a change. She no longer watched
Sarah sharply with pursed lips, as she had done for the first few weeks
after the Pearsons's departure.

In the middle of that month however, this calm status quo came
to an end. Within a twenty-four hour period Sarah received two
unrelated phone calls. She didn't realize the repercussions of either
one immediately, but they were destined to completely shatter her
hard-earned facade of normalcy.

🍂 🍂 🍂

The first call came on a Thursday evening. It was from a man
called Trevor Williams, who introduced himself as one of the judges
of the harp competition at the International Eisteddfod. He was
calling from Chester (a city about 50 miles north of Pen-y-Bryn), on
behalf of the city's Rotary Club. They were organizing a Christmas
concert for local charities, and were wondering if she would be
willing to perform for them. Sarah checked her calendar, made a
mental note of how much practice time she would need, asked a few
detailed questions about the location, facilities, and type of music
they wanted. Then to the obvious surprise and delight of her caller,
she promptly accepted the invitation. She hung up the phone, still
smiling at Trevor William's effusive words of thanks.

Sarah returned to the kitchen to tell her mother about the invitation, but they didn't talk for long. Annie Lewis, although obviously
interested in the Christmas concert, excused herself to go to bed. She
was fighting a sore throat and beginning to feel a little achy.

By the next day, Sarah diagnosed her mother with a bad case of
the flu and admonished her to stay in bed and to drink lots of fluids.
Sarah went to work but called home every couple of hours to check
on her mother, and hurried home at the end of the day. It was then
that the second phone call came.

This time Sarah recognized the voice on the other end of the
phone immediately. It was Gwyneth Rees, old Aunty Sally's daughter.

"I'm so sorry to bother you, Sarah, but I'm afraid Mam seems to
have got herself into rather a tizzy over something. I can't for the life

of me figure out what it is she wants. She just keeps saying that I have to call and have your mother come over straight away."

Sarah's forehead wrinkled with concern. "Oh dear, I'm sure she'd be happy to come, Gwyneth. But she's in bed with the flu. I don't suppose she'll be up to visiting for a few days yet."

"Oh, poor thing! I am sorry. Dear, dear what am I going to do with Mam? I've rarely seen her so concerned about anything."

"Did Aunty Sally give you any idea of why she wants to see my mother?"

"No, not really. She just keeps saying 'I have to tell her about the box before I forget again.' If I ask her what she's talking about she just says, 'Go and call Annie Lewis!'"

Sarah was as baffled as Gwyneth was. "D'you think it would help if I came over instead?" she asked.

"Oh could you, Sarah? That might just do the trick. I really can't understand it at all."

"Alright." Sarah glanced at her watch. "I can come in about twenty minutes. I probably won't be able to stay very long. I don't want to leave Mam alone any more than I have to."

"Of course. I understand. Thank you Sarah. We'll see you soon." Gwyneth Rees hung up the phone and Sarah replaced her receiver.

She ran upstairs to her mother's room. Annie Lewis was lying in bed with her eyes closed, but she opened them when she heard her daughter's approach.

"That was Gwyneth Rees on the phone," Sarah said. "Aunty Sally's been asking for you. Something about a box she needed to tell you about."

Annie shook her head. "I can't think what that would be," she whispered in a hoarse voice. Sarah patted her mother's hand as it lay on the quilt.

"It's alright. I told Gwyneth I'd go over and see if I can be of any help. Will you be alright here for a little while?"

Annie gave a small smile and nodded again.

"I'll do my best to be quick, but you know how it is . . . " Sarah left the sentence hanging. Her mother smiled and nodded again. Explanations were not necessary. Everyone knew how Aunty Sally loved to talk. Annie closed her eyes and Sarah slipped out of the room.

ॐ ॐ ॐ

It was soon after seven P.M. when Sarah walked the quarter of a mile distance between her home and Aunty Sally's. It was already dark and there was a nip in the air. The road glistened from the rain that had fallen earlier in the day. It would fall as snow before too long, Sarah reflected.

Gwyneth was watching for her and opened the door at Sarah's approach. She took Sarah's coat from her. "This is awfully good of you Sarah. I just can't imagine why Mam's in such a tizz. Something really seems to be worrying her."

Sarah gave what she hoped was an encouraging smile. "Well, I don't know that I'll be of much help, but I'll try."

She followed Gwyneth down the hall and into a small sitting room. A coal fire was burning merrily in the fireplace. The light reflected off the brass ornaments on the mantlepiece and highlighted the fine handmade tatting and lace work draped over the backs and arms of the armchairs. The creator of all the fine handiwork was sitting in the armchair closest to the fire.

Aunty Sally was a small woman, bent over with age. Her thin, snowy-white hair was pulled back into a tiny topknot. Her bright blue eyes twinkled behind the glasses that she wore perched at the end of her narrow, beak-like nose. A large magnifying glass and table lamp sat on the small coffee table at her side, and a smokey-grey siamese cat lay at her feet. Aunty Sally's gnarled hands were not idle. They moved deftly with a narrow silver hook, creating a ribbon of fine lace that fell from her hands to drape across her knee.

Without so much as a slight pause in her work, Aunty Sally looked up as Sarah and Gwyneth entered the room.

"Mam, you have a visitor," Gwyneth announced with a cheerful smile.

Sarah stepped closer. It had been several months since she had last been to see Aunty Sally, but she saw little change in the old lady. Aunty Sally for her part was intently studying Sarah's advance over the rims of her glasses. Abruptly she turned to her daughter and glared at her.

"Gwyneth," she said in a disparaging tone, "There may be days when I am a little forgetful, but I am not yet in my dotage. This . . ."

She turned to face Sarah once more ". . . is not Annie Lewis!"

Gwyneth Rees, although an elderly lady in her own right, blanched at her mother's reproof.

"I know that, Mam," Gwyneth said, obviously fighting to maintain a conciliatory tone to her voice. "I did call to ask Annie to come over and see you, but she's not well. Sarah kindly offered to come instead."

Both women turned their eyes on Sarah, who felt distinctly uncomfortable and wondered whatever had possessed her to come. She cleared her throat awkwardly then said, "I'd be happy to take a message to my mother for you, Aunty Sally. But I'm afraid she won't be up to visiting you for a few days yet."

"Hmm." Aunty Sally pursed her lips. "Bad is she? Sorry to hear that." She paused, then raising her claw-like hand, she beckoned Sarah closer. "Come here, bach. Seeing as you're here, come and sit down and have a cup of tea."

Gwyneth recognized her cue immediately. "That's right, Sarah. Sit yourself down here by the fire and I'll go and make a spot of tea." She scurried out of the room without a backward glance.

Sarah sat down in the large overstuffed armchair opposite Aunty Sally and pinned an encouraging smile on her face. "Was there something in particular that you wanted to talk to Mam about, Aunty Sally?"

Aunty Sally's eyes were blank. "Something in particular? Well now let me see . . . " She paused reflectively ". . . dear me . . . there was something . . . but I can't quite . . . oh my, I tried so hard to remember what it was and seeing you here instead of your mother, well, it's gone clean out of my head!"

Sarah tried to hide her frustration, knowing only too well that the elderly lady before her must be even more frustrated than she was.

The sound of clinking china drew their attention to the door. Gwyneth was entering with a tray. She carefully placed it on the low coffee table near the women.

"Now then, Sarah, milk and sugar?" Gwyneth sat with her hand poised over the sugar bowl.

"Yes, please." Sarah took the proffered cup and stirred the steaming brown liquid, glad of a distraction.

When all three ladies had been served their tea, Gwyneth turned to Aunty Sally and said "What was it you needed to tell Annie, Mam?"

Aunty Sally took another sip of the hot tea.

"I'm afraid she is having a hard time remembering," Sarah explained to Gwyneth quietly.

Gwyneth looked troubled. "You acted like it was terribly important Mam. Something about a box." Gwyneth was obviously as much in the dark as Sarah was.

Aunty Sally screwed up her wrinkled face with concentration. "A box . . . a box . . . well of course, that's it!" Her expression lit up as memory returned. She turned to Sarah eagerly. "I can't think why it didn't come to me when they were here, but I only thought of it a few days ago, and then I knew I needed to let her know. Of course it may be long gone. Or it may be nothing at all. But you never can tell. No, you never can tell!"

Sarah hoped that she didn't look as confused as she felt. Her only consolation was that Gwyneth was obviously as perplexed as she was. "I'm not sure that I follow you, Aunty Sally," she said with as much patience as she could muster.

Aunty Sally leaned forward and placed her gnarled hand on Sarah's knee. "I need your Mam to tell that nice lady from America that at one time there was a box full of papers belonging to Reverend Williams in the chapel. Mind you, whether it's still there, I couldn't say."

It was all Sarah could do not to spill the scalding tea. With trembling hands she carefully placed the cup down on the coffee table and turned her full attention to the woman at her side.

"Why . . . why don't you tell me about it, Aunty Sally," Sarah suggested. She was amazed that her voice showed none of the turmoil she felt inside.

Aunty Sally leaned back in her chair. "I hadn't given it any thought in years. Never seemed very important really. Not until your Mam and her visitor came to see me. Such a nice lady she was too."

Aunty Sally gave a small sigh and her eyes got a faraway look. "We got to talking about the old days. My, she was interested in everything. We had a lovely chat. She wanted to know about Mary and Glyn Jones. Wanted to know if I'd known them or their families. I hadn't, of course. I was too young. But everyone in Pen-y-Bryn knew about them. I told her what I knew, but was right sorry that I couldn't help her more. She was related to them somehow, I think."

Sarah nodded and Aunty Sally continued. "I don't get many new visitors these days, so I must have had her in the back of my mind, even after she'd gone.

"Then a little while back, Gwyneth told me that some of the ladies were going over to the chapel to do some cleaning. It set me to thinking about the days that I used to do that. It was when the late Reverend Jenkins was minister."

Sarah made a mental note that Reverend Jenkins had replaced Reverend Williams (Mary's father) and had been the predecessor to their current clergyman, Reverend Davis. Reverend Jenkins had watched over the Pen-y-Bryn parishioners for several decades.

Aunty Sally continued. "There was a time when I'd go in and help Reverend Jenkins once a week. He wasn't married, you know. Sad really. He needed a bit of help with his housekeeping at home and at the chapel. I was happy to do it, and it did give me a bit of extra spending money when the war was on. My word, and every little bit counted then!

"One day Reverend Jenkins asked me if I'd go through some of the cupboards in the office at the chapel. You've never seen such dust. Goodness only knows how long it had been since someone had tidied up in there. But I set to work. It seems to me that it took me a few days to get through all the paperwork. A lot of it was old hymn books and prayer books. But I did find some other papers and some of them were quite old. Some were letters and a few of them were addressed to the former minister, Reverend Williams.

"I have to confess, I wasn't sure what to do with them. They were there because no one seemed to know where Reverend Williams had gone, so they couldn't be forwarded. But I have to say, I didn't really feel that it was my position to throw them away. I mean, they weren't mine, were they? And they weren't Reverend Jenkins's either."

Aunty Sally paused and glanced at her rapt audience. Her small smile showed that she was enjoying the telling of this tale as much as her two listeners were enthralled by the hearing. Sarah felt nervous tension build within her as she waited for Aunty Sally to continue. Was it possible that they could find a clue for the Pearsons, even now?

"What did you do with the letters, Aunty Sally?" Sarah's question was almost a whisper.

"It was the only thing I could do," Aunty Sally replied. "I gathered them all together in a big envelope, put them in a box, and put the box back into the cupboard!"

Sarah stared at her. "You mean they've been there all this time?"

"That I don't know, bach. They were there last time I was cleaning. Mind you, that's a good twenty years ago now. I don't know who Reverend Davis has cleaning for him. The whole box may be long gone."

"I think Nia Hughes goes in once a week." Gwyneth's voice startled Sarah. She'd almost forgotten that there was anyone else in the room.

Aunty Sally gave a snort. "Well, unless she's changed her ways, there's not much deep cleaning going on at the moment!"

Gwyneth gave Sarah an embarrassed look. Sarah tried hard not to giggle. Aunty Sally had long since decided that she was old enough to say whatever she wanted. It was Gwyneth's job to smooth over the ruffled feathers afterwards. This time however, Sarah was not the least bit offended by the elderly lady's remark. Indeed, she fervently hoped that it was accurate.

Turning back to Aunty Sally, Sarah said, "D'you think Reverend Davis would let me see if the box is still there?"

"I don't see why not. Unless it's already gone, he'll probably be glad to get rid of it. Especially if he knows it's going to Reverend Williams' family. Why, he'd probably be very pleased."

Aunty Sally paused. It was as though mention of the family had triggered another thought. A look of concern crossed her lined face. "You will be sure to get it to that nice lady won't you? Dear me, I wish I could remember her name!"

"Mrs. Pearson. Iris Pearson."

"That's it! Pearson. Make sure she gets it. She was so anxious for any little bit of information. Those letters may be just what she needs."

Sarah glanced at her watch. With shock she discovered she'd been there over an hour. She rose. She wanted to go straight over to the chapel and start looking, but it was late and she knew she needed to return to her mother. Besides, she'd have to contact the minister first.

"I'll go over to the chapel first thing in the morning, Aunty Sally. If I find anything, I'll make sure it reaches the Pearsons."

"Oh, thank you dear. I'll be glad to have it off my mind. Something just kept nagging at me after Mrs. Pearson's visit. Until I remembered that box. Well, it may come to nothing. But you never know, do you?"

"No, Aunty Sally." Sarah smiled down at the old lady. "Thank you. I'll let you know what I find."

"That's right! You do that." Aunty Sally reached out and gave Sarah's hand a pat. "You're a good girl!"

Sarah smiled. She picked up the coat that she'd draped across the arm of the chair and followed Gwyneth to the door. As she left the room she turned. "Good-bye Aunty Sally!" But the old lady's eyes were already closed and her white head was nodding gently.

"Thank you, Sarah." Gwyneth said sincerely. "I've rarely seen her so worked up about something. It's really been bothering her."

"She's the one we should thank, Gwyneth, not me. Wouldn't it be marvelous if those letters are still there!"

"Yes, indeed. Well, you let us know."

"I will. Thank you Gwyneth."

Sarah stepped out into the damp, cold darkness. She waved at Gwyneth standing in the doorway, then lowered her head and began to walk briskly toward home. She was glad that every step of the way was so familiar. She gave no thought whatsoever to her route. Her mind was whirling with questions, her body tingled with nervous anticipation, and her heart pounded as she thought of the Pearsons and what this might mean for them.

As soon as she got home, Sarah ran lightly up the stairs. She tiptoed to her mother's door and opened it a crack. She could hear her mother's even breathing. The small reading light on the bedside table radiated a warm glow over Annie's sleeping form. Sarah slipped inside and gently withdrew the open book from her mother's fingers. She set it on the table, switched off the lamp, and left as quietly as she had come.

Sarah debated about calling the minister. Would she be calling too late? What if he were already in bed? But she didn't want to risk missing him in the morning. Even that was too long to wait.

She dialed Reverend Davis's number from memory, and, to her relief, he answered on the second ring. Sarah quickly explained her visit to Aunty Sally and the information she'd received there. The minister remembered Iris Pearson well and enthusiastically suggested that he meet Sarah at the chapel at nine o'clock the next morning. He was more than happy to help.

❦ ❦ ❦

The rain was still falling the next morning when Sarah awoke. But the gloomy skies and gray pallor did nothing to dispel her excitement. As soon as she was dressed, she knocked softly on her mother's bedroom door. Immediately Annie's voice called, "Come in!" Sarah entered. Although she was still very pale, it was readily apparent that Annie was feeling better. The twinkle was back in her eyes. Sarah walked over and kissed her mother's forehead.

"Your temperature's come down," she said with a smile and sat down on the edge of the bed. Before her mother could respond, she popped a thermometer into her patient's mouth.

"How did you sleep?" Sarah asked.

"Better," was the mumbled response.

Sarah grinned and withdrew the thermometer. A quick glance at it confirmed her intuition.

"Back to normal," she said.

"Oh good!" responded Annie with feeling. "There's so much I should be doing."

"Not yet, you won't!" Sarah placed a restraining hand on her mother's shoulder. "You need at least another day in bed, or that fever will be right back where it was yesterday."

At her mother's chagrined expression, Sarah chuckled. "It's about time you learned how to pamper yourself," she teased. "I'll bring you up a nice cup of tea and some toast. And then I've got some really interesting news for you."

Annie's eyes lit up. "Interesting news?"

"Not yet!" Sarah laughed. "Give me five minutes." And she hurried downstairs.

Ten minutes later Annie had her tea and her news, and had perked up no end. "Oh Sarah, just think if it's still there!"

"I know, Mam, but I keep telling myself that it's been years since Aunty Sally saw it. Anything could have happened since then. I don't want to be disappointed."

"I wish I could go with you."

"I know you do. But don't worry, I'll come straight home and let you know if I find anything."

Annie sighed. "Alright. But don't be long!"

Sarah laughed. "Yes ma'am!"

She gave her mother a teasing salute that brought a smile to Annie's lips.

"Go on, you little imp."

Sarah glanced at her watch. "Yes, I'd better run. Reverend Davis is going to meet me at the chapel. You stay in bed and rest, alright?"

She leaned over and tucked her mother's bedclothes around her. Then she handed her the book from the bedside table and dropped another kiss onto her forehead. Annie smiled up at her.

"Good luck, Sarah!"

"Thanks, Mam. Get some rest. I'll be home before long."

Sarah closed the door gently behind her, then left all pretense of calm behind. She flew down the stairs, retrieved her raincoat and sturdy shoes from the boot room, then headed straight outside and into the rain. In less than ten minutes she was at the chapel.

The minister was already there. She had seen his dark figure appear just minutes before she turned into the chapel yard. By the time she reached him, he had opened the heavy wooden doors and he ushered her in before him.

"My word, bit damp today isn't it?" Reverend Davis was a master of understatement.

"Yes, I'm afraid I'm dripping all over the chapel floor, Reverend." There were small puddles of water forming around Sarah's feet.

"Oh, not to worry. Why don't you give me your coat and we'll hang it up here."

Sarah handed him her limp, soggy jacket. He hung it beside his own on a couple of wooden pegs just inside the main doors. They turned together and entered the chapel. It was cold, and Sarah wished she still had on her coat. The wooden floor and wooden pews were polished to a glowing luster. The walls and vaulted ceiling were whitewashed, and a tall, impressive lectern stood at the front of the room. The lectern was approached on both sides by a set of steep stairs covered in a rather worn crimson carpet. Small arched windows let in the weak morning sunlight, but most of the chapel remained shadowed. A few spots of color were visible on some of the benches, where families had left hand-tatted prayer cushions.

Sarah's eyes were instinctively drawn to the pew where her family always sat. She knew every hairline crack in the plaster walls and every knot in that wooden bench. As a child, she had studied them every Sunday, her imagination distorting the shapes into fantastic creatures. For years she had sat on that bench, with her legs not long enough to reach the ground, not old enough to appreciate the words of the eloquent ministers, but even then, relishing the majesty of the Welsh voices united in song.

"Come on through, Sarah. It will be a bit warmer in the office."

Sarah followed the minister through the wooden door at the back of the chapel into a narrow hallway. She looked around with interest. She had never had occasion to enter this area before. The walls were lined with dark wooden panels. A single lightbulb hung from a long cord above her head. They passed two doors. Sarah assumed from their close proximity to one another that they must lead to cupboards, a toilet, or a washroom.

At the end of the hall was another door. Reverend Davis took out a large key and unlocked it. He ushered Sarah inside and turned on the light. Immediately in front of them was a large wooden desk, littered with piles of paper. A small lamp sat on one corner to augment the weak light from a second suspended lightbulb above. There was a large wooden chair behind the desk.

To the right were two ancient armchairs in a muted green fabric. A filing cabinet and set of three tall, wooden cupboards lined one wall. Another wall displayed a simple brass crucifix between two small windows. A long counter ran the length of this wall. On one end there was an electric kettle and a selection of mismatched mugs.

The rest of it held piles of books and papers. The third wall was bare except for a long coat rack that displayed not only an old coat and umbrella, but also a couple of cassocks and other formal clerical attire.

The minister walked over to the desk and pulled out an electric space heater that was hidden behind it. The heater fairly sparkled—a remarkable contrast to the faded, worn appearance of everything else in the room. The chrome and white enamel gleamed, and it had all the latest dials and buttons.

Reverend Davis plugged it into the wall socket and turned to Sarah with an almost guilty expression.

"It's my one concession to old age," he said patting the heater. "I'm afraid these bones are starting to feel the cold more than they used to."

Sarah smiled at the kindly man before her. He was of average height and build, with a thick thatch of white hair, and eyes that were nearly hidden beneath bushy white eyebrows and round wire-rimmed glasses. A careworn face showed obvious laughter lines, blending with the wrinkles brought on by anxiety for the individual members of his flock. The reverend wore the dark shirt and white collar of his ecclesiastical order, along with grey flannel trousers and black shoes. He beckoned her to sit in one of the arm chairs. "Sit down Sarah. Now, tell me again what Aunty Sally told you."

Sarah sat down opposite Reverend Davis and rehearsed her experience of the evening before to him. He listened intently and did not speak until she had finished her story.

"About twenty years, you say." Reverend Davis stroked his chin thoughtfully. "I came to Pen-y-Bryn about eleven years ago. Mrs. Nia Hughes was already doing the chapel cleaning then—and still is. It seems likely that she took over from Aunty Sally." He paused in thought again.

"The only place that I can imagine keeping a box like the one Aunty Sally described is in one of these big cupboards." He indicated the three cupboards behind him. "I'm ashamed to say that I've never sorted through them myself. And to the best of my knowledge, Mrs. Hughes hasn't either. But twenty years is a long time. We'd better not get our hopes up too high, before we've checked."

The minister heaved himself out of the chair and walked over to the desk again. He opened one of the desk drawers and retrieved a large ring of keys. He fingered the keys, searching until he found three small ones placed together. Then he walked over to the first of the solid wooden cupboards. Sarah got up and stood beside him.

Her heart was racing as the Reverend pulled open the first door. It had to be here. It just had to be! The door creaked as it opened. They both took an involuntary step back as a musty smell assailed them.

"Dear me! I'd say this hasn't been sorted out for quite some time!" Reverend Davis understated again.

The lower shelves held an assortment of old hymnals and prayer books, with a few leaflets strewn seemingly at random amongst the books. The upper shelves contained a variety of items: dingy white fabric (possibly old table cloths or curtains); some glass vases in various sizes and shapes; some ancient newspapers, yellowed with age; an oil lamp; and one small box. Everything was covered in a thick film of dust.

Sarah eyed the solitary box. It did not look promising. Nevertheless she reached for it, standing on tiptoes to do so. Its contents moved as she displaced it. As soon as she had it in her hands, both she and the minister peered inside. It was full of rectangular slats of wood, about 3" x 5". Each one was painted white with black numbers on one side.

"An extra set of hymn numbers!" said the Reverend with surprise. "Fancy finding those here."

Sarah thought it a very logical place to find them, but refrained from saying so. "D'you want me to put them back?" she asked.

"Yes, we'll put them back for now, but it's nice to know we've got another set isn't it?"

Sarah murmured her agreement.

The second cupboard revealed more of the same neglected paraphernalia. It included a box of outdated parish literature and a box of white ceramic cups, saucers, and plates, presumably donated by the Women's Institute for chapel functions. To Sarah's eye, everything looked suspiciously dust free. It didn't take much intelligence to realize that this cupboard had been tidied within the last decade! She fought a wave of discouragement. There was only one cupboard left.

When the Reverend opened the last door, Sarah's heart sank. There was no creak. The door moved on recently oiled hinges. There was no telling film of dust. Everything on the shelves immediately in front of her was tidily arranged and neatly stacked.

"Well, this looks more promising!"

There was excitement in Reverend Davis' voice. Sarah looked at her companion in confusion. His focus was above her head on the highest shelf of the cupboard. She followed his gaze. Sitting side by side, stacked to the top, were half a dozen cardboard boxes.

Minutes later all the boxes were on the floor. Reverend Davis and Sarah sifted through piles of yellowed paper together. Sarah sneezed as the dust rose around them. Before long, the floor was covered in a thin layer of dry, crackling paper. But not one of the many envelopes bore an American stamp or Reverend Williams's name.

Sarah sat back on her heels and gave a sigh of disappointment.

"I'm sorry, Sarah!" The minister looked as dejected as she felt.

"Oh well, it was a long time ago. Too much to hope that they'd still be here I suppose." It was easy to say. Easy to rationalize. But Sarah was illogically let down. She tried to hide it. "Thank you for all your help Reverend."

He nodded his head sympathetically and looked down at the carpet of littered paper they had created. "It's just too bad!"

Dispiritedly, they both began gathering armfuls of paper to refill the boxes. "I really must go through all this," Reverend Davis muttered. "It's very silly to put it all back. But I have to confess, I don't feel much like sorting through it today."

The ringing phone made them both jump.

"Dear me! I wonder who that could be?" The minister rose stiffly and walked over to the desk. Sarah continued collecting the scattered papers. The minister's side of the conversation revealed very little—just "yes, no, and dear me." But he ended it with "I'll be there as soon as I can!" and put the receiver down with a worried frown.

"That was Dai Evans. His mother's in very poor health and is asking for me. He sounded quite worried." He looked at Sarah apologetically. "I think I'd better run over there, Sarah. D'you think you can finish up here?"

"Of course! I'll put these boxes back and lock the office door on the way out. Will that be alright?"

"Splendid! Thank you Sarah. So sorry to leave you like this . . . "

"Don't worry. I'll be fine. It'll only take me another few minutes. And thank you, Reverend."

"You're welcome my dear. Only wish we'd had more success. Good-bye now."

The minister walked over to the door and gave a small wave before leaving her alone in the office.

15 August 1883

Dear Father,

By the time you receive this letter, Glyn, William, and I will have left our home in Logan. Leavetaking will be most difficult. We have come to love this beautiful area and the many friends and neighbors nearby. Bidding farewell to Will and Catriona Evans will be especially painful, but Glyn and I feel assured that it is the right thing for us to do at this time.

Glyn has met a man in Logan by the name of Thomas E. Ricks. Brother Ricks has been commissioned by our Church leaders to establish a settlement of the Saints (for that is the title with which we refer to fellow Church members) north of here, along the Snake River in Idaho Territory. He has told Glyn of the vast, fertile farming land available there.

Although anxious to have us join him and the small group of other settlers going north, Brother Ricks has told us, most forthrightly, that conditions there may be considerably more taxing than we are currently accustomed to. The settlement is yet in its infancy and the winters are quite severe.

However, Glyn and I are both young and strong and feel that we can withstand much if we but face it together, with the Lord at our side. Glyn yearns to return to working the land as he did in Wales. He has become a skilled cabinet maker, but owning his own farm has been a lifelong dream. We have been promised some land not far from the main settlement. We hope to begin a homestead with some hardy sheep and perhaps a milking cow.

William has grown into a sturdy young lad. He is anxiously awaiting the birth of a sibling early in the new year. I will write to you again once we are established in Idaho.

Your loving daughter,
Mary.

Chapter 9

It took Sarah another fifteen minutes to pick up all the papers. There had not seemed to be any logical system to the way that they had been organized originally, so she just dispersed them evenly between the boxes and closed the lids once more.

She found that she was able to lever each one back onto the high shelf without the aid of a stool until she reached the last box. It was a tight squeeze between the edge of the cupboard and the boxes already sitting on the shelf, but Sarah knew it should fit—after all that's where it had come from. Nevertheless, despite all her shoving, she could not get it all the way in.

Frustrated, she finally admitted defeat, grabbed the desk chair and dragged it over to the cupboard. Standing on the chair she realigned the box and gave a big push. The box moved in a little further but still hung over the edge of the shelf by about three inches.

"Come on, you stupid thing!" Sarah banged the box with her fist. It didn't move. "There has to be something jamming it," she muttered to herself. She yanked the box out again and lowered it to the floor. Then standing on tiptoes on the chair, she leaned into the cupboard.

Trying to ignore the film of dust and occasional cobweb, she ran her hand along the back corner of the shelf. Sure enough, within seconds, she felt a wad of paper scrunched up against the back. She pulled on it. It was wedged in tightly. Sarah wiggled the box that she'd placed next to the open space. Just moving it a fraction of an inch did the trick. The wad of papers came loose. She withdrew it with a satisfied sigh. "Finally!"

She looked down at the offending object. It appeared to be a mangled large manilla envelope stuffed with papers. She lowered herself to a sitting position and smoothed the envelope out on her knee. Then she took a sharp breath. In a spidery, black script someone had written two words across the front of the envelope: "Reverend Williams."

With shaking hands, Sarah turned the envelope over. It was not sealed. She peered inside. There appeared to be several smaller envelopes within. Carefully she tipped the large envelope over and poured the contents onto her lap. Not one of the letters that fell out had been opened. There were four, each addressed in a different hand, with local postmarks. And there were ten bearing a foreign stamp. Nine were addressed in the same handwriting, the tenth on the same stationary but written by another, more rudimentary hand.

Sarah picked up one of the foreign letters for closer inspection. Her heart was beating so fast she thought it would burst. In the top right-hand corner she saw the post mark: The United States of America. She looked at the handwriting. It was a woman's. She was sure. Mary Jones! It had to be Mary Jones!

Sarah's first thought was of Iris Pearson. Finally they had a real clue. Something concrete that could perhaps answer some of the questions the Pearsons had wondered about for so long. Then her thoughts turned inevitably to Brian. He would be thrilled too. Sarah could imagine the enthusiasm with which Brian would receive the news of this find. She must send it to them immediately.

Quickly Sarah slid the letters back into the large envelope and placed it carefully on the floor. She heaved the solitary box back onto the shelf and pushed it into place. This time there was no difficulty. It sat on the shelf, flush with the others. After a quick glance around the room to be sure that she hadn't left anything behind, Sarah closed the cupboard door and turned the key.

She replaced the chair behind the desk, picked up her precious envelope, turned off the light, and let herself out of the office. Out of deference for her surroundings, she forced herself to walk slowly through the small hallway and the rear of the chapel. But once she had on her coat and was outside, it was as though she had wings on her feet. She stopped long enough to tuck the envelope under her coat to keep it dry, then, heedless of the cold rain falling in sheets, she ran all the way home.

She burst into the kitchen gasping for breath and dripping water all over the floor. After quickly depositing her shoes and coat in the boot room, she took the stairs two at a time, coming to a halt outside her mother's bedroom. Taking a deep breath to calm herself, Sarah knocked at the door.

Annie's voice reassured Sarah that her mother was still awake. She stepped into the room. Annie was sitting up in bed, and as Sarah entered she dropped the book that she'd been reading onto the quilt. She took in her daughter's appearance with one swift glance. The wet hair, pink cheeks, and breathlessness all told a tale. But the verification was the wrinkled package Sarah clutched in her hands. Sarah saw her mother's eyes fix upon it and watched her pale face light up.

"Sarah! You've found something!"

Sarah could only nod. Silently she sat on the edge of the bed beside her mother and handed her the envelope. Annie Lewis took it from her. With questioning eyes she glanced from Sarah to the object in her hands.

"Look inside," Sarah said.

Two minutes later the letters lay scattered on the bed quilt.

"We must send them to Mrs. Pearson today," Sarah said.

Annie nodded but Sarah could tell that she didn't have her mother's full attention. She watched as Annie picked up one of the American letters and pressed her fingers across the thin paper. Annie peered at it curiously through the reading glasses that she'd forgotten to take off. After a minute of careful scrutiny, she gave a satisfied grunt.

"What ever are you doing Mam?" Sarah was quite mystified.

"Well, a thought occurred to me just now," said her mother. "And I think I'm right." She handed Sarah the letter that she'd been holding. "Remember the trouble the Pearsons had with the chapel records? I think they're up against the same problem now. I can't read much through that envelope, but I can make out a few words. I think it's written in Welsh." She looked at the envelopes scattered across the bedspread. "These letters will be no use to the Pearsons at all, unless someone over there can translate them."

Sarah felt her excitement ebb. "That's not very likely is it?"

"No, it's not." Annie began gathering up the letters in businesslike fashion. "And that's why we're going to call Iris right now and ask her if she wants you to translate them before we mail them off!"

Sarah stared at her mother. "Call her? Mam, do you have any idea how much that will cost?"

"No! And it's probably a good thing too! But we must do it Sarah. Now help me find that number. I know she gave it to us before she left."

Annie Lewis threw the covers off her bed and went to stand up.

"Slow down, Mam! Remember, you've been ill." Sarah's warning was almost too late. Annie's weak legs wobbled as she put weight on them. She clutched the bedside table and reached out for her daughter. Sarah helped her mother back onto the bed.

"Now, tell me where to look and I'll go and find the number."

It wasn't until she'd tried three possible locations that Sarah finally thought to check the guest book. Sure enough, Iris Pearson had filled out her address and phone number next to the dates she'd stayed with them. Ruefully thinking that she'd sorted through enough boxes, drawers, and letters that day to last a lifetime, Sarah carried the guest book back to her mother's room.

"It looks like you'll have to make the call, Sarah," Annie said regretfully. "If I can't make it across the room, I'll never make it down the stairs."

Sarah battled a sudden wave of emotion. It was always possible that Brian would answer the phone. While part of her longed to hear his voice again, another part, the larger part, didn't want to risk penetrating the facade she had built up carefully over the months since his departure. She couldn't risk opening that wound again.

"Why don't we wait a day, Mam? Then you could make the call and talk to Iris yourself."

"No, we mustn't wait, Sarah. Besides, if you talk to her you can tell her all about your visit to Aunty Sally and finding the letters."

Sarah had to concede that her mother was being logical. She knew Iris had a right to be told immediately. She also knew that she would want to hear all the details of the discovery. Sarah tried to ignore the qualms that churned within her.

"Alright. I'll try." Sarah walked to the bedroom door. As she slowly closed it, she heard her mother call out.

"Give Iris my love!"

☙ ☙ ☙

Sarah's hands trembled as she dialed the number. She had checked with the local operator about placing a trans-Atlantic phone call. The numbers were all clearly written on a piece of paper before her. Within seconds of dialing the last digit, she heard a few clicks then a ringing sound. It was a different type of ring than she was used to, but she assumed her call was going through. She felt her nervousness increase with each ring. Suddenly there was another slight click and a distant voice.

"Hello!"

Sarah cleared her throat. "Hello! May I speak with Mrs. Iris Pearson?"

"This is she."

"Mrs. Pearson, this is Sarah Lewis calling from Pen-y-Bryn."

There was a slight pause.

"Sarah! Sarah, is that really you?"

Sarah laughed at the excitement in Iris's voice. "Yes, it is!"

"Oh my dear, I'd have recognized your voice straight away if I hadn't been half asleep. How are you?"

Sarah experienced a pang of concern. "I'm fine. But did I wake you up?"

"It's only four-fifteen in the morning here, dear. But I'm so glad you called. It's lovely to hear your voice."

"I'm terribly sorry. I didn't even think about the time difference. I can call you back later."

"Goodness me, no! How's your mother? We think of you all so often."

"Mother's just getting over the flu I'm afraid. But she's well on the mend. I think she'll be up and around very soon. She wanted me to send you her love."

"Please give her my love too. Oh I wish Brian was here. He'll be so sorry to have missed your call."

Sarah felt a stab of disappointment followed by an easing of her former tension and nervousness. As she relaxed, her natural enthusiasm began to surface.

"I had to phone to let you know some very exciting news!"

Sarah could hear the interest in Iris's voice. "What's that, dear?"

And so Sarah began her tale. She told her about Aunty Sally's summons, the minister's help, the search at the chapel, her discovery at the back of the cupboard, and her dilemma now.

"I can put all the letters in the mail today. The only reason I haven't done just that is that we think the letters are written in Welsh. We weren't sure if you have anyone there who could translate them for you."

There was a long pause on the line. Sarah started to worry.

"Mrs. Pearson, are you there?"

"Yes! Yes! Oh Sarah, I can't believe it! I'm in shock! I can't believe you did all that . . . and you found them. Oh, I can't believe it!"

Sarah couldn't help warming to the joy in the older woman's voice.

"It's very exciting. Mam and I are thrilled for you. I only hope the letters help to answer some of your questions."

"Wouldn't that be great!" There was another slight pause. "Sarah, would it be asking too much to have you translate them for us?"

It was Sarah's turn to pause. "Well, I can try. I'm not really a linguist . . ."

"You're totally bilingual and I can't think of anyone I'd rather have do it. We'd pay you for your time of course."

"You most certainly will not!" Sarah's indignation made Iris Pearson laugh.

"Okay, we'll put that discussion on hold for now! Will you do it for us?"

"I'll start on them today and get the letters and translations in the mail to you just as fast as I can."

"Thank you Sarah. You're a doll."

Sarah smiled at the Americanism.

"Good-bye Mrs. Pearson."

"Good-bye dear. Thank you so much."

Sarah put down her receiver. The loud click emphasized the quiet of the house. Sarah wished she could magically make Iris Pearson appear. The hall seemed cold, dark, and lonely without the American's cheery voice. Sarah tried to shake off the melancholy. If speaking with Iris Pearson for a few minutes affected her this way, she didn't want to think about what speaking to her son would have done. Sarah felt another wave of relief that she had been spared that ordeal.

"Well?" Annie Lewis had been anxiously awaiting Sarah's return.

Sarah smiled. "Well . . . she was thrilled! Couldn't believe it! And she asked if I'd translate the letters for her."

"What did you say?"

"I told her I'd do my best."

Annie looked pleased. "Good for you, bach! I'm sure you can do it."

Sarah gave a small moan. "I wish I had your confidence." She looked at her watch. "I'm going to run downstairs and make us both something to eat." She picked up the battered old envelope. "Then I'd better get started on these. I mustn't keep Mrs. Pearson waiting too long."

"I can hardly wait to hear what the letters say." Annie's face was full of anticipation.

"Mam!" Sarah used a cautionary tone. She knew her mother's penchant for gossip. "This is not our story to tell." Annie's expression fell. "Don't worry; you'll have plenty to talk about just telling people how we found the letters!"

Annie looked unconvinced but Sarah smiled. "I'll be back in a few minutes with your dinner." Carrying the precious package in one hand, she slipped out of the room.

❦ ❦ ❦

An hour and a half later, Sarah sat cross-legged on her bed. The letters were spread around her in a semicircle. She had tried to place them in chronological order by scrutinizing the faded, blurred dates stamped on the envelopes. Gingerly she picked up the first one and sliced open the top of the envelope as carefully as she could. There

were two onion-thin sheets of yellowed paper within. She drew them
out and gently unfolded them. A quick glance told Sarah everything
she needed to know. The date in the upper right-hand corner read:
"15 Mai 1881" (15 May 1881). On the left side of the paper were the
words "Fy Nhad Annwyl" (Dear Father). The signature at the bottom
was "Mary." The letter was over 100 years old. It was written in
Welsh and it was from Mary Jones. With bated breath, Sarah began
to read.

Sarah didn't stop reading until she had read each letter twice.
Leaning her head against the backboard of the bed, she marveled at
this woman she had come to know, and was amazed at the bond she
felt with Mary Jones. Instinctively, she knew that had they lived in
the same time period, they would have been close friends. She felt
overwhelming admiration for the woman's courage and faith. Did
she, Sarah Lewis, possess such integrity?

The thought made Sarah squirm. She had received an offer to
leave home and family for the love of a man. She'd rejected it,
cleaving to the security of all that was familiar. But that was different,
she rationalized. Mary had known without doubt that she loved Glyn
Jones. Sarah's feelings for Brian were in their infancy when he made
his proposal. She hadn't had enough time.

And what about Mary's change of religion? Mary, the daughter of
a Methodist minister, had become a Mormon! How could she turn
her back on her very upbringing like that? Sarah picked up the letter
again.

'Please believe that it was not an easy decision, or one that I took
lightly. We had not long been in Logan before Glyn and I came to feel great
admiration for the people of the Mormon Church. They are hard workers,
generous and kind. They seem to truly be striving to live Christ-like lives.
As a people they have suffered and sacrificed more than any I know, but
they have retained a cheerfulness and optimism in the future without the
bitterness that often follows such persecution.

'I was curious to read the Book of Mormon that they spoke of so
lovingly and mentioned this interest to my good friend, Catriona Evans.
She loaned me her book. Glyn and I read it together each evening. As we
read we became more and more convinced that it contained great truths.

There is a power to the book that I have never experienced before. By the time we reached the last page, Glyn was ready for baptism. . . '

The Book of Mormon. Wasn't that the book that Brian had given her when he left? What had she done with it? Sarah scanned her bedroom, but not seeing anything that immediately triggered her memory, she returned to the letter.

'. . . *You were in my thoughts constantly at that time. I could not do anything more that might hurt you, who I love so dearly, without total conviction that I was choosing the right course. I prayed as I have never prayed before. The answer came, Father. I cannot deny it. I was filled with a burning warmth that encompassed my whole being. I have never known such joy. It is true! It is true!*
'*I was baptized into the Church of Jesus Christ of Latter-day Saints on 23 August 1882 in the Logan River . . . '*

Sarah could only imagine how hard it must have been for Mary to pen this letter, knowing that her conversion to the Mormon faith would surely further ostracize her from her father and Welsh village. Was joining another church that important?

Glancing over at the window, she saw that it seemed to have stopped raining. She got off the bed for a better look. The sun was breaking through the clouds, and the trees and bushes were glistening with moisture. Even though dark puddles covered the ground, she would go for a walk, clear her mind, then return home to begin the translating.

❦ ❦ ❦

Sarah was up late into the night on Saturday—reading, translating, and writing. It was a laborious process, because she wanted to make her effort as accurate as possible. But she also wanted to transmit in English the love and longing conveyed through Mary Jones's Welsh words.

Since Sarah's thoughts were consumed with this project, it came as rather a shock the next morning to realize that ordinary life had to go on. She attended early-morning chapel services and spoke to

Reverend Davis briefly after his sermon. He was surprised and extremely pleased to hear of her find in the chapel office after his departure the day before. When she told him she would be forwarding the material to the Pearsons, he nodded his approval; but they had no opportunity for further discussion before someone else came up to speak with him.

Annie continued to steadily recover. By Monday morning, when Sarah ran downstairs after another long night of translating, her mother was already up and making breakfast. Sarah had no time to do more than kiss her mother on the cheek, grab a piece of toast and her coat and set off running for the Primary School. By the time she arrived home again at 4 P.M., she'd decided that burning the candle at both ends was not for her. She was exhausted.

Nevertheless, she allowed herself no more than half an hour for a cup of tea and a chat with her mother (whom she was pleased to see resting in the sitting room), before heading back to her room to continue her work.

By Wednesday night it was finished. As Sarah gathered the papers together, she felt as though she had just completed a marathon. She had read and reread each sheet meticulously and felt sure that she could do no better. At this point, she felt so close to Mary that she almost thought of her as the sister she'd never had. And while she was anxious for the Pearsons to get to know their ancestor as she had done, she was loath to relinquish her connection to the woman she had come to admire so much. She looked at the papers in her hand and was struck by an idea. For safety's sake, she would make a copy of the original letters and her translation. She couldn't bear to think of them getting lost again. It was sound logic and it gave her an excuse to keep a record of the letters herself.

It was only as she was replacing Mary Jones's letters into the battered manilla envelope that she remembered the other letter sent from the United States in another person's handwriting. She found it still in the original envelope, unopened. Carefully she slit apart the top and extracted the fragile sheets. It appeared to be the same type of paper that Mary had used. Sarah sat down beside the lamp. The letter was dated 17 February 1884. It was also written in Welsh but the penmanship was more difficult to read.

Dear Sir,

Whether you will ever receive this letter I know not, but I promised my beloved Mary that I would write it. Mary passed from this life on 13 January, 1884, while giving birth to our daughter. Her last words were of you and of her sorrow over ever having hurt you.

Only now can I truly understand your loss when I took her from her Welsh home. I live only for the day that I can be with her again.

Yours in grief,

Glyn Jones

Sarah let the tears fall. Her heart went out to a bereft husband in America and a lonely father in Wales. It was for all the world as if she, Sarah Lewis, had lost a loved one that day.

Early on Thursday morning, before school began, Sarah copied the papers on the school Xerox machine. With utmost care she unfolded each of Mary's letters and the one from Glyn. Then she went through each sheet of translation, including the new one she had done after reading Glyn Jones's letter.

She placed all the originals in a padded envelope carefully addressed to Iris Pearson; when the time came for her lunch hour at school, she walked over to the post office and sent the package on its way. It was like sending off part of herself. Her only consolation came in imagining Iris Pearson's joy when the manuscripts arrived at their destination.

Chapter 10

Everyday life seemed very mundane after that. Only the minister and her mother knew what she'd been doing. Sarah had made a conscious decision not to tell others. As she had told her mother, it wasn't really her story to tell. She told the minister that the package had been mailed off, and he was satisfied. Her mother begged for some details as to the contents of the letters only once. When Sarah refused to elaborate, Annie had protested, "But Sarah, I'm your mother!"

Sarah had smiled and added, "Yes, and you're also someone's aunt, sister, grandmother, friend, neighbor, niece, and so on. I know how it would be, Mam!"

Annie's sheepish expression betrayed the fact that Annie also knew how it would be. No more was said on the subject.

Sarah did go to see Aunty Sally again. She wanted to thank her. But Aunty Sally remembered nothing of the incident. It was as though she knew that she had discharged her responsibility and her part was over. All thoughts of old letters were promptly and completely forgotten.

Not so for Sarah. She tried desperately to keep her mind occupied, but working on Mary Jones's letters had caused memories and feelings to surface that she thought she'd put behind her. At night, Mary, Glyn, Iris, and Brian flitted through her dreams at random. Especially Brian. She wondered for the millionth time if he ever thought of her.

Meanwhile, she tried to spend every spare minute with her harp. The day of her first rehearsal for the Christmas program in Chester

was drawing close. She was to play two solo performances and partici-
pate as part of the orchestra. Her selections had already met with
approval from the organizers. The director, Trevor Williams, had sent
her copies of the orchestra music, and while most pieces were familiar
to her, she was anxious to get together with the other musicians to be
sure that her interpretation of the music complemented theirs.

Mid-morning on the last Saturday in November, Sarah set off for
Chester in the shop van, with the harp (duly loaded by Kevin) in the
back. It was a cold, damp day with an overcast sky, but no rain. She
was grateful for the dry roads. It was two weeks since she had run
through the pouring rain to the chapel and found Mary Jones's
letters. She had heard nothing from the Pearsons, but was hoping
that no news was good news.

The journey to Chester was blissfully uneventful. Road improve-
ments had shortened the travel time considerably, and the straight
dual-carriageway made travel with a harp much less worrisome than
the twisting, winding roads she often had to negotiate. She arrived at
the city with half an hour to spare before the scheduled rehearsal
time.

It had been a few years since Sarah was last in Chester. She had
always loved this city with its downtown area still surrounded by the
ancient city wall. Many of the buildings were whitewashed with dark
wooden beams running in stark contrast across the eaves and around
the windows and doors. There were already Christmas decorations in
many of the shop windows, and the city was buzzing with Saturday
shoppers.

Sarah again consulted the address she'd been given and strained
to hunt for road signs. She followed a likely-looking street for a few
miles until she began to think that she'd made a mistake. Then she
rounded a bend in the road and saw the sign for the Civic Center
immediately ahead. With a sigh of relief and a quick glance at her
watch (she still had ten minutes to spare), she drove into the
parking area.

Trevor Williams met her at the door, and soon organized a crew
to help unload the harp and set her up on stage. After brief introductions, the rehearsal began. Unused to playing as part of a larger group,
Sarah found the experience musically taxing, exhausting, and utterly

glorious! She thrilled in the magic of creating music as a team, marveling at how each instrument wove its unique color into the larger tapestry of the orchestra as a whole. Time sped by. She was stunned when Mr. Williams brought the rehearsal to a close and she realized that three and a half hours had passed.

As the musicians began packing away their music, stands, and instruments, two ladies came out with a big urn of hot tea and a plate of sandwiches. Everyone was glad of the refreshment. Sarah enjoyed chatting with the lead violinist and percussionist as she drank her tea. Mr. Williams joined them.

"It's a long way for you to come, Sarah. We really appreciate it."

"I enjoyed it very much, Mr. Williams. Thank you for asking me."

He looked a little troubled. "We'll be having another, longer rehearsal next Saturday since our performance is the next day. I hate to have you travel all that way two days in a row. I've been wondering how you would feel about staying here in Chester overnight; we could put you up in a hotel nearby."

Sarah was sure that her surprise showed on her face. "Thank you, that's very nice of you. To be honest, I haven't given it much thought yet, but I will. Can I let you know closer to the time?"

"Of course, of course! We can always make a provisional booking at the hotel and change it at the last minute. Whatever's best for you!"

Sarah smiled her gratitude. "Thank you. I'll let you know then."

"Right. Now, let me see about getting some help to move your harp."

Trevor Williams set off in search of a moving crew, and Sarah excused herself from the others on stage and gathered up her belongings.

Dusk was settling in as she started the van. She was concentrating on heading out in the right direction, so it was not until she was pulling out of the parking area that she noticed the building across the road. It was built of cream brick and appeared to be fairly new. The design was very simple, but a single spire, now illuminated, suggested that it might be a church. The sign attached to the wall of the building was also illuminated. Sarah read: "The Church of Jesus Christ of Latter-day Saints. Visitors Welcome."

She clutched the steering wheel in shock. It couldn't be! Here in Chester! With shaking hands Sarah maneuvered the vehicle into the road, then cut across into the parking area next to the church. Taking a deep, steadying breath, she left the van and walked over to the front of the building. She gave a small tug at the double glass doors. They were locked. She shielded her eyes from the street lights behind her and peered through the glass. All was darkness. She could make out a carpeted hallway, a coat rack and several wooden doors leading off from the hall.

Anxious not to appear to be loitering, she took a couple of steps back. A sign on the door announced a meeting schedule. Something called "Sacrament Meeting" began at 9 A.M. Sunday School was at 10:20 A.M. and "Priesthood/Relief Society" at 11:10 A.M. Sarah recognized the last words. Brian had spoken of "priesthood" and Mary Jones had written about a women's group called "Relief Society." But was it really the same thing, functioning here in Wales? Sarah walked back to the van slowly, her head buzzing with unanswered questions.

ॐ ॐ ॐ

As the week wore on, Sarah found herself often thinking about the church she'd seen in Chester, and her curiosity grew. She wasn't convinced that she had the courage to go to one of their church meetings alone, but she couldn't let the idea rest. By Thursday, the weather forecasters were predicting storms for the weekend. Seizing this information as the excuse she needed, Sarah presented it to her mother.

"Mr. Williams has offered to put me up in a hotel on Saturday night. If the weathermen are right, it might be best if I wasn't traveling too much."

Annie was quick to agree. So Sarah found herself setting off for Chester the next Saturday with her harp and an overnight bag. Annie had glanced anxiously at the bank of clouds moving slowly over the mountains as Sarah left.

"Aunty Lil and I will be there for the concert tomorrow unless a big snow storm moves in."

"Alright, Mam. I'll watch for you. I'll call you tonight from the hotel."

"Yes, do that, bach. Then I won't worry about you."

And so Sarah made the journey to Chester again. She spent a long but productive day rehearsing, then checked into a nearby hotel, leaving her harp under lock and key at the Civic Center. She called her mother that evening. Pen-y-Bryn had received a skiff of snow during the day, but the roads were still clear.

By morning however, it was a totally different story. From her hotel window Sarah surveyed a sparkling white world. Puffs of smoke came from chimney tops and floated up into an azure sky. The few townspeople who had ventured out early were busily shoveling off their driveways and uncovering their cars. Sarah watched for a few minutes, amazed at how completely transformed the world became with a blanket of snow. Then she hurriedly placed a phone call home.

The snow had reached the Pen-y-Bryn valley too. The pass over the Berwyn mountains was closed, and it was unlikely that her mother and aunt would make it out. There was even a remote possibility that Sarah wouldn't make it back. She would make another phone call later in the day to determine road conditions that evening.

It didn't take Sarah long to dress. She was glad that she'd packed her soft, warm, wool knit dress. Slipping a narrow brown leather belt around her small waist, she surveyed herself in the mirror. The rust-colored fabric brought out the golden highlights in her long dark hair. She ran a brush through her shining mane and pinned it back with a tortoise-shell clip.

Shoes were going to be a bit of a problem. She eyed the high-heeled shoes she had packed—one slip on the snowy roads in those and she'd be a goner. Her only alternative was the casual shoes she'd worn with her jeans the day before. Sarah put them on and stifled a giggle. Well, she wasn't going to win any prizes for fashion, but hopefully she'd arrive in one piece. She picked up her other shoes and stuffed them into her handbag.

A quick glance at the clock told her that she didn't have time for breakfast, but she wasn't too worried. No breakfast wasn't that different from half a grapefruit anyway. She grabbed her coat and let herself out of her room, locking the door behind her.

The lobby was quiet. Not many people surfaced before 9 A.M. on a Sunday morning. Sarah couldn't quite believe she'd done it either.

She was not usually an impulsive person. But then she didn't really consider her actions this morning impulsive. She was being driven by something within—something that had been working on her ever since she first saw the church across the street from the Civic Center. She was going to go to that church this once and put to rest all her curiosity and questions.

Outside, the peaceful serenity of an hour ago had been replaced. Wet slushy sounds accompanied every car as tires spewed grey sludge in their wake. Sarah slithered her way to the van. After depositing her handbag within, she found an old rag (part of the harp packing material) and brushed off all the windows.

To her relief, the van started on her first try, and soon she was moving gingerly out into the road. Within five minutes she was in the church parking area. This time there were several cars parked there and a few others had followed her in. She watched a young couple herd their three young children out of an old blue car and into the building. The children's pink cheeks and noses and their excited voices as they bounded ahead of their parents brought back fond memories for Sarah. She remembered going to the chapel in Pen-y-Bryn with her parents and brothers on cold, snowy winter Sundays. It didn't seem like there were as many young children going now as there were then.

An older couple walked by, each carrying books. Sarah suddenly felt very alone and vulnerable. She knew none of these people. What was she doing here? She clutched the steering wheel in indecision. Part of her wanted to run back to the hotel right then, before she became at all involved. But another part, the real Sarah, knew that she would not rest until she'd done this. Fighting her fears, she changed her shoes, stepped out of the van, and, noting with relief that someone had cleared the pavement of snow, she followed the other people into the church.

She entered the main lobby that she had seen indistinctly through the doors the week before. The floor was covered in a light grey commercial carpet. A handful of people were talking softly to each other, but most were walking directly through a set of double wooden doors into what Sarah assumed was the main chapel area. She could hear the sound of a piano being played each time the door opened. There were a lot of coats hanging along the far end of one wall. A few boots were also sitting beneath the coats.

As she paused to take this in, two young men wearing navy blue suits, white shirts, ties, and black name tags approached her. One offered her his hand. She shook it automatically.

"Hi! I'm Elder Mitchell. You must be a visitor here today?"

Sarah was momentarily taken aback. He sounded just like Brian. Not his voice exactly, but his accent was just the same.

"Yes," she responded, trying to pull herself together. "I'm just in Chester for the day. I saw your church and thought I'd come. I hope that's alright?"

"That's great! We're glad to have you." Elder Mitchell was enthusiastic. He indicated the man beside him. "This is Elder Sorenson."

The other man shook her hand.

"I'm Sarah. Sarah Lewis," she said.

"I'm very pleased to meet you. Where are you from, Sarah?"

Sarah decided this experience was going to be one surprise after another. She didn't need to be a linguist to know that Elder Sorenson was neither from Britain nor the United States.

"I'm from Pen-y-Bryn." Both men looked blank and she smiled. "It's a small village on the other side of the Berwyn mountains. About an hour and a half from here." She turned back to Elder Sorenson. "Where are you from?"

His blonde hair and name should have been clues enough. "Norway."

"There are Mormons in Norway too?" Sarah couldn't contain her amazement.

Elder Sorenson grinned. "Of course! That's where the best ones come from!"

A speaker located in the corner of the lobby crackled to life. "Good morning Brothers and Sisters!" Sarah jumped. She and the two men looked up at the box on the wall.

"The meeting is starting. Shall we go in?" Elder Mitchell asked.

Sarah nodded and followed him to the door. He held it open for her. Sarah stepped inside, then stopped. The chapel floor was a light-colored wood. The walls were white and most of the light came from large flourescent light strips on the vaulted ceiling. Along the far wall were long narrow windows covered with fine net curtains in a gold tone. At the front of the chapel was a raised platform with a lectern, seating for about 20 people, a piano, and a small organ. To one side of the raised area was a small table covered with a white lace cloth. Three men and two women sat behind the lectern. Two teenage boys sat behind the small table.

Perhaps what was most noticeable however, was what was missing. There were no stained glass windows, no crucifix, and no wooden pews. The congregation was seated on rows of plastic chairs. The rows had been set up to facilitate a large central aisle and two narrower ones on both outer edges of the room. Sarah noticed that a few of the chairs were already a little out of alignment, particularly those being used by the many children in the room.

The man standing at the lectern wore a slightly faded grey suit, white shirt, and paisley tie. As Sarah watched, he turned and joined the other men seated behind him. One of the ladies on the stand rose and stood beside the piano. She raised one arm as the pianist began to play, then led the congregation in singing. To Sarah's surprise, the congregation remained seated throughout the hymn. It made her feel all the more self-conscious as she followed Elder Mitchell to a seat near the back.

The whole meeting was a kaleidoscope of new and strange experiences. Sarah watched as another lady took the stand and bowed her head in a simple, unrehearsed prayer. She sat in wonder as the congregation raised their hands to agree to names and positions that meant nothing to her. Then she watched, somewhat discomfited, as young boys passed trays of broken bread and small cups of water down the aisles towards her. Not once did the congregation stand, kneel, or walk to the front. Three different men spoke. Each had their own style and message. Sarah recognized a few of the quoted scriptures and one of the hymns, but otherwise she felt as though she was in a totally different world.

Occasionally one of the babies in the room would cry, and many of the young children wiggled and whispered loudly. The Church meeting lacked the total quiet and rigid solemnity that she was used to. But despite that, despite all the strangeness, there was something there that attracted Sarah. She couldn't say what it was. In fact, her feelings baffled her.

The meeting closed with a prayer and suddenly there was movement all around her. Chairs were being moved and a large partition was drawn across the room. The young men beside her stood and she followed suit.

"They're preparing this area for a Sunday School class," Elder Sorenson explained. "If you'd like to come with us we can find a quiet area and answer any questions you may have."

He led the way out of the chapel. Several people stopped Sarah as she passed them. They shook her hand, introduced themselves, and welcomed her. Sarah couldn't help but be impressed by their genuine interest and friendliness. She was positively brimming with questions. She waited only until they reached the foyer.

"D'you usually have a minister who takes the service?"

Elder Mitchell smiled. "We have no paid clergy. Members of the Church are called by those in authority over them to serve in the area where they live. Clive Edwards is the bishop here in Chester. He's the man who was conducting the meeting today. He's a builder."

Sarah looked incredulous. "You mean he has no formal religious training?"

"None at all. But we believe he's called of God to lead this ward right now."

Sarah took a step back. This was all too much. "Ward? What ward?" The only wards she knew were in a hospital.

Elder Sorenson intervened. "A ward is what we call a Church unit. Elder Mitchell means that Bishop Edwards looks after the welfare of the Church members in the Chester area."

Before Sarah could say anything more he opened one of the doors leading off from the foyer. It led into a small office. "Come in. We'd like to tell you more about the Church."

An hour and a half later Sarah and the two missionaries (for that is what she had discovered they were), emerged from the office. They had reviewed much of what Brian had told her about a man called Joseph Smith who claimed to have seen an angel, God the father, and Jesus Christ. This man, whom Mormons revered as a prophet, had organized the Church in America and translated the Book of Mormon from an ancient record given to him by an angel.

Sarah had peppered the missionaries with questions. Some were questions that she'd harbored since Brian had spoken to her about his Church; others were from the recent meeting she'd attended; and still others stemmed from the material the two young men presented. She was sure that her skepticism was obvious during portions of the discussion, but the missionaries didn't seem to be the least daunted by her reservations. And much to her own surprise, she realized that despite her misgivings, her curiosity was still piqued. Indeed she was intrigued by some of the new concepts presented to her.

She felt suddenly anxious to leave, to think things through alone. A glance at her watch told her that she just had time for a quick lunch before the final rehearsal at the Civic Center.

"I must go now," Sarah said to the missionaries by her side.

"Okay." Elder Mitchell shook her hand. "It was great visiting with you, Sarah. Be sure to read the Book of Mormon we gave you."

Sarah wasn't sure what to say, so opted to say nothing. She turned and shook Elder Sorenson's hand also.

"Good luck at the concert tonight. We'll be in touch with you," he said.

"Thanks." Sarah wondered fleetingly if it had been a mistake to give these two men her phone number, but thought it unlikely that they'd call. Chances were slim that she'd be back in the Chester area for a long time. This was her one opportunity to be inside a Mormon church. She'd done it. Now it was time to get back to her own life.

She left them quickly. It was still cold outside, but the early-morning crispness was gone. The roads were wet and slushy but the pavements had been cleared outside the hotel. Sarah hurried to her room, changed into her casual clothes once again, ran a brush through her hair, and gathered up her music. She paused and picked up the navy-blue book that she'd dumped on the bed beside her handbag: The Book of Mormon—Another Testament of Jesus Christ. What ever could this book contain? What made it so unique? Its history was so fantastic, so farfetched. And yet, so many people seemed to believe in it. How could so many people believe such a ludicrous story? Still wondering all these things, Sarah slipped the book into her music bag, grabbed her handbag and let herself out of the room.

She ordered a sandwich and a cup of tea at the hotel restaurant. She allowed her gaze to traverse the room. There weren't very many people around. It was still too early for Sunday dinner and rather late for breakfast. A teal-green carpet matched the upholstery of the dining chairs. Wooden tables of various sizes were scattered around the room, many of which were already set with cutlery, glasses, and serviettes. A few tables had yellow 'RESERVED' cards in the center. The windows faced the back of the hotel and looked out upon a small patio surrounded by shrubs that had become unidentifiable fluffy white blobs. The inside walls were decorated with oil paintings depicting fox-hunting scenes. There were expanses of English countryside and red jacketed riders astride magnificent horses. Above the doorway of the restaurant hung a brass bugle similar to those used during a hunt.

It didn't take the waitress long to bring Sarah her food, and it took Sarah even less time to eat it. She still had about 30 minutes before she needed to be at the Civic Center so she ordered another cup of tea and took the Book of Mormon out of her bag. Idly, Sarah flipped through the pages. The names on the chapter headings were strange: Nephi, Mosiah, Alma, Helaman. The missionaries had highlighted a few sections with a red pencil. She turned to one. It was under the heading 3 Nephi and Chapter 11. She began to read.

By the time Sarah reached the end of the chapter her neglected tea was stone cold and her fascination captured. Could an American farm boy have written this? It seemed extremely unlikely. But the alternative was unthinkable. Sarah's thoughts were in a whirl. She had to put all this out of her mind or she would be unable to focus on her performance that evening. She looked at her watch with a gasp; if she didn't change her focus immediately, she would be late for rehearsal on top of playing poorly.

❦ ❦ ❦

Sarah was profoundly grateful that a final rehearsal with Mr. Williams proved so demanding. It took every ounce of her concentration. He worked the whole orchestra hard and demanded their best efforts. Even the volunteer stage hands were scurrying to keep up with the program changes.

When Mr. Williams finally dismissed them, they had less than two hours before the performance was to begin. It was just enough time for Sarah to call her mother and learn that word had just arrived in Pen-y-Bryn that the mountain pass was open. Sarah would be able to make it home. Sarah's relief was only offset by the fact that the news had reached her mother too late to allow her and Aunty Lil to make it to the concert.

Sarah checked out of the hotel and returned to the Civic Center to change. Since she was not in the habit of performing with an orchestra, she didn't have the traditional black attire. She had brought her burgundy velvet dress, and hoped that she wouldn't stand out too dramatically among her fellow musicians. As she stood in front of the mirror and swept her hair up, she couldn't help but think back to the last time she'd worn the dress. It had been at the Eisteddfod in Llangollen. Brian had been there. Her hands, affixing pins to her chignon, trembled. Sarah sighed. Would she ever be able to think of him without emotion?

Someone walked by in the hallway and bumped the door ajar. Sarah could hear the familiar cacophony of instruments being tuned. Without further thought for her appearance, she slipped out of the changing room and onto the stage.

☙ ☙ ☙

As Sarah lay warm and snug in her very own bed five hours later, her time in Chester seemed another world away. If it had not been for the dark bulk of her overnight bag silhouetted beneath her night light, she could easily have believed the last two days had been nothing more than a dream.

The concert had been a resounding success—the murmur of the audience followed by their rapt attention, the bright lights and almost tangible anticipation, the magnificent music and the applause—it had all been like magic. Sarah had been thrilled to be a part of it. She had floated home encompassed by a joyful glow created by the spirit of Christmas music and kind words.

Sarah purposefully pushed back any thoughts of her other activities of the day. Memories of her time at the Mormon Church and her discussion with the missionaries would only release a plethora of questions, concerns, and the seeming need to make some decisions. That pandora's box could remain closed until the light of morning.

As it happened, Sarah managed to keep it closed for several days. Monday morning brought the beginning of a flu epidemic at school. Sarah found herself taking children's temperatures, administering medicine, and calling parents throughout the day. When she arrived home exhausted from her third day of it, her mother told her that she'd received a phone call from a foreigner. A man. The curiosity in Annie Lewis's voice was obvious. But Sarah could not appease it. She had no idea who the man could be. They'd have to wait until he called back.

He did call back the next day. This time Sarah was home from school and recognized the voice immediately. It was Elder Sorenson.

"Sarah, how are you?"

"I'm fine, thank you." Sarah's voice was guarded. Whatever had possessed her to give the missionaries her phone number?

"We wanted to call to see if you've had a chance to read any of the Book of Mormon yet?"

"A little."

"How do you feel about it?"

"It was very interesting." Even to her own ears, Sarah could tell that her answer was weak at best. There was an infinitesimal pause before Elder Sorenson continued.

"I'm glad you thought so. Did you pray about it?"

"No."

"Would you try reading it again Sarah? And this time pray about what you read."

Sarah hesitated. She didn't want to make any kind of commitment, but it was hard to say no to this man.

"I'll try," she said lamely.

"Great!" Elder Sorenson's enthusiasm made it sound like she'd promised him the crown jewels. "Listen, we've checked with our mission president and there are no missionaries in your area. Is there any way you can meet us again in Chester so that we can tell you some more about the Church and answer your questions?"

"I think that's unlikely," Sarah responded. "I don't have any plans to be in Chester any time in the near future. It's quite a drive and the road conditions can be bad this time of year."

It seemed to Sarah that a person would have to be cast in stone not to acknowledge that rebuff, despite her pleasant tone. Elder Sorenson, it seemed, was a man of granite.

"I understand. But just in case your plans change, let me give you our number. Give us a call a day or so before you come and we'll make sure that we can meet with you."

Reluctantly Sarah copied down his number and thanked him for calling.

"No problem," was Elder Sorenson's reply. "We'll be in touch again soon."

Sarah put down the phone wondering just how soon 'soon' was.

It was not difficult to quell her mother's interest in the mysterious foreigner. Sarah just told her part of the truth. She told Annie that he was someone she'd met while in Chester and that he was from Norway. When Annie made the assumption that he was a member of the orchestra, Sarah did not correct her. Sarah told her that it was very unlikely that she would see him again. And that appeared to be that.

By the next afternoon, Sarah was coming to realize that the pervasive flu strain that had claimed so many of her young charges had found another victim. That evening found her in bed with a fever. She alternated between feeling boiling hot and freezing cold. Her head throbbed and she ached all over. Saturday was not much better. It passed in a fog of discomfort, and she had vague memories of her mother forcing water down her along with an occasional tablet.

When she awoke on Sunday morning, her temperature had finally dropped to normal. Sarah felt terribly weak but had an overwhelming desire to get out of her sick bed, even if it was only for a minute or two. Her legs shook precariously when she tried to stand. By clutching the head of the bed and then leaning against the wall, she made it over to the window at a snail's pace. She pushed the window open a crack and inhaled the cold outside air. The small breeze puffed tingling freshness into her warm stuffy bedroom.

Sarah pushed the window open a little more. Then she gingerly lowered herself onto the chair beside the dressing table. She tried to ignore her bedraggled appearance in the mirror and focused instead on a cheeky little red-breasted robin perched on a branch outside the window. He was hopping up and down, fluffing his feathers against the cold. Every few minutes he would stop and send up a trill song to the world around him. He cocked his head to one side as if listening for a reply. When none came he would sing again.

"Sarah Lewis, you'll catch your death of cold! It's like a fridge in here!"

Annie's voice made Sarah jump. She hadn't heard the soft knock at the door. Annie walked over to the window and pulled it closed.

"What ever are you thinking, child? It's perishing out there."

She put her hand on her daughter's forehead. A look of relief crossed her wrinkled face.

"It's down. Thank the Lord!" She bent and kissed Sarah softly on the top of her head. "That was quite a bout you had my girl! How're you feeling now?"

Sarah grimaced. "Weak!"

"I'm sure you are. You haven't eaten in two whole days. Come on, back to bed with you!" Annie helped pull Sarah to her feet and led her slowly back to bed. "Now you stay put. No more communing with nature or what have you. I'll be right back with some breakfast."

"Thanks Mam." As Annie turned to leave, Sarah called out, "Mam, not a big breakfast please. Just some toast and a cup of tea."

Annie pursed her lips, then with a quick shrug of her shoulders conceded the point. "Alright, toast and tea to start with. But we'll have to see about building up your strength with something else a bit later."

Sarah managed a feeble grin. They never would see eye to eye on breakfasts.

The day passed slowly. Sarah was tired of being in bed, but was incapable of doing much else. Her mother checked on her quite regularly which helped dispel the feeling of being in solitary confinement. By mid-afternoon, out of desperation to ward off total boredom, Sarah picked up the Book of Mormon she'd brought back from Chester. This time she started reading at the beginning.

Sarah heard her mother's footsteps on the stairs and the chink of cutlery hitting china. Tea time? She looked over at her small bedside clock in amazement. She just had time to slip the book under her covers before her mother entered the room carrying a tray.

"How are you feeling?" Annie asked as she gently set the tray on Sarah's knees.

"Better. I should be able to go to work tomorrow."

"You will not be going to work tomorrow!"

"But, Mam . . . "

"No buts! I saw the headmaster at chapel today. I told him you'd been down with the flu. He's not expecting you back until Wednesday."

"Mam!" Sarah's voice was filled with indignation.

Annie laughed. "You may be twenty-three Sarah Lewis, but I'm still your mother. I'll not have you going back to that school to be surrounded by an army of germs before you're well enough to deal with them. And that's final!"

Sarah didn't have the strength to argue. Besides, deep down she knew that her mother was right. Annie sensed victory and smiled down at her daughter.

"Now you eat your tea and enjoy being pampered for a change!"

ॐ ॐ ॐ

Sarah spent the next two days reading the Book of Mormon. When she wasn't reading it, she was thinking about what she had already read. She was drawn to the book in a way she had never experienced before—almost as if she recognized the stories while knowing that she'd never heard them. A feeling of comfortable familiarity enveloped her even as she encountered startling new concepts.

Thoughts of Mary Jones also consumed her. Knowing that Mary had studied and come to love this unique book was another motivating force behind Sarah's voracious reading. She wondered, not without misgivings, if her own positive response to the book was similar to Mary's. Was she too being led to acceptance of the doctrine it contained?

She was careful to put the book out of sight when her mother came to check on her, but it was hard not to let slip the words, pictures, and ideas tumbling through her thoughts. There could be no doubt that her mother would not approve of her reading material. She knew that the day would come when she would tell her mother about it. But she wanted to be more sure of her own feelings before she shared anything with anyone else.

On Wednesday morning before leaving for work, Sarah made a phone call. She'd lain awake in bed the night before thinking it through. It was a simple, plausible plan if only the missionaries could work around it.

"Hello, Elder Mitchell speaking!"

Sarah cleared her throat nervously. "Elder Mitchell, this is Sarah Lewis."

"Sarah! We were going to call you this evening. How's everything going?"

"Well, I'm hoping to go Christmas shopping in Chester on Saturday and I wondered . . . I wondered if I could meet you and Elder Sorenson sometime during the day?"

"You bet! We'd love to. What would be a good time for you?"

"How about three o'clock?"

"That would be great. Shall we meet you at the church?"

"Yes, if that's alright?"

"You bet! We'll plan on it. We'll meet you there on Saturday at three."

"Alright. Thank you. Elder Mitchell."

"Thanks for calling, Sarah. Bye!"

"Goodbye!"

Sarah stood and stared at the telephone in shock for a few seconds after she'd replaced the receiver. She could scarcely believe she'd done it. The enormity of what she was getting herself into terrified her if she allowed herself to think about it. She tried to tell herself that she had just arranged a casual meeting to clarify some things that she'd wondered about during her recent reading. She wasn't too sure however, that that was a truly honest appraisal.

Later that day, Sarah broke the news of her pending trip to her mother.

"Mam, I've decided to go to Chester on Saturday to do some Christmas shopping."

Her mother looked at her in surprise. "Chester? That's quite a drive. Can't you find what you need closer to home? In Oswestry maybe?"

"Perhaps. But Chester's such a lovely place to shop. I didn't get a chance to look around when I was there for the concert. So I thought I'd go back." It was true—to a point. But it didn't stop Sarah from feeling extremely uncomfortable. She'd rarely kept the truth from her mother, and didn't like doing it now. She hoped that her mother would not sense something amiss.

"Well alright dear. If that's what you want to do." Annie continued to look a little mystified. "Just be sure you watch the weather forecast in case any more storms are on the horizon."

"I will, Mam." Sarah paused. "D'you want me to get you anything there?"

Annie's interest quickened. "Well, now that you mention it, I might put together a little list for you."

Sarah groaned. "Just make sure it is a *little* list!"

Annie laughed. "Alright! Alright!"

Chapter 11

Sarah left early on Saturday morning. She carried her handbag (with the Book of Mormon safely stowed inside), her own Christmas shopping list, a medium-sized list from her mother and a request for a particular brand of knitting wool from Aunty Lil.

The journey passed quickly. Once in Chester, she was fortunate to find a centrally located parking spot downtown. The city was already filling up with Christmas shoppers. The store fronts were glowing with lights, decorations, and tempting wares. Sarah was soon caught up in the madding throng. She thoroughly enjoyed wandering through one shop after another, casting her eyes about for just the right gift for the people on her list.

She spent over an hour in a toy shop deliberating over what to buy for Aled. She finally decided on a large set of wooden dinosaur figurines that came with three different backdrops. She thought it ample fuel for his vivid imagination and hoped it would fill some of the quiet times winter weather would enforce on the farm.

She found a beautifully handcrafted set of pottery casserole dishes for her mother. Annie was always pleased to receive something that she could use with her infrequent bed and breakfast guests.

While hunting for the specific wool that Aunty Lil had asked for, Sarah found some other yarn. It was a pale lavender color and made of the softest lambs' wool. It would make a perfect shawl for Aunty Lil. Sarah knew that she didn't have the skill to do the yarn justice, but Aunty Lil did. Aunty Lil filled many winter hours knitting. She would love the feel of this wool and enjoy making something beautiful out of it.

It wasn't until her stomach growled loudly that Sarah realized how late it had become. She stopped at a bakery and bought a Cornish pasty and after only a moment's hesitation, treated herself to a chocolate eclair too. She made her way slowly back to the car loaded down with purchases. She was tempted to store them in the boot and go back to the shops again, but it was not in her nature to break her commitments. She had promised to meet the missionaries, so regardless of her cold feet, meet with them she would.

To Sarah's surprise, Elder Mitchell and Elder Sorenson were not the only ones at the church when she arrived. There were several cars in the car park. The building doors were unlocked and as Sarah entered she could hear the sound of children's excited voices through the doors that led to the back of the chapel. The missionaries met her in the foyer. They must have seen the curiosity in Sarah's eyes.

"They're holding a Primary Quarterly Activity in the cultural hall," Elder Mitchell said.

He may as well have been speaking Greek. Sarah smiled blankly. Elder Sorenson saw her expression and grinned.

"What Elder Mitchell is trying to say is that once every three months or so the children get together for an activity day. The back of the chapel is closed off and forms a large gym or hall. That's what they're doing in there today."

"It sounds like they're having a good time," Sarah said as the children's chatter turned to song.

"Come and see," invited Elder Sorenson.

They walked over to the heavy double doors. Elder Sorenson opened one a fraction and moved back so that Sarah could see inside. About a dozen children were sitting cross-legged in a semi-circle. A dark-haired lady was standing in front of them, leading them as they sang. Sarah recognized the song immediately. It was "Away in a Manger." Behind the children, three large tables had been set up. They were covered in a multitude of objects ranging from colored pieces of paper and ribbons to crayons, glue, and cotton balls. Judging by the general disarray, Sarah guessed that the children had already worked at the tables. Her guess was affirmed when she looked back at the children. Several of them were clutching homemade tree ornaments and fluffy white decorative snowmen.

Sarah stepped back and Elder Sorenson allowed the door to close softly. They walked over to the office where they had met before. With the sound of the children's voices raised in song as a muted background, Sarah and the missionaries knelt in prayer and began another discussion. They spoke of Christ, of faith, baptism and repentance, then the gift of the Holy Ghost given after baptism. Sarah was intrigued by the different perspective given to her on the Godhead and the purpose of life. She was particularly touched by what the missionaries told her about their belief in the next life, the importance of families, and the possibility of being with loved ones even after death. She thought of her father. Was he watching over her now? If he was, how did he feel about her investigating this new religion? She wished she knew.

Rather to her own surprise, Sarah realized that she had enjoyed talking with the missionaries. There had been a good feeling between them. Then, as their discussion came to a close, Elder Mitchell ruined it all.

"Sarah, we'd like to set a date for you to be baptized. Would next Saturday be a good day for you?"

Stunned, Sarah could only gape at him. Elder Mitchell, aware that her reaction was not all good, played for time.

"Elder Sorenson and I feel that you have the beginning of a strong testimony in your heart. You understand the concepts we've discussed with you and feel good about them . . . "

"Elder Mitchell," Sarah interrupted him, her initial shock replaced by indignation. "I'm not getting baptized on Saturday! I'm still not sure how *I* feel about your Church, so I have no idea how you can! I have to admit that I've found what you've told me fascinating, and I agree with a lot of it, but that doesn't mean I'm ready to commit to be baptized. I take my commitments very seriously. One this important isn't something that I decide on a whim or in a hurry."

As Sarah spoke the words, memories of a similar conversation flooded into her mind. Brian's crazy proposal had been done in a similar, overconfident, even overbearing manner. What was it with these Mormon men?

"I'd better go now. I've got a long drive home." Sarah rose and the two young men followed suit.

Elder Mitchell appeared crestfallen as he took her hand. Elder Sorenson however, beamed with pleasure and shook her hand enthusiastically. Sarah caught the puzzled glance Elder Mitchell threw him.

"I'm really glad that you can sense just how important this is, Sarah," Elder Sorenson said. "I also took my time coming to recognize the truthfulness of the gospel before I was baptized. Like you, I wanted to be sure. Maybe we Europeans are a bit more cautious than our American brothers and sisters!" He smiled at her with encouragement. "Take this extra reading material. Continue to read the Book of Mormon. And pray. Pray always that you will come to know what is right."

Elder Sorenson handed her a small stack of pamphlets and another book. The title read "Doctrine and Covenants." Sarah accepted them, but not without some reluctance.

"All we ask of you, Sarah," Elder Sorenson continued, "is that you seek to know if the Book of Mormon is truly the word of God. When you come to know this, as Elder Mitchell and I do, then will you promise to be baptized?"

Sarah could see no gracious way out of this corner. She nodded her head. "If," she placed great emphasis on the word, "I find that the Book of Mormon is what you claim it to be, then I will be baptized. But other than that I'll make no promises!"

Elder Sorenson shook her hand again. "Thank you Sarah. We will be praying for you."

🕉 🕉 🕉

The next two weeks sped by in a flurry of Christmas preparations. Sarah was kept busy at school with various childhood ailments, and also spent several hours helping at the shop. Even the local shop experienced a boom in sales during the Christmas season—especially in baking supplies and last-minute small gift items.

Her discussions with the missionaries and what she had read of the Book of Mormon were never far from her mind, but she had no chance to do any more reading during that time. Her mother mentioned once that the 'foreign man' had called again while she was out. Sarah had been rather relieved that she had not had to talk to him. She wasn't ready for that exchange yet.

Christmas morning arrived with three inches of fresh snow on the ground. After eating breakfast, Annie and Sarah bundled up warmly and walked through the pristine whiteness towards the chapel. Their feet crunched and their breath came out in puffy cloudbursts. They met other friends and neighbors heading the same way. The air rang with calls of "Merry Christmas" and the joyful laughter of children. A couple of little boys, who just couldn't contain their exuberance, let a handful of snowballs fly. They were quickly called to order by a stern word from their father walking a few yards behind them. Sarah gave them a conspiratorial wink as she passed by. They gave her answering grins.

"Merry Christmas, Miss Lewis!" they called in unison.

"Merry Christmas, boys!" she replied.

The chapel was full. Sarah was pleased to see that Kevin, Mair, and Aled had made it, despite the slippery roads. Aunty Lil had arrived just ahead of them. They squeezed onto the family bench together.

"Aunty Sarah, Father Christmas came!" Aled's excitement permeated his whisper.

"Did he really?" Sarah whispered back with feigned amazement, unable to conceal a smile at his obvious delight.

Kevin hushed his young son, who pulled a face and reluctantly turned to face the front. The pulpit had been decorated with evergreens, red ribbons, and white candles. The chapel was redolent of pine. The organ music came to a crescendo, the congregation stood, and the singing began. It was glorious. Sarah would not have been surprised to see the roof of the chapel raise a few inches. The strong male voices blended with the women's in a rich harmony of parts. It didn't matter how many times Sarah heard the familiar Christmas carols, she loved them every time.

Reverend Davis read the New Testament account of Jesus Christ's birth, and preached a short sermon on loving one another. He read a special Christmas prayer and dismissed them all to their homes.

Sarah soaked it all in. She loved the tradition. She felt secure with a chapel, a minister, and a congregation that she had known since birth. There were no startling changes here. Everything moved on slowly as it had done for centuries before. She wondered how she could even consider breaking out of this mold. She was worshiping God with good Christian people. Surely that was all that was important?

At the close of the service, the villagers gathered outside the chapel to chat for a few minutes. Most people didn't stay long. They were drawn home by something in the oven, impatient children, or a desire to return to their warm fireplaces. It saddened Sarah that the warm, joyful feeling she'd experienced during the service dissipated so fast. It was almost as though once outside the chapel, all thought of religious things were left behind. It didn't seem right somehow. Especially on Christmas day.

She found Aled's mittened hand and grasped it.

"Come on Aled, let's go and see if there's anything for you under the tree at Nain's house!"

Aled needed no second bidding. Hand in hand they skipped and slithered back to the house.

It was not long before the rest of the family joined them. They spent a happy time opening gifts and eating a wonderful Christmas dinner together. After the meal, everyone took turns speaking to Sarah's brother John and his wife Eileen on the phone. They were spending the holiday with Eileen's family in south Wales.

Aled was thrilled with the dinosaur collection that Sarah had purchased in Chester. It kept him busy most of the afternoon. During a lull in the conversation, and between T-rex battles, Aled called out to her, "Hey Aunty Sarah! I got a card from Brian yesterday!"

Coming out of the blue like that, Sarah was unprepared for her own reaction. No one had mentioned Brian for weeks, including Aled. She felt her heartbeat quicken and, to her fury, felt her color rise. She tried to appear nonchalant.

"That's nice, Aled! What did he say?"

"Oh, he said he'd been really busy learning to be a doctor and there's lots of snow where he lives."

Somewhat deflated, all Sarah could say was "Oh."

Aled picked up another dinosaur and prepared to launch another great battle. Over his shoulder he added, "Oh yeah! He said to say 'Hi' to you!"

Sarah looked down at her hands. She shouldn't have allowed herself to expect anything more. After all, she'd heard nothing since he left, and she was the one who had closed the door with a resounding slam on that relationship.

"Oh Sarah, that reminds me! Something came for you from Iris just yesterday. I was so caught up with getting today's dinner ready, I forgot all about it. Let me get it for you."

Sarah raised her head as Annie picked up a white envelope that had been propped up beside the Christmas cards festooning the mantelpiece. She was momentarily disconcerted to find Aunty Lil's penetrating gaze upon her. She wondered, uncomfortably, just how perceptive Aunty Lil really was. She appeared to be the only one really interested in Sarah's reaction to news of either of the Pearsons.

Sarah eagerly grasped the letter from her mother's outstretched hand, opened it quickly, and began to read.

Dear Sarah,

How can I ever thank you? Mary Jones's letters were more than I had ever dared hope for. Thanks to your marvelous translation, I feel that I have finally come to know my grandmother.

I have made copies of the original letters and your translation for each of my children. It will be their best Christmas gift ever.

Thank you so much.

All my love,

Iris.

Sarah carefully refolded the short letter. It warmed her to know that her efforts had been so appreciated. More than that, she was glad that Mary Jones would at last receive the appreciation she deserved. She had been a remarkable woman, and one that Sarah had come to admire deeply. Sarah sighed.

Aunty Lil's soft voice made her jump. "Everything alright, Sarah?"

Aunty Lil was still watching her. Sarah smiled. "Yes, thanks, Aunty Lil." She had a sudden urge to share the whole story of the letters with Aunty Lil, but before she could say or do anything, there was a clink of china and her mother set down a tray laden with teapot, teacups, and turkey sandwiches.

"I'll pour and you pass them out, Sarah," Annie directed.

The moment with her aunt was gone.

ૐ ૐ ૐ

The next day was Boxing Day. There was a feeling of life slowing down to its normal even keel once more. After spending the morning writing a few thank-you cards and helping her mother clear up the post-Christmas debris, Sarah donned her coat and boots and headed outside.

She didn't give much thought to her direction. She wandered down the lane, enjoying the crisp, clear air. The sky was cobalt blue. A few wispy clouds painted trails across the mountain tops. The snow crystals glistened in the sun. All was very quiet. Sarah caught sight of an occasional hardy bird, but they were out for serious food-gathering and had no time for song. The livestock were all gathered in barns and sheds, so even the familiar lowing of cattle was missing.

There was only one sound breaking the slumbering silence. Despite the thin sheet of ice along its bank, the river still chortled its way through the village. The fast-moving water had never, in Sarah's lifetime, frozen completely. On this day as she walked along the lane that followed its course, the water positively pranced its way downstream. The clear liquid shimmered in the bright sunlight, and tiny rainbows danced beside the icicles that hung from the shrubs nearby.

Sarah reached the wooden footbridge and stood leaning on the handrail and watching the river below. Not too much further downstream there was a fork in the river. Both branches of the river could be followed by footpath. As children, her brothers had always wanted to follow the right-hand fork. The river bed became wide there and the water calmed to a moderate flow. It was an idyllic fishing spot. It was also a perfect place to practice skimming stones across the placid river surface. Kevin and John would spend hours trying to outskim each other.

Sarah had always preferred the left fork of the river. There the river narrowed to not much more than a stream. As a child, Sarah had always thought that the water that took that turn was happier. The riverbed was rocky, and the river leaped over the stones in its path sending out spurts of white foam. It gurgled and sang and raced on its way. With her childish imagination, Sarah had been convinced that the river was laughing in fun.

Standing on the bridge, Sarah acknowledged that she had reached a fork in her life. Somehow circumstances, curiosity, and a powerful inner urging had brought her to a point that necessitated making some serious choices. If she spent too long considering them, she felt weighed down by the burden. But she had put it off too long. She knew she wouldn't be free of that weight until a decision was made and her course set.

In the peaceful atmosphere of that solitary setting, Sarah tried to organize her thoughts. By far, the easiest course would be to turn her back on all she'd read and learned about the Mormon Church and just continue on with her life as she had been doing before the Chester concert, Mary Jones's letters, or even the Pearsons's visit. Sarah sighed. Life had been so simple then. She'd loved being back in the village. She loved her work with the children. She felt she was where she belonged.

Now it seemed that she was fighting an unfamiliar restlessness. First Brian had burst into her life, had awakened feelings she'd never known before and had left as quickly as he'd entered. Without knowing it, Brian had caused Sarah to really question her happiness. Would she always be content living in the village with her mother and then, in years to come, alone? Her brief time with Brian had forced Sarah to look at her life as a single adult. If she was totally honest with herself, she knew that was not what she wanted forever. She wanted to love and be loved. She wanted a husband and children. She wanted to create a home of her own. Her opportunities for those things were bleak at best if she remained at Pen-y-Bryn.

Then there was the Mormon Church itself. Brian and his mother had torn down many of her preconceived notions about the Mormon Church. Then Mary Jones's indomitable spirit, courage, and conviction had reached out to her through her letters. Visiting the church in Chester, the missionaries, their discussions, her reading . . . Sarah didn't think she could really put all that behind her as though none of it had ever existed. But if she continued to learn about this new religion, if she were to embrace it . . . whatever would her mother say? Her brothers? Aunty Lil? Sarah shuddered. Surely it wasn't worth the anguish?

And so Sarah's thoughts churned on as she absently watched the water flow by. The river chose its course at the fork. Sarah needed to choose hers too. She longed for someone to confide in. Someone with whom to share this load.

"I wish you were still here Dad," Sarah whispered the words out loud. "What would you tell me to do?"

Apart from the omnipresent sound of the river, the silence around her was complete. Sarah looked downriver again. It was Boxing Day, she reasoned. New Year's Eve was a week away. A time for new beginnings and resolutions. She'd give herself that one week. She would read and make a real effort to know if the Mormon Church was for her. If she was not convinced in one week, she would put it behind her and move on with her life.

Filled with new resolve, Sarah's steps were lighter as she made her way back home. For a week at least, she had a productive course to follow.

ʚ ʚ ʚ

Sarah was true to her word. Over the next three days she spent a lot of time in her room reading the Book of Mormon. Although there were many parts that she struggled to understand, she couldn't deny how drawn she felt to it. She felt good as she read it, and that positive feeling stayed with her long after she closed the pages.

It was not until the fourth day however, while digging through the bottom drawer of her chest of drawers, that Sarah found the other book. She was trying to find a light-blue wool sweater that Aunty Lil had knitted for her a couple of years before. She hadn't worn it for some time but she was pretty sure that if she dug deep enough she'd find it in that drawer. She did, and as she pulled it out, another object, hard and rectangular, came with it.

It fell to the floor as she unfolded the sweater. Sarah froze and for a few short seconds just stared at it. Then, with a small cry she reached out and picked it up. She ran her hand across the soft, leather cover before tracing the gold embossed letters with a trembling finger: *The Book of Mormon — Another Testament of Jesus Christ. Brian D. Pearson.*

She opened the book. A small piece of paper fluttered out. Memories flooded back as Sarah read it. *Dear Sarah, Please forgive me for not being more sensitive to your feelings. I hope you will accept this book. I know that nothing can bring you more happiness than living by the teachings it reveals—and more than anything, I want you to be happy. I will never forget you or the time we spent together. With love, Brian.*

Sarah felt a lump rise in her throat. She had spurned his gift; had all but thrown it away. Carefully she opened up the cover. The pages felt soft from much use. As she began slowly turning them, she noticed how many were marked with colored pencil. Notes had been written in tiny print along the margins. Sarah felt a rush of pleasure as she realized that she recognized most of the references Brian had inserted. Nephi, Alma, Mosiah, Mormon, and Moroni—these were all names she knew now.

As she continued to flip through the pages in her hand, she began to gain a sense of what Brian had given her. She could only imagine how many hours he had spent reading, marking, and cross-referencing this book.

Pictures flitted in and out of Sarah's mind. She saw the two leather-bound books sitting on the table in the guest room. She remembered knocking on his door at night. He'd been awake reading. In her mind's eye she saw this book in Brian's hands. He had quoted it from memory at Pystill Glas.

Looking down at it now, Sarah had no doubts. Brian Pearson loved this book. It was perhaps the most precious possession he had with him while at Pen-y-Bryn. And he had given it to her.

She began to pick out sections that Brian had underlined. She followed his notes and tried to glean some understanding from his insights. Time stood still. For the first time, Sarah felt that she had someone beside her as she read, someone trying to guide her through the new concepts, someone opening her eyes to all that this book could reveal.

As the shadows began to lengthen in her bedroom, Sarah came to a section in Moroni. It was Chapter ten, verses four and five. She read the underlined words once. Then, as their impact reached her she read them again:

And when ye shall receive these things, I would exhort you that ye would ask God, the Eternal Father, in the name of Christ, if these things are not true; and if ye shall ask with a sincere heart, with real intent, having faith in Christ, he will manifest the truth of it unto you, by the power of the Holy Ghost.

And by the power of the Holy Ghost ye may know the truth of all things.

That was it. Suddenly Sarah understood what she needed to do. The desire for counsel and guidance that she had experienced so acutely on her walk to the footbridge was real. Her error had been in limiting her scope. There really was no other person who could aid her completely. She needed to go to a higher source. She must ask God.

It was easier said than done. Prayers for Sarah had been learned by rote and recited by rote. She had yet to formulate her own prayer and express a personal need. She wished she knew exactly what to do. As she sat, feeling her confidence ebb until it bordered on despair, another image of Brian came unbidden into her mind. She saw him kneeling beside a large boulder on the mountainside near Pystill Glas. The rain was falling. She was beside him and he was praying. He was praying for Aled, that they would find him.

The image was so vivid that Sarah wrapped her arms around herself. She felt the cold and damp and fear again. But Brian's prayer had been like a blanket of peace covering her frightened being. He had used simple words, filled with sincerity. Surely she could do that too. Her desire was real and intense. If what Brian and the missionaries had told her was right, God would overlook her inexperience.

Before she could allow herself to talk her way out of it, Sarah knelt down beside her bed. She bowed her head and began to pray. At first her words were stilted and awkward. She searched for the correct opening address and phraseology. After verbally stumbling for a few minutes, she knew it would not work. She let go of the restrictions that had bound her prayers since childhood and poured out her heart. She recounted her experiences of the last few months. She tried to explain the mixture of emotions that teemed through her and the conflicting loyalties vying for dominance.

She had come to realize that, like Mary Jones, she could not leave behind her Welsh Methodist heritage and family traditions without being sure that what she was doing was right. She feared hurting those she loved. Only total conviction would give her the strength to move away from all that was familiar and to stand up to possible criticism. She had to know that this new religion was truly what it claimed to be: the restored Gospel of Jesus Christ.

Emotionally spent, Sarah laid her head upon the bed. She was still on her knees and still had her eyes closed when she felt the change. It was as though a glowing warmth was filling her chest. The heaviness that had weighed down her shoulders for so long was lifted. She experienced a wave of overwhelming joy that coursed through her. Scarcely able to believe what was happening, Sarah raised her head and opened her eyes. Even the room that minutes before had been so shadowed by the coming dusk seemed brighter and full of radiant light.

Sarah reached out for Brian's book and clutched it to her. For the first time in her life she knew that her individual prayer—her own communing with God—had been heard and answered. She was filled with awe and overwhelming happiness.

భ భ భ

Sarah was sure that her mother would notice something different when she finally went downstairs. She still felt as though she was glowing.

"Hello Mam!"

Annie was stirring a pan of custard at the stove. She turned her head at Sarah's voice.

"Sarah! Whatever have you been doing upstairs for so long? I was going to come and check on you."

"Reading mostly," Sarah replied in a noncommittal tone. Her experience and feelings were too tender to share yet. She wanted to keep them close and savor them alone a little while longer.

Annie clucked her tongue and shook her head. "I've never known anyone to forget the time the way you do when you read or play the harp. You probably haven't eaten anything since breakfast, have you?"

When she stopped to think about it, Sarah realized with surprise that she actually hadn't had any breakfast either. She pulled a face. "Sorry Mam, I forgot!" She tried to erase her mother's frown "But dinner will taste even better because I'm so hungry now!"

"You'll waste away to nothing, you will!"

Sarah smiled at Annie's warning. She'd heard it too many times before.

Later that evening, while Annie was watching the news on the television, Sarah phoned the missionaries.

"Hello, Elder Sorenson speaking."

"Elder Sorenson, this is Sarah Lewis."

"Sarah! How are you?"

"Fine, thank you!" Sarah didn't want to prolong this. "I'd like to meet you again, if I may." She took a deep breath. "I'd like to talk to you about getting baptized."

The joy in Elder Sorenson's voice when he spoke again made Sarah smile. His undeniable Scandinavian accent overshadowed the American lingo.

"That's so awesome! You bet!"

🐛 🐛 🐛

A trip to the January sales in Chester was the excuse Sarah used for her appointment with the missionaries. If her mother was surprised, she didn't show it. The January sales were a legitimate draw for any bargain lover.

Sarah did spend the morning browsing through some of the larger department stores before meeting the missionaries at the church once again. Their enthusiasm was contagious. Sarah felt a thrill as they discussed the concepts of eternal families and temple work. She thought about her father. Had he already heard and accepted this message too? She wanted to think so; it made her feel less isolated. She promised to keep the Word of Wisdom. Alcohol and tobacco would not be hard. They had never held any attraction to her. But tea—that was another matter entirely. How was she ever going to explain this to her mother?

Then the missionaries brought up the subject of her baptism. As they each bore their testimony of the truthfulness of the Gospel and of the rightness of her decision, Sarah felt a return of the warm glow she had experienced after her prayer at home. It was not as intense this time, but it was there nevertheless. Grateful for this personal reaffirmation, Sarah accepted the missionaries' suggested date.

She knew that the next thing she needed to do was to tell her mother. It wouldn't take Annie long to notice that Sarah was no longer drinking tea. Sarah also wanted to be able to drive to Chester for Church functions without needing a deceptive excuse. She had not liked keeping the whole truth from her mother. It had always been something that she'd avoided in the past. All reason pointed to telling her mother as soon as possible. Reason however, did not take into account maternal emotions. Sarah was pretty sure of how her mother would react—and she was not looking forward to the experience.

She was right. It wasn't helped by the fact that the calm, peaceful environment that she'd hoped for didn't materialize. She broke the news over breakfast the next morning, after she'd refused her mother's third offer of a cup of tea.

"Mam, I'm afraid you're going to have to get used to this. I'm not going to be drinking tea any more."

Annie looked at her as though her daughter had gone mad. "What on earth are you talking about?"

"I'm not going to be drinking tea any more," Sarah repeated, "or coffee either."

Annie still looked as though she was hearing things. Sarah took a deep breath and ploughed ahead. "I've decided to join the Mormon Church."

Annie's face blanched and she put the teapot down with a thud. "You've decided what?" Her voice was not much more than a harsh whisper.

Sarah clenched her fists beneath the table. This was not going to be easy. "I'm going to join the Mormon Church. I've done a lot of reading. I've listened to the missionaries' message. I've even prayed about it. I'm going to be baptized next week."

Annie pulled out a chair and plopped into it like a doll with all the stuffing knocked out of her. "The Mormons! Whatever are you thinking? Are you mad?"

Sarah felt her indignation rise. "No! I am not mad! How can you say such a thing? You know I'd never do anything like this unless I was sure I was making the right decision."

"Up until one minute ago I'd have said you'd never do such a thing at all!" Annie's voice was rising.

Sarah bit back a bitter retort. Using all the self control she could muster, she continued. "I'm getting baptized next Sunday in Chester. It would mean a lot if you'd come."

"Chester! Is that why you've been going there so much? Sarah how could you?"

"Mam, I know this is a shock, but I really feel like I'm doing the right thing."

"The right thing!" Annie shouted. "You've been brainwashed! What will all our friends and neighbors think? What will they say?"

Sarah stared at her in disbelief. "Is that all you care about? What your friends and neighbors think? What's it got to do with them anyway? D'you have any idea how many of your friends's children don't even go to church? Is that what you'd prefer? You'd rather have me be an agnostic or even an atheist than worship at a Mormon Church?

"Just because it's socially unacceptable not to drink alcohol or tea doesn't make me some sort of outcast. You didn't throw the Pearsons out, did you?"

Annie looked up, nonplussed. "The Pearsons?"

"Yes, Mam. The Pearsons are Mormons. And I know you liked them."

"Did they set you off on this craziness? They're Americans. Americans are always doing strange things. You're Welsh. You have no right ignoring all your family's past and joining some American cult."

"It's not a cult! Give me some credit! It's the fastest growing Christian church in the world. And I believe it's the true church. And anyway, just because I'm joining another church doesn't mean I'm giving up my heritage."

Annie's face was an implacable mask. "You've already been baptized. You don't need to be baptized again!"

Sarah could see that this conversation was getting her nowhere. It would be better to bring things up again than continue at this point. Fighting discouragement she said, "I'm sorry, Mam, but I've made my decision."

Annie Lewis didn't say anything. She remained seated as Sarah got up and picked up her coat.

"I'll see you after work," Sarah said as she walked to the back door. Annie's lips remained pressed tight. Her only acknowledgment of Sarah's departure was a small, mute nod.

Sarah left the house wanting to weep. She'd rarely seen her mother so upset. Would she ever come round to Sarah's way of thinking, or had Sarah just opened an irreparable rift between them? Was joining another church really worth all this pain? Even as a student nurse in faraway Birmingham, Sarah had never felt so alone.

The never-ending pile of paperwork and demand for plasters and throat lozenges at school helped keep Sarah from dwelling on the morning's confrontation. During her lunch break she took a few minutes to read from Brian's Book of Mormon. It boosted her spirits. Nevertheless, her steps slowed as she made her way home at the end of the day. She wasn't sure what to expect from her mother.

To Sarah's amazement, Annie greeted her as though nothing had happened. Encouraged, Sarah exchanged a few words with her before running upstairs to change. Her pleasure was short-lived however. When they sat down to their meal she noticed that her mother had set a cup of tea for them both. Sarah recognized the signals. Annie had used the method before—if you ignore it, it will go away! Her mother was going to treat Sarah's announcement that morning as though it was nothing more than a childish, passing fad.

Had Annie but known it, her actions had the opposite effect than she'd hoped for. Sarah was starting to feel the strain of having been without tea for twenty-four hours. The smell of the freshly brewed beverage was almost more than she could bear. Frankly, she had found her deep craving for the drink during the day to be quite eye opening. She was amazed at how much she had come to depend upon tea to pick her up. At this late hour, she was dying for just a little sip.

Now she looked at the cup beside her plate and felt a stirring resentment fight for advantage over her craving. She was a full-grown, independent woman. She did not deserve to have her feelings or decisions treated as if they were nothing—especially by her own mother. Without saying a word, Sarah picked up the cup and walked over to the sink. She poured the steaming brown liquid down the sink, rinsed the cup out and filled a clean glass with water. She then returned to the table with glass in hand, sat down, and began to eat.

The remainder of the meal passed in stony silence. Sarah was relieved to have it behind her. She helped clear up, then took refuge in the front room with her harp. She soothed her frayed emotions with her music.

The remainder of the week followed much the same pattern. Sarah's conversations with her mother were stilted at best. Her mother continued to try to unobtrusively undermine Sarah's decision without ever coming right out and talking about it. The cups of tea continued. An invitation to give a harp recital at the Welsh Methodist chapel seemed just a little too serendipitous. The minister was invited to tea without Sarah's prior knowledge, and gave her a mini-sermon on the evils of Mormonism. Then as if in a last ditch effort, the big gun was brought in. Annie asked Kevin to come over on Saturday evening.

Although somewhat fortified by a short conversation with the missionaries a little earlier, Sarah viewed the inevitable protests from her brother with foreboding.

Kevin had never been one to beat around the bush. As she entered the kitchen where he and her mother sat at the table, he came right to the point.

"What's all this Mam's been telling me about you wanting to join some American cult, Sarah?"

It was only the obvious concern in his voice that prevented Sarah from turning around and walking right back out without so much as favoring him with a response. Instead, she stood still and met his eyes. She'd never come out on top in an argument with her brother in the past. He was bigger, older and therefore (in his estimation) wiser. He always put her on the defensive. She realized that with his aggressive question, he'd instinctively put her there again now. She would get no where with Kevin if he backed her into a corner. She must not let it happen. A flash of inspiration hit her, and as it did so she knew what she must do.

Without dropping eye contact she said, "Kev, of all the men you know, tell me some of the ones you admire the most."

Disconcerted, Kevin looked at her blankly. "What?"

"Give me the names of the men you know that you admire the most," Sarah repeated patiently.

"Reverend Davis," Kevin countered with a small smile.

Sarah nodded her agreement. "Who else?"

Kevin shook his head. "Come on Sarah! Stop trying to change the subject."

"I'm not changing the subject. I'll answer your question as soon as you've answered mine. Now, who else do you admire?"

Kevin rolled his eyes. "Dad!"

"Alright, who else?"

"How many d'you want?"

"I don't know. Just give it some thought."

"The Prime-minister, John Wayne . . . "

Sarah shook her head in frustration. "No, Kevin. They have to be people you know personally!"

"Good grief, girl!" Kevin thought for a minute. "Alright, how about John, Mair's Dad, Huw Jones . . . " He paused again then added, "the doctors that worked on Aled. And Brian Pearson. How's that!"

Sarah broke into a beaming smile. "Perfect!" she said. "Now I'll answer your question. I'm not joining an American cult. I'm joining the Church of Jesus Christ of Latter-day Saints. It's a world-wide Christian church that is growing fast, quite simply because it's true." Then, unable to completely hide her sense of victory, she added, "It's also the church that one of the men you most admire belongs to!"

"What on earth are you talking about?" Kevin looked totally perplexed by his sister's response.

"Brian Pearson is a Mormon," Annie said in a lifeless voice.

Kevin stared at his mother, then swiftly turned back to Sarah. "Did he put you up to this?"

Sarah was startled to hear a hint of anger in Kevin's tone. "No he didn't! I've had no contact with him at all since he left here. Even Aled can tell you that.

"I only brought up his name to prove to you that I'm not joining a cult full of weirdos. It's a church full of good Christian people who are trying to do the right thing."

"You've been going to a 'church full of good Christian people who are trying to do the right thing' all your life!" Kevin countered.

"I know that!" Sarah took a deep breath. "But at chapel we don't have *all* the truth." She struggled to phrase her feelings so that she could communicate without offending either her mother or brother. "I've always loved going to chapel. My spirits are lifted when I hear the singing and minister's messages. But then we leave and it's all gone.

"There's nothing to hold on to all week. I feel like I've been living two lives: my normal life every day and my religious life for an hour on Sunday. I don't think it's supposed to be that way. I think we're supposed to carry something with us all the time.

"I don't know if you noticed it, but there was something about Brian Pearson. Have you ever seen the people of Pen-y-Bryn respond to a stranger like they did to Brian? Usually they're so reserved, especially with English speakers.

"Maybe you think it was just him. And perhaps you're right. But I've met other people who are members of his Church now. And they have that same 'something' that Brian had.

"I've done a lot of reading. I've talked to the missionaries and I've prayed. I'm convinced that what they have is the whole truth. By living the way their Church teaches them, they're able to keep that religious or good feeling with them all day, every day. And we respond to it, without even knowing what it is. They have an inner peace and happiness that comes with their religious understanding and lifestyle.

"I want that peace and happiness too." Sarah's voice broke.

Kevin rose and turned to his mother. "You've got yourself a real problem this time, Mam. You've raised a daughter as stubborn as yourself. She knows what she wants and whether or not you and I agree with her, I for one am not going to stand in her way. I can't understand all this religious stuff at all. But the only time I've seen her this worked up was when she wanted her first harp—and look where that got her!"

Kevin walked over to Sarah and put his hand on her shoulder. She looked up at him in wide-eyed amazement. She'd been bracing for an onslaught. She was unprepared for this.

"I'd say you were off your rocker Sarah, but that's what I said about the harp, so I'll reserve judgement for now." Then his tone became more serious. "But I'll tell you this; if I find out this church of yours is anything less than what you've led me to believe, I'll be on you like a ton of bricks."

Sarah managed a tremulous smile. "Thanks, Kev."

As Kevin picked up his coat and prepared to leave, Sarah stole a glance at her mother. She was obviously as stunned by Kevin's response as Sarah had been.

"Kevin, is that all you're going to say to her?" Annie's voice was incredulous.

"There's not much more I can say, Mam. I know Sarah well enough to tell when her mind's set."

"But Kevin . . . Mormon?" Annie spoke the word as though it was an insidious disease.

"I didn't say that I like the idea, Mam. I just said that arguing with Sarah right now isn't going to do any good. Like I said, if it ends up being something other than the Christian religion she's told me about, then we'll have another, much longer conversation with one another!" Sarah recognized the warning directed her way, but Kevin's next words totally superseded it.

"I trusted the life of my son to Brian Pearson and he came through like no one else I know could've done. I guess I'm willing to trust his judgement on religion too."

With that, Kevin turned, waved, and was gone. He left both women staring at the door he closed behind him.

There was nothing more that Sarah could say. She took advantage of her mother's shocked silence and made a hasty, albeit quiet, retreat. She walked up the stairs to her room marveling at what had occurred in the kitchen. By the time she reached her room, Sarah had come to realize that another of her prayers had been answered.

Chapter 12

Sarah hummed as she drove towards Chester the next morning. The blue sky was bright with promise, and she was filled with nervous excitement. She sensed that this day would be a turning point in her life, and she wanted it to be wonderful.

The only real blot on her day was the knowledge that she was acting directly against her mother's wishes. Annie had been cold and brusque with her at breakfast. It was completely counter to the warm relationship they usually enjoyed. It worried Sarah enough that she wondered if she was really doing the right thing. She had to work continually to control her residual fears. When they threatened to engulf her, she focused on the warm feelings she had experienced each time she'd prayed about her decision to join the Church of Jesus Christ of Latter-day Saints. Just the memory of those feelings sustained her.

Kevin's parting words the night before had done a lot to bolster her confidence too. She allowed her thoughts to rest on Brian. He had obviously made an even greater impression upon Kevin than she had realized. Would he be pleased with her decision to join his Church? Unbidden, words from the note in his Book of Mormon came into her mind:

' . . . I know that nothing can bring you more happiness than living by the teachings it reveals— and more than anything, I want you to be happy. . .'

Yes, Sarah thought, no matter what Brian's feelings were for her now, she knew he would be pleased.

Elder Sorenson and Elder Mitchell were waiting for her at the Church. Sacrament Meeting was just beginning as they took their seats. Sarah tried to concentrate on the speakers's messages and the words of the prayers. She sang the familiar hymns with vigor and sight-read the others. She couldn't help but feel rather daunted by how much she had to learn, how much she had to adjust to. Even referring to other members of the congregation as "brother" or "sister" was alien to her. But she hoped, given time, she would feel more comfortable with such differences.

When her own baptism was announced over the pulpit, Sarah was surprised. She smiled ruefully to herself as the bishop invited anyone to attend. She knew no one but the missionaries, so she was expecting a very quiet service with merely the three of them in attendance.

She met with the missionaries again after Sacrament Meeting. They introduced a few more principles of doctrine to her. The payment of tithing came as a bit of a shock, but she accepted it as part of the commitment she'd already promised to make (while privately hoping that there weren't any other similar surprises still in store). Elder Sorenson then introduced her to two other missionaries visiting Chester that day. He called them Zone Leaders, and they spent a few minutes with her, discussing her upcoming baptism.

As they left the office where they'd been talking, other meetings were ending. People milled through the foyer, a few of them exchanging greetings with Sarah. All were pleasant and welcoming, and Sarah felt cheered by their open acceptance of her.

Before long however, the temporary congestion in the foyer dissipated. People left for home. The missionaries guided Sarah over to the man who had conducted the two Church meetings she had attended. He was standing talking to another couple, and when he finished his conversation, Elder Mitchell extended his hand. The older man shook it immediately.

"Bishop Edwards, this is Sarah Lewis. She's getting baptized this evening."

The older man shook Sarah's hand enthusiastically. "Sarah! I'm very pleased to meet you. We're so pleased to have you joining our ward."

Sarah smiled. "Thank you." This time she knew what was meant by a "ward."

"The missionaries tell me you're from down Bala way?"

"That's right. Pen-y-Bryn. It's just on the other side of the Berwyn mountains from Bala."

"I know it. A beautiful part of the country. Quite a drive for you though." He looked concerned.

"It is, but the roads were clear today. The sunshine makes a big difference."

Bishop Edwards smiled at her. His green eyes crinkled. Sarah could tell that the lined face smiled frequently. "It does indeed. But tell me, you're not planning on going back home before your baptism are you?"

"Well no." Sarah glanced down at her feet to hide her embarrassment. "I was hoping it would be alright if I waited here. I could do some reading perhaps."

"You're more than welcome to stay at the chapel if you'd like to," Bishop Edwards said kindly. "But my wife and I were rather hoping that you'd join us for dinner."

Sarah was momentarily speechless at this show of generosity to a total stranger. "That's very kind of you, but you really don't have to . . . "

The older man raised his hand to stop her. "We'd love to have you. It will give us a chance to get to know you better. The missionaries have already accepted, so you'll have a couple of familiar faces there too."

Sarah smiled at the older man. "Thank you, I'd like to come."

"Splendid!" He said. He looked past Sarah and surveyed the emptying foyer. "We'll see if we can find my wife here somewhere, and you can drive home with us."

"I can follow you in my car," Sarah suggested. "Then you won't have to bring me back."

"That's no problem. We'll be coming back for your baptism anyway."

Sarah decided this was to be a day of surprises. "Are you sure?"

Bishop Edwards chuckled. "Of course. Wouldn't miss it for the world!"

❦ ❦ ❦

Sister Edwards untied the apron covering her ample figure and patted her faded gray hair into place.

"Well now," she said with a pleased sigh, "I do believe we're ready to eat."

The table was laden with a wonderful spread. There was roast beef with peas, carrots, roast potatoes, and Yorkshire pudding. Everything looked delicious. But what impressed Sarah the most was that once everyone was seated, a blessing was offered upon the food.

The Edwardses and the missionaries spoke easily with one another. At first, Sarah was content to sit quietly and listen to the conversations going on around her. Much of the talk at the table revolved around Church matters, but no one appeared overly pious or pompous. There was much laughter and a great feeling of friendship.

Before long, Sarah was drawn into the circle. They asked her about her background and showed genuine interest in her family, her work, and her recent struggle over conversion to their faith. She was moved by Sister Edwards's empathy when the older lady leaned over and patted her hand.

"Try not to fret over your mother, dear. It's hard for her to see her little girl growing independent and moving away from things she thought would never change. Just give her some time. When she realizes you're happy and she's not losing you to a mind-washing cult, she'll come round. Just give her time and continue to show her that you love her."

Sarah bit her lower lip to prevent tears from falling at hearing her wise words. She wished her mother could meet these good people. Perhaps that would help remold her negative opinions.

Bishop Edwards was as perceptive as his wife. He was quick to notice Sarah's distress and deftly steered the conversation onto another topic.

"The missionaries tell me you are musical, Sarah?"

"I enjoy music very much," replied Sarah modestly.

It didn't take long however, before he'd peeled away the layers of Sarah's natural reserve and learned about her talent with the harp and her ability to play the organ. Sister Edwards was ecstatic.

"Oh Sarah, d'you think you could play the organ for our services?"

"Well, some of the hymns are new to me, but I could try." Sarah replied.

"If you could. . . oh, it would be marvelous! We've had an organ for over a year now but we've never even heard it. No one in the ward knows how to play."

Sarah looked at her in amazement. "Is that all! I wondered if there was a special religious reason it wasn't used!"

Bishop Edwards started to chuckle. Before long the others, including Sarah, were laughing too. "I'm sorry," Sarah gasped. "I must seem so silly and naive."

"Not at all!" Bishop Edwards gave her an encouraging smile. "You should hear some of the mistakes I made when I was investigating the Church." He proceeded to regale them all with funny stories from his early days as a Church member.

The time sped by and Sarah could scarcely believe it when Elder Sorenson looked at his watch and announced that it was time they headed back to the church.

The surprises continued when they arrived back at the church. By the time Sister Edwards had found Sarah some white clothing, helped her to change, and walked her into the chapel to join the missionaries, there were about twenty people already seated there. Sarah looked around in wonder.

"Are they all here for my baptism?" she whispered to Elder Mitchell, who was also dressed in white, and was waiting for her at the front of the chapel.

He smiled and nodded.

"But they don't even know me!" she whispered again.

"They consider you a sister already! They want to share this special time with you," Elder Mitchell whispered back.

Sarah didn't know what to think. The short service passed in a blur. Within minutes it seemed, she was being led to the baptismal font. Elder Mitchell was waiting for her in the water. He held her arm in one hand and raised his other to the square. There was a prayer, then she was under the water and up again. It was over.

She shook the water from her eyes. Joy filled her heart. She looked up at the people standing beside the font. They were wreathed in smiles. Some had moisture glistening in their eyes. She turned to Elder Mitchell.

"Thank you!" It was all she could say, but he understood. There was moisture in his eyes too.

Sister Edwards was waiting for her at the top of the stairs, with a large white towel. She wrapped it around Sarah's shivering form and gave her a hug.

"Congratulations, Sarah!"

Sarah smiled. "Thank you."

Once Sarah was dressed, Sister Edwards escorted her back to the chapel. There Elder Sorenson, with Elder Mitchell and Bishop Edwards assisting, confirmed her a member of the Church and bestowed the gift of the Holy Ghost upon her. With Elder Sorenson's pronouncement came the incredible glowing warmth that Sarah had experienced during her first prayer. It filled her whole being and moved her to tears. When the prayer ended and the three men stood back, she rose and silently shook each one's hand. No words were necessary. They all sensed and respected the sacred nature of the moment. Sarah wished the feeling could last forever.

It was hard to leave the warmth of that meeting and the friendly acceptance of the people there. Sarah's only consolation was that she still felt the glowing light within, and was convinced that with time, study, and Church attendance she could nurture it and keep it bright.

Her happiness was dampened considerably, however, when she arrived back home. The dour expression on her mother's face did not bode well.

"I was beginning to wonder if you were ever coming home!"

Sarah felt as if she'd been slapped in the face. She battled to keep calm. She wanted to retain the joy she'd felt earlier. She knew that anger and harsh words would send it fleeing faster than almost anything. Desperately she tried to see past her own hurt feelings and view things from her mother's perspective.

"Sorry, Mam. I'd have called if I'd known you were worried."

"That's right. My only daughter drives off to join some American cult, and I'm not worried!" There was bitterness in Annie's voice. Bitterness that Sarah hadn't heard since her father's death. This was affecting her mother deeply.

Sarah took a deep breath. "Mam, for the hundredth time—it's not a cult! Nothing is going to change that much. I'll still be here with you, working at the school, helping at the shop. . ."

"Not drinking tea, going off to Chester every Sunday, standing out as different in the village!" her mother interrupted.

"Mam, if anyone notices any differences in me, I hope they'll be changes for the better."

"Well I liked you more before all this Mormon falderal!" Annie's harsh words cut to the quick.

"Mam!" Sarah's cry was full of anguish. It succeeded in penetrating her mother's anger. Annie took a step forward.

"Sarah, I. . ."

But Sarah was walking out of the room. As she closed the kitchen door behind her she heard her mother call after her.

"You don't understand, Sarah! You can't do something like this and expect everything to be the same as it was before!"

Sarah held her head up high and kept right on walking, all the way upstairs and into her room. Once there however, she threw herself onto the bed and dissolved into tears.

ॐ ॐ ॐ

It was probably for the best that Sarah had no notion of how prophetic her mother's warning would be. For a few weeks, things did fall into a calm routine. Her work at school continued as it had always done. Somewhat mollified by the prevailing lull, Annie and Sarah slipped into a state of armed neutrality at home, with all religious subjects avoided.

Sarah read from Brian's Book of Mormon every day. She referred to his copious notations often. It was the way she tried to stave off feelings of isolation. She left for Chester each Sunday morning and arrived home in the early evening, cherishing the time she spent at Church each Sunday. Contact with the other members did much to fortify her for the following week.

She had been asked to play the organ for sacrament meeting the first Sunday after her baptism. Since then she had also been asked to play the piano for the children's Primary. She loved being there. In addition to the joy of being with the children, she found the messages and talks given in those meetings helped her understanding of the gospel to grow. The concepts were presented in simple, uncluttered ways to help the children grasp them, and Sarah found herself learning right along with each boy and girl. And as she learned, Sarah's young testimony took root and began to grow.

Then almost overnight, things in the village began to change. It all began innocently enough. A teacher at the school stopped by Sarah's office during her lunch hour. Eliza Thompson was a regular chapel attender and had noticed Sarah's absence at the Welsh Methodist services. Since she'd known Sarah all her life, she knew this to be unusual behavior. She broached the subject with Sarah that afternoon.

"I've missed you at Sunday services, Sarah. Where have you been all these weeks?"

Sarah's heart started thumping. What should she say? Up until now only her mother, Kevin, Mair, and Aunty Lil knew where she went on Sunday. But it couldn't stay that way indefinitely, Sarah rationalized. And Eliza was an old friend. She mustered her courage.

"I've been going to church in Chester," she replied as casually as she could.

"Chester?" Eliza's tone was incredulous. "Why ever would you want to drive all that way to go to church?"

"Well, because that's the closest congregation to Pen-y-Bryn," Sarah said, knowing full well that more explanation would be necessary.

"What ever do you mean?" Eliza was mystified. "There's a chapel and a church right here in the village."

Sarah nodded. "I know that, Eliza. But I've joined the Church of Jesus Christ of Latter-day Saints. Their nearest church is in Chester."

Eliza's mouth opened, closed, then opened again. Finally she squeaked, "You've joined what?

"The Church of Jesus Christ of Latter-day Saints." Sarah looked at her friend anxiously. "It's sometimes called the Mormon Church."

Sarah saw the instinctive recoil immediately. It showed in Eliza's eyes and in her stiffened body.

"You've joined the Mormon Church?" Eliza's voice was not more than a whisper. "But why? Why ever would you do such a thing?"

"Because," said Sarah, trying to remain congenial, while angered that she was always asked to defend her decision, "it teaches the true Gospel of Jesus Christ."

Eliza sat back in her chair and stared at Sarah. "You really believe that?"

"I know that!" Sarah stated emphatically.

Eliza gazed at her friend with bewilderment, then turned and hastily gathered up her belongings. "Well, I'd best be on my way. The bell will be ringing in a minute."

Sarah glanced up at the clock on the wall. There were still twenty minutes before school was to resume, but she made no comment.

"Thanks for dropping by, Eliza."

"Oh yes! Well, you're welcome. Bye." It was, Sarah reflected sadly as she closed the office door, as if Eliza couldn't leave fast enough.

Sarah didn't dwell on her conversation with Eliza unduly, because over the next few days a number of strange incidents required her attention. First she noticed that her office was not as busy as it usually was. In fact, as the days wore on and her patients dwindled to one or two, Sarah even called the school secretary to see if absenteeism was up. She was informed that numbers were normal.

She started leaving her office door open and watching the children walk by in the hall. A few ran past her office with their heads averted. Others slowed down, whispered, and pointed. One child came limping by crying, with blood pouring from a grazed knee. Sarah immediately stepped out to assist her. The little girl saw her coming and half ran, half limped away from her, crying even harder.

Sarah couldn't understand it. Even the sweets that she left well within sight on her counter, remained untouched. She saw no sign of her regular young visitors. The only boy who consistently stopped to talk to her was Aled. He had long since discarded his crutches and showed no indication of ever having had a severe leg injury. But he was still in the habit of dropping by her office.

Then at the end of the week, Aled's visit was more than just social. He entered her office doubled over. Sarah rushed to his side and eased him into a chair. There was no one else with him.

"Aled! What is it?"

Aled raised his face to hers. His right eye was swollen and beginning to discolor. He continued to clutch his stomach.

"I got in a fight!" he said between clenched teeth.

"Aled!"

With deft fingers Sarah gently prodded Aled's side and abdomen. She was pretty sure there were just bruises. She urged him to lie down and went to get some ice for his eye.

As she applied the cold pack, she asked, "And what does the person you were fighting have to show for it, may I ask?"

Aled gave her a crooked grin. "I think he lost his wobbly tooth!"

"Aled Lewis, this isn't funny! What will your Dad say?"

Aled turned his face away from her. "He'll be proud of me!" he said with conviction.

"Proud of you?" A fear began to gnaw at Sarah. "Aled, what were you fighting over?"

Aled remained silent.

Sarah cupped his chin in her hand and turned his face towards her. "Aled, this is your Aunty Sarah speaking. Now's not the time to start keeping secrets from me. What were you fighting over?"

Aled sniffed and ran his hand under his nose. "Nothin' important."

Sarah was unconvinced. "Well, why isn't the other boy who was fighting over 'nothing important' in here too?" She was starting to get an inkling of what might have occurred and it was giving her a sick feeling inside.

Aled shrugged his shoulders and avoided eye contact. "I don't know. Didn't want to, I suppose."

Sarah began mentally piecing together other incidents and their timing. Nothing unusual had happened until after her conversation with Eliza Thompson. Since then the children had been acting . . . well, they had been staying away. They had been avoiding her! Why?

"Aled, did this fight have anything to do with me?" Even as she asked the question, Sarah knew the answer. It was all starting to make sense.

Aled sniffed again and hung his head. Sarah put an arm around his small shoulders.

"It's alright, bach. You can tell me. You've been defending your aunt, haven't you?"

Slowly, he nodded his head. Sarah wanted to cry along with him but she knew that for Aled's sake she must appear strong.

In a broken voice, Aled said, "It was that stupid Derek Pugh. He kept saying awful things about you. Big lies." Aled paused to sniff. "He said you'd sold your soul to the devil!" Another sniff. "I told him he was a big fat liar. . . an' then I biffed him!"

Sarah gave his shoulders a squeeze. "Thank you Aled. I love you."

Aled threw his arms around Sarah and wept. She rested her head on his and held his shaking body.

When Aled had composed himself once more, Sarah left his side and placed two phone calls. The first was to Mair.

"Mair, this is Sarah. D'you think you could come and pick up Aled from school early?"

"Of course." There was a hint of panic in her voice. "Is he alright?"

"He'll be fine. He just got involved in a bit of a scuffle on the playground. I'm afraid he's going to have quite a shiner to show for it. I don't think he feels up to going back to class."

"Oh dear! Thanks Sarah. I'll leave right now."

"Thanks Mair. I'll keep him here at the office until you arrive."

When she replaced the receiver Sarah stood and stared at it for a few minutes. The next call would not be so easy. She knew she would need every ounce of self control to prevent the fury seething within her from bursting forth.

She dialed the headmaster's office number.

"Mr. Roberts? Sarah Lewis here."

"Ah yes, Sarah. What can I do for you?"

Was it her overactive imagination, or did Mr. Roberts sound a little uncomfortable?

"I need to talk to you and was wondering if you had some time this afternoon that I could drop by your office?"

Mr. Roberts cleared his throat. "Uh, yes . . . let's see. Would half past two be convenient?"

"I don't think I'll be busy then," Sarah said drily.

If Mr. Roberts noticed anything, he chose to ignore it. "Very good, then. I'll see you at two-thirty."

"Thank you Mr. Roberts. Good-bye."

When she turned back to Aled, he was looking at her with a stricken expression. "You're not going to report me for fighting are you, Aunty Sarah?"

Sarah tousled his hair gently. "No, you silly goose. My conversation with Mr. Roberts has nothing to do with you."

That wasn't absolutely true, but Sarah had no qualms about keeping Aled blissfully ignorant of the subject she wished to discuss with the headmaster.

🍂 🍂 🍂

With Aled safely discharged into his mother's care and her office as quiet as she had anticipated it to be, Sarah walked down the hall to the headmaster's office at the appointed time. Mr. Roberts responded immediately to her knock.

"Come in. Sit down." Mr. Roberts stood up behind his desk and indicated the chair opposite him. Sarah sat down obediently but did not relax. She remained perched on the edge of the seat.

"What can I do for you, Sarah?" Mr. Roberts asked.

No matter how long Sarah had thought through this conversation since her initial phone call earlier in the day, she had not come up with a diplomatic way to confront the issue. So she decided to come right to the point.

"Mr. Roberts, there is something that I don't understand going on at this school that involves me. What I do know is that no children are coming in to see me, even if they're hurt. I also know that my nephew just got in a fight with another pupil because he was trying to defend me. Defend me from what? Again, I don't know. I'm hoping that you do, and that you will tell me."

Mr. Roberts cleared his throat nervously. "Hum . . . I see . . . well yes. I have to confess, this matter was brought to my attention by someone else very recently—not the fight you understand—but the issue of the children not using the nurse's office."

Sarah could see that the headmaster's discomfort was increasing. She prodded him on.

"Do you have any idea why they are avoiding me?"

Mr. Roberts positively squirmed in his seat. "I dislike being the one to broach this subject," he began, " but it seems that someone has been spreading malicious rumors about you within the school."

Sarah did not let her eyes drop, although she felt her heart sink.

"How the children ever got started on this in the first place is beyond me. You've always been such a favorite with them. However, it appears to have taken hold. I am very sorry about it Sarah. I would be pleased to hear your suggestions as to how to deal with it."

Sarah struggled to keep her voice normal. "Would you mind telling me exactly what is being said?"

Mr. Roberts' face reddened. "Well . . . I . . . uh . . . "

Sarah sighed. "Mr. Roberts, if I don't know what is being bandied about, I won't know how to deal with it."

"You're right of course," Mr. Roberts said with regret. "Well, I believe they are saying that you're a Mormon."

Sarah nodded. "And along with that, that I've sold my soul to the devil and will be after their souls next," she added.

It was Mr. Roberts's turn to nod. "You've heard!"

Sarah shook her head. "I guessed!"

"I can't tell you how sorry I am, Sarah," Mr. Roberts repeated, shrugging his shoulders helplessly.

Sarah felt her temper rise. "Sorry" wasn't really good enough. "Yes, well I'm sorry too! Sorry that my illusions about this country were just that—illusions. I honestly believed that we were free to choose our own religion and that the era of witch hunts was long gone!"

Mr. Roberts, totally unprepared for this outburst, looked utterly confused.

"You see, Mr. Roberts," Sarah continued, "you were right. The rumors are malicious. They are unkind and unwarranted. But, as with most rumors, they are based on truth. I am a Mormon. I became a member of the Church of Jesus Christ of Latter-day Saints in January."

If Mr. Roberts had been confused before, he was now completely stunned.

"I see . . . uh, I see!" He obviously didn't see anything, but had no idea what else to say. "Well, uh. . . this sheds a rather different light on it doesn't it?"

"Does it?" Sarah asked. "In what way?"

"Well . . . " Mr. Roberts blustered, "I suppose it's possible that some parents may have got wind of this and don't feel very comfortable with it."

Sarah just stared at him. Mr. Roberts could not meet her gaze. He strummed his fingers on the desk nervously. When it became apparent that Sarah was waiting for him to make the next move, he spoke again.

"It's Friday! Let's take the weekend to let everyone's emotions calm down. Perhaps things will have blown over by Monday."

"And if they haven't?"

"We'll cross that bridge when we come to it!" was his weak reply.

Mr. Roberts pinned an encouraging smile on his face and rose to his feet. The interview was over. Sarah recognized her cue and came to her feet too.

"Thank you, Mr. Roberts," she murmured automatically.

"Thank *you*, Sarah," he replied.

Sarah left, feeling more discouraged than when she'd come.

⚜ *Chapter 13* ⚜

Now that she was aware of what was being spread abroad, it wasn't difficult for Sarah to see the signs. There were fewer friendly greetings as she walked through the village. Some people she'd known all her life blatantly ignored her, or stared as if she'd grown horns. Maybe they thought she had, Sarah thought ruefully. She tried desperately not to let it bother her, but it did. It hurt terribly.

On Saturday afternoon she went to help at the shop. For once she was grateful that her aunt assigned her backroom work. She was well out of range of any curiosity seekers. As she worked, Sarah wondered what her aunt thought of all the changes in Sarah's life over the last few months.

She had told her aunt about her baptism the weekend that it had occurred. Aunty Lil had just listened quietly with an expressionless face. At the end of Sarah's explanation she had continued to show very little reaction. Her only comment had been, "You've always had a good head on your shoulders, Sarah. I just hope this time you haven't let your heart lead it astray."

Sarah had been surprised that she hadn't shown more opposition. It was almost as though she'd had time to resign herself to the idea before it even surfaced. As impossible as it seemed, Aunty Lil acted as though she had known all along it would happen.

The jangling shop doorbell brought Sarah's attention back to the job at hand. With a sigh, she resumed unpacking boxes of canned goods. But not for long. As Mabel Jones's strident voice pierced the air, Sarah froze. She knelt before the half-empty box, as if suspended in time.

Mabel had presumably reconnoitered the shop, ascertained that there were no other customers, and had decided it safe to launch her gossip on her sole audience, Aunty Lil.

"Well, Lil, what ever do you make of this business about Sarah?" Mabel didn't bother waiting for a reply. "I must say, it doesn't surprise me a bit. Any time these young people go off to the big city like she did for her nursing, they get caught up in the wickedness there. You know I've always liked Sarah, but this really is too much. It's just too bad. It really is.

"Mind you, now that folks are warned, I can't see her spreading her wickedness around here too much. People here'll be right careful around her now to be sure. Of course, it makes it a bit hard, having her at the school with all the little ones. But that's Mr. Roberts's problem, I'd say.

"If you were to ask me though . . . "

Lil's voice was as cold and brutal as a razor-sharp steel knife. She cut Mabel off midstream. "I didn't ask you, Mabel! And if you don't mind, I'd rather not hear any more of your idle chatter. It's your gossip that's wicked—not Sarah!"

There was total silence from the shop for a few interminable seconds. Then came Mabel's voice again, brimming with righteous indignation, "Well! I've never been so insulted in my life!" And with a humph she stalked out of the shop, slamming the door behind her.

Sarah felt as though she'd been hit in the stomach. If she had not already been sitting she would have been forced to do so. She closed her eyes. Surely this was all some horrendous nightmare.

The penetrating cold of the cement floor began to filter through her jeans. When she opened her eyes there was no blissful awakening. Her surroundings were unchanged. Misery enveloped her. A slight noise at the doorway caused her to raise her head. Aunty Lil stood there gazing down at her. She wore an expression of deep concern as her faded grey eyes searched Sarah's face.

"You heard that meddlesome woman's tripe?"

Sarah could only nod. A lump the size of an orange was forming in her throat.

"Now Sarah, you listen to me!" Aunty Lil took a couple of steps into the room. "If you give any mind to the rubbish that Mabel Jones spouts off, you're playing into her hands. She's just a frustrated old woman who wants nothing more than for everyone in the village to look up to her as the fount of all knowledge. She's not and she never will be. So she just invents things to keep people listening to her."

Again Sarah nodded. No words would come. She lowered her head and noticed that her hands were shaking. Aunty Lil must have noticed too. Within seconds she was beside Sarah and had taken Sarah's slim shoulders in her work-worn hands. She gave Sarah a gentle shake.

"Listen to me, Sarah Lewis!"

The urgency in her voice forced Sarah to raise her eyes once more.

"I all but ruined my life because of gossip. I will not see the same thing happen to you. D'you understand? You're a beautiful young woman, inside and out. Don't you dare let some snide whisperings from a bunch of ignorant villagers let that beauty wither and die!"

"But Aunty Lil, what can I do? Everyone stares at me or ignores me. The children are scared of me or point at me. The truth's distorted. The lies are growing. What am I to do?" Sarah's voice broke on a sob. She buried her head in her hands and let the tears fall.

The older woman continued to hold her niece with one hand and ran the other down her silky chestnut hair. Aunty Lil continued her rhythmic stroking until Sarah's weeping began to subside. "It's alright, bach. It's best to get all that hurt out. Don't let it fester. Things will get better. I promise."

Sarah wiped the tears off her tear-stained face. "I just can't see any way out of this. I feel like I'm living a nightmare."

Aunty Lil patted her back reassuringly. "There'll be a way. It may not be easy. But there's always a way." She paused, as if measuring her words. "The obvious answer of course, would be for you to come back to chapel with us."

That brought Sarah up in a flash. "No!" She saw the faint hope in her aunt's eyes die and quieted her voice. "I can't do that, Aunty Lil. It would go against everything within me—everything I've been taught about standing up for what's right."

Aunty Lil nodded her head. "I rather thought that would be your answer, but I thought it worth asking. I don't understand it, but I'm proud of you for holding firm to your convictions Sarah. You're going to need to be strong—stronger than most young people are." Then almost as an afterthought, she added, "Stronger than I was at your age."

Sarah looked at her curiously. What was it in her past that Aunty Lil kept alluding to? Sarah knew very little about her aunt's personal life other than the general family history that she shared with Sarah's father, and that her everyday life centered around the shop. Although Aunty Lil had never made any attempt to share past experiences with her, Sarah suddenly felt ashamed that she had never had the genuine interest to ask. She really knew very little about this lonely woman who cared so much about her.

Their thoughts must have been similar, for Aunty Lil gave Sarah's hand a reassuring pat and said, "Why don't you leave this now?" She indicated the half-empty box of cans at their feet. "Go upstairs and put the kettle on. I'm going to close the shop early." At Sarah's startled expression, she raised her eyebrow. "I think I'm entitled to do that once every ten to fifteen years, don't you?"

Sarah gave a faint smile.

"That's better!" Aunty Lil said patting her hand again. "Now, like I said, you go and put the kettle on and I'll join you in a minute. I think it's time I told you a little bit of family history you may not have heard before." She paused, and Sarah could sense her hesitation. "That is, if you can bear to hear an old woman's rambling?"

Sarah squeezed her aunt's hand. "Of course. Thank you, Aunty Lil."

Sarah's answer seemed to relieve Lil. She nodded and gave a satisfied sigh. Then she turned and walked back into the shop. Sarah was still for a few minutes, listening to her aunt's clipped footsteps across the wooden floor. She heard the key in the front door turn and the sound of the blinds being lowered, one by one. Then Sarah left and made her way through the back door and up the narrow stairway that led to her aunt's small home.

෯ ෯ ෯

By the time her aunt arrived, Sarah had the tea brewing and had made a drink of orange squash for herself. She had found the rather ancient bottle of concentrate at the back of one of her aunt's cupboards. She guessed it was kept on hand for Aled's infrequent visits.

It wasn't long before both ladies were seated together on the two overstuffed armchairs before a small coal fire. Lil's cat had curled up on his mistress's knee and was purring with contentment. It didn't move an inch when Lil leaned over to place her tea cup and saucer on the small coffee table beside her.

Sarah stared into the flickering flames but did not see them. She felt numb with misery, and despite her aunt's presence, she felt terribly alone. She longed for someone she could turn to who understood her fledgling faith and had the strength to stand beside her and help her overcome this unjust attack. Someone like Brian . . .

"It just about broke your heart when he left, didn't it?"

Sarah jumped at her aunt's voice and turned to stare at her. How had she known? How had Aunty Lil known she was thinking of him?

Lil sat absently stroking the purring feline on her knee and looked at Sarah with a tenderness that Sarah had never seen in her aunt's face before.

Sarah opened her mouth to speak, then closed it again. She didn't know what to say.

"It's alright, bach. You don't need to say anything." Lil averted her gaze and focused instead on the contented cat. "I haven't always been a white-haired, old spinster woman." Lil gave a faint smile. "In fact at one time my hair was as long and shiny and chestnut as yours!"

Sarah looked at her aunt with interest. She'd known that her coloring came from her father's side, but she'd never even tried to envision Aunty Lil as a young woman. Sarah remained quiet, waiting and watching as her aunt gathered her thoughts.

"There was a young man in my life once."

Sarah tried to keep her amazement contained at this revelation. It was hard to imagine Aunty Lil ever being young and in love. Somehow Sarah had always thought that she'd not had time for such frivolity, and had even disdained such emotion as immature foolishness.

"I was just a couple of years younger than you are now when he came to the village. Robert Bennet was his name. He came as a substitute headmaster when old Mr. Ellis died."

A shadow of sadness crossed Lil's face. "We were just getting over the war. We'd lost so many good men. It was hard to find qualified teachers and headmasters, especially those willing to come and live in an isolated Welsh village.

"Someone on the county council knew Robert's father—through his business, I think. Robert hadn't finished his degree at the time so he didn't qualify for the post on a permanent basis, but they asked him to come, to hold the school together like, for the time it took them to find a replacement. So he came. He was here almost three months."

Lil gave a small sigh. Her eyes were seeing another time, another place, and another person. "He was tall and had dark brown hair." Sarah saw a fleeting smile cross her aunt's lips as she remembered. "His eyesight wasn't very good—maybe that's why he showed interest in me! He had to wear thick glasses—the kind with the big black rims. I suppose he was a bit of a bookworm really, and even a bit unsure of himself with the girls, but I thought he was grand! He was so different from all the farm boys I knew. He was a cultured man, and in my eyes, his proper English accent proved it!"

"We met for the first time at the shop. I remember he came in twice a week for quarter of a pound of lemon drops." She gave a faint smile at the memory. "He was so bashful. Didn't say too much at the beginning. But eventually he plucked up enough courage to ask if I'd like to take a walk with him. We walked together a lot after that. He even asked me to the harvest festival dance at Deniol Hall."

She paused as the memories played out and Sarah waited, not daring to speak for fear of breaking the spell that had loosened her aunt's tongue and opened her heart.

"I suppose that's why the gossip flared up again—being there at Deniol Hall where it all began." Lil's voice had lost all animation. It was tinged with bitterness, regret, and unwilling acceptance.

Sarah had to ask. "What gossip?"

"The gossip about Mary Jones and my father, your grandfather."

Sarah sat back in her chair and stared at her aunt in astonishment. Lil acknowledged her expression.

"I know it sounds far-fetched now. But at the time it was a big thing. You see, I'd always been a bit sensitive about that whole story.

It never seemed to die. I hated the fact that my father was always made to look like the man who couldn't get the girl. And even more than that I hated the fact that it made my mother look like second best.

"It sounds foolish, but I really didn't want Robert to hear it. How I thought I could prevent it, I don't know." There was undeniable bitterness in her voice now. She looked over at Sarah apologetically. "I think we both have a pretty good idea of how impossible it is to keep back the floodgates of gossip in this community."

Sarah said nothing, but looked down at her hands unhappily.

"Well, it didn't take long. Within a week Robert had heard about ten different versions of the story. Some of the more graphic ones included Mary running away to escape my father's abuse, my mother bribing Glyn to take Mary away, and Glyn Jones stealing all my father's money.

"He came to see me, to ask me about it, and I flew off the handle. I let all my frustrations over the silly story pour out on poor unsuspecting Robert. I told him if he had any feelings for me, he wouldn't listen to such rubbish. I even went as far as to tell him that a real man would stand and defend my name and my family's name."

Lil groaned, ran a worn hand across her face and slowly shook her head. "I didn't once tell him the real facts behind the story—scant though they were. Instead, like an idiot, I ranted on until I'd convinced him that I really did have something to hide. He was too unassuming to stop my tirade. He just sat and took it all. Then he left. I found out three days later that the council had told him his replacement had been found and that he had returned home to Wrexham. I never saw him or heard from him again."

Lil's voice became quiet. "All my girlish dreams and part of me left when he did. I suppose, looking back, I didn't handle my disappointment very well. I withdrew from others. None of the other boys could ever quite match up to Robert in my eyes, so I stopped socializing with them. I became bitter, and refused to get excited about any other direction my life could have taken. Instead I stayed where I was safe and alone—at home, with the shop."

She looked over at Sarah and must have noticed the sorrow in her eyes. "Don't misunderstand me, bach. It's not that I've been unhappy all these years. I've had a good life. I've enjoyed working in the shop and being close to my family here. But I do sometimes wonder, if I'd done things differently, if my life would have been more full. If perhaps I could've had my own children . . . "

She left the sentence hanging. Sarah rose and knelt beside her aunt's chair. "I'm so sorry, Aunty Lil!" Sarah's voice caught in her throat. Her own recent heartache gave her special empathy with the older woman's story. She thought of the many, many times during her growing up years that her aunt had been a surrogate mother for her. Sarah realized that she, for one, had never taken the time to really appreciate the strength and support that had always been there from this dear relative.

"Now, now! I didn't mean to upset you. It's all water under the bridge and I came to terms with it long ago." Aunty Lil transferred her stroking from the cat's back to Sarah's silky head. The cat must have sensed that his turn was over. He jumped off Lil's knee and slunk into the kitchen. Sarah inched forward and rested her head against her aunt's leg.

"I've never been much of a talker, Sarah. But I do see and hear a lot in my own quiet way." She paused for a moment, then continued gently. "I saw how it was with you and Brian—and I won't say it didn't worry me."

Sarah raised her head suddenly. "Is that why you didn't want to meet the Pearsons?"

Aunty Lil shook her head. "That didn't get past you did it? No, that wasn't the reason." She averted her eyes from Sarah's questioning face. "After Robert left I felt so disappointed and betrayed that I had to find something or someone to blame. Mary and Glyn Jones were the obvious choice. It was rumors about them that had triggered the problem. They weren't here to take offense, so I blamed them. I'm ashamed to admit that it almost became a hatred.

"When the Pearsons arrived I was afraid to meet them. Afraid that if I didn't like them, my feelings about their grandparents would show through. And even more afraid that if I did like them, I'd come to see how wrong I'd been. No one likes to admit they're wrong— especially someone my age! I knew I'd have to find someone else to blame for what happened so long ago—and deep down I've known for years that the true culprit was me."

"But you did meet them." Sarah's voice was filled with anxiety.

Her aunt smiled at her and patted her head affectionately. "It's alright! I liked them!" Sarah felt a small load lift off her shoulders at her aunt's words. She had hoped that was how it was, but she'd not been sure.

Her aunt continued. "I think perhaps the time for blaming has passed. It's time for accepting and moving on." She tucked her hand under Sarah's chin and turned her face upward. "And that, young lady, is my advice to you! Don't you go waiting fifty years to figure it out. You learn from my experience. I don't want you bowed down over this stupid gossip. I don't want you becoming a recluse and destroying that joyful personality because your heart aches or the people around you are unkind. You decide what's important to you—and if that's this new religion of yours, so be it—and you move forward."

Sarah stood up and put her arms around her aunt. She kissed her soft, lined cheek. "Thank you, Aunty Lil," she whispered. "You've always been so good to me." She held her close for a few minutes. "I wish I could do more for you!"

"Don't be silly. You've done plenty already. All your help in the shop, all your visits, sharing in your accomplishments. You've been a joy Sarah. I know I haven't showed it enough, but you've been a joy!"

Without warning, Sarah pulled away from her aunt's arms. "Wait!" she said. "Aunty Lil—there is something!" A spark of excitement lit Sarah's face.

Her aunt looked at her, noting her sudden change of mood with concern. "What ever are you talking about?"

"I have something to show you." Sarah didn't stop for further explanation. She squeezed the older woman's hands. "I have to run home for a minute, but I'll be right back. Stay here." And without waiting for further response, Sarah turned and dashed towards the door. She took the narrow stairs two at a time and ran all the way home.

ॐ ॐ ॐ

It took Sarah less than ten minutes to arrive home, bound up the stairs to her room, and retrieve the large manilla envelope. There was no sign of her mother, so she was able to slip out of the house again unhindered.

She was getting a side-ache from over-exertion by the return trip. She half jogged, half briskly walked her way back to her aunt's flat. A couple of people watched her activity with curiosity but Sarah didn't have the time or inclination to offer excuses. She reasoned ruefully that they would just chalk it up to another strange eccentricity that she'd developed since becoming a Mormon!

Lil was sitting in the same armchair when Sarah returned. She had made a fresh cup of tea and looked up expectantly at Sarah's brief knock and entrance.

"Good gracious me, child! You haven't been home and back already? What did you do? Run all the way?"

"Just about!" Sarah panted.

Lil indicated the other chair. "Sit down and catch your breath." Sarah flopped into the chair gratefully. "Now what on earth is all this fuss about? You bolted out of here like a scared rabbit!"

"Not a scared one—an excited one!" Sarah corrected with a smile. "I want to show you something . . . " She paused, trying to infuse some diplomacy into her selection of words. "I haven't shown these papers to anyone—not even Mam. They're very private letters, and I think they should stay that way. But I think she'd want you to read them."

"She?" Lil looked puzzled.

"Mary Jones," said Sarah. Lil stared at her, tongue-tied. "Mam told you I'd found them, didn't she?"

"Why . . . yes! But since she didn't say anything more, I assumed you'd just packaged them and sent them off to the Pearsons."

"I think that's what everyone thought. And that's for the best. But when I called Iris Pearson to tell her what I'd found, she asked me if I'd translate them for her before I sent them. They were all in Welsh, you see." Sarah saw understanding illuminate her aunt's face.

"So you read them all and translated them into English?"

"Yes, then I made copies of everything, just in case they got lost in the post or something. These are the copies." Sarah held up the manilla envelope in her hand, then leaned over and placed it on Lil's knee. Lil said nothing. She did not touch the envelope. She just sat and stared at it, as though it had the power to jump up and bite her.

Sarah noted her reluctance. "Please read them, Aunty Lil. They will answer many of your questions and help you understand what really happened. These letters affect you more directly than anyone else still living here at Pen-y-Bryn." Lil still made no move to open the envelope, so Sarah continued. "Mary Jones would've wanted you to read them. I know she would . . . and I know you won't . . . " Sarah trailed off awkwardly.

Lil guessed her meaning immediately, and completed the sentence. "Talk about them!"

Sarah felt color flood her cheeks. "I suppose I don't feel that it's my place to start talking about other people's families when they're not here."

Lil nodded. Then with a touch of asperity she added, "Unlike ninety percent of this community, I agree with you!"

Sarah caught her meaning and gave a wan smile. "I'll leave them with you and come and get them tomorrow after Church."

"You're going to Chester again?"

"Yes."

Lil nodded and held out her hand. "You stick to your guns Sarah. Don't let the Mabel Joneses of this village get you down. Things will be better before long."

Sarah sighed. "I hope so." Her tone was anything but hopeful, but she put on a brave smile and gave her aunt a parting kiss. "Thanks Aunty Lil."

"I'll see you tomorrow, bach."

Sarah walked over to the door. As she let herself out, she looked back at her aunt. Lil had picked up the envelope. Sarah smiled to herself. She was sure that by reading Mary Jones's tender words, her aunt would find some of the peace and understanding that she'd been missing for so long.

ੴ ੴ ੴ

Annie Lewis was already home when Sarah arrived back. Sarah could hear the pots banging before she entered the back door. When she saw how the defenseless potatoes were being savagely peeled and thrown into the waiting pan of water, Sarah knew that her mother was seriously out of sorts. She was tempted to slip back out and return later, hopefully after her mother simmered down, but before she could act, Annie saw her.

"Sarah! I'm glad you're home."

Sarah's initial reaction was one of relief. It didn't appear that she was the object of her mother's wrath this time. She was right.

"I'll tell you, Sarah, I've decided you can't trust anyone these days. Here I've been good friends with Mabel Jones for over forty years—and does it count for anything? No it does not! It doesn't matter that I've always been there for her. Oh no! The minute she has some juicy bit of news . . . "

"Gossip" interrupted Sarah.

Her mother gave her a sharp look. "Gossip" she corrected. "The minute she has some juicy bit of gossip, she's off spreading it around the village no matter whose family it's damaging!

"Of course, she won't say anything to my face. Oh no! I go into the post office and she's as nice as you please, asking after every member of the family. Like she's really interested!" Annie gave a rather un-lady-like snort. "She's probably just hoping I'll let drop something else that she can tell every other customer who comes in!"

Sarah sat down on one of the kitchen chairs wearily, and let her mother's tirade continue. She didn't need to respond; she just needed to appear to be listening. Sarah let most of it just wash over her. She felt totally drained, as if trapped in a box with no energy left to devise a way out.

In the end it was the doorbell that roused Sarah from her pit of despair and stemmed Annie's spate of words. Reluctantly Sarah rose, walked slowly down the hall, and opened the front door. Bishop and Sister Edwards stood on the door step.

"Hello, Sarah!" Bishop Edwards said with warmth and extended his hand to shake hers. "I hope we're not interrupting anything."

For a few seconds Sarah could only stare at them both disbelievingly. "No! No, of course not. I just can't believe you're here. Come in! Please, come in!"

She led them into the front room and asked them to sit down. As they did so, Bishop Edwards said, "I know this visit is unexpected, Sarah. I'm afraid it was made on rather short notice. I've felt very strongly that we needed to come and see you today, but I kept ignoring the feeling because I thought I'd see you at Church tomorrow. When the feeling persisted and I mentioned it to Helen here, she insisted that we take a drive to see you." He paused and looked at Sarah intently. "How are you?"

For the second time in as many minutes, Sarah was momentarily speechless. She thought that after her weep-fest at the shop, there were no tears left in her, but she was mistaken. As the impact of the bishop's words sank in, tears began to flow again. She felt as though someone had just thrown her a life preserver.

Between sobs, Sarah told the bishop and his wife about the gossip being spread around the village. She told them about how it was impacting her work at school and the effect it was having on her family members. They sat quietly as Sarah shared her feelings, her blossoming testimony, her fears and her guilt for having brought all this upon her mother in particular. It was a much-needed catharsis for Sarah.

The Edwardses didn't need to say much. Just the empathy in their eyes, their listening ears, and their presence in her home was enough to lift the overwhelming feeling of isolation that had threatened to engulf Sarah. But the bishop had one more source of immense comfort to offer.

"Would you like me to give you a blessing, Sarah?" he asked.

Sarah looked startled. A blessing had not even crossed her mind. Before she could respond, Bishop Edwards continued. "I know that you're not ill, but priesthood blessings can be given at other times too—like times when you need comfort or direction in your life."

Sarah nodded. She was remembering the only other time she'd participated in a priesthood blessing. She'd been up on Mynydd Mawr with Brian and Aled. Before he'd left to get help, Brian had given Aled a blessing. As she thought about it, she remembered that not only had Brian blessed Aled at that time, he had also asked for protection over her. Even then she had sensed the power in that blessing. Sarah nodded again.

"I think I'd like that."

Bishop Edwards looked pleased. But before he could say anything more, their attention was drawn by a sound at the door. Annie, obviously curious as to why Sarah had not returned to the kitchen, had come to investigate. Sarah got up immediately and moved towards her.

"Mam, this is Mr. and Mrs. Edwards from Chester. Mr. Edwards is my bishop." She turned to the Edwards. "Bishop, Sister Edwards, this is my mother, Annie Lewis."

They stepped forward with warm greetings, seemingly oblivious to the guarded expression on Annie's face. Sarah watched their interaction anxiously. At first their exchange of pleasantries appeared stilted and awkward. Her mother did little to help the conversation along. Sarah's anxiety deepened until, out of nowhere, Sister Edwards hit a master stroke.

"I have to say, Mrs. Lewis, that I couldn't help noticing your rose bushes on the way in. They are so beautifully shaped and already in leaf with blossoms budding. How ever do you manage to keep them looking so wonderful?"

Sarah wanted to hug her. The rose bushes were Annie's pride and joy and Sarah had yet to see her ever turn down an opportunity to talk about them. She was not to be disappointed this time either. Annie's countenance lit up.

"Why thank you. They are lovely aren't they?" Then she bent her head and lowered her voice conspiratorially. "I'll let you in on a family secret. Tea leaves! That's the trick. When I rinse out the teapot I pour the old wet leaves under the rose bushes. It works like a charm."

Sister Edwards made no mention of the lack of tea leaves (or teapots for that matter) in her home. Instead, she expressed suitable surprise and interest. Sarah mentally applauded her. She noted Bishop Edwards's eyes were brimming with mirth but he was manfully maintaining a straight face. Annie, oblivious to her faux pas, had moved on to discussing the strengths and weaknesses of the various strains of rose bushes in her garden.

Before many more minutes had elapsed, Annie had invited Sister Edwards to tour her garden, and Sister Edwards was more than pleased to comply. As they closed the door behind them, Bishop Edwards looked over at Sarah questioningly.

"Would this be a good time to give you a blessing?"

Sarah nodded her assent and sat down on the chair beside the bishop. She folded her arms tightly, closed her eyes, and bowed her head. Then she tried to shut out everything but the words spoken by the man behind her.

She felt as though a huge burden was being lifted off her narrow shoulders as the bishop spoke of the love and watchful care that Heavenly Father had for her as an individual. (Surely the Edwards's presence in her home was manifestation of that.) A feeling of peace and comfort seeped through her.

She listened as the bishop moved on to words of counsel. He told her not to be afraid of change, but rather to look for the good and growth opportunities in change. He exhorted her to stay close to the gospel and to listen to the prompting of the Holy Ghost. He then promised her that if she did so, her relationship with family members would improve, and great blessings would be hers.

Sarah took all this to heart. When the blessing ended, she felt renewed. She was not naive enough to think that all her troubles were over, but she was strengthened and encouraged by the knowledge that she did not stand alone. Her testimony that a loving Heavenly Father was mindful of her and would help guide her through the rough spots ahead was redoubled. The future didn't look so bleak any more.

Minutes later, the two older women's voices could be heard talking animatedly in the hallway. When they came into the room, Sarah was thrilled to see that her mother's normal cheery disposition had been restored. She threw Sister Edwards a grateful glance. The kindly lady smiled at her, then turned to her husband.

"Mrs. Lewis has graciously asked us if we'd like to stay for dinner."

Sarah looked at her mother in surprise, but Annie's attention was with the Edwardses.

"Please do. You can't possibly make that long drive home without dinner first. It's just beef stew, but we've got plenty," Annie encouraged.

To Sarah's delight, the Edwardses were pleased to accept, and they were soon sitting down together over one of Annie's hearty meals. Apart from the initial awkwardness over beverages, a positive, friendly feeling pervaded. And when the time came for the Edwardses to leave, even Annie seemed genuinely regretful. As she and Sarah returned to the house after waving them off, she said, "Well, they seemed to be very nice, ordinary people, Sarah."

Sarah's heart positively sang. Never had the words "nice" or "ordinary" had such grand meaning.

ॐ ॐ ॐ

Sarah stopped by Lil's house on Sunday evening. She had never seen her aunt cry but when Lil handed Sarah back the envelope full of letters, there was moisture in her eyes.

"Thank you, Sarah," she said with feeling. "I think I understand now." She paused. "It means a lot to know that she did care about my father." Another pause. "I even thought last night . . . what if it had been me and Robert instead . . . perhaps I would have . . . well, you understand . . . " Lil stopped and seemed unsure of what else to say. But for Sarah, who had followed similar trains of thought with Brian in mind, she'd said enough. She gave her aunt a hug, then said good-bye. She could tell that her aunt was not in the mood for small talk. She had much to ponder and reflect upon and was needing time alone to think things through.

At work on Monday, Sarah had plenty of time for reflection too. Not one person came to her office the entire day. Even the faculty and staff seemed to be avoiding her. By the afternoon Sarah had tidied her supplies, updated all her paperwork and ordered more bandages through the school office. There was really nothing else left to do.

She sat by the window watching the children outside playing. She had loved this job from her very first day at work. She loved the children, the school, and the village. She always would. But she knew that she could not go on as things were now. She sighed and rested her head against the cold windowpane. It was bad enough to be shunned, the object of gossip, and feared by the children. There was not much she could do about that without the healing passage of time.

It was a whole different matter to be totally useless at work— sitting alone in the school nurse's office all day. Her own sense of worth was going to suffer, along with the health of all the children who refused to be seen by her. Surely this was something that she could alter. But how? In what way? Unanswered questions spun in never-ending circles within her head. She gave a small moan and closed her eyes to the sights and sounds of the school yard. "Heavenly Father," she prayed, "help me know what I should do."

Nothing had changed when she opened her eyes. With a heavy heart, Sarah waited for the final school bell before making her weary way home. She was relieved to find her mother gone when she arrived. She just could not have borne the "I told you so" look in her eyes.

As she had done many times before, Sarah took solace in her harp music that evening. She sifted through familiar and well-loved sheet music, then dug deeper for something new. Buried at the bottom of the pile she uncovered the music she had played at the International Eisteddfod. She sat and stared at it for a few minutes. So much had happened since then. Slowly she got up and positioned the music on the stand. She took her place behind the harp and plucked the first string, then another and another. As the music swelled, she was immediately transported back to the competition and, inevitably, the Pearsons's visit the previous summer.

Memories came in a collage of pictures and words: the audience's applause, Brian's kiss, eating fish and chips, Aled's excitement, Iris's kind eyes, Pystill Glas, cowering on the cliff, safety in Brian's arms, the hospital . . . Abruptly Sarah's fingers froze. The hospital! Why ever hadn't she thought of it before? In her mind's eye she saw herself there waiting with the Pearsons to see Aled. Dr. Robinson had been there. What was it he had said about her? "We lost one of our best nurses . . . " Sarah's heart began to thump. Did he really feel that way or was he just flattering her? How would he feel about getting her back, she wondered? She glanced at her watch. It was too late to call the hospital administration office now. She'd have to wait until morning. She turned back to her music, but it was no good. She couldn't concentrate any more.

Sarah lay awake long into the night. The thought of moving back to Oswestry Orthopedic was daunting. It wasn't that she hadn't enjoyed her time there. It was just that she'd always imagined herself at Pen-y-Bryn. This was her home and now she was in danger of being uprooted for good. However, despite her trepidation, the more she thought about it, the more right it seemed. If she left the village, the gossiping would die. Her family members's lives could resume their former peaceful paths. She could feel fulfilled at work once more and the school could hire another nurse with whom the children felt secure.

Why was making a change so hard? Sarah thought about the bishop's counsel when he'd blessed her just a few days before. There was a lot of good that could come out of this change. She admonished herself to have more trust in the Lord. She finally fell asleep still praying for courage, guidance, and faith.

Chapter 14

Less than one week later, Sarah was driving home from the hospital with a new job in hand. Even now, she could hardly believe how everything had fallen into place. As she negotiated the narrow, winding country road, she offered up another one of many prayers of gratitude.

She had called the hospital on Tuesday and spoken with Maggie Thomas in the administrator's office. Maggie remembered Sarah well and was only too pleased to pass her inquiry on to Dr. Robinson. Sarah had no idea how many strings he'd pulled, but within two days he'd succeeded in getting her an interview with Claire Alexander, the Head Nurse of the children's ward.

Sarah had driven to the hospital after school on Thursday. She'd known that she would like working with Nurse Alexander as soon as they met. She was a short, plump lady with light brown hair that was fading to gray. She somehow managed to exude both kindness and practicality simultaneously. She got straight down to business, but did so in a way that made those around her feel comfortable. Sarah had been put at ease by her manner immediately.

Her questions had been direct and probing with regard to both Sarah's medical skill and character. But Sarah felt that the interview had gone well, and it seemed that Nurse Alexander thought so too. At the end of their time together, she had referred obliquely to a glowing report she'd received from Dr. Robinson, shook Sarah's hand and expressed pleasure at the prospect of working with her. Sarah was to begin the day shift on the children's ward in a week's time.

Sarah's emotions followed the hilly road she drove: up one minute, then down the next. She felt sadness over leaving her posi-

tion at Pen-y-Bryn, particularly as it was not a decision that she
would have made had circumstances been different. She felt apprehension over breaking the news to her mother. Would she be upset or
glad? Sarah wasn't sure. She also felt a stimulating mixture of
nervousness and excitement over her new post. It would be a fresh
challenge, and she wanted to do well.

She rounded a bend in the road and slowed her speed as she
entered the village. Within minutes she had parked outside her
home. She walked around to the back door. As soon as she opened it,
the smell of frying fish assailed her. Her mother was standing at the
stove with spatula in hand.

"Hello Sarah! You're home late today."

"Sorry Mam. I had to go to Oswestry right after school." Sarah
hung up her coat as she spoke. When she turned around she noticed
that her Aunty Lil was seated at the kitchen table. She smiled at her.
"Hello Aunty Lil!" Despite the fact that Aunty Lil made no pretense
of understanding her desire to join a different church, Sarah felt that
in her she had a level-headed ally. She was glad that she was to be
here when she broke the news of her new job to her mother.

Her mother was looking at her with surprise. "Oswestry? Oh, I
wish you'd told me. I'd have had you stop at the butcher's there."

"I didn't go downtown," Sarah clarified, "I went to the hospital."

Annie's look of surprise was replaced by one of concern. "Dear
me, did one of the children get badly hurt today?"

"No, it was nothing like that," Sarah hastened to reassure her
mother. She took a deep breath and continued, "I had an interview
there. I've been offered a job working on the children's ward." Sarah
watched a myriad of reactions play across her mother's face within a
matter of seconds. Before Annie could say anything, Sarah ploughed
on. "I've accepted. I'll be starting the day shift there in a week."

It was out. She'd said it. Sarah waited anxiously for her words to
sink in. She offered up a last, silent, short, but fervent prayer that her
mother would receive the news well.

For a few moments there was absolute quiet in the room. Then
Aunty Lil spoke up. "Good for you, Sarah!" Her uncharacteristic
vocalness caused both Sarah and Annie's heads to turn. She didn't
flinch at their stares. "Much as we loved having you at Pen-y-Bryn,

you're too good a nurse to be hidden away here. You'll be able to help a lot more people over at the hospital."

There was really nothing Annie could say to that. To argue against it would have been to suggest that Sarah was not the wonderful nurse Lil believed her to be. She walked over to her daughter and caught hold of her hands. "Are you sure that's what you want to do, Sarah?"

Sarah looked into her mother's anxious face and nodded. "Yes, Mam. I think it's for the best."

Annie gave a sigh. "I thought you loved it here—wanted to stay!"

"It'll always be home, Mam!" Sarah hoped that her mother's words would not reduce her to tears. "But I think it's time I moved on. The hospital will be more challenging for me. It's important that I don't stagnate."

Annie dropped her hands and gave a small nod of acceptance. "Will you live there too?" She asked in a quiet voice.

"I think it might be best." Sarah had thought through a logical excuse for removing herself completely from the village and its gossiping occupants. "I'm on day shift now, but that might change at any time. I don't really want to be driving the country roads at night. Especially in the winter."

Again Annie nodded but her face was full of sadness. Sarah stepped forward and gave her mother a hug. They held each other tightly. After weeks of restraint between them it was wonderful to feel loved again. When they parted, Annie wiped her eye with the corner of her apron. "I'm sorry to be so daft," she said. "After all, it's not like you're going to Timbuktu is it?"

Sarah gave her a smile. "No, you'll see plenty of me on the weekends. And I can always come home for an evening every once in a while."

"You'd better come home for a decent meal on a regular basis!" Annie warned with fake ferocity. Sarah laughed. The thought of food reverted Annie's attention to the now extra crispy fish in the pan behind her. "My lands! The fish!" She hurried to salvage what she could.

Sarah walked over to her aunt. She took her hand and gave it a squeeze. "Thanks Aunty Lil!" She didn't need to say more. Lil understood.

"You're doing the right thing, bach. I'm proud of you! It won't be long before these pigheaded people realize what they've lost. Mark my words—they'll rue the day they started on at you the way they have!"

Aunty Lil stayed for dinner that evening, but it was a rather somber affair. Each woman had much to think about, and they kept most of their thoughts to themselves.

Sarah wasted no time the next morning in seeking out the headmaster. Mr. Roberts was in his office shuffling paperwork when Sarah entered. Sarah had been concerned about the fact that she would only be able to give one week's notice at the school. But when she explained the situation to Mr. Roberts, the look of relief on his face swept all feelings of guilt from Sarah. He did little to hide the fact that he was glad to be rid of her and the awkward problem she presented.

When her interview was over, Sarah closed the office door behind her feeling like she was also shutting the door on part of her life. But she knew, even more assuredly after speaking with Mr. Roberts, that despite the heartache, she was doing the right thing. She swallowed the bitterness that threatened to infiltrate her thoughts as she looked back. There was no time for self-pity. She would make the same decisions again if she had to. The gospel meant more to her than anything else—certainly more than the opinion of Mr. Roberts, Mabel Jones, and the like!

As Sarah returned to her own office, she resolved to look ahead with optimism and try to focus on the happy memories at Pen-y-Bryn school. She sat down in the quiet room and opened up Brian's Book of Mormon. Just reading it for a little while helped bring a feeling of peace to Sarah's soul and encouragement to her heart.

౿ ౿ ౿

Within six weeks Sarah was used to her new lifestyle. She loved her work on the children's ward. She felt that she was really able to make a difference in the lives of her young patients. She enjoyed the other nurses that she worked with and, as she had guessed, found Claire Alexander to be a fair, kind supervisor. She derived great satisfaction from working as a team with the doctors, nurses, and other medical professionals at the hospital. It opened her eyes to just how isolated she had become from others in her field while working at Pen-y-Bryn.

Not that she didn't miss home. She had found a small flat, located near the hospital, that she shared with two other nurses. It was adequate accommodation, but not home by any stretch of the imagination. She didn't work the same shift as her roommates so she rarely saw them. She had to creep around the flat in stocking feet when she was there, so as not to disturb their sleep. To her sorrow, playing the harp was out of the question. The harp remained in her mother's front room, where she played it each time she visited.

Whenever she was off duty on a Saturday, she visited her mother and Aunty Lil for a few hours. Her mother tried to coincide her trips with at least one hearty meal. Often, Kevin, Mair, and Aled were invited too. Sarah always enjoyed seeing them. Aled kept her updated on happenings at the school. She took rather mischievous delight in hearing about the new school nurse. She was apparently an older lady from one of the neighboring villages. Much to Sarah's amusement, the children had nicknamed her "Sergeant," and apparently, she lived up to the title. Privately, Sarah wondered how Mr. Roberts was dealing with the new regime.

As Aunty Lil had surmised, the local gossip swirling around Sarah had subsided somewhat since her departure. It made life easier for her family members, and for that Sarah was glad. She herself did not feel that the scourge had been totally lifted. Longtime neighbors and friends still acted coldly towards her on the few occasions that they met. But Sarah tried hard not to let it affect her. It was easier to put it behind her now that she was not faced with it day in and day out.

To Sarah's relief and pleasure, her move seemed to smooth things over between herself and her mother. Their relationship slipped back into something resembling the comfortable standing it had held before Sarah had been baptized, although by unspoken agreement, religion was never mentioned between them. Since Annie didn't have daily reminders, such as Sarah's observance of the word of wisdom, she didn't dwell on her daughter's new faith. It helped, too, that Sarah drove to her Church meetings in Chester from Oswestry.

Annie didn't see her go or wait for her return. Even her absence at the local chapel was not as much of a sore point, since it was accepted that she no longer lived at home.

The Chester ward was a great source of strength to Sarah, and she felt truly integrated there now. The Sunday meetings buoyed her up and helped her cope with all the daily challenges during the week. On the few occasions that she missed Church because of a Sunday shift at work, she felt the loss sorely. With her regular scripture study, daily prayer, and focus on personal progress, this new religion was becoming a part of her very being, twenty-four hours a day, seven days a week. And Sarah was glad.

A few of her coworkers had shown curiosity over the fact that Sarah never drank tea or coffee on her breaks. But other than mild interest and an occasional jibe, it was hardly ever mentioned. Sarah was grateful for their nonjudgmental acceptance.

🐚 🐚 🐚

It really seemed to Sarah, as she drove to Pen-y-Bryn on a Saturday several weeks later, that her life had fallen into a satisfying routine. She had her window rolled down and was enjoying the light breeze on the warm, sunny day. Looking out at the peaceful, pastoral scene around her, it was hard to imagine the misery and turmoil she had felt only a few months earlier. Gratitude filled her heart. Her prayers had been answered many times over.

Sarah passed very little traffic on the road. Subconsciously she relaxed her grip on the steering wheel a little. Out of the corner of her eye she saw the new lambs bounding around in the fields. The air was filled with their high-pitched bleating and their mothers's low-pitched reply. The blue, cloudless sky emphasized the vivid green of the meadows and hedgerows. Sarah took a deep breath. She was a country girl at heart. As much as she enjoyed working in town, her heart would always be in the rural hills and valleys. She missed the open spaces, the closeness to nature, and the farm sights and sounds. She missed her solitary rambles by the river.

She slowed the car as she turned the last bend in the road before entering the village. It would be a shame to spend her whole afternoon in the car and in the house on such a beautiful day. Sarah determined that when she arrived home, she'd change her shoes and take one of those favorite walks she missed so much.

Sarah was surprised to see a small blue car parked outside her mother's house. She looked at it curiously as she got out of her own car, but she was none the wiser. As usual, she made her way around to the back of the house. She noticed that her mother's vegetable patch was coming on nicely. The runner beans had grown considerably since her last visit and had been staked up. Bees were humming busily around the lavender bush, and a neighbor's cat was sunning itself on the kitchen windowsill.

The kitchen was uncharacteristically quiet when Sarah entered. "Mam! I'm home!" she called as she opened the door. There was no answering response.

As soon as she walked in she saw the note propped up against the salt and pepper shakers on the kitchen table. Sarah picked it up. It read: "Sarah, Gone to the shop for a few things. Won't be long. Love, Mam." Sarah smiled. Just how long her mother would be gone depended entirely upon who else she ran into at the shop or on route. She knew from past experience that her mother's shopping jaunts were rarely brief.

She picked up the pencil that still lay on the table and wrote on the bottom of her mother's note: ' Mam, Sorry to have missed you. Have gone for a walk. See you soon. Sarah.' She propped it up in the same position that she'd found it and walked back to the boot room.

It didn't take her long to find her sturdy walking shoes hidden behind her mother's wellies. She had just finished putting the first shoe on when she heard the door between the kitchen and the hallway swoosh open. She froze. Her mother never came in through the front door. Who else was in the house? Then she heard a chair's legs scrape the floor. With her heart beating violently, she opened the door leading from the boot room to the kitchen and stepped inside.

He was standing with his back to her. Sarah gasped and clutched the doorknob. At the sound, he swung around and faced her.

"Hello Sarah!" he said.

Sarah felt the color leave her face. "B . . . Brian!"

He stepped forward then. Sarah's feet were rooted to the spot and her hand was glued to the doorknob. Was she hallucinating? He was just as she remembered him—the same tall, strong physique, blonde hair, deep blue eyes. But there was something . . . Sarah struggled to put her finger on it . . . something was not quite the same. She looked up into his face as he drew nearer. It was thinner. He'd lost some weight. And despite his smile, his former aura of carefree enthusiasm was missing.

The cold red tiles beneath her feet finally penetrated through her sock and Sarah realized with embarrassment that she was still clutching a shoe in one hand and the door with the other. She dropped the shoe and let go of the doorknob simultaneously. The shoe clattered to the floor noisily. Brian smiled and extended his hand to her.

"Sorry to have startled you!"

Sarah shook his hand self-consciously. "I had no idea . . . I mean . . . When did you get here?"

Brian glanced at his watch. "About an hour ago. I just drove in from Manchester airport." That explained the blue car parked outside. "I saw your mother and she was nice enough to give me a room." Sarah mentally applauded her mother's innate hospitality for rising above her religious prejudices. "I thought I'd better rest a bit to try and get over the jet lag." He grimaced and ran his hand through his hair. "But even though I know I'm tired, I can't seem to make sleep come."

Sarah could see the weariness in his face. "I'm sorry," she said sympathetically. She'd never experienced jet lag but she imagined it was a lot like starting the night shift after months of day shift. And that was awful.

"Is your mother here too?" she asked.

"No, I'm on my own this time. She told me to be sure to send you her love, though."

Sarah smiled. Then, because she wasn't sure what else to say, she played for time and bent over to retrieve her shoe. She tried to tell herself that her shaking hands were purely a factor of the big shock she'd just received. However, she knew she wasn't being honest with herself. It was not so much the shock of seeing Brian so unexpectedly, but the shock of realizing that almost a year after she'd last seen him, he could still evoke an inner longing so strong that it caused her to tremble.

"Are you on your way in or out?" Brian's voice startled her out of her self analysis.

"Both, really," Sarah replied with a shaky laugh. "I just arrived from Oswestry, but it's so beautiful outside that I couldn't face the thought of being indoors. I was going for a walk."

"Would you . . . " Sarah heard the hesitation in his voice. "Would you mind if I joined you?"

There were many times during the dark weeks after the Pearsons's departure that Sarah had dreamed of going for another walk in the countryside with Brian. She had always awakened filled with sorrow that the joy of her dreams could not be a reality. But her dreams had never included the fear that was threatening to overpower her now. She could not allow this man to break down all those carefully built walls around her heart. She knew from her initial reaction to his presence that she was about as far from being immune to him as she'd ever been. If she was to open herself up to him again, only to have him leave for America in a few days . . . Well, she didn't think she could live through the experience again.

She stood up and looked at him. The uncertainty and hope in his eyes made her waver. "Of course you may come," she heard herself say. He smiled again, and this time it lit up his whole face, erasing the tired lines that had been so prominent only seconds before. She led the way out of the house in a daze, convinced that she'd wake up any minute.

By unspoken consent, they headed off toward the path that ran alongside the river. They walked in silence for a few yards, then with admirable, totally unfounded nonchalance Sarah asked, "What brings you to Pen-y-Bryn this time?"

This time Sarah did see the old spark of enthusiasm light up Brian's face. "I'm here to work!" he announced and laughed at the look of astonishment on Sarah's face. "Well, not in Pen-y-Bryn exactly, but at the hospital in Oswestry."

Sarah was so stunned she stopped walking. "The Orthopedic hospital you mean?"

"Yes," Brian replied. "The one where Aled was treated."

"But I . . . " Sarah couldn't finish her sentence. Brian was so anxious to tell her everything.

"It's quite simple really. When I went back to medical school I met up with the two doctors that Dr. Robinson mentioned when we were visiting Aled." Sarah nodded. Brian didn't realize that she too had reason to remember that conversation well. "They had been hoping to do some collaborative work with someone over here and had already thought of contacting Dr. Robinson. The more I talked to them and the more I studied their work, the more fascinated I became with their research. At the eleventh hour I decided to make orthopedics my specialty and have been involved with their research ever since.

"As I got to the end of my fourth year at the University of Utah, Dr. Hansen and Dr. Young helped me coordinate with Oswestry Orthopedic. And to cut a long story short, they've made it possible for me to do an internship here under Dr. Robinson."

Sarah could only stare at him. Where she had at first tried to dampen the spark of joy she'd felt in seeing him again, she now gave it fuel. She felt it begin to glow and strengthen. "But that means you'll be here for . . . "

"At least a year!" Brian finished the sentence for her.

"Oh Brian, that's wonderful!" Sarah could barely contain her happiness.

His face lit up. "D'you really feel that way?"

"Of course!"

Brian really smiled then, a smile that reached his eyes. And Sarah saw some of the strain leave his face. "I wasn't sure . . . when I left . . . I never heard from you . . . I . . . " Brian was having difficulty finishing a sentence.

"You aren't the best letter writer either!" she accused, trying to divert his stumbled queries about her feelings.

Brian had the grace to look embarrassed. He turned away from her and gazed off down the lane. Then in a quiet voice he said, "I was doing my best to try to forget you."

Sarah remained silent for a few minutes. The gurgling river rushed on beside them, but Sarah felt as though she were suspended in time. Eventually she ventured, "And did you manage it?"

They had reached the wooden footbridge. They stepped onto it together and Brian leaned over the railing. He looked down at the dancing water, sparkling in the sunshine. Sarah stood beside him, her hands on the wooden handrail tense, waiting for his reply.

He spoke softly, and Sarah could tell that he was picturing a time months before, and a place an ocean away. "I tried hard. I threw myself into my studies. I tried to block out everything else. And for a while I'd think I'd been successful. Then a friend would set me up with a date. I'd go and spend the whole time wishing I was with you—and then feel like a heel for not giving the other girl my attention. It was the pits!" Brian lowered his head as though his shoulders still felt the burden of that time.

Sarah wasn't sure what "the pits" was, but she thought she could guess. She looked at the remarkable man beside her. Apart from her obvious pleasure at the news of his internship, she had told him nothing of her feelings or of all that had happened to her since they were last together. And yet he had the bravery to admit how hard their separation had been for him. With little promise of reciprocation, he was willing to wear his heart on his sleeve. She felt the ice she had so carefully packed around her own heart begin to thaw.

She reached out and put her hand on his shoulder. Brian felt her touch immediately and turned to face her. "Brian, a lot has changed in my life since you were here." Sarah saw the spark of hope in his eyes flicker and fade at her words. She smiled at him, hoping to dispel his discouragement. "Come and sit over here." She led him to a grassy bank beside the river. As they sat down, Sarah was very aware of his presence beside her. She plucked at a few blades of grass nervously.

"I'm not quite sure where to begin," Sarah started. She thought about how honest Brian had been with her and knew that she could not, in good conscience, dissemble. "The first few weeks—no, few months—after you left were torture. I tried to fill my days and ignore the feelings of loneliness, blame, guilt, and frustration. Half of me desperately wanted to hear from you. The other half wanted you out of my system altogether. I was convinced that I'd never see you again, and wanted my life back the way it was before your visit."

Sarah threw a handful of plucked grass into the river. "I really thought I was over the worst when, out of the blue, Aunty Sally led me to Mary Jones's letters. It was hard to find and read those without memories of you and your time here flooding back." Sarah sighed as she thought about the impact those few sheets of paper had had on her life.

"Those letters meant so much to my family." Brian's comment brought a smile to Sarah's lips.

"They were wonderful, weren't they?" Without waiting for a reply, Sarah continued. "About the time I found the letters, I was invited to play the harp at a Christmas concert in Chester. That's a town about an hour and a half drive from here. The first time I drove there to rehearsals, I saw the church right across the street from the concert hall."

It was Sarah's turn to get a faraway look in her eyes. "Perhaps the fact that I'd just read Mary Jones's letters and knew that another Pen-y-Bryn woman had joined the Church gave me extra courage. I don't know. But somehow, I found myself there, talking to the missionaries."

Brian sat up straighter. "Wait! You mean it was an LDS Church?"

Sarah looked at him and smiled. "Yes, it was an LDS Church." She hadn't the heart to keep him in suspense any longer. "I was baptized in January."

"Sarah!" His joy-filled eyes never left her face. "Why didn't you tell me?"

"I . . . I hadn't heard from you and I'd told myself that you'd gone on with your life—that I wasn't part of it anymore."

"Oh Sarah!" His voice was an agonized whisper.

Sarah reached out her hand and touched his arm. "No, Brian, you don't understand. I knew that you would be happy for me. But I was having to deal with a lot of changes in my life, and I suppose I thought I couldn't risk rekindling my feelings for you, too. Especially since I thought it was a vain hope." She paused as she felt the color rise in her cheeks again, but went on regardless. "I've read your Book of Mormon every day. I've imagined you here, teaching me as I've studied your notes and cross-references. It's helped me feel less alone."

"Has it been really hard?" Brian's expression was filled with concern.

Sarah bowed her head. "There was a time when it was awful." It was hard to keep the quiver out of her voice. "I've never known Mam so upset. She couldn't understand why I'd do such a thing. Then to make matters worse, her friends and neighbors in the village found out I'd become a Mormon and some rather hateful gossip started to fly." Sarah raised her head and flicked her long hair back over her shoulder. She gazed out across the peaceful, rural scene before her. "I don't suppose things will ever be as they once were for me here. The villagers still treat me with disdain or distrust." She tried to instill some enthusiasm into her voice. "But it's improved a lot since I left."

"You left?" came Brian's startled response.

Sarah nodded. "I couldn't work at the school anymore." She looked over at him. "The children were afraid of me. Most of them believed I'd sold my soul to the devil!"

The compassion in Brian's eyes threatened to destroy Sarah's fragile composure. "But you loved that job! You loved the kids!"

Sarah nodded again. "Yes, but I love the gospel more—and it had pretty much come down to one or the other! As difficult as it was, I knew it was the right thing to do. And I've been very blessed since then. I have a new job I enjoy, and moving away has been good for me and my family. I'm not quite such a black sheep in their eyes anymore!" At the thought, Sarah glanced at her watch and gasped. "I may have spoken too soon. If I don't get back home fast I will most definitely be in my mother's black books!"

She stood up and brushed the grass and leaves off her clothes. Brian stood up too, but put out a restraining hand. "Wait, Sarah! You haven't told me where you've moved to. Where are you working now?"

"Oswestry Orthopedic!" she said, and laughed as she saw the look of incredulity then delight cross Brian's face.

"You're kidding!" he exclaimed.

Sarah shook her head. "Children's ward. Day shift."

"And you're living in Oswestry too?"

"Yes," she said. "In a small flat by the hospital."

"Then . . . then I'll see you often?" Brian asked cautiously.

Sarah couldn't help teasing him. "Off duty or on, Dr. Pearson?"

Her lighthearted ribbing brought a twinkle to Brian's eyes. He caught hold of her hand and gave it a gentle squeeze. "Come on, beautiful black sheep! I think I can smell your mother's pot roast from here!"

ಞ ಞ ಞ

Sarah lived through that evening as though in a dream—the happiest, most wonderful dream of her life. Kevin, Mair, and Aled drove into the driveway as she and Brian returned from their walk. They had picked up Aunty Lil on their way. Aled shot at Brian like a cannonball from a gun.

"Mr. Pearson! Mr. Pearson! You came back!"

Brian laughed delightedly, scooped up the young boy and swung him high into the air. "Hey, how's my best buddy? Doesn't look like that leg's slowed you down a bit!"

From that point on, no one could get a word in edgewise. As they entered the house, Aled filled Brian in on all the news about Mot, his new pet rabbit, the sheep that kept trying to escape the shearers, and the newest fads at school. Sarah seized the opportunity to flee to her bedroom. She looked at her starry-eyed reflection in the mirror— afraid to pinch herself for fear that she would wake up. She brushed her hair until it shone like burnished copper, put on a little lipstick, and made her way into the kitchen.

She did her best to help her mother with final dinner preparations, but found it almost impossible to concentrate on the simplest of tasks. Aunty Lil walked in just in time to prevent Sarah from adding sugar to the gravy. The older woman assessed the situation in one piercing glance and pulled Sarah away from the stove. She gave her startled niece a reassuring pat on the cheek and turned her to face the hallway.

"You've been apart long enough. Go on into the front room and be with him. I'll help your mother in here." Then, almost as an afterthought, she added "Besides, someone has to save him from Aled. He's now started in on how Davie Hughes got three nosebleeds in one day!"

"Oh no!" Sarah groaned and hurried off to the rescue.

Dinner was much the same. Aled insisted on sitting next to Brian. But Sarah didn't mind. More than once she felt Brian's glance upon her, and when she met his look, it was as if they were the only people in the room.

Everyone was in good spirits. Kevin, Mair, and Aled were genuinely pleased to see Brian. Aunty Lil was glad for Sarah. Even Annie rose to the occasion. Without fuss, she refrained from offering Brian or Sarah the obligatory cup of tea at the end of the meal.

Much later, although obviously loathe to leave, Kevin managed to persuade Aled that he needed to go home to bed—but only after Brian had promised to visit them at the farm the next evening. They offered to drop Aunty Lil off on their way, and she happily accepted the ride. Sarah looked at the clock and pleased her mother no end by asking to sleep in her old bedroom rather than make the long journey to Oswestry so late at night. Annie hastened upstairs to prepare her daughter's bed.

Sarah sat in one of the armchairs in the front room. Brian was sitting in the other armchair near the fireplace. Now that their guests were gone and he'd had a few minutes to sit quietly, his long journey and exhaustion had caught up with him. His eyes were closed and his breathing deep. Sarah felt her heart contract as she looked upon him. It amazed her that she could still feel so much for this man. It amazed her even more that after all the time of doubt and denial, those feelings might still be reciprocated.

Quietly she got up and walked over to her harp. She touched the strings softly, then impulsively sat behind it. She closed her eyes and began to hum one of the Primary songs she accompanied at Church. She had never played it on the harp before, but her fingers seemed to pluck the notes right out of the air. As they did so, she began to sing softly.

When the song ended, she raised her head to find Brian watching her. The emotion in his eyes affected her more than any words could have done.

"I'm sorry," she whispered. "I didn't mean to wake you."

"It was beautiful," he said with reverence. Without another word, he stood up and walked over to his jacket, hanging on a coat rack behind the door. When he returned, he was carrying a long, thin, white box. He handed it to her. "I made this for you," he said simply.

Intrigued, Sarah took the box from his hand and lifted the lid carefully. She pulled back a layer of white tissue paper to expose the gift.

At first she could only gaze at it in wonder. Then she touched it; and finally, with gentle fingers, she withdrew it from the box. It was a perfect Welsh love-spoon. The wood had been carved, sanded, and smoothed until it shone. The handle began with an intricately worked harp. Beneath the harp were two interwoven hearts. And beneath the hearts was an open book.

"Oh Brian!" Sarah breathed. "I've never seen a lovelier one. It's truly a work of art. Did you really make it yourself?"

Brian glowed at her praise. "I found the wood when I was hiking in the Tetons."

"Your favorite hike?" Sarah asked, remembering what he had told her about his outings with his late father.

"Yes, near Jenny Lake." He seemed pleased that she hadn't forgotten. He touched the spoon cradled in Sarah's hand. "I sure came to appreciate this old tradition." He paused then mused, "I often wondered if Glyn Jones made one for Mary."

"It was probably one of Mary's most prized possessions," Sarah said with feeling.

He smiled at her. "Working with this wood was a wonderful outlet to express . . ." He paused, then continued more hesitantly, ". . . my feelings." He paused again. "I wanted something I could see and touch that represented the things we shared."

He pointed to the harp. "This was your gift to me. Your beautiful music." He pointed at the open book. "This was my gift to you. The Book of Mormon."

Sarah could only hold the spoon and marvel at the hours of work and love that had gone into its creation. Anything she could say seemed inadequate. "Thank you, Brian. It's beautiful!"

He met her eyes. "You're beautiful!" was his quiet reply.

Sarah rose and went to him then. She buried her face in his shoulder as Brian's arms wrapped around her and held her tight.

"Oh, Sarah!" he whispered, and she heard the catch in his voice. "We've been given another chance—and more time."

She knew he was thinking of their falling out last summer. "Don't remind me of what I said to you that day," she warned. Brian shook his head.

"It's ingrained in me now. I can't tell you how many times it's replayed in my mind over the last year. I'm so ashamed of how brash I was. I was arrogant and way out of line. Can you ever forgive me?"

"If you can forgive me for being so blind and so faithless," she replied.

"I love you, Sarah!"

"I love you too!" she said.

Their lips met in a kiss that became a voiceless communication. It cleansed two tender hearts of past hurt and misunderstanding. It dared to hope, and ended with beautiful promise.

As they drew apart, Brian cupped his hands around Sarah's face. "I'll never leave you again, Sarah. Never!"

A single tear of joy rolled down Sarah's cheek. Brian wiped it away gently with his thumb and smiled tenderly at her. "The third gift on the spoon is our love for each other," he whispered. Nothing more needed to be said. They both knew that at last it had been given freely and accepted gratefully.

ABOUT THE AUTHOR

Siân Ann Bessey was born in Cambridge, England, to Noel and Patricia Owen. After her father completed his doctoral work there, the family returned to their Welsh homeland. Siân grew up among the austere mountains and verdant hills of North Wales. At the age of ten, she joined the Church along with her entire family. Siân left Wales to attend Brigham Young University and graduated with a bachelor's degree in communications.

Forgotten Notes is her first novel, although she has written several articles that have appeared in the *New Era, Ensign,* and *Liahona* magazines. Siân and her husband, Kent, are the parents of five children. They reside in Rexburg, Idaho.

Siân is the Welsh form of Jane, and is pronounced "Shawn."